THE HONEST AFFAIR

BOOK THREE OF THE ROSE GOLD SERIES

NICOLE FRENCH

raglan

Copyright © 2020 by Raglan Publishing

ISBN: 978-1-950663-10-1

Cover Design: Raglan Publishing

PROLOGUE
SEPTEMBER 2018

Matthew

A storm was brewing in New York.

Just four days after Labor Day, the city was drowning in heat. New York was originally built on wetlands, and on days like this, in the last throes of summer, humidity lounged over my shoulders like the sweaty arm of a drunk too far gone, while clouds roiled with anger and dripped with disdain.

It wasn't quite five in the morning when I parked my beat-up Accord outside the squat concrete and brick building that housed the eighty-fourth precinct of the NYPD. I'd gotten the call thirty minutes earlier. For anything else, I'd have said "fuck off" and gone back to sleep. But for Derek Kingston, the investigative detective I'd been working with for years? For this specific case?

Yeah, I jumped right out of bed.

As I reached the interrogation room, I was pulling my sticky shirt away from my skin, uncomfortable in the air-conditioning of the station.

"Jesus," Derek said when I entered the observation side. "What the hell happened to you?"

Okay, so I wasn't exactly in my Sunday best. But Derek knew me as a man who generally took pride in my appearance, even at this hour. My colleagues teased me for looking more like Cary Grant than a public servant, thanks to a sister who owned a men's vintage clothing store. Maybe it was a carry-over from my military days, but I liked the precision of a uniform: a tailored suit, shoes I could see my reflection in, a perfectly knotted half-Windsor, and a fedora for the street.

Not this morning, though. Right now I looked like any average bum in the t-shirt I'd been sleeping in and the jeans off my bedroom floor.

"It's a swamp out there," I replied. "You said get down here, and I got down here. Has she signed anything yet?"

Derek shook his head. "She's been waiting on you."

"Not her own lawyer?"

He shrugged. "She said she doesn't have representation yet. But she will. You know they always do."

"So she's martyring herself," I muttered.

We both turned toward the window to look at the woman whose appearance at the precinct an hour earlier had brought us here.

Nina Evelyn Astor de Vries Gardner.

It was a whole lot of names, but then again, she was a whole lot of woman. Even sitting, she was taller than most, with a swan-like neck, ramrod posture, and the kind of cool, competent grace that comes from generations of breeding. Only I really knew how that pristine exterior masked fathomless layers of passion and pride. Nina was like a pool of glassy water dying to be touched. And I knew the exact pattern of her ripples. Hell, even now, I was dying to dive in, despite knowing I'd be burned in a lake of fire.

According to Derek, Nina was here to confess for abetting the very crimes we had charged her husband with not quite four months earlier: racketeering, bribery, tax fraud, and, most damningly, sex trafficking. We knew all about him and the operation he had worked with. Girls missing from a Brooklyn housing project. Witnesses to several men running people, guns, and drugs out of a safe house in The Hole, one of the worst neighborhoods in the borough. Photographs of Gardner himself outside the house with notorious kingpin John

Carson, who had been shot and killed last spring. And lastly, the name of the Delaware shell corporation used to run every dollar in and out of those operations and mask those involved.

And then, three days ago, Nina had confessed her involvement in all of it. Told me a story about how her husband had forged her signature on a number of legal documents ten years ago. Implicated her in a scheme to sell false papers and smuggle illegal immigrants from Eastern Europe.

She wasn't innocent, but at first it seemed clear that she'd been used as a front for the larger operation, a fact which freed her from her husband's claims of spousal privilege in his trial. I didn't think she knew anything else beyond what was on the papers. Honestly, it would have been great for the case and my career to have such a coup of a witness.

It would have been all those things if I hadn't been in love with her. And if I hadn't known she was lying.

Moments after Nina told her story, Derek sent me a giant cache of videos he had received from colleagues in New Jersey, Connecticut, and Massachusetts. It turned out that Gardner's trafficking ring went well beyond Brooklyn. And in video after video, I watched in horror as a gorgeous blonde whose legs had been wrapped around my waist more than once guided scared young girls in and out of ramshackle houses all over the greater Northeast. I watched her make contact with the other associates we had identified as part of Gardner's ring. I watched her hand them envelopes and accept their money in return.

She was the lynchpin. The one who made it all happen.

And it broke my cold, jaded heart.

Now Nina sat in the interrogation room, cool as a fuckin' cucumber and ever the lady, swathed in designer clothes as spotless as snow. A white sundress showed off her pale, sun-kissed shoulders. Slender legs crossed daintily at the ankles. White-tipped fingers folded over the table, the golf ball-sized diamond on her finger glinting under the fluorescent lights while she remained perfectly still.

Unlike most people, Nina didn't fidget. Me, I was always grabbing at shit when I was agitated. My tie, my hair, my pockets. Even now, I was pulling the collar of my old Springsteen t-shirt like it was choking me. But despite the fact that she was locked in a room where criminal after criminal was interrogated daily, Nina looked like a queen waiting for her court to arrive. Like I was a jester sent in there to entertain.

Fuck. That.

"She's lucky I was even here," Derek said. "Most of the guys don't even know about this case."

I nodded. "I know."

We had pursued this case secretly for the better part of a year. Given the number of obvious bribes Carson and therefore Gardner had at the FBI, the CIA, and the U.S. attorney's office, we could never trust anyone else completely to help us with the case. The smaller the circle, the better. Until, of course, I fell for the defendant's wife.

"So…you want to talk to her? Or should I?"

I was about to answer when my phone buzzed loudly in my pocket. I looked at the number and swore.

"What is it?" Derek asked.

"Cardozo," I said. "At five in the morning? I have to take this."

I turned my back on Derek and walked out to the hall. The voice of Greg Cardozo, executive assistant district attorney of the Kings County office, chief of the organized crime and racketeering bureau, and my boss, blared through my phone's tinny speakers.

"Zola, you want to tell me what you're doing down at the station? I called the chief last night to let him know you're off the Gardner investigation, and now he wakes up me, my wife, and my schnauzer to ask if I changed my mind. Because apparently, you're at the fucking station!"

I frowned. Apparently the cat was out of the bag. Yeah, okay, only yesterday I'd handed Cardozo my resignation due to my involvement with Nina (who was officially a suspect now). But then he had apparently notified the entire NYPD about everything?

So much for secrecy. At this point, Gardner was already as slippery as an eel. We were basically giving him a two-day head start with this shit.

"I—it was late," I said weakly. "And I'm not *technically* on leave yet. You said yourself that you had to send the paperwork to HR today, and—"

"Get the hell out of there!" Cardozo shouted. "Look, Zola, you did the right thing coming to me and submitting your resignation. Don't make me accept it by sticking your nose back where it doesn't belong. Leave it to Derek and Cliff and me. Your part is done."

"But—"

"I'm on my way down now to question Mrs. Gardner," my boss said. "If you're still there when I arrive, you're fired, Zola. End of discussion."

The line went dead. I walked back into the observation room. On the other side of the mirror, Nina still hadn't moved.

"What did he want?" Derek asked.

I sighed and rubbed the back of my neck. "To remind me that I am off this case and, as soon as HR processes everything, on unpaid administrative leave for the next six months. Minimum."

Derek reared. "*What*? Why? What the fuck did you do?"

I didn't need to answer, though. His eyes flew between me and Nina, who was still sitting at the interrogation table, hands folded calmly in front of her like she was waiting for someone to bring her a mimosa, not take her confession.

"Zola," he rumbled. "Tell me you didn't…"

I shook my head with obvious regret. "I have to go. King, can I have a minute with her first?"

He frowned, looking a lot like *Nonna* when I dragged muddy shoes all over the house. "If you're off, I really shouldn't…"

"Just a minute, cameras off? Cardozo said he's on his way, and if he catches me down here, I'm fired for good. But I need to talk to her. I need to say…fuck, man, I need to say goodbye."

Derek looked like he wanted to say no. I understood. I was putting him in a tight spot. But the other side of it was that I was one of his best friends, someone who had pulled all number of strings for him over the years, and he knew it.

"All right," he said, resigned as he moved to the cameras and flicked the off switch. "One minute, Zo. That's it."

"That's all I need."

She looked up when I entered, and the expressionless ice was immediately replaced by a flurry of emotions I had come to know so well. Eagerness. Shame. Remorse.

Lightning-bolt attraction.

Goddammit. A million questions flew through my mind as those silvery gray eyes lasered through me.

Why had she lied to me for as long as she did?

What the hell was she doing here?

Why did she have to be so crazy beautiful?

I had told Cardozo that I was off the case because I *was* in love with Nina de Vries, with the full conviction that the emotion was firmly in the past and had been since the moment I discovered her deception. *Who the fuck are you kidding?* I thought as I looked at her. *You* are *in love with Nina de Vries.* Then. Now. Forever.

The fact made me that much angrier.

"Hello, Matthew." Her voice was low, almost husky, like she hadn't had enough sleep or had maybe just woken up. It *was* pretty damn early.

Her sleek blonde hair was tied back, away from her clean, ice-sculpted face that included those big gray eyes, long nose, and full, pink lips that I knew turned the color of ripe plums when I sucked on them hard. She looked a far cry from the sex-tousled siren I'd left in Boston just a few days prior.

"Nina," I said as I let the door close behind me. "What the hell is this? Some plea for attention? Trying to lure me back into your web?"

Neither of us mentioned the several dozen calls and texts she had sent me since Tuesday. All of them unanswered.

She refolded her hands. "I thought it was clear. I told Detective Kingston I was here to turn myself in."

"For what, exactly?"

She looked up, and her eyes landed on me with the force of a gavel. "Well, I'm not sure about the correct legalese, but I believe it will be something along the lines of conspiring in sex trafficking, possibly of minors and illegal aliens."

I raised a brow. "That wasn't the story you fed me Tuesday night, doll."

"Matthew, as you so judiciously pointed out at Skylar and Brandon's guesthouse, I am part owner of over fifty houses used to abuse and transport young women across the greater Northeast."

"Yeah, but you didn't know it!" I blurted out without even thinking.

Something like relief fluttered over her fine features.

"Didn't I?" she asked softly. "You seemed to think I did."

It wasn't until that moment I realized that deep down, I wanted to believe her. I'd been so angry about what I'd found. Felt so blindsided by the measures her husband had taken to traffic what had to be hundreds, maybe thousands of girls to other slimeballs, that even the thought of the woman I loved being a knowing accessory to those actions made me feel physically ill.

But now, a few days after the truth had sunk in, a few days after my skin still yearned for her touch, my heart still hollered for hers, even in my sleep…I didn't know what to believe. On the bed, when I'd shown her the videos, she had looked horrified. Terrified. And I knew that woman on the screen. I knew her hair, her legs, the shoes she had been wearing the night we met.

But I still remembered her response: *It isn't me.*

"I—I don't know," I said, sinking into the chair across from her.

Nina unfolded her hands, turning one over so it reached toward me, palm up. I stared at it. I wanted to take it. Just the touch of her, that impossibly smooth skin. But right now, this close, her inimitable scent of roses and light drifting toward me…

No. I couldn't. I was confused enough.

"Do you—do you still have the video on your phone?" she asked. "The one where I…meet…this Ben Vamos?"

I ground my teeth at the thought of the skeezy bastard whom Derek and I had discovered was a family connection of Gardner's from back when his name was still its original Hungarian, Károly Kertész. They had been working together for years, with Vamos running the houses through which they had trafficked girls from Eastern Europe into the country. With, apparently, Nina's help.

Still, I nodded curtly. The IT guys had deleted all evidence from my hard drive, including my access to the secure file server where we could view digitized evidence. But I'd rebelled and saved one to my own device, if for no other reason than to remind myself of the truth. That Nina was a liar. A traitor.

Wasn't she?

"May I look at it, please?"

I frowned. What was her game here? But I still pulled my phone from my pocket and flipped to the video in question. Nina showed no surprise I still had access to it. I placed it on the table and tried not to inhale that floral aroma when Nina leaned in with me to watch.

I'd seen it at least a hundred times. The black Escalade pulling to the curb of a shitty New Jersey townhouse. The back door opens, and out walks Nina in her prim white dress, her sleek blonde hair tousled around her face. I knew exactly how many steps it took for her to walk from the sidewalk, through the gate, and up the porch steps. She knocks on the door, and it's opened by Vamos, a thick middle-aged man with gray hair buzzed close, a stained shirt the color of old socks, and a permanent frown etched onto a reddened face.

They talk, and after a few minutes, she enters the house. Later, she leads a parade of girls from the house to the Escalade that will take them to a private airport, where they would disappear from the investigator's lens.

Knowing all of this, I scowled as Nina greeted Vamos like a friend. Kisses to the cheek. Smiles and touches. The whole deal.

I wanted to punch a hole through the concrete walls surrounding us.

"Pause it." Nina's voice was a soft-spoken command, but a command nonetheless.

Scowling, I obeyed and stopped the video. "What?"

"Matthew," she said, and this time her voice cracked. "How could you not know?"

I stared at the video, which, for all intents and purposes, still showed a woman that looked exactly like Nina. I honestly didn't know what she meant.

"How could I think otherwise?" I answered, feeling like my throat was constricting as I looked back up and felt the hurt and pain in her eyes.

God, I wanted to believe her. I wanted to believe she had nothing to do with this. That this woman, this beautiful siren who had warmed my cold, callous heart over the last six months wasn't capable of conspiring to sell women like cattle into sex slavery.

And yet, there she was, clear as day, wearing those sleek high heels, at least three inches high that tapered into deadly stilettos, smoothed over her feet in waterfall-colored leather. The exact same shoes she had been wearing the night we met. The same shoes she was wearing now.

The legs of her chair screeched on the concrete floor as Nina pushed back from the table. She strode to the door, then turned to stand in the frame.

"Stand up, please?"

I frowned, still staring at the screen with blood boiling in my chest. Still, I did as she asked, shoving my chair hard enough back that it practically screamed through the small room.

"What?" I snarled as I stepped closer. "You want to look me in the eye when you're lying, sweetheart?"

"Look at him," she said calmly as if I wasn't spitting like an alley cat in heat. "And look at her. Then look at me now."

I did as she asked. And then did it again. And on the third time, I started when her meaning was suddenly crystal clear.

The doorway next to us was about average—maybe eighty inches tall, just four inches over my height of six-two. The man in the video—whom we had also seen face-to-face at her house in Newton—was much shorter, maybe five-ten in boots. His barrel chest and thick middle perhaps gave an illusion that he was larger than he was, but I remembered it clearly.

I stared at the video. The Nina in it barely came up to the guy's forehead, even in these same heels. Both of their heads were at least eight or more inches below the entryway to the house. But here with me, in the exact same shoes, Nina's eyes were perfectly level with mine. She had, as always, the grace of a gazelle...but the height of someone much, much taller than the woman talking to Vamos.

"Oh, fuck," I whispered. "Nina, I..." I shook my head again and again.

"I said it wasn't me," she said sadly. "But you didn't believe me."

She closed her hand over the phone, silently bidding me to put it away. "Why didn't you believe me, Matthew?"

My mouth just opened and closed like a damn fish, my heart pounding so loud I could practically hear it banging like a drum. Fuck. Oh, *fuck.*

"If you had waited a few more moments. Answered *any* of my calls, we could have figured it out together. But you left. You ran away. And now..." She drifted off, as hopeless as I felt.

I blinked again and again between her and the photo. "So, it's..."

"That is my friend," she said quietly. "And someone you know... intimately. Her maiden name is 'Caitlyn Calvert,' although I believe she goes by Shaw now. Some people, myself included, have been known to call her Cait." She raised a sleek blonde brow. "I have wondered if that might correspond to another Kate you've been looking for. She's from Paterson too, you know."

I blinked. Derek had said as much on the phone when he called me here, but I hadn't really believed it. Not until now. And I hadn't even thought to ask Caitlyn herself about her relationship with Nina's husband—fucking idiotic, considering she had been right in front of me less than two weeks ago in the Hamptons. Given our history, I had spent most of that day trying to avoid someone I saw as an obnoxious, desperate try-hard, but it was clear now what Caitlyn was trying so hard to be. She wasn't just attempting to become a member of Nina's class and station. She was actually attempting to *be* Nina de Vries herself.

And this was why.

"Jesus," I murmured.

"Convincing, isn't she?"

"So...I don't get it," I said. "What are you doing here, then? If that's not you, what are you turning yourself in for?"

Nina tipped her head, eyes full of resolution. "Because I still know things, Matthew. It's still my name on the deeds. On the company. Is it not?"

"You said yourself those weren't yours. Caitlyn was obviously the one who showed up to sign those papers, Nina. It's identity fraud, not your conspiracy."

"Yes," she said, a hell of a lot more calmly than I would be if I found out my childhood best friend had literally stolen my identity. "But just the same..." She shook her head. "For a moment, I thought I would have to be here anyway. Calvin called me just after you left, wanting to waive spousal privilege. But last night, his attorneys talked him out of it again. And I drove back from Boston right away."

She turned to look down at her hands, which were folded in front of her skirt again. For a moment, I thought I saw the shadow of a bruise on her neck, just under her ear. But before I could say anything, a scratch of static indicated that the room's speakers were turned back on.

"Zola. He's on his way up."

I glanced toward the mirror, behind which I knew Derek was standing. "Shit."

"This is what's going to happen," Nina said calmly as if we were still having the same conversation. "I'm turning myself in for the crimes I mentioned. Maybe that makes me an accessory to this whole disgusting scheme. Maybe it doesn't. I looked it up. Identity fraud or not, I'm still part owner of a variety of real estate used to traffic young women into sex slavery throughout the tristate area. So, I'm going to own it. Because that's how I can help put Calvin where he belongs. You said it yourself, didn't you?"

I glanced toward the door, half expecting my boss to come tearing through any second. "I said..."

"You said the only way around it was if I was an accessory to the crime. Well, I am, as I just discovered. So I'm turning myself in."

I nearly dropped my phone as I shoved it back into my pocket. "Nina, before you do anything, you need to call your lawyer. The new prosecutor on this case is here to—"

"New prosecutor?" she interrupted. "What do you mean, new prosecutor?"

"I recused myself yesterday. Told my boss about you and me, and as of yesterday, I'm off the case."

"You—you *what*?"

"I recused myself," I repeated, this time impatiently. "Nina, I had to. I should have done it from the start. And because I didn't, technically I'm on administrative leave. I'm not even supposed to be here. *We shouldn't even be talking.* I just—"

"Zola," Derek interrupted sharply with a knock on the glass. His meaning was clear.

I frowned at the mirror, then turned back to Nina. "Look, Cardozo is solid, but he doesn't know you. Get a lawyer, Nina. Now. Do not put yourself through a deposition. Do not say a word until you have someone to advise you legally. Please. Do it for Olivia, if not yourself. Do it for—for me."

There was a knock on the glass, which I took to be my final warning.

"I have to go, Nina," I said. "Fuck, I'm...I'm so goddamn sorry."

Her eyes widened again, as if she was just registering that I was going to leave her once more. "You know, I could have borne anything if I'd thought you believed me."

A tear fell down her cheek, cutting a red flushed line down her porcelain skin. I felt like it was cutting me through completely.

"I'm sorry," I whispered again.

And then, because I could already hear the sounds of Cardozo's voice booming to the receptionist on the other side of the barriers, I let the door close and ran in the opposite direction, to escape out the back door like the rat I was.

It killed me to leave her there alone. Unprotected.

But it was the only thing left to do.

PRELUDE

"Page Six"
The New York Post
September 9, 2018

Socialite Surrenders to Scandal & Splits!

Heiress Nina de Vries Gardner, granddaughter of the late Celeste de Vries and cousin to De Vries Shipping CEO Eric de Vries, pled no contest to accessory to human trafficking and identity fraud this morning at the Kings County criminal court.

"Ms. de Vries is a law-abiding citizen, which is precisely *why* she turned herself in the moment she discovered her inadvertent part in the scheme as a co-property owner," said her lawyer in a statement outside the courthouse. "Her only desire now is to cooperate with law enforcement and do everything she can to bring real justice to the true villains of this case, starting with her husband."

Sources confirmed that early this morning Mrs. Gardner filed for divorce and a legal name change from her husband of ten years, Calvin Gardner, who was indicted on similar charges of human trafficking last May. She was also granted a six-month no-contact order from Judge Stratford, which will prevent Mr. Gardner from contacting his wife or daughter, who reportedly attends a boarding school in Massachusetts. It's rumored that Mrs. Gardner may have accepted a plea deal in exchange for offering testimony against her husband. Mr. Gardner pled not guilty at his arraignment and is awaiting trial at his residence on the Upper East Side.

Though notoriously low profile, the de Vrieses, one of New York's oldest families, have been plagued by scandal in the last year. It began with Eric de Vries's wedding upset, then shocking charges of insider trading (later dropped), and the kidnapping of his wife last January, and the shooting of arms mogul John Carson inside their apartment following the Met Gala last May. Mere weeks later, Calvin Gardner was indicted on charges thought to be related to John Carson's underground arms networks in Brooklyn.

Mrs. Gardner left the courthouse with her head held high, wearing a suffragette-white vintage Chanel skirt suit. Perhaps a gesture toward her newfound freedom? Or a sign that the Gardner divorce is about to get *very* ugly?

"It's an heirloom," she replied when asked. "It belonged to my grandmother, Celeste de Vries. She always looked very striking in it."

And in this gossip columnist's humble opinion, "striking" also runs in the family—at least when they are wearing Chanel.

The Brooklyn DA's office, represented by Greg Cardozo, officially had no comment.

———

The Newark Star-Ledger
October 8, 2018

Four charged in multi-state human trafficking ring

Four New Jersey and Brooklyn residents indicted for a simultaneous, multi-state human trafficking ring this morning. Concurrent charges were filed in New Jersey, New York, Connecticut, and Massachusetts in one of the largest interstate cooperative efforts on record between local law enforcement agencies.

New Jersey investigators arrested Ben Vamos, a Paterson landlord, as well as his girlfriend, Gloria Adami, while Brooklyn authorities arrested local gang members Kevin "K-Money" Reynolds and Devon Carter for their alleged roles in the scheme. At four different houses co-owned by Vamos and Pantheon, LLC, an anonymous shell corporation registered in Delaware, investigators found drugs, weapons, forged immigration documents, as well as seventeen women held captive in the basements. In addition to trafficking charges, Vamos has also been charged with the intent to distribute illegal narcotics and weapons trafficking.

Vamos, the leader of the alleged ring, was born in Hungary and emigrated to the United States in 1969 following the failed revolution. He owns a number of properties across New Jersey, several of which were identified as locations through which potentially hundreds of women have been funneled since the early eighties.

"We believe this effort began initially as a way for Vamos and others like him to help friends and family escape the Eastern Bloc before the Iron Curtain fell," said New Jersey Attorney General Patrick Johnson in a press conference.

"But since the nineties, it seems to have morphed into an entry point through which women from Eastern Europe are funneled into prostitution all over New England."

Johnson was not able to offer a specific number or any other names in conjunction with the case.

"This operation makes the Epstein case look like a walk in the park," said one officer who chose to remain anonymous.

No other names have been released in conjunction with Pantheon, but Patrick Johnson assured reporters this was just the beginning.

"This is a sign that local government can and will get things done," said Derek Kingston, the NYPD detective who headed up the investigation in conjunction with the Brooklyn DA's office, the Newark DA, and investigative units from New Haven and Boston.

He did not answer questions about why federal charges were absent, though another anonymous source inside the Brooklyn DA's office speculated that federal agencies as well as other judicial appointees may be involved as well.

———

The New York Times
November 8, 2018

U.S. Attorney for the Southern District of New York resigns

In a surprise announcement, Seymour Taft has resigned as U.S. attorney for the southern district of New York. Speculation about Taft's potential corruption was rife when he was tapped to replace Sanjay Ramamurthy after the 2016 election, but grew louder when his office declined to prosecute former munitions contractor John Carson on federal charges of arms and human trafficking. Carson was killed in May, but last month a hack of Taft's files revealed he had been gifted several large stock holdings from Carson two months before his appointment, and that his portfolio was subsequently reinvested in a fund managed by Calvin Gardner, who is facing charges of human trafficking as a part of Carson's operation.

Rhonda Klein, a deputy attorney in the southern district, will be the acting U.S. attorney until another is appointed by the district judges, a process that could take months.

"I have no connection to John Carson, Jude Letour, Calvin Gardner, nor any other members of the alleged trafficking ring in the Northeast that has caught the attention of the public in recent months," she said in a statement outside the U.S. attorney's office in Brooklyn, only two blocks from the district attorney's building at 350 Jay Street. "Human trafficking is a massive problem in this country, and I will not rest until I am certain this office has done everything it can to cooperate with the local authorities who have valiantly pursued this case, beginning with the Brooklyn district attorney's office tomorrow morning. This is a human rights issue, and certainly a federal one. We will not stand idly by."

Jude Letour and Calvin Gardner were both arrested in May, while a larger trafficking ring across New England and the tristate area, headed by Ben Vamos, was broken up last month. While no official connections have been made between the two, Mr. Gardner's child-hood relationship to Vamos emerged last month and has provoked questions about whether or not Gardner and Vamos had been working together from the start.

Mr. Gardner and Mr. Letour both await trials due to start within the next few months.

———

The New York Times
November 15, 2018

Socialite sentenced in trafficking case

New York heiress Nina Astor de Vries was sentenced today on charges of accessory to human trafficking and fraud. Despite remaining married to financier and real estate investor Calvin Gardner, de Vries has reassumed her maiden name after filing for divorce.

The judge agreed with the DA's request for relative clemency, awarding only forty-five days of jail time and three hundred hours of community service to Ms. de Vries. She checked into Rikers Correctional Facility earlier this morning and is expected to serve only a short time of her sentence.

"Relief," she said sharply when asked how she felt. "And gratitude."

Although Executive Assistant District Attorney Greg Cardozo declined to comment on the sentencing, many suspect that Ms. de Vries made a plea bargain with the DA in exchange for testimony against her husband's involvement in a larger human trafficking operation.

Calvin Gardner's trial was delayed again after his wife confessed to her crimes. A new date has not yet been announced.

I

PRIMI

CHAPTER ONE

NOVEMBER 2018

Nina

The doors closed on a whisper, not a bang.

Even so, I stumbled slightly as I exited the Rose M. Singer Detention Center—one of the eleven jails housed at Rikers Island—with the wobbly grace of a newborn foal on the heels I hadn't worn in more than two weeks. Under my arm, I carried the purse I'd brought in with me, just before I'd been stripped down, searched, and forced to trade the demure Chanel shift dress and wool coat for a brown jumpsuit.

Despite having been kept in a storage locker for the mere fifteen days I'd endured of my forty-five-day sentence, all my clothes still smelled like the jail, like sweat and concrete and mildew and bleach. Like misery and anger. Hopelessness and despair. I'd burn them all as soon as I could find replacements. But for now, I just wanted off this godforsaken island.

I held up a hand to block the sun that was unnaturally bright for so late in November. Or was it just that I hadn't seen it in over a week? Regardless, the light was blinding, and I squinted as I looked for the stop for the shuttle to the central hub of Rikers, from where I could call a car to take me…somewhere.

"Cos."

My head snapped up at the sound of a familiar voice. I turned to find a tall blond man dressed in an impeccably cut navy suit, standing in front of a familiar BMW sedan.

"Eric?" I asked incredulously.

As my eyes adjusted to the light, I found I wasn't just hearing things. It was my cousin—Eric de Vries, Chairman and CEO of De Vries Shipping Industries and one of the busiest men in New York—waiting patiently for my release.

"What—how do you—what are you doing here?"

"I came to pick you up," he said as if it weren't obvious.

I glanced around at the few vehicles in the lot. "I mean, how did they let you drive in here, though?" Already I had steeled myself for a ride through the complex on one of the crowded shuttles, then expected to call a cab or something similar to pick me up from the entrance to the facility.

"They'll do a lot with a few well-placed donations to the complex. Here's to your freedom, Nina. Welcome back."

He leaned in with a smile to deliver a customary kiss to my cheek, but I immediately held up a hand.

"No, don't," I said. "I reek of that horrid soap."

Eric made a face and backed up. "Oh, yeah. That stuff makes your skin feel like chalk. I remember."

I pressed my lips together. My cousin had his own holiday in another jail on the island while being detained for insider trading. A farce, all of it. But it left a scar just the same.

"I suppose now being jailbirds runs in the family," I said wryly.

Eric snorted. "Talk about a rite of passage. Come on. Let's get out of this dump."

I followed him into the back of the car, which was manned by his driver.

"How did you know?" I asked as we took off.

My cousin shrugged good-naturedly. "Barney told me after your parole hearing."

I frowned. That he had spoken to my attorney wasn't so strange—after all, Eric was bankrolling my criminal defense. "But you came?"

Eric's face remained calm, but beneath that cool facade lurked a ripple of something darker. "I remember what it's like. No one should come out of here alone." His eyes widened as something else occurred to him. "You weren't expecting someone else, were you?"

I shook my head. "No. No, I wasn't. Thank you."

I didn't tell him that as I had walked outside, temporarily blinded by the sun, a part of me *had* in fact wondered if another might show. Someone with black hair and a rakish grin. Someone with a taste for vintage suits and old-fashioned fedoras. Someone I hadn't seen in months, since I'd turned myself in for the very crime that had earned my lovely stay here at Rikers.

Matthew Zola. My heart's enemy. And yet somehow still my heart.

I had never imagined it was possible to love and hate someone at the same time. But here I was.

"So, how was it in there?" Eric asked as casually as if he was wondering about the weather.

"Manageable."

He nodded knowingly. "I heard things...about Rosie's."

I stiffened at the use of the common moniker for the center where female detainees and short-term sentences were housed here on the island. Like the peeling pinkish paint that covered the squat building, the name covered all multitude of sins quite inadequately.

"Barney was able to negotiate for a solitary cell," I said. "Instead of the dormitory. I mostly just...stayed there."

No one had argued. Such were the kinds of allowances people like us got. Unfair, perhaps, but at the same time, we were greater targets. During the few times I'd been forced to mingle with the rest of the prison population, I'd received a total of forty-two threats that would have undoubtedly come to fruition had I spent my nights with the rest of the women in my wing. But given my high profile, my assault wasn't something the ailing prison, with its already questionable reputation, could afford. Solitary became a forced luxury.

Eric nodded. "I had the same. It's something, I suppose."

"I suppose."

I wasn't going to detail the fears that had prevented me from sleeping more than one or two hours in a row during my time here. Especially after the third night, when a guard, unaware of my status, crept into my cell and had just slipped his hand under my thin blanket when the warden took his own stroll through our wing. The guard vanished as fast as he had appeared, but it didn't stop me from wondering what he might have done otherwise. Two nights later, I didn't have to wonder anymore. I could hear others' responses to him, their hoarse whispers loud and clear only a few doors away.

Begging like that stays with you. Not for pleasure, but for mercy. I doubted the word "please" would ever sound the same again.

I rubbed absently at my knee. My skin had been crawling for days. I wasn't entirely sure I hadn't contracted lice, though I hadn't found a thing.

"Well," Eric said as the car finally turned onto the Queensboro Bridge. Somehow, we had already made it through Queens. The Manhattan skyline loomed. "Where to?"

I knew what he meant. There was no way I was returning to my Lexington Avenue penthouse. Calvin's lawyers argued that by leaving it the way I did (jail or not), I had effectively ceded residency rights until ownership was settled. I didn't care enough to fight it. For the last decade, that foppish hatbox of an apartment had been its own jail cell. I wanted to be as far from the Upper East Side as I could. Right now, I wanted to put this entire city behind me and pretend I'd never seen a single cement square of it ever.

But I had a few more things to tie up. First and foremost was ridding myself and my daughter of the man who had been nothing but an abusive leech. Second was providing the testimony in a criminal trial that would ensure he could never harm us again.

No small tasks. But I'd had plenty of time—the past fifteen days, in particular—to prepare myself. For now, there was the waiting.

I sighed. "The Waldorf, I suppose. Or the Plaza. It doesn't really matter." Eric could take me to the nearest shelter for all I cared.

"A hotel? I figured Aunt Violet's. Or maybe Long Island."

I shuddered. "Mother's?"

The idea of the overwrought townhouse where I had grown up

myself honestly hadn't even occurred to me. Nor had our family's massive Long Island estate, despite the fact that my horse and the stables there would probably do me good. Unfortunately, both places involved my mother, who would probably be too doused in gin and chardonnay to bother giving me the appropriate amount of space or support. Meanwhile, the cooks, maids, butlers, and all the other household staff would be happy to earn an extra dollar by offering anonymous interviews to the tabloids. I hadn't been in the papers this much since I was a teenage debutante; the paparazzi had been incessant in the month following my sentence. It was the one way Rosie's had offered some reprieve.

"No," I said. "I think a hotel will be best." Another cell. Another version of solitary, perhaps. But at least this one came with a concierge and room service.

Eric was quiet as the car stopped in the traffic entering Manhattan. "Well, there is another option, if you want it."

The world outside my window seemed like a gleaming ice cube. Or maybe that was just me, living inside the warped glass of a fishbowl. "Oh? What's that?"

"Well, Jane sort of mentioned that if I didn't bring you home, she'd make kimchi with my testicles."

I turned. "She—what?"

Eric's wide mouth quirked into an impish smile that only his wife and her peculiar sense of humor seemed to be able to bring out of him. "What can I say? She's taken a shine to you." He lifted a hand, then hovered it awkwardly over my shoulder before pulling it back, seeming to remember my earlier reticence to being touched.

Do you know how long it's been since someone held my hand?

Unbidden, a memory flashed through my mind. I asked Matthew that very question the night we met, lonely and aching for someone's, *anyone's* touch. For a moment, I allowed other memories with him to wash over me like a cool rain. The fleeting rendezvous in the hotel, the woods, even his small, spare bedroom. Each time, I had allowed myself to believe that for once in my life, to just one person, I would come first. That I was precious and whole and worth loving beyond measure.

And just as quickly, I remembered the look on his face when he had decided, despite my protests, that I was a liar and a fraud. And thus, had promptly shattered my heart.

"What about you, though?" I asked finally. "Do *you* want me in your home, Eric? You and Jane just moved back there, did you not? I don't want to intrude."

Our family was private. Maybe too private. We saw each other frequently, but everyone had their designated spaces. We barely touched, hardly shared compliments. Conversation was determined by decorum over substance.

Yes, a family like ours had rules to follow. And by spending fifteen days in a jail cell, I had promptly broken many of them.

But then again…so had Eric.

"You won't," he answered quickly. "I—we *both* wanted you to know you're welcome to stay with us for as long as you want. And if you'd rather go somewhere else…well, you know I'll help with that, too."

He was being kind not stating the obvious: that the assets I shared with my husband were frozen, and the bulk of my inheritance was still tied up in probate court following Grandmother's funeral nearly a year ago. It was an issue Eric didn't have once he had been formally hired as CEO and chairman of the board—even without his inheritance, his salary alone was astronomical. I, on the other hand, had a small allowance from the trust set up by my father, but it wasn't anywhere near enough to live on. Despite a storage room full of couture and jewelry, I was all but penniless these days, dependent on the good will of others to keep me afloat. An heiress with absolutely nothing but a record and the Chanel on her back.

Pathetic.

"Why don't you stay through the holidays, at least," Eric continued. "We're having a bit of a Christmas party next week, and after that, Jane will want to see Olivia when she comes home for the holidays. She wants to spend a little more time with kids because…well…" He tipped his head back and forth, causing his straight blond hair to flop from side to side. "She'll probably kill me for telling you this, but, yeah. We're trying for a baby again."

I sat up straight. "You are? Since when?"

"Right after Thanksgiving. The doctor thinks we have a good chance of conceiving naturally, even after everything she went through in Korea."

"Oh, but that's…" I trailed off remembering the horror of Eric and Jane's loss of their first pregnancy at the hands of a complete and total monster. Jane was nearly dead when Eric found her. "Eric, that's *wonderful!*"

My cousin's long, straight nose pinked visibly at the end, the only sign of any anxiety as he nodded. "Yeah. It is. But I'm sure you understand that she's feeling…a little fragile. We haven't told anyone else. Not even Skylar and Brandon."

I nodded with a small smile. I had come to like the Sterling family, Eric and Jane's Boston-based friends, during my brief stay with them in September. They often opened their home to others during the holidays especially. Eric and Jane had also visited for Thanksgiving in part so they could see my daughter, Olivia, who attended school not far from Boston, in my stead.

But then another thought occurred to me.

"Did Matthew go?" I wondered, unable to help myself completely. Matthew was friends with the Sterlings too.

Eric glanced at me, but then kept his gaze trained almost completely on the traffic ahead of us. "He did not. You know we haven't heard from him since September either. But Brandon mentioned that he was still on leave. Working at a bar downtown while he waits, I guess."

I kept my face perfectly still. Matthew? At a bar? The idea of that beautiful, intelligent man wasting his time pouring drinks was painful.

I didn't have time to ask more as the traffic started moving. Eric had reached out again, and this time actually clapped his hand on mine and squeezed. "Jane could use you being there. I know I could too."

I didn't have to think twice.

"Of course I'd love to stay," I said, and was genuinely surprised by how much I meant it.

CHAPTER TWO

DECEMBER 2018

Matthew

Drip. Drop.

D Freezing cold raindrops smacked the collar of my trench coat and splashed my cheeks. A storm was threatening from the New Jersey side of the Hudson, darkening the skies over the Statue of Liberty. From this crumbling cement block of an abandoned Red Hook dock, I had a front row seat.

It was the first day of December, and Mother Nature was celebrating with a harsh drizzle that could easily turn into the first snow of the year. The rest of the streets in my lonely corner of Brooklyn were suspiciously empty—people had already gone to work or else had hibernated at home.

But I hadn't moved for the last three hours, since I'd returned to my side of New York after finishing my latest shift at Envy, the Lower East Side lounge where I currently had a job as a part-time bartender.

Job. Ha. More like a joke. Once I was a Marine. An officer, even. Captain fuckin' Zola before I became Matthew Zola, ADA. I had medals, degrees, accolades and honors. Now I was slinging drinks for Wall Street assholes and the women they wanted to fuck, night after night while I waited for the powers that be to decide if I could, in fact, still be a prosecutor in the city of New York.

And who fuckin' knew when that might be.

With a swig from the flask of bourbon I'd been nursing since clocking out sometime past four, I stared at the front page of the *Post* I'd found abandoned on the subway on my way home. A few more rain drops stained the newsprint, from which shone two familiar faces caught in the bright flashes of paparazzi outside the Brooklyn courthouse where I litigated case after case for nearly eight years. Eric de Vries and Nina de Vries...Gardner.

I almost spat out my drink. Just thinking that name put a bad taste in my mouth. Instead, I took another swig and swallowed heavily, ignoring the buzzing in my head.

The de Vrieses were a good-looking family, I'd give them that. Side by side, the cousins certainly bore a clear resemblance to one another. Same long nose, same flaxen blond hair, same piercing, almost hawkish gray eyes. Despite the generations of polish, ruthlessness lurked behind the designer clothes and perfectly straight teeth. Shadows of the Viking ancestors who had conquered most of Northern Europe at one point, burning and pillaging wherever they went. People who would do anything—and I do mean *anything*—to protect what they believed was theirs.

Eric in particular looked like he had just seized another town. I understood why. The case against Jude Letour was a big one, and the fact that it was going to trial this quickly, just six months after the guy was arrested, was big news. Even bigger when the key witness was one of New York's ten richest people.

But where most people with de Vries-level clout might be content to move behind the scenes, asserting their power like a puppet master, it was obvious that Eric wanted to be a part of this particular display. After all, it was personal.

Letour was the second-most-powerful man in a ring of extremely powerful men, a secret group known as the Janus society. They were stupid rich sociopaths who attended Ivy League colleges before inheriting some of the most powerful positions and wealth in the world. People who say the United States doesn't have an aristocracy are wrong. Wealth and power are generational, and the Janus society was proof.

It also seemed they were having a bit of a civil war. The first-in-command was dead, shot last May in self-defense by Eric's own hand. The Viking had protected his own—in this case, his wife. Letour, though, was responsible for a lot of what had happened to them. He was complicit in the near constant targeting of Eric over the past decade, through the murder of his first fiancée, the abduction of his wife, and even Eric's own kidnapping. Mob tactics, plain and simple. You don't just go after your target—you make them heel by attacking the ones they love.

And when Eric had gone to war with members of the Janus society, I had served as his general. Af few months ago, this had been *my* case. *I* had been working tirelessly and secretively for nearly a year to put this motherfucker away. People like Letour didn't come down easily. The members of Janus had the feds, congress, even the president in their pockets. So I alone had filed all the papers, arranged the stings, worked lock, stock, and barrel with Derek Kingston and Clifford Snow, the single investigative unit who knew about this case. And in the last year, we had identified Jude Letour and John Carson as part of one of the largest human trafficking rings ever in the Northeast. But they were smart enough not to put their names on the thing —just use it, apparently. No, the ring itself was headed by someone outside the Janus society. A man named Calvin Gardner. Nina's husband.

I took another heavy drink. Fuck. Breaking up the white-collar criminal ring that was the Janus society would have all but guaranteed me a promotion, probably bureau chief in another year or two. Instead I was sitting here on this crumbling dock, drinking at seven in the morning next to the river to avoid going home and facing the void my life had become. And for what?

A woman, that's what.

I drifted my thumb over Nina's face, tracing the stark lines of her cheeks, the graceful contour of her lips. She still looked beautiful. More beautiful than any woman I'd ever seen. But unlike Eric, she looked sad. She wasn't wearing red anymore. She hadn't on the night we met, but after I'd mentioned it, I'd only seen her with her lips painted crimson since. Until now.

Yes, I'd sacrificed my future, fucked up my life, for the defendant's wife. And in doing so, I'd also convinced myself that she was just as guilty as he was...and for that, she'd never forgive me. Any wisp of a future disappeared the moment she looked at me in that interrogation room like I'd killed her puppy and kicked it into the river. After everything, I hadn't believed her. I hadn't trusted her the way I had come to realize she had trusted me.

Instead, I'd used her to gain as much as I could for the case against her husband, and possibly against her too.

Now, I had next to nothing.

A shitty job that barely paid my grocery bill.

A mortgage that was quickly eating up my savings.

A sister and niece who would soon be homeless if I didn't figure something out fast.

"Zio!"

Speak of the devil.

I turned at the sound of my niece's bubbly voice, but not before I took another glug of bourbon and tucked the flask into the breast pocket of my trench coat, then tipped the brim of my gray fedora a little farther over my brow to hide the glaze in my eyes. Drunk at seven in the morning isn't a good look for anyone. Sofia didn't need to see me like this.

My sister, however, wasn't giving me a free pass.

"Bit early for that, isn't it?" Frankie asked, glancing at my hidden breast pocket as they approached.

See, this was why I didn't want to go home. My sister was a third-grade teacher at a school in Carroll Gardens—she spent half her days tracking down forbidden crap her students brought to class.

I shrugged as I gave Sofia a quick kiss. "I'm just getting off work, right? Call it my nightcap." I couldn't keep the resentment out of my voice. "Time doesn't exist anymore anyway."

"Well, if that's the case, you won't want your birthday present."

"What?" Sofia looked between us, aghast. "Why wouldn't Zio want his birthday gift?"

I glared at Frankie. "You just had to go there, didn't you?"

She frowned, then turned to Sofia. "Sof, go throw rocks for a second, okay? Can you count ten and see how far they'll go?"

"I can count twenty!" she shouted jubilantly, scampering to the small beach next to us. "Watch!"

"Kid's got it made," I remarked. "If we could all just be happy skipping rocks, maybe the world would be a better place."

"Hmph." Frankie frowned as she came to stand next to me. "Well, while you feel sorry for yourself, open that. Happy birthday, big brother."

I looked down to find a small package pressed onto my lap. "What's this?"

"Just something little. And unmedicated. Open it."

Obediently, I pulled the ribbon off the small black box, then opened it to find a scarlet paisley tie folded neatly inside.

"It's—" Something thick lodged in my throat as I saw a similar fabric tightly binding a pair of snow-white wrists to a headboard. "It's nice, Frankie. Thank you."

"You burned that other red tie, so I figured you could use a new one. Sofia helped me pick it out."

I blinked, taken back to the day I'd arrived home from Boston, gone straight to the kitchen, and burned the red tie in my pocket. The one that had still singed for four hours from the remnants of passion and rage all at once.

"It's great, Frankie. Thank you."

"Don't sound so happy about it. That's real silk, you know."

"I'm sorry." I shook my head. "I'm a little down, that's all."

"I'd say down is an understatement." She sank to the cement block beside me, keeping one eye on Sofia. "Everyone's worried about you. *Nonna* told me to drag you to Mass this weekend kicking and screaming if I had to. I told her I can only manage one toddler at a time."

I shrugged, my hand moving automatically to the cross dangling over my shirt. I hadn't been to confession in months. I hadn't stepped foot in a church in just as long, and had been avoiding the calls from

Nonna, Lea, and just about everyone else I was related to for more than eight weeks.

"This just isn't where I expected to be at thirty-fuckin'-seven, you know?" I said. "A disgraced lawyer, bartending while I'm on unpaid administrative leave. And for what? A fuckin' broad."

Frankie snorted. "Okay, now I know you need to lay off the hard stuff. You keep talking like Sinatra, and I'm going to drag you over to AA."

"No, no, no," I said, but allowed her to reach into my jacket pocket and remove the flask. She was right. It only made me that much more pathetic.

"Have you heard from her?"

"Who?"

Frankie rolled her eyes. "Hilary Clinton. Who do you think? It is your birthday."

"You think she's going to, what, send me a card? Drop off some balloons?" I snorted. The idea of a princess like Nina de Vries strolling down our cracked sidewalk with a dozen multicolored balloons was laughable. "Nah, that's all done with."

Frankie glanced at the paper on my lap, then back at me. "It is?"

I scowled, crumpled the paper, and hurled it toward a garbage can a few feet away. It missed.

Frankie sighed. "Are you working again tonight?"

I nodded. "Yeah. I need to make the bills somehow."

"What time? I could be home a little early. Get a cheesecake from Junior's if you want. It won't be *Nonna's*, but it's something…"

Frankie trailed off. Her meaning was clear. I'd stalwartly ignored any attempt to lure me up to the Bronx to celebrate getting older with my sisters and grandmother, who loved a party more than anyone.

"I have to be at work by five," I lied. My shift didn't start until ten.

Frankie's brow rose. She could clearly see right through me, but didn't say anything. Instead, she waited a moment more before speaking again.

"Mattie?"

"Yeah?"

"Are we…are we going to be okay?"

I frowned. "With what?"

"With…look, I have to ask. I noticed the mortgage is due in a few days, and, well, I know Jamie's only been able to give you part-time shifts, and—"

"We're fine," I said a little too sharply. "Don't worry about that."

Frankie looked unsure. "I mean, I could probably pick up some shifts at Tino's too, like I used to. *Nonna* could watch Sofia; I'm sure she wouldn't mind—"

"I said we're fine," I cut her off again. "Frankie, I promise. This is your and Sofia's house too. I'm not going to let anything happen to you two, all right?"

Even as I said it, a heavy weight lodged in my gut. I hated that she even had to wonder. I hated that we were both back where we started —Frankie working odd jobs because her teacher's salary couldn't pay for her and her little girl, me struggling to make mortgage payments I was way under-qualified to have. We had a tenant below who helped defray some of the costs of the red brick house off Van Duys Avenue. But it didn't cover everything. Not even close.

"*Zio!*" Sofia interrupted as she scampered back over from the water. "Did you like it? I helped Mommy pick it out."

I looked down at the tie in my lap, and immediately felt like shit. "Shi—shoot, kid. Yes, I love it. You did good, Sof. Real good."

Sofia's face split with a wide grin, minus two teeth. "See, Mommy! I knew it!"

She ran back to the water to continue throwing rocks.

"Okay," Frankie said. "Well…if I don't see you. Happy birthday, Mattie."

I glanced at Sofia to make sure she wasn't looking, then drained the last of my bottle. "Sure. Yeah. Thanks, Frankie. Thanks."

CHAPTER THREE

Nina

"I don't understand. Why can't I just give him what he wants and be done with it?"

Four pairs of eyes all blinked, none of them surprised.

I continued pacing on the other side of a marble-topped coffee table.

Jane and Eric sighed simultaneously from their places on their new olive-green Poltrona Frau sofa (I had to give Jane credit—her style was far more adventurous than mine, but she certainly made it work) while Barney Clay and Delia Hibbert, the two attorneys representing me in what was turning out to be a far more contentious divorce than anyone had anticipated, continued scratching notes on identical legal pads. They came highly recommended by Skylar when I decided to file for divorce in New York instead of waiting a year in Massachusetts. I just couldn't stand to be married to my husband one moment longer than I had to.

Two months ago, the same day that I had pled guilty to charges of accessory to trafficking and identity fraud, I had also officially filed for divorce from my husband of ten years. That, however, was just the start. Getting the man to sign any sort of agreement was quite another —particularly when I had agreed to testify against him as a result of my plea deal. Greg Cardozo, the attorney from the Brooklyn DA's office now prosecuting that case, had not yet provided the information to Calvin's counsel, though eventually he would have to. But all the lawyers I was working with thought Calvin likely suspected it, as did the newspapers. And subsequently, he was planning to use our divorce to prevent it at all costs.

Barney and Delia had come tonight with the bad news that yet another offer had been turned down by Calvin's representation.

"Because, Nina," Jane said as gently as she could from where she was currently curled up under Eric's arm. "What he *wants* is everything."

"Not to mention the impossible," Eric added dryly.

He had arrived home from work just as Delia and Barney were finishing up their review of my case. My cousin still hadn't even loosened his tie, but he was more than happy to nurse a vodka soda and cuddle with his wife. My own glass of pinot grigio sat untouched.

I turned from my place in front of the fireplace.

"Still," I said to my attorneys. "He can't be serious. Two *billion* dollars in DVS shares? A seat on the board? He knows my net worth. He knows I don't have anything close to that."

"He also knows you'll do anything to retain full legal custody of your daughter," Delia replied.

"Ms. de Vries," said Barney, "if you might consider sharing at least *some* custody—"

"Absolutely not."

"Fuck, no."

"My cousin will *never* do that."

Jane, Eric, and I all spoke at once. My heart thumped a few times in anger, but just as soon quieted. It was good to know my family felt as vehemently as I did.

I strode forward, collapsed onto a thick white ottoman, and pushed my face into my hands. "I don't know what to do. We've offered the penthouse, the property in Aspen, that ridiculous hut in the Maldives he insisted on buying because all his friends swore by vacations on atolls. Do you remember that?"

Eric looked at me blankly. I had forgotten for a moment that he had actually been absent for most of my marriage.

"My entire stock portfolio and more than seventy percent of my liquid funds," I rattled on. "You would think taking nearly *all* my assets would appease the man. It's worth much more than the hundred million coming in my inheritance and what's left in my trust."

"The problem is that he knows there's a lot more behind it all," Barney said. "Mr. Gardner was there for the reading of your grandmother's will, Ms. de Vries. He knows what the family is worth. And his other attorney is still doing everything he can to challenge the will in probate."

Eric muttered something unintelligible behind me that sounded like "Don't I fucking know it." I gathered the probate issue had caused him some headaches at work once he had assumed leadership of DVS.

"But he's not even a family member!" I burst out. "Tell me again how he managed to squirm his way out of the prenup, Barney? I cannot possibly believe that my grandmother would have *ever* let this happen!"

Delia and Barney both traded bemused, slightly terrified looks that weren't unlike so many other traded glances I had seen around Celeste before she died.

"Well, as we've been over, Ms. de Vries, Mr. Gardner signed the prenuptial agreement less than two days before your wedding," Barney said uneasily.

"We were engaged for less than a month, though," I argued.

"Indeed," Delia replied. "And he's using that to argue that he signed under duress. Unfortunately, it also sounds like the judge may be inclined to agree with him."

I groaned into my hands. "This is ridiculous. No one actually named in the will is arguing Grandmother's state of mind or the document's validity, but somehow he can get away with that too in probate? Calvin should have absolutely no standing here."

"Well, considering your marriage lasted ten years, he may have more than you think," Delia countered gently. "Mr. Gardner's argument is that he has a right to maintain a similar lifestyle to which he has grown accustomed, which is larger than what he was offered in the prenuptial agreement. And the judge may sympathize. Now he's not going to accept some real estate and a few million dollars and walk away, even if it is worth everything you have. Not when your family is worth billions and they have supported you both for years under, as he claims, the logic that until Mr. de Vries returned to the family fold, you were originally going to inherit the de Vries fortune. Not Eric."

"That's all that's in your original trust?" Eric asked. "A few million dollars?"

"Really?" Jane piped up next to him. "Is that what's important here?"

I frowned back at him. "Thirteen, to be exact. There was more, but I gave some to Calvin when we married to start his first investment company. But I'm only given a percentage of the interest as an allowance. Any more than that, and I have to request special permission. My father named Grandmother the head of the board of trustees when I was a girl. When he left for Europe. You should know this, Eric, considering you inherited that position along with everything else."

I couldn't help the resentment. It was one thing to be a teenage girl asking my grandmother for money for seasonal fittings or an extra trip to Paris with friends. Had I been given full access to my trust at that age, it would have almost certainly disappeared in a matter of years, if not months. But now I was thirty-one. And still begging my cousin, who was more like a brother, for pocket money.

Yet another cage from which I longed to be free.

"I—I didn't realize," Eric said, looking a bit ashamed.

"Didn't realize that Grandmother held nearly all the purse strings and then handed them to you?" I replied dryly.

Eric swallowed and turned back to the attorneys. "Okay, so he's tying things up because he thinks I'll pay him off. For the record, I'm not against it—"

"Eric, no," I put in, but he held up his hand, steely-eyed and suddenly resembling our grandmother more than I'd ever seen.

"Nina, it's the least I can do. I wasn't there for you when you needed me. Maybe if I had been, you'd never have gotten wrapped up with the bastard." He turned back to Delia and Barney. "Billions, no. I'll have to speak to my finance guys, but I think we could put together a package worth up to five hundred million, likely including some stocks in other companies, possibly a subsidiary that we can let go. The penthouse and that creepy island. But no ownership of the company. That's a hard line. Can you feel out his interest? Don't name the number."

Delia and Barney both frantically jotted down the details Eric had listed. My mouth was dry. Inheritance or not, five hundred million was *far* more than I was ever going to call my own. Calvin would be a fool not to take it. And perhaps that made Eric a fool for even offering.

Every iota of resentment I'd felt before melted away…and immediately turned to guilt.

"Of course, Mr. de Vries." Barney nodded, and Delia shoved her notes into her briefcase.

I stood up and walked to a window looking onto West Seventy-Sixth Street, watching the occasional car drive past, a few people walking quickly home from work. They had places to be. Homes of their own. Refuges to return to.

I was tired of this. So, so tired. For the first time in over ten years, I had energy to fight, to do something more than lie back and allow whatever misfortune to wash over me like a dirty tide. Yet, once again, I was powerless. Despite only just having been freed from one actual cage, I was still a trapped animal. The world was out there, so close, waiting for me to touch it, and I was tired of everyone else holding the keys to my freedom but me. I wished desperately I knew how to pick the locks.

"It's kind of strange, you know," Jane said. "All the changes Celeste made before she died."

I turned around. "Like what?"

"Like changing the terms of your trust so that you couldn't access it until you were forty."

I grimaced. It had been a lovely surprise last spring to learn that my thirtieth birthday no longer marked full ownership of my assets. I'd paid for it too when Calvin found out. Absently, I rubbed my elbow. That bruise had taken months to disappear.

"And then when she funneled all of your shares of the company out of your name and into Eric's," Jane added.

"Yes," I said wryly. "It almost seems like she didn't think she could trust me with my own money."

"Or she knew this was going to happen, Nina. She knew that rat would try to take it all."

I crossed my arms, hugging my thin frame, which had gotten even thinner over the last few months. Everything tasted like sawdust. I could barely swallow seltzer water.

"Then why did she let me marry him in the first place?" I asked bitterly. "Grandmother hated Calvin. That was never a secret. If she liked to control everyone so much, why not that too?"

Eric shrugged as he crossed one ankle elegantly over his knee and toyed with a loose lock of Jane's hair. "Well, you never did tell anyone that he wasn't Olivia's father. So far as we all knew, he was. She probably just thought he had the right to his own family, at least."

An awkward silence descended over the table. Eric and Jane had taken the news that Olivia wasn't Calvin's biological child in stride, but I did wonder if my cousin was a bit hurt that I had kept up such a lie after his return to the family fold. They had, however, agreed not to say anything to Olivia until I found the right time. The problem was, I wasn't sure when that would be.

"There is...one other option here," Barney ventured.

The lawyer withdrew a document and set it on the table. I walked closer to examine it and immediately recoiled. It was a nondisclosure agreement that effectively forced me to do nothing but take the fifth if and when I was called to the stand in Calvin's trial.

"Absolutely not," I said.

"Ms. de Vries, your testimony in Mr. Gardner's criminal trial is arguably worth more than anything. If you agreed not to testify—"

"*No*," I said viciously. "That was the entire point of taking the plea, was it not? The whole reason I suffered the last two weeks was to be able to put him away."

"It was part of her plea deal," Jane supplied helpfully, having been a prosecutor herself at one point. "And if she breaks it, she'll be taken back to court."

"We may be able to renegotiate that," Delia replied. "I still think there's an argument for spousal privilege."

Jane shrugged. "If it were me, I'd subpoena her regardless, and I'd probably win. Most judges won't uphold spousal privilege if said spouse is accessory to the crime. Nina already confessed. And served her time for it."

Which I appreciate more than you know, doll.

I closed my eyes at the sound of the familiar voice that even now still rumbled in the depths of my conscience, two months since I had last seen him. Truth be told, I was still furious with him. And tremendously hurt. The look on his face when he had come storming into the bedroom where we had just made love only to accuse me of acting in concert with my husband to traffic young women across multiple states had cut me through like a sword. Even more once I had had a moment to really *look* at the so-called video evidence.

Caitlyn Calvert, my former best friend, yes. She might have tried, but she was no me. Not even close.

I had thought the love of my life would have recognized that almost as quickly as I had.

I shook his voice away. Regardless of my feelings for Matthew, I still believed in the importance of his former case. My husband was a monster. My home was riddled with lies. It was long past time for me to do whatever was needed to escape them both and deliver justice where it was needed.

Delia and Barney, Eric and Jane all traded glances. It was no secret that everyone in this room clearly thought that particular decision had been foolhardy in the extreme. I didn't care. The Brooklyn DA had treated me fairly, and the defense attorney Eric had hired as soon as he found I was there had negotiated terms that were better than I had expected. I was sentenced to forty-five days in prison, had served only a few weeks. Was I now technically a felon? Yes. But I wouldn't really suffer, and it would allow me to do the right thing: indemnify my husband, the man who was *really* at fault here.

But if I signed an NDA, it would all go away. Then who knew what he would do to me?

"I want to make something very clear," I said, taking the time to look each of them in the eye. "I only care about coming out of this with two things: my ability to testify against my husband, and my daughter's future intact. I don't care about the money. Any of it. He can have all of my inheritance. Every piece of property. All of it as long as I get to walk away with what's left of my father's trust and enough to get myself through school so I can support Olivia somehow."

My voice carried through the room. The truth was, I was terrified at the idea of being out on my own. But it also seemed like the right thing to do. If anything, Grandmother's postmortem machinations only convinced me that much more that I could not depend on this family.

"Nina," Eric started once more.

"No," I interrupted. "Eric, I know you think I'm just some spoiled socialite raised with a silver spoon—"

"Nina, I didn't say that. But come on, look at you. You're...well, you're obviously used to a certain kind of lifestyle. And now you're saying you want to go without?"

I looked down at my clothes—an icy gray Givenchy blouse and skirt combo I'd purchased two years ago off the runway. Lovely, yes. But not a necessity.

"This is all Grandmother. You have to know that," I replied. "The way she made me in her image. She thought she was teaching me the skills to live this life, but really she was just gilding my cage."

"And the penthouse?" Eric countered. "You live in one of the nicest homes on the Upper East Side—"

"It's a decrepit hatbox that smells like old rose water," I retorted. "I've always hated it, and I always will. He can have it. Next."

"It's a penthouse apartment on Lexington Avenue," countered Delia not-so-gently. "It's worth nearly as much as Celeste's bequest with its value growing. If for some reason the will is challenged successfully, it's a good insurance policy for you."

"I. Don't. Want. It," I practically gritted through my teeth. What was so difficult to understand about this? I turned to my cousin, pleading. "Eric, you left and made it on your own. Why shouldn't I?"

"Because no one's asking you to," he said, but I wasn't done.

"I would wear nothing but rags and raise my daughter in a cardboard box if it meant I could be free of him forever," I said. "That's all I want. That's it."

"Well, luckily, it won't ever come to that," Jane put in as she returned carrying a tray of badly needed glasses of wine for us and the lawyers, plus a straight vodka for Eric.

Warmth flooded through me. The way these two continued to care for me was utterly baffling. I hadn't expected this much. Ever.

My attorneys, however, seemed to have something else on their minds. Neither of them even touched the proffered drinks.

"Er, Ms. de Vries. Might we speak with you in private?"

Eric frowned. "Nina?"

"Come on, Petri dish," Jane cut in. "We don't need to be voyeurs on every single one of Nina's conversations, you know."

She popped up from the couch and proceeded to tow Eric out of the room by his tie. He didn't look altogether unpleased by his wife's sudden attention.

I turned back to Barney, who had made the request. "It's getting late."

"Yes," he said. "But we wanted to speak to you about...well, about the other option here. Of getting Mr. Gardner to be more...amenable."

I frowned. "There's another option?"

Delia sighed. "We didn't think you would want to discuss it in front of Eric and Jane. But, Ms. de Vries, if you *did* file on grounds of abuse—"

My head snapped up. "On grounds of *what?*"

Both lawyers remained quiet. They looked almost sorry for me, and their expressions were exactly why I had never told anyone at all about the things Calvin had done.

But that day in their office, caught as I was on a tidal wave of truth that seemed to be crushing every aspect of my life at the moment, I had told them. I had shown them the pictures I had taken over the years. I had recounted time and time again that Calvin had hit me, kicked me, beaten me so hard my ears rang and I saw stars, sometimes for hours after he was done. I showed them the X-rays with cracked ribs, another with a deep contusion just below my kidney. They had seen everything.

"If you file on grounds of physical abuse, it may speed up the process. Particularly given the fact that with the dates of some of these events, Mr. Gardner may face criminal charges if you wanted to pursue them."

"And if he counters with grounds of adultery?" I asked.

"You said he was not aware of your relationship with ADA Zola," Barney replied. "Was that true?"

"I—yes, I believe it was. But—" I cut myself off this time. "No, I'm not going to do that. It's too much. Olivia will find out. My family will learn of it. No. The answer is no."

Delia folded her lips together, clearly disagreeing. "Please just think about it, Ms. De Vries."

"I'm paying you the earth, or at least my cousin is, Delia. I'll think about it, but I'd ask *you* to think about more creative ways to get me out of this marriage. As soon as possible. Please."

"Ms. de Vries—"

"I need a break," I said suddenly, and stood from the couch, sweeping past Eric and Jane as they reemerged from the upstairs.

"Hey," Jane said. "We were just going to make dinner."

"I'm going for a walk."

"Nina, come on, it's raining," Eric said. "You can go to Jane's workshop if you need some space—"

"Going for a walk!" I practically squawked as I grabbed my favorite cashmere coat from the rack in the front hall and swept out the front door.

"Take Tony!" Jane called before the door swung shut.

But I just kept walking, where neither Jane's voice nor her hulking security detail could follow.

CHAPTER FOUR

Matthew

"I'm going for a smoke."

One brow rose on Jamie Quinn's face, but my best friend (and my current boss) didn't say anything. I knew what he was thinking. Jamie was wondering what the hell was so bad that I was smoking for the first time in ten years.

Nah, fuck that. He knew the answer to that, too. And the fucked-up thing was, neither of us had an answer to the problem. So we were, as they said, letting sleeping dogs lie. Or in my case, reacquaint themselves with nicotine.

It was almost midnight on a Monday, and I was only halfway through my shift. The lounge was all but dead, with a few couples nestled in the far booths and the last remnants of the NYU crowd hanging off some of the barstools. There would be one more influx as the 24/7 folks clambered in before last call. Until then, there wasn't much else to do.

Avoiding Jamie's latent judgment, I took advantage of the lull and headed out the back entrance to the alley. Leaning against the cold brick wall, I pulled the crumpled pack of Camel Lights out of my back pocket, lit one, and took a long drag, then exhaled with a sigh of relief.

It was a bad habit I'd picked up on tour. Like a lot of other service-men, I grasped at anything that would help harden my pounding heart, calm the swirl of anxiety that constantly seemed to beat there when IEDs killed one of my men every other day and the threat of insurgents loomed on every horizon.

Maybe it was the nicotine. Maybe the curling smoke. But some-thing about a cigarette calmed the nerves, something I needed these days. Badly. This city was a war zone. Except the bombs going off weren't IEDs—they were memories of her.

That corner over there. A restaurant two blocks down. The hotel penthouse that loomed overhead. Even this fuckin' bar, where every night, I'd stare at the barstool where I'd first seen her, sipping on red wine, pinky raised and all.

How could you have not known? she'd asked, pain cutting through her silvery eyes like a knife.

It had cut through my chest, too.

And why didn't I see it, huh? If I hadn't been so busy looking for her guilt, I might have noticed proof of her innocence. I'd broken the first rule of justice: innocent until proven guilty.

I'd turned it all around out of fear, too scared to trust the woman I loved. And now I was paying for it, a blast to the heart, on every goddamn corner.

Boom. Boom. Boom.

Liver or the lungs. One of them was going down while I tried to let go of my regret. And let go of her, too.

I finished the cigarette and headed back inside, grateful for the slight haze that now clouded my thoughts. The bar was full again, right on schedule. In another hour, it would peter out for the last time. Jamie would do last call around two, then he and I would clean up, and I'd head home at the relatively early hour of three instead of four thirty or five.

Some schedule. Some fuckin' life.

"You want me to take the door end?" I asked as I washed my hands at the sink next to the register.

Jamie finished ringing up a new tab. "No, I got it. You take the inside section. There's someone there for you anyway."

I frowned. "Who?"

For a moment, I wondered if it was one of the ladies who some-times still left breathy voicemails, dreaming of "that one night" we had spent together and begging for one more. Some people might have found them pathetic, but these days, I only felt that about myself. A year ago, I would have taken those calls and thought nothing of it. Met them at some hotel out by the airport, where their husbands wouldn't find them.

Now the thought just made me ill. Because as much as I hated it, there was only one woman I had eyes for anymore. Married or not, she had stolen my soul, along with any faith I had in the institution of marriage or even love.

And I'd fucked it all up.

Shit. Maybe I needed another smoke.

"I think you know." Jamie handed me a newly opened bottle of his most expensive red wine. A wine I knew very well, considering I'd once shared a bottle of it with—

"Shit."

"Don't pussy out now. Although you might want a breath mint. You smell like a pool shark, Zola."

"It's a bar, Quinn," I snapped even as I grabbed one of the Altoids we kept under the register.

He just chuckled. "Whatever you say. But if I had that waiting for me, I'd take at least four of those bad boys. And I wouldn't keep her long."

My friend turned to help a crowd of college students on the other side of the bar. I sighed, taking a second to adjust the rolled-up sleeves of my plain white shirt, the cheap black tie, the old black pants that were appropriate for a job where spills happened every few minutes, courtesy of over-excited patrons.

I felt strangely naked without a full suit. This was a woman who went through designer threads like she picked them up at the Good-will. I'd never seen her anything less than perfect unless I was the one mussing her up. I wasn't her equal in a lot of ways, but right now, the idea that I was no better than one of her servants hurt my pride more than I wanted to admit.

Or maybe you're just delaying the inevitable, asshole.

I rolled my eyes. Yeah, even my conscience wasn't putting up with my bullshit tonight.

I checked my breath, and when I finally turned around, I was immediately struck with the strongest déjà vu of my life. Nina de Vries was sipping wine at the end of the bar right where Jamie said she was, looking almost exactly the same as when I'd first met her in an elegant gray cashmere coat partially covering a white silk dress. Under the dim lights, her smooth, pale skin seemed to glow. One long leg was crossed over the other, a silver-colored high heel dangling off her foot. Her blonde hair gleamed, and her lips were stained with drink.

For a moment, it was the same dark and stormy night eleven months ago. I was knocking back gin like it was my job, feeling lost and alone for reasons I couldn't comprehend. She sat at the other end, fingering the stem of her wineglass. An angel in white. A beacon in the dark.

This time, though, the angel was staring a hole through me and looked really fucking mad. Angel of mercy, I'd hoped for. More like the angel of death.

Still, it was her. Nina, in my bar. Nina, out of jail.

Nina…free.

"Excuse me?"

The palm of a short, snappy woman found the bar top with a flat, hard smack. Shit. Nina already had her drink, but there were at least four customers waiting to be served. As much as I wanted to ignore them, I couldn't. I was working. And frankly, I needed the tips.

"Hey, handsome," said the twentysomething woman, whose businesslike blouse was unbuttoned a few too low. "Think we could get some drinks?"

I blinked. "Sorry, ladies. Sure. Just caught in my thoughts for a second."

"I like a daydreamer," said her friend with a sly grin. "So long as he shows me what he's thinking later on."

She slid her jacket off, baring a thin black shirt that was a lot too tight, and batted a pair of eyelashes that looked like the ones my sister Joni glued on her eyelids every now and then. I told her they made her look like Betty Boop and that no man wanted to feel plastic butterfly wings smacking his cheeks when he was kissing his date. She told me to take my chauvinist male gaze and shove it up my ass.

Some manners.

I didn't argue. Still, a man could have his preferences.

I nodded at Betty with a fake smile, conscious of the much more alluring siren to my right watching us with silver daggers.

In the two months since I'd last seen Nina in that interrogation room, I'd about given up on her. Us. Anything. After that little stunt I pulled, I had been told in no uncertain terms that I was not to approach her until she was sentenced, unless I cared to be disbarred completely. And even though Cardozo never said it, talking to her at all until her husband was locked up was probably a bad idea too.

But apparently I was a glutton for self-punishment. I had tried to visit her at Rikers only to be told that Ms. de Vries was not accepting visitors other than her attorneys. Since she was released, her phone number was disconnected too. She had a lot of very good reasons for the distance too, I supposed. Like that I'd broken her fucking heart.

Maybe that was the reason she looked like she wanted to claw my eyes out. Or maybe she was just acting the same way I felt as a couple of men eyed her overtly on their way to the restroom.

Jealousy really is a sneaky bitch.

So yeah, maybe that's what made me wink at my new customers like a teenage boy on the prowl. I had an audience. And for the first time in months, it was making me feel a bit more alive.

"What can I get you ladies? Something sweet or something spicy?"

Okay, not my finest, I'll admit. Still, the two girls giggled like hyenas. The white figure in my peripheral vision remained perfectly still.

"Can you make a cosmopolitan?" asked Betty, eyelashes batting hard enough to cast a small wind across the bar.

"Like a champ," I told her with a grin. "And for you, miss?"

"A lemon drop, please," said Blouse Buttons.

"Sweet and sour," I confirmed. "The very best combination."

The girls glanced at each other and grinned. "We like to think so," one of them said. "Especially with the right...mixer."

A loud yet incredibly ladylike cough sounded from the other end of the bar. I didn't look her way—not yet—and just smiled more broadly to myself.

"We'll be in the far booth if you want to join us," said Betty as she and her friend sashayed away. "We hope you do."

"Cheers, ladies." I turned to the next customer only to find Jamie already there.

"That was a very nice show you put on there, Casanova," he said dryly as he poured a couple of drinks. "Now do us both a favor and take care of that one before she burns my bar to the ground."

I snorted, busying myself with drying some glasses. "She wouldn't do anything like that."

"Tell that to the napkin and three coasters she just ripped to shreds. Zola, stop being a fuckin' pussy and go talk to her. As your boss, that's an order."

I sighed. Not much to say to that. I tossed the bar towel over my shoulder, grabbed the bottle of wine Jamie had opened, and headed over to meet my doom.

"Of all the gin joints in all the world..." I started as I approached.

"Save it," Nina snapped. "I finally watched that movie, you know, and it's not nearly as good as you think it is."

I slapped a hand to my chest like she had shot a bullet through my heart. "You didn't like *Casablanca*? How is that even possible? Who doesn't love Humphrey Bogart?"

"He doesn't even fight for her. She's married, sure, but she was in love with him. And he just lets her go."

"He was being noble. He knew she'd be better off."

"He was a coward and a cad. And he didn't deserve her anyway," Nina cut back, then tipped back the remainder of her wine like it was a shot of cheap tequila.

I couldn't help but wonder if she was still talking about Bogart...or someone else. "Well, so much for lightening the mood. Hello to you too, duchess."

"What are you doing here?" Nina demanded without reservation.

I frowned. "Come again?"

"I said, what are you doing here? Working or whatever. If that's what you'd call it."

She looked over her shoulder at the two girls now giggling away with a pair of investment bankers who had joined them in their booth instead of me. I could have kissed her for the unbridled jealousy.

"I don't give a shit about them and you know it," I said as calmly as I could as I started polishing a set of wineglasses that definitely didn't need polishing.

Nina turned back, her hair swishing around her shoulder as she did. "Then what was that all about?"

"What was what all about?"

"You know."

I raised a brow. Suddenly, I had no intention of making this easy on her. Two months I'd settled for newspaper clippings and secondhand information. There was an elephant in the room, and she didn't want to deal with it. But somehow she thought *she* could interrogate me?

Think again, doll.

"What's that?" I asked instead of answering her question.

"The—" She did a pretty admirable job of miming the girls' idiotic body language, followed by my own tendency of leaning on my forearm across the bar with a knowing look.

"I do not do that," I said.

"You absolutely do. Usually when you're trying to 'charm' some-one. I should know."

The acidity in her voice burned. I didn't like the insinuation, though I knew what it meant. She thought I had tried to play her too. And she was right. Sort of.

"Fine. Maybe I do," I said, unable to keep my own bitterness at bay. "Paying a mortgage on tips is a lot harder than it sounds, princess. Not that you'd know."

She recoiled visibly at the pet name, and because I knew why, I did too. Her husband used that name for her. I heard him do it once, and I'd wanted to beat the shit out of him right there and then.

I hadn't meant to use it. She was just sitting here like goddamn royalty, looking down her long nose at every person in the place, including me. Who was she to get pissed at whatever I needed to do to pay my bills? Female bartenders could show off their tits. So I had a few nice lines and a smile women seemed to like. I wasn't breaking any laws here.

Still. That name was a low blow, and I knew it.

"Sorry," I muttered. "I didn't mean it."

"Yes, you did. And I deserved it." She also had the grace to look dejected. "But I would appreciate it if you wouldn't use it again."

I nodded in a funny kind of half bow. "You got it, duchess."

We stared at each other in a funny, awkward kind of silence. I grabbed another perfectly clean wineglass and started polishing.

"Well, are you going to take them up on their invitation?"

I snorted. "Are you kidding?"

"I don't know. They seemed quite eager, don't you think?"

Suddenly, I was done with the games. I didn't want to trade jibes anymore. Not when every one of them felt like a punch to the gut.

"Nina." I stopped what I was doing, set the glass on the bar top with a clink, and fixed her with a steady gaze. "Why in the fuck would I bother with a poster print when I've got the original here in front of me? Even when you clearly want to slap me silly, you're still the most beautiful woman I've ever seen."

Nina's mouth dropped, and I fought not to stare. I lost. Her lips closed, and she bristled. And finally looked away.

"I didn't think you would be here," she said quietly. "I left the house tonight somewhat…frustrated. I wanted a drink. And I ended up here. Call it nostalgia, if you like."

"You didn't think I would possibly show up at my best friend's bar?" I asked incredulously.

"Well, I didn't *exactly* know you worked here until tonight, if that's what you're asking." She blinked coyly, though it was obvious she had given up on hiding her innocence. "But really. Why *are* you working here?"

I shrugged, glancing down the bar to make sure Jamie didn't need help. Things had calmed down again, and he was busy at the register. Everyone else in the joint had a drink.

"Like I said, I have to pay the bills somehow, don't I?" I pulled out the bottle of wine I'd brought over. "Another?"

Nina bit her lip—which certainly didn't help me to stop looking at it—but then cautiously nodded.

"Why, though?" she persisted as she watched me pour. "Why are you doing...this?"

"I'm on leave, remember? I tried to quit all together, but my boss wouldn't let me. Four more months of this, or so I think. Really depends on how the trial goes. I doubt I can come back until your husband's locked up. Or worse, let off."

"But you're a lawyer. You should—can't you get work in another office?"

"Not for a year, at least. I signed a non-compete when I was hired." I looked regretfully around the bar. "You know, after I finished law school, I really thought I was done with this kind of grunt work. But then again, I didn't think I'd meet someone like you, either."

"What's that supposed to mean?"

I shrugged as I stowed the bottle back under the bar. "Someone worth throwing it all away for."

Nina softened for a moment. "No one asked you to do that."

"No one had to. I'd do it again in a heartbeat."

We stared at each other for a long second, unsure of what else to say.

A million questions danced between us, all unspoken. I wanted to ask her a million things, but couldn't.

Did you take the plea the papers say you did?

Are you really getting divorced from that scumbag?

Did any of those motherfuckers at Rikers touch you?

Have you forgiven me for not believing you?

Have you forgiven me for not being there when you got out?

Will you ever forgive me...for all of it?

But before I could get up the nerve to ask anything, Nina reached into her purse and pulled out a pink envelope decorated with green heart stickers.

"Olivia made this for you," she said quietly. "It came in the mail last week."

With one slim finger, Nina pushed the letter across the bar toward me. "She wanted you to have it in time for your birthday. I apologize for not getting it to you sooner."

I took the letter, which had my name scrawled across the front in a little girl's naive, looping script. I tore it open and pulled out a hand-drawn card that had pictures of baseball and pizzas on it, along with the following written inside:

DEAR MATTHEW,

I HOPE *you're having a good birthday and had a really big cake with your sisters and your family. I hope I get to meet them someday too and see you again.*

XOXOXOXO,
 Olivia

I STARED at the note for a long time, trying to understand why such a short, perfunctory card from a nine-year-old girl I'd only spent a few days with seemed to tear my chest in two. I had received a few other "cards" for my birthday from my nieces and nephews. Equally child-like, with the same kinds of simple drawings and wooden messages.

But this one, sent of her own accord from the little blonde girl with soulful dark eyes…the one who called me Matthew like her mother and who fell asleep on my chest like it was the most natural thing in the world… Yeah, this one meant something more.

Then it occurred to me that I'd never told Olivia my birthday. But I had told her mother.

"You remembered," I said. "My birthday, that is."

"I remember everything about you, Matthew." She didn't sound like she was glad of the fact.

Yeah, well. I knew the feeling.

Her eyes were bright, but still disturbingly hardened, even in the bar's dim light. So different from the soft, silky gray I had always found there, begging to wrap me in their warmth.

But there were other differences too. Her hair, though still glossy and bright, actually looked a bit duller than I remembered, and more than a few strands were out of place. Her lips were full and plump, but plain and unpainted. Under her eyes, shadows carved fatigue into her porcelain face.

"Hey," I said as I reached out a hand. "Are you all right?"

She looked at my hand on the bar, but didn't take it. Still, the pretense fell.

"It's been difficult," she admitted. "Very difficult. I don't suppose you've been following the news—"

"Every word," I cut in. "You don't have to tell me anything you don't want to."

"Then you know. About the plea deal. And the divorce. You know things are...moving forward."

I nodded. "I read something about it. But your case was sealed, right?"

She nodded.

"Good. So Cardozo won't have to give it up to Calvin's attorneys until later. But you had to go to Rikers, didn't you?"

Nina shuddered. "Yes. I did. Fifteen days."

It wouldn't matter if it was for an hour or a lifetime. Any time spent in that shithole would never be okay.

"Are you all right?" This time I set my hand on top of hers. "Now, I mean."

"I'm so...oh, Matthew, I'm so *angry* at you still. But...I miss you." Her head dropped, like she was deeply ashamed. "I do."

Words bubbled up before I could stop them. *Fuck*, I wanted to hold her so badly.

"Nina, I'm so sor—"

"Don't."

I frowned. "Why the fuck not?"

She sighed, staring at our hands entwined. Our fingers weaved together, light and dark.

"Because. I'm not ready to hear it." Before I could stop her, she pulled her hand away. "This was a mistake. I shouldn't have come here."

She slid off the stool like a stream of water, set an embarrassingly large bill on the bar, and started toward the door before I could stop her.

"Shit," I muttered. "Nina, wait. One more thing!"

She turned. "Yes?"

I gulped, grasping for straws. And then, by some miracle, I found one. "Eric and Jane's Christmas party. Are you going to be there?"

She stilled. "I—yes. Why? Were you invited?"

"Well, yeah. They are friends. Would you mind if I came?"

She swallowed, and for a moment, I thought she might say yes. I told myself it didn't matter. I wasn't planning on going to the party in the first place, since I figured she'd be there and wouldn't want to see me anyway. If I was smart, I'd just lie low for a while and definitely away from the Gardner case and anything to do with it.

But I wasn't smart. When it came to Nina de Vries, I was the dumbest man in New York. All she had to do was crook her little finger, and I'd come running.

After all...what more did I *really* have to lose?

"No," she said. "I wouldn't mind."

Relief flooded me. "Well, all right then. I guess I'll see you there."

I turned toward the other end of the bar with every intent of using other patrons to make my cool exit.

"But, Matthew?"

I looked back. "Yeah, doll?"

The nickname made the side of her luscious mouth twitch, but she didn't smile.

"You're not forgiven. Not even close."

Maybe not, I thought to myself. But for the first time in months, I found myself able to see a possibility of a bright side. Maybe the fact that she was bringing it up meant that it could change. Maybe there was hope after all.

CHAPTER FIVE

Nina

I t had been a sudden decision to change the color and style I'd worn essentially for at least a decade. Jane and I had been trying to decide what to wear for the Christmas party she and Eric were throwing. While she was mostly concerned with trying to hide the baby bump she was convinced was already evident (it was not), I was trying unsuccessfully not to hear the sound of Matthew's voice every time I held up a dress in front of the antique twin mirrors mounted in the guest-room closet.

"Everything I own is white," I complained once I had cycled through every piece of clothing I had taken out of my storage unit to their house. "I look like that Disney princess. The one who makes the ice in that movie Olivia loves. *Frozen*, I think."

"Elsa?" Jane chuckled as she looked me over. "Actually, that's not a bad comparison. But I think technically, she was an ice queen." She had only laughed harder when I fixed her with a glare. "You look just like Eric when you do that, you know. And it only makes me tease him more."

I held up a white sateen frock that was once one of my favorite pieces. It glittered with tiny mother-of-pearl beadwork that shimmered when I walked. The perfect winter white, like a snowflake.

It was very...me. Icy. Colorless. Lifeless.

Classic, doll.

With another scowl, I threw the dress on the bed. I didn't want to be his *doll* right now, whether it was at a bar or in my own head. Right now, when I looked in the mirror, I saw only a woman who was played for a fool—by a charming Italian-American prosecutor, my best friend, my grandmother. Classic was fine. Icy too. But apparently they were too easy to imitate. So much that the man who swore he loved me more than anything was fooled by a few pictures.

And just like that, I was seething all over again.

"Nina, are you all right?" Jane reached out tentatively. "I'm sorry about the joke. I didn't mean anything by it, really. You don't look like Elsa, I swear."

I just shook my head, swept up my purse, and started for the door. I needed to get out of there. Go...somewhere. "Do you think Eric would mind terribly if I purchased a new dress for tonight?" I immediately hated myself for even having to ask.

Jane frowned. "Nina, you don't need his permission or mine to use your own money. That's why he put it in your account. So you wouldn't have to ask at all."

"Well, if it came from you, it's not really mine, is it?" I snapped, then wilted completely. "I'm sorry, Jane. That was unforgivable."

Jane put her dress on the bed next to mine, albeit much more carefully than the way I'd hurled the priceless piece. Then she strode to me and placed a hand on my shoulder with a light squeeze.

"Absolutely no apologies needed," she said firmly. "I can't blame you for being irritated. I'd probably have destroyed this entire room by now."

"Sometimes I feel like all of this is her punishment from beyond the grave," I said. "Like there was some sort of test for my life, and by choosing the way I did, I failed. And she'll never stop punishing me for it."

Jane just looked on sympathetically. "I know I'm still relatively new to this family...but I really don't think Celeste wanted to punish you for anything. If anything, I think she would be happy to see you becoming more independent."

"Ha." The sharp laugh flew out of my mouth on a bite. "By independent, do you mean wearing orange instead of black? Or smudging the pristine de Vries name with my gorgeous record?"

The hand on my shoulder rubbed more insistently. "I think she'd be impressed that you did whatever you believed was right. It took guts. Everyone knows that."

I stared at myself in the mirrors again. Despite being of similar heights—Jane was also close to my nearly five feet, ten inches—we were polar opposites. Her hair was a deep black brown, but streaked with a few colorful riots on one side that tended to change with her moods. Right now they were aqua and green. Her gold cat-eyed glasses gleamed atop her bright hazel eyes and the slash of red she always wore on her lips. In slim black jeans, the sturdy combat boots, and the bright red top that wrapped around her torso like a snake, she was an explosion of contrast and color, daring anyone to ignore her. Meanwhile, I was as colorless as the dress I'd discarded. Between my light blonde hair, one of hundreds of white silk blouses, light gray wool pants, and the tasteful makeup designed to look as natural as possible. Everything was impeccable, of course. Products of the very best designers and the very best salons and the very best stylists. And yet, I practically disappeared into the walls behind me.

Suddenly, I couldn't bear it any longer. I wanted to scratch my own eyes out for hatred of their plain, distant gray.

"Go," Jane urged with a light tap on my back. "Spoil yourself a little. Just take Tony with you—otherwise Eric really will be angry when he gets back."

I nodded. When I'd fled the apartment, I had been rid of Davis, the Calvin-assigned driver, as well as my assistant, Moira, and anyone else who could have potentially told him more about me. I was content to trade one babysitter for another. For now.

"I'll be back before the party," I said, then pushed my purse up my shoulder and left.

―――――

THREE HOURS LATER, I was turned around in the chair at my favorite salon to face myself in the mirror.

"Okay, this color looks amazing." My stylist, Marco, practically gleamed as he fluttered his hands over my freshly shampooed hair, tucking and petting as he examined his work. "The lowlights will look fabulous once we blow it out. Just that hint of bronze underneath, and your natural color comes to life, my love."

I smiled grimly in the mirror. "But it will be darker now, right?"

"Not so much that it won't blend with your natural hair. Just a little more gold and caramel. Much warmer than before. I know you wanted to go full brunette, but with your complexion and eyes, babe, you really would have ended up looking like you rose from the dead."

Still, as I turned my chin back and forth, examining the way the salon lights reflected off the new shades, I could see he was right. When I'd asked for him to dye it black, Marco had shaken his head and said absolutely not. Blonde I'd always be. But I could still look different.

I nodded. "Point taken. Now, chop it off, please."

Marco sighed, then, standing behind me, grasped two solid locks of hair on either side of my face and pulled them to my chin. "Really?"

"To here." I held my hand to my chin, indicating I wanted twelve inches or so gone. "At least."

"Are you sure? Your long hair, it's so lovely. Like a pri..."

At my suddenly fierce expression, Marco trailed off. I could tell he wanted to say princess, but didn't. He had caught my wrath for that particular comment more than once over the years.

"To the chin," I ordered. "Or else I'll ask Sara to give me a pixie."

Marco's mouth dropped in horror as I gestured to one of the other stylists in the salon whose chair was currently empty. "You wouldn't! Don't even joke about such a thing."

He gathered my wet hair into a ponytail at the base of my neck, pulled it straight, and picked up his scissors. It took only a few moments, but eventually, the tension gave as the blades sliced through the last few strands. *Snip, snip.*

I smiled genuinely now, enjoying the way the jagged edges of my newly shorn hair bounced around my chin. Gone was the princess, icy or not. In front of me was someone else entirely. I was eager to discover who she was.

———

IT'S NOT FOR HIM, I tried to tell myself as I fingered yet another red dress in the Oscar de la Renta boutique at Bergdorf's. I wasn't attracted to the boldest color in the spectrum simply because a certain devastatingly handsome Italian was planning to attend this little soirée. Or the look on said Italian's face whenever he saw me in this color. No, no connection at all.

I pulled a short red velvet minidress off the rack and held it up against my body while I looked at one of the mirrors mounted on the walls.

Do you ever wear red? Matthew's deliciously lazy voice echoed through the back of my mind.

"*No,*" I told it sharply. "And certainly not for you."

"N?"

I jumped and opened my eyes to find a familiar face peering at me from the other side of a slender white mannequin. "Caitlyn?"

"My God. I thought I heard you talking to someone, but it wasn't until you turned around that I really recognized you. That hair!"

She scampered around the other side of the mannequin, revealing a wrinkled shopping bag in one hand and her Birkin in the other.

Reflexively, I touched the edges of my hair. "Oh, yes. I, um, just got it cut." I looked around, suddenly wishing I had taken Tony up on his offer to accompany me up the escalators. Eric's chief of security was waiting for me by the concierge desk, where he could watch both entrances. "I—Caitlyn, what are you doing here?"

She glanced at her bag, then back at me. "I—well, shopping, I mean, okay, yes, I have to return something. But please don't tell anyone." Her words were a quick stumble, and her embarrassment was palpable. "It's nothing, really, just an absolutely hideous sweater Kyle's mother bought me for my birthday, and I absolutely hate it. Since when do you buy off the rack, by the way?"

"Oh, well…" I shrank, suddenly even more uncomfortable. "Given the circumstances, I thought I should try to save a bit of money."

I could hear Matthew's snort in the back of my mind. Yes, I was aware of the irony of saying that any shopping on Fifth Avenue characterized saving money. But considering the couture I usually wore to events like these cost sometimes ten or twenty times as much as I would pay here, Bergdorf's was downright frugal. And it wasn't as though Eric would want me mingling with his business associates in dime store garbage.

"Eric must give you a nice allowance." Caitlyn's voice was just slightly tinged with sourness.

I scowled. "I don't know if that's any of *your* business."

She held up her hands in surrender, and it was then I noticed a few other things that were off. Her nails were unvarnished, short at the tips instead of long and polished. Her hair, too, was growing out, with her dark roots evident, ends split and dried.

"It was just a comment," she said. "Everyone knows you're living with him and…*her*."

"I'm staying with Eric and Jane because they asked me to, if you must know. It's quite nice. *She* is quite nice."

I used the same slanted tone Caitlyn had used to refer to Jane. Caitlyn's eyes narrowed, but she seemed to give up the fight, slumping with a heavy exhale.

"Good for you," she said quietly. "Good for them."

I studied her for a moment, then hung the Oscar de la Renta I was holding back on the rack, suddenly ready to go. I could borrow something of Jane's, or make do with white.

"I need to go," I said. "We shouldn't be talking, given everything that's going on."

"Oh, please, N. Don't."

There was something in the pathetic tenor of Caitlyn's voice that stopped me.

"Please," she whispered. "I'm so sorry. You have no idea how awful it's been."

I stared at the hand on my arm until it fell again.

"*I* don't have any idea how *awful* it's been?" I repeated more caustically than I thought. "Did you think they rolled out the red carpet for me at Rikers Island? I suppose it doesn't matter. You'll discover the pleasures of the place soon enough, I should hope."

I didn't have to add that on top of everything else, Eric had insisted on suing Caitlyn for damages regarding identity theft. Neither he nor Jane had any love for her, and at the moment, neither did I.

Caitlyn's lower lip trembled as her large blue eyes filled with tears. "I had—I had no idea that you were going to do that, you know! Calvin said you'd never breathe a word of it. He said in my own way, I was protecting you!"

"You thought you were protecting me by—" I cut myself off, shaking my head as my voice rose untenably. I wasn't used to this. Losing my cool. Losing my temper. And in a place like this. I took several deep breaths before I could continue, still gritting my teeth. "You thought you were protecting me by pretending to *be* me?"

Caitlyn's eyes shimmered, oceans of regret. *Or so she wants you to think,* I told myself. I couldn't believe anything this person said to me anymore. Or ever had.

And like she knew it wasn't an argument worth having, Caitlyn just shook her head sadly. "I...well, I suppose if things don't go well, I might take your place in there anyway." She sniffed. "Kyle certainly seems to think so. He filed for divorce. On grounds of fraud, if you can believe that. I wouldn't have contested it—he just wants to humiliate me."

I swallowed. "I'm sorry to hear that."

I wasn't. That Kyle Shaw, the latest aging billionaire Caitlyn had cornered for herself, had demanded a divorce—with *grounds*, no less— barely six months after their wedding was the least of the justice she deserved.

"It wasn't always a lie, you know." Like she could hear my inner doubts, Caitlyn cut through my thoughts at precisely the right moment.

I reared like a shy horse. "*What* wasn't always a lie?"

"Our friendship," she said softly. "When we first met...all those years ago..."

I didn't reply, but couldn't help the cascade of memories that accompanied her admission. The moment when we had met—both of us at eight, both painfully shy for entirely different reasons. She was marked as an outsider, her scholarship status evident in her grubby secondhand uniform and the thick New Jersey accent that took her close to ten years to smooth over. I, on the other hand, stuck out on the other end, the only child of Violet de Vries Astor, daughter of a dynasty, and just as friendless as any princess. I remembered how badly I had wanted a *real* friend in a world where everyone I knew only seemed to care about my family. Here was this girl from outside the city who didn't know me. Didn't know my names.

I cringed.

Or so I'd thought.

"When?" I asked, unable to help myself. "When did you start...was it from the beginning? Back when we were only children?"

Her eyes widened, and she shook her head vigorously. "Oh, oh *no*, N! No, I promise, it—I had no idea who you were."

I wasn't sure I could believe her, but somehow, it still made me feel better.

"Calvin is my cousin," she said. "Second, I think, or maybe third. By marriage. You know all of this already, I expect."

I stared at her, unwilling to look away. I did, yes. A private investigator had gone to Hungary and made short work of the connections between Károly Kertész —otherwise known as my erstwhile husband, Calvin Gardner—and Katarina Csaszar, an orphaned two-year-old girl who had gone back to Hungary in 1990 and returned less than a year later in the care of her mother's cousin. But only after the two of them had legally changed their names in Budapest to Sara and Caitlyn Calvert.

"He was much older than me," she said. "You know that, too. But he was always around. When I was given the spot at the academy, it was such a relief..." She shuddered, as if trying to shake off some nameless memory. "And then he went away, too. Went to some business school, I think. Honestly, I don't really even know. It wasn't until he came back to the city and got that job with your father. I remember when he came home for Christmas. He asked me about you. Said he met you at a Christmas party or something like that, and that you and I went to the same school. I didn't think anything of it at the time. I just knew...I knew if I didn't answer his questions, he would...punish me."

I didn't push to ask what she meant. I could imagine. I had borne the brunt of Calvin's "punishments" more than enough over the years, as Caitlyn well knew. And if Caitlyn had grown up with it, no wonder she always acted as though she understood exactly what I was experiencing. She did know. Perfectly.

"He said he loved me," she whispered. "Like a...like a brother. Of sorts."

It sounded innocent, but there was something about the way she paused that made me look up.

"A brother. Hmm. But did he ever..." I couldn't finish the sentence. I couldn't even think about the possibilities for that kind of relationship.

Her lower lip trembled. But then, slowly, she nodded. "Just a few times. When I was younger. Before you left for college."

My stomach turned. We had been girls. Teenagers, still in high school. Caitlyn was younger than me—she didn't turn eighteen until the fall after we graduated. Which meant that Calvin had been sleeping with her when she was only a child.

"You were what he really wanted," she continued. "But he said you thought you were too good for him."

"That's because I am."

For once, I had no shame in saying what others had whispered for the last ten years, what had caused Calvin to rage at me so terribly behind closed doors. Maybe it was the time, maybe it was finally meeting Matthew, or maybe it was having family members who saw my worth again, but I had no problem admitting the truth: I *was* too good for my husband. And I always had been.

"So, is that it?" I asked acerbically. "He met me at my father's party and the two of you planned to entrap me in this scheme when we were, what, fifteen?"

"No!"

Caitlyn stepped back, like she knew the importance of calming herself. The store was quiet. We would attract attention sooner rather than later.

"No," she said again. "It was—it was after he ran into you in Queens. The day you…" She glanced down at my stomach, then back up at me. "The day you decided to keep Olivia," she finished softly.

I examined her hard. More and more of those conversations came back to me these days as I tried to retrace my mistakes. The random ways Caitlyn and I had "run into each other" following my return from Florence. The way she had skillfully feigned surprise when I'd confirmed my engagement to Calvin. The way she had so subtly urged me to go through with it.

The entirety of it made me sick.

"I have to go," I said as I turned away.

"Wait."

She reached out and grabbed my arm before I could slip around the racks of clothing.

"We were friends, Nina," she pleaded. "*Best* friends."

"We absolutely were *not*." I shook her off me. "And we certainly aren't now, nor will we ever be. Let's be *very* clear about that."

Again, her lower lip trembled. "All I wanted was to be a part of your family."

"I think you mean you wanted to *be* my family." The statement was acid on my tongue. "Specifically me, correct?"

"He said I had to," Caitlyn whispered. "He said I had to, or else he would…Nina, you know what he does. T-to those girls. My guardian died when you were in Italy. Don't you remember? He promised—he said I'd be one of them if I didn't do what he—he said I'd disappear, and no one would ever care about some no-name from Paterson! It was why I took up with Florian, remember him? I was trying to escape, just like you are now. But he's never let me go, not ever!"

"Keep your voice down!" I hissed, suddenly aware of the perking heads of the saleswomen on the other side of the boutique. The last thing I needed was a scene. Not when half the paparazzi in New York were still on the lookout for me daily.

Caitlyn swallowed. "I—okay. I'm sorry. I'll get myself under control."

"And I am going to leave," I said, turning once again for the exit. "And you are *not* going to follow me."

"Wait, Nina! Please!"

"What?" I hissed as I whirled around. "What else could you possibly want from me?"

"Calvin. He's angry. And mean."

"Do you think I don't know that?" I demanded. "You, of all people? I know his temper, Caitlyn. I wore the marks of it for *ten years*."

"I know that," she replied. "But, Nina, you've never seen this side of him. The side that plans. The side that did this." She gestured up and down her general person, clearly to indicate all the changes in her appearance she'd been forced to assume. "That's the side you shouldn't underestimate. He's smarter than you think. And when he wants something—vengeance—he'll do anything until he gets it."

We stared at each other for a long time. Blue eyes locked with gray. I searched for the signs of the duplicity I knew was there. But Caitlyn didn't look away. She didn't waver. Not once.

"Okay," I said at last. "I'll keep that in mind." I turned to leave, but found I couldn't. Not without saying one more thing. "You should— Caitlyn, would you ever consider…what he did to you, it isn't right. You should come forward. Tell your story."

She blinked, looking very much like a blue-eyed owl. "Oh, no. I could never do that. And you can't make me, N, so don't even try."

"Why not?" I shook my head. "Why would you go to jail for someone like him?"

"Because," she said. "He's the only family I have left, for better or for worse." She cocked her head. "I'm sure you know how that feels."

We examined each other, shocked to find one last thing we had in common.

Caitlyn nodded. "Okay. I'll—I'll see you, N."

I blinked. "Yes—well, probably not, actually."

Caitlyn opened her mouth like she wanted to argue. But eventually it closed, and she nodded in defeat. "All right, Nina. If that's what you want."

CHAPTER SIX

Matthew

"Goddammit." I yanked the silk through the knot for the fourth time in a row while glowering at myself in the slightly warped full-length mirror next to my closet. "Kate!" I shouted. "Can you come in here a second?"

I wrestled with the tie until my sister trotted across the hall from my niece's room.

"I thought I was here to babysit Sofia, not you and Frankie," Kate said as she entered. "What's wrong?"

"This tie. My fat fuckin' fingers forgot how to make a half-Windsor. Can you do it?"

Kate smirked as she came to stand between me and the mirror. Yeah, yeah, yeah. My sister just *loved* when I had to admit she knew more about men's fashion than I did. But considering she probably tied about a hundred of these a week onto her mannequins, she did have more practice. And I wasn't about to head uptown looking like a slob.

"There, all done," she said. "Smart. I like that you went with the pinstripes. They're very festive."

I pulled on the jacket that with its thread-thin white stripes over midnight blue matched the pants and vest of the three-piece suit. "You don't think I look like a gangster?"

"Oh, you definitely look like a gangster. But in the best possible way." Frankie pulled slightly at the red silk pocket square tucked into my jacket, then stood back to look me over. "The red makes it work with the holidays. And since you actually listened to me and skipped the wingtips, I'd say you walk the line perfectly."

"How about now?"

I grabbed my favorite fedora off the bureau, but before I could put it on, Kate plucked it away.

"Hey!" I protested. "Give me that."

"Mattie, I know you love *Nonno's* hat, but if you put that on, you're going to look like Al Capone. Trust me on this. Coco Chanel always said you should take off the last thing you put on. I'm just doing it for you."

I grunted, but didn't argue. Nina liked Chanel. No, it didn't have anything to do with that. Or maybe it did.

"I need help too."

We both turned to find Frankie, my other sister, striding into the room followed by her daughter, Sofia. "Kate, can you zip me up?"

"When did my room become everyone's damn dressing room?" I sputtered, even as I sat on the bed to allow Sofia to climb onto my lap. "Hey, watch the collar, Sof. I don't need your paw prints on my shirt, all right?"

Sofia made a face at me and shook her black curls from side to side. But she did keep her hands to herself.

"Whose party is this again that I'm babysitting for?" Kate said, doing as Frankie asked.

"You don't need to babysit," Frankie said as she took my place in front of the mirror. "I'm thinking maybe you should go with Matthew, Katie, because I'm not."

"Yes, you are," I said for what had to be the fourth time that evening. As a single mom and third-grade teacher with next to no free time, Frankie didn't exactly get out much. "You deserve a night out, Frankie, and since you badgered me into taking one, you're coming." I looked down at Sofia. "Don't you think your ma needs a night away from you?"

Sofia grinned, displaying the gap between her teeth. "Why would she need that?"

I ruffled her hair and gently picked her up and placed her on the bedspread. "Eh, you'd chain her to the stove if you could, you little gremlin."

"I'm not a gremlin! It's the *boys* that's gremlins!" she protested, referring to her cousins uptown. "What's a gremlin, anyway?"

"It's a monster that never lets its mommy do anything fun," I told her.

At that, Sofia's smile dropped, and her eyes began to water. "Mommy?" She turned to Frankie, who was trying to keep still while Kate played with her hair and dress. "Mommy, am I a gremlin? Am I no fun?"

"Mattie!"

Frankie turned around, and a moment later, I was dodging her purse.

"Okay, okay!" I laughed. "You're not a gremlin, Sof. Maybe just a baby troll."

"Oh!" She perked up. "I can be a troll!" She slithered off the bed and scampered out of the room singing some terrible song at the top of her lungs.

Frankie caught my mystified expression and giggled. "It's from a movie," she clarified. "The trolls are cute."

"Then I rest my case," I said with a shrug. "And if you know more about a kids' movie than going out with people your own age, you definitely need to get out more, Fran."

"You *both* do," Kate clarified as she finished the final touches on Frankie's dress. "Whose party is this anyway?"

"Some friends of mine uptown," I replied, glad they weren't looking at me when I answered. I didn't want to say who else might be there. Or the fact that she was going to be surrounded by friends and family that made me want to bring my own security.

That was me. Big, bad Matthew Zola bringing his little sister to a party as a bodyguard.

"*Rich* friends," Frankie said pointedly. "They own a *house* on the Upper West Side. They're going to think I'm a hobo." She eyed herself nervously in the mirror again and sighed. "At least Derek never expected me to wear anything other than jeans and a t-shirt."

I didn't reply, feeling a bit uncomfortable. I had encouraged Frankie to go out with my friend and former investigative partner last spring. It hadn't lasted long, but I had never pried into what happened. I didn't want to get in between two good people.

"That's because Derek's idea of a good date was Chinese takeout and watching the Mets game on the couch," said Kate, who didn't have any such compunction.

Frankie turned. "He wasn't *that* bad."

"He was nice," Kate admitted. "But he wasn't for you. You said so yourself. There was no...zing. No za-za-zoo."

"What the hell does that mean?" I asked. "It sounds like one of those spells Sofia makes up when she's pretending to be my fairy godmother."

"It's the thing," Kate clarified, and to my surprise, Frankie nodded in agreement.

"Electricity," she chimed in. "That spark. *You* know, Mattie. Like how you and blondie couldn't stop setting off fireworks all over the city this year."

"Yeah, well," I said. "Look how that ended."

Both of my sisters quieted down, sensing the jokes were over.

"Here we go again," Frankie muttered.

"You know, maybe I should take your place, you grump," Kate said to me. "I could talk up my shop to all your rich friends. Or at least make some good contacts to pick up product. I bet a lot of these guys toss out their Armani like it's day-old chicken."

"*No!*" Frankie and I both chimed in unison.

I stood up, suddenly ready to leave. Frankie grinned at me, and for the first time in weeks, I managed to smile back. Yeah, a night out was definitely what the doctor ordered.

———

THAT FEELING, however, had completely disappeared by the time we were walking up the steps of Jane and Eric's brownstone after an hour and a half on the subway.

"Frances. Francesca," I said.

Frankie rolled her eyes as we approached the double doors to the big townhouse off Central Park West. "I know you're nervous when you use my full name. What is it?"

"Nothing," I lied, then nudged her on the shoulder. "You just look pretty tonight."

And she did, too. I forgot sometimes that my sisters were all lookers in their own right. Especially Frankie. She was the shortest of all of us, taking most after *Nonna* with her slight build that barely even reached my shoulder at five-three in heels. Usually she lived in a uniform of child-friendly jeans and t-shirts, maybe a nice sweater if she had a staff meeting that day. Tonight she'd actually taken the time to let down her dark hair over her shoulders in soft curls, put on a black satin dress, and looked like a lady for a change.

I wasn't sure what I thought about that, but Frankie's cheeks pinked as she patted her dress. "Nonna let me borrow it. She said it reminded her of Audrey Hepburn when she bought it."

I nodded in approval. "Yeah, you could be on the set of *Breakfast at Tiffany's*."

Frankie beamed. "Thanks, big brother."

I knocked on the double doors, which were opened by one of Jane and Eric's security guards.

"Zola. Good to see you."

"Been a while," I confirmed as I shook hands with Tony, Eric's head of security.

The big man looked down his list of people—the guestlist for this shindig was tight. No surprise there. Eric didn't take any chances with his family's security.

"Who's this?" he asked, nodding at Frankie.

"My sister, Francesca Zola," I said, waiting for him to locate Frankie's name on the list. I'd messaged Jane about bringing her as a plus-one earlier this week.

"Got it. Have fun." Tony winked at Frankie, who immediately turned red.

We walked into a party in full swing, and our coats were immediately checked by someone who introduced herself as Eric's assistant. The party was also apparently a dual Christmas housewarming party of sorts since Eric had surprised Jane by purchasing the entire building and remodeling it top to bottom. They had been staying primarily with Eric's mother since the shooting last May, returning here only when they needed space.

"Wow," Frankie breathed as she looked around the massive dining room, which had been decorated in Jane's signature eclectic style. The furniture was a mix of classic mid-century pieces combined with punches of color and textures, including several mural-sized pieces of modern art on the walls.

"See that one?" I pointed across the room. "That's an original Gustav Klimt."

Frankie's eyes bugged. "You're kidding."

"It's the most comfortable museum you'll ever visit," I confirmed. "But I promise, the de Vrieses are good people."

"Drink, sir?"

We turned to find one of the cater waiters holding a tray of champagne flutes.

"Please," I said, taking two for Frankie and me. "Hold on a second, kid."

As one, my sister and I both downed the contents of the glasses like they contained shots of Cuervo, not Cristal. I quickly exchanged them for two more.

"Thanks," I told the waiter. "Keep 'em coming."

"I can't believe you hang out with these people all the time," Frankie said as she accepted her other glass.

I shrugged after taking another sip of champagne. "I wouldn't say it's all the time. I see them occasionally. Not for months, now."

She continued looking over the crowd, then turned to examine me. "You know, you fit in here."

I snorted. "Pull the other one, why don't you."

"No, you do," she insisted. "We always make fun of you for your hats and your suits, but I'm looking at you. And in here, with all these fancy people. You blend right in, Mattie. You really do."

"Give or take a billion dollars," I joked back.

"It's smaller than you think."

Frankie turned to the crowd, who were all busily chatting and laughing. Eric and Jane were buried somewhere near the back. I caught Jane making large, animated movements with her hands. Her gold-rimmed glasses glinted under the lights of a modern chandelier, and when she saw me, she raised one hand and waved wildly, indicating for me to join them. I waved back, but I wasn't in the mood to shove my way back there.

"Is she here?" Frankie asked.

"Who?"

Frankie gave me a look. "You know who. *Her*."

I swallowed. I guessed I hadn't been as discreet as I'd thought. Because no, I wasn't scanning the crowd looking for famous faces from the *Post*. I was only interested in one face. A perfect face that had been scowling at me just a few days ago.

I frowned. We were almost two hours past the start time of the party. The visible living room and dining rooms that had been cleared for guests were jammed with people. Still, nowhere did I see the tell-tale gleam of bright blonde.

"I don't think so," I said. The churning in my stomach didn't stop.

"Good. You deserve a night off from the misery that woman brings you."

I looked down. "What's that supposed to mean?"

But before Frankie could answer, we were interrupted.

"Francesca?"

At the sound of her full Italian name (she was Frankie, Fran, or Frances pretty much everywhere but at our grandmother's house) spoken in a suspiciously deep, clearly British voice, my sister froze. We both turned to find the tallest man in the room, who must have been close to six-five, weaving his way through the crowd with a shocked, yet determined expression. I couldn't deny it: the guy, whoever he was, had a presence. He had that black-haired, blue-eyed look that, judging by the number of women (and a few men) whose heads swiveled as he passed, seemed to be pretty damn pleasing to the eye. If you liked that sort of thing.

"Do you know him?" I asked Frankie.

"Go," she ordered through clenched teeth. "You should go."

I did no such thing.

"He looks familiar." I tipped my head, trying to figure out where I had seen him before. A magazine, maybe? Was he one of those people in *Page Six*, someone I'd seen on local tabloids? Half of the city had hard-ons for these rich assholes.

Then he smiled at Frankie, and I knew *exactly* where I'd seen that face before. Or at least another version of it. It wasn't in the paper. It was at my kitchen counter, eating breakfast cereal. Tossing a baseball. Talking about Doc McStuffins. I saw that face every day in my own damn house.

"Frankie, is that Sofia's—"

"Hush!" Her hand pressed into my chest, shoving me a full step away from her.

I frowned as the man approached. He was staring at Frankie with the kind of awe I felt whenever I saw Nina. But it didn't make sense. Was this the guy who had abandoned her and Sofia? The deadbeat, possibly married man who shirked his daughter and left my sister crying?

If that were true, then why did he look so damn excited to see her?

"Frankie," I started again, but I was cut off by the exact same look *Nonna* used to give me whenever I came home with stains on my white shirts.

Message received, loud and clear.

"Yeah, yeah," I said, brushing out any creases she might have left on my lapels. "But you're answering that question later, little sister."

"Get lost!" she hissed.

"Going. But my two cents? He's too tall for you anyway."

"Francesca?" I could hear him ask as I walked away. "Is it really you?"

"Hello, Xavier."

Yeah, she was *definitely* going to have some explaining to do on our way back to Brooklyn.

Deciding to make my way to where I'd last seen Jane, I started pushing through the crowd, ignoring the bored, curious looks, especially from some of the women. Yeah, yeah, ladies. I know you like. It didn't matter. I was only here to see one of them, and she was nowhere to be found. I'd say hello to the hosts and get the hell out of here, back to where I *actually* belonged.

A cascade of shoves ended with me bumping into a woman on my left, who dropped something as she turned around.

"Beg your pardon, miss. Let me get that."

I crouched to the floor and retrieved the small leather purse, but then froze when confronted with shiny black heels, delicate ankles, and a pair of intensely long legs.

Slowly, I looked up, noting the slight curves of her calves, then the knee-length dress. It was demure at first, solid black broken by a white lace panel that traveled from the hem all the way up her body. And as my gaze traveled too, it became very clear that there was absolutely nothing under that lace but miles and miles of butter-soft skin. And I was intimately familiar with all of it.

Even so, I nearly fell over when I found those bright gray, almost silver eyes looking down at me, full of imperious, almost haughty irritation.

"Nina," I murmured.

"Hello, Matthew," she said. "Are you coming back up, or are you going to stay down there all night?"

CHAPTER SEVEN

Matthew

I cleared my throat, then finally managed to pull myself back up to standing. It was hard, though. I couldn't stop looking at her. *All* of her.

It was Nina, but like I'd never seen her. Her hair, which used to fall about six inches past her shoulders, now stopped just below her chin in blunt waves the color of amber—still blonde, but several shades darker than the sunny gold I remembered. Her mouth was painted a deep, oxblood red, and her eyes were lined in black, lending a ferocity that reminded me of the female jaguar I'd seen at the zoo with Sofia. Elegant, yes. But with a lot of bite.

And then, of course, there was the dress—all black, except for that transparent lace and the skin that was more evident through it the longer I looked. So different from the white and grays she usually wore (and yes, the one red dress). Ironic, really, that the most delicate part of it was most revealing.

Good fuckin' God, that was her hip bone right there. And the swell of her perfect, pert ass, the curve of her art-worthy breast.

I gulped and tugged at my collar. Anyone who took a good look would see most of Nina's body in profile. Could feast their eyes over her long, lithe muscles, subtle yet powerful curves. Gone was the demure socialite. Lace or not, she looked ready to fight.

"Jesus, doll," I whispered. "You, um, want to borrow my jacket or something?"

She smirked as she took back her purse. "Why would I do that?"

I swallowed, unable to look away from the slight tip of a berry-shaped nipple only *just* evident through the black silk. "Ah...you look cold."

But when I managed to tear my gaze back to meet hers, what I found was ice...laced with fire.

"I'm fine," she said shortly. "Thank you for your concern."

Only the rich knew how to make gratitude feel like a slap across the cheek. Yet again, I felt like I'd failed some kind of test. Nina had been here the entire time, and I hadn't even recognized her.

This time, however, I had an excuse.

"You changed your..." I trailed off. I wanted to say everything, but that wasn't true. Not exactly.

"My hair, yes." She gestured toward her head with an almost bored movement.

"To say the least." I looked her up and down again, and this time she had the decency to blush under the heat of my inspection. "You look good, doll. Better than good."

I almost said I liked her better before, but that wasn't quite true either. I liked her no matter what, but the most beautiful Nina ever looked was in the morning when she woke up after a long night of letting me tire her out. When her hair was tousled and she wore nothing at all except the afterglow of passion.

She was still her, though. Whatever made her the most beautiful woman I'd ever seen had nothing to do with what was on the outside. Darker hair or not. Blackened eyes or just pure gray. Nina de Vries could paint her face green and wear nothing but trash bags; I'd still follow her around New York like a lost fuckin' puppy.

She seemed to understand what I couldn't express, because somehow, her face softened as we stared at each other

"Oh, Matthew," she whispered in that exact way that melted my cold, jaded heart.

I opened my mouth to tell her exactly that, to say we should just ditch the party and find somewhere to talk for real. Walk through the park like we used to. Get lost with nothing but the trees for company.

But before I could, we were rudely interrupted.

"Well, well, well, if it isn't our resident jailbird."

Nina and I both jerked like we'd been yanked by the hair. With a snarl on my lips, I turned to the intruders: two cocky men with impeccably fitted, if boring, gray suits, matching floppy brown hair, and razor-straight noses that only those from a certain class have. The kind who sparred in fencing matches, not schoolyard battles.

I took a long drink of champagne to hide my irritation. Nina simply resumed the bored expression I'd come to recognize as the trademark mask of the rich and useless. I fucking hated it. It was so at odds with the vibrant, intelligent woman I knew. The woman who was capable of so damn much—if she and everyone else would only give her a chance.

"Chase. Sawyer."

She greeted the men courteously, but with a caustic edge that either I was the only one to hear, or else they were too self-absorbed to notice. As I caught the flicker of her expression when each man leaned in to kiss her cheek, I was pretty sure it was the latter.

She didn't, however, introduce me.

"Hey, gorgeous," said the first jackass as he smoothed back one side of his hair and straightened his tie. "God, look at you. A vision. We were hoping you'd make your triumphant return tonight."

"And without the ball and chain, no less," added Jackass Number Two as he examined Nina in her dress like she was something on display at the butcher shop. He actually licked his thin lips before taking a drink of his champagne.

Jackass Number One nodded. "We were all taking bets on how long you and Gardner would last, you know. Grayson had ten years, the bastard. I owe him that fifty grand now, thanks to you. Did you know Gardner's nickname around the club? Chase here called him

'The Grub' once, and it stuck! So, for a while, I guess that made you 'Mrs. Grub.'"

He grinned like she was in on the joke, and the other one laughed outright. Nina bared her teeth in a polite smile, but her jaw tightened. I wanted to punch both of them in their flash-bulb veneers. As satisfying as it was to know other members of Nina's social circle thought Calvin Gardner was unfit for this goddess (and resembled a wormy little scavenger), the way they had all been casually betting on her marriage like she was a thoroughbred was infuriating. Where were they, I wanted to ask, when she was being conned for everything she was worth? Where were they when she practically signed away her life and had gotten wrapped up in his schemes?

Where were *any* of these smug motherfuckers then?

"So, Nina," said Jackass Number One (I couldn't remember either of their names, and I really didn't give a shit either). "How was the big house? Bigger than *your* house?"

"Did you get lucky on the inside?" added Jackass Number Two as his eyebrows popped up and down like overly groomed caterpillars.

"What a fantasy that is," said Number One. "That'll keep me in business for a good while, if you know what I mean. Thank you for that, *Mrs.* Gardner."

"Oh God, yes," agreed Number Two. "Every morning in the shower for the next six months at least."

Were they for real? Were these two pigeon-shaped hot air balloons actually saying they were going to jack off to the idea of Nina in jail? To her face? What in the ever-loving *fuck* was wrong with these people?

I opened my mouth to tell both of them to have some fuckin' respect or I'd teach it to them myself, but Nina spoke up first.

"That's enough," she said sharply.

"Come on, now, Astor," taunted Number One. "It's just a friendly joke."

He used what I recognized as her father's surname—the one she'd given me when we met, but which she'd also shunned as a teenager. Which meant she must have known these jokers long enough for them to have used it regularly back in the day. I didn't care how long they'd known her. They deserved to have their teeth knocked in regardless.

"It's disgusting, and you're disgusting when you tell it," Nina retorted. "Frankly, Sawyer, I'm surprised you'd bait me like that. Particularly when you might find yourself in a similar situation one of these days."

The smug grin on Jackass One's face disappeared. "Excuse me?"

Nina took a step closer, and her voice dropped, thick and husky. "I think you know. The thing about being married to a grub...I know exactly which carrion he devours. Like your father's company, Sawyer. And the ways in which Calvin may have curried *your* favor."

It was a bluff. I knew it was a bluff. Until last September, Nina had known only the basics of Calvin's operation, and nothing about its prostitution side.

But the look on both these men's faces told me they weren't so sure...and that ten to one, they had made use of Calvin Gardner's little operation over the years.

Nina stepped back and took a calm sip of her champagne. "You might want to consider that before you make me the object of your schoolboy fantasies." Her face remained placid, but her voice sounded tight, like a string pulled past its capacity. My hands clenched. Something told me this string was about to snap.

"Whatever," said Jackass Number Two. He nudged his friend. "Something tells me that after ten years, you're probably used goods anyway."

I almost flew forward with a punch right there, but once again, Nina beat me to it. Her glass flew out of her hand, and champagne coated the man's face, tie, and expensive suit before the flute fell to the ground with a smash that was only just hidden by the loud music and hum of the party.

"Bitch!" Both men jumped back, as if the action would allow them to step out of the sopping mess of champagne covering their clothes. "What the fuck, Nina!"

A few of the people around us turned with bored expressions to see what was happening, but it was soon clear that watching these gentlemen have drinks thrown in their faces was nothing new.

Jackass Number One raised his hand, ready to retaliate. This time, I did step in front of Nina and pushed her solidly behind my back. Her hands rested against my shoulder blades, fingers quivering with tension.

"Just try it, son," I growled, low enough that I was only heard by the four of us. "Touch her, and I'll knock every one of those pretty teeth out."

"Oh, really?" sneered Jackass Two as he shook out his tie. "And who are you, her white knight? Or just her mangy guard dog."

"I'm whoever the fuck she wants me to be," I snarled. "And if you'd like to learn more, I'm happy to make an introduction outside."

Both men looked like they wanted to take me up on my offer, but before either could say anything, the music was shut off and a high-pitched ringing of silver tapping crystal filled the room, catching everyone's attention.

"Stop." Nina's voice was barely above a whisper, her breath warm against the back of my ear. "Thank you. But you can stop now."

I was shaking with anger. Anticipation. I hadn't wanted to fight this badly since I was in the Marines. I hadn't realized until now how deeply that need was ingrained in me, how being a DA had given me a place to channel it. And now I didn't have it anymore.

But Nina's touch brought me back from the brink. I turned around to face her; the only thing I saw was gratitude. Well, it was a hell of a lot better than the irritation I'd seen before.

Now apparently more concerned with missing the gossip than with being taught a lesson from yours truly, the two jackasses turned with the rest of the crowd to face Eric, who was standing on a stool that elevated him about two feet above everyone else. Jane stood next to him at regular height, looking resplendent in a bright red dress, a few matching stripes of color shooting through her black-brown hair.

"Everyone," Eric called out from the head of the room. "First of all, we'd like to thank you for coming tonight. It's a hell of a housewarming, I'll give you that."

There was a round of hoots and hollers, though the people in the room who seemed the loudest also seemed to be the youngest. Eric had more friends than I'd realized. Or maybe that's just who comes out of the woodwork when you inherit seventeen billion dollars.

"This gorgeous woman and I are thrilled to announce that Jane has just been accepted on early admission to the Fashion Institute of Technology!"

There was a gasp behind me, then another round of deafening cheers, though I doubted any of these people really cared about Jane's triumphs. I was happy for her, though. Jane needed this more than most, and she was talented. Better her than anyone else.

I turned to Nina to say as much and found her staring at Eric, eyes bulging, face reddened. While everyone shouted their well-wishes to the couple, she looked anything but happy.

Fuck distance. Fuck space.

"Hey." I slipped a hand around her waist and pulled her close enough to hear me. "Are you all right?"

"Oh." Nina pressed a hand to her heart as if she were in pain. "Oh, *God*."

I didn't have to know why she felt the way she did. Only that she did. And that I needed to help.

"Please," she begged suddenly. "Out. Matthew, I need to get out."

"You got it," I said as the crowd swarmed forward to Jane and Eric. I grabbed her hand and immediately started towing her through the crowd, mindless of who or what I might be knocking aside with my shoulders and a few pointed elbows.

With a few curious glances, Tony and the security team allowed us past the barrier to the upper floors of the townhouse. Up, up, up we climbed, beyond the noise of the party, past the third-floor bedrooms where John Carson had been shot. We continued to a door at the very top, which opened onto the newly renovated rooftop patio. The rush of Central Park West and Seventy-Sixth Street were reduced to whispers, and the chilly air and cold night seemed to wrap around us both like a blanket.

"Here," I said, immediately stripping off my jacket and wrapping it around Nina's thin shoulders. "You'll freeze without that, baby."

Nina didn't reply, just continued to gasp for several minutes, like she'd just emerged from under water.

"Lord," she said as she sank against the now-closed door. "I just—oh, God, I just couldn't."

"You don't want them to have a baby?" I asked, somewhat confused.

She looked up, that beautiful ferocity returned. "What? No! I already knew, actually. I only…"

Then her head drooped, full of shame. Quickly, I crossed the space between us, and tipped her chin up so she had to look at me.

"You what?" I asked quietly. "You can tell me. I won't judge."

She looked like she wasn't sure about that, then exhaled again. Her breath was sweet, white in the cold December air, tinged with champagne. Suddenly I wanted to kiss her. Actually, I *always* wanted to kiss her.

"It was envy. And hate." Nina shook her head. "Aren't those some of the seven deadly sins?"

"Just envy. But I think unless you start Single White Femaling Jane, you're not going to hell or anything. You're allowed to feel jealous for a minute before you feel happy."

"I *am* happy for them. I love them—so much. And they deserve every bit of happiness they are getting. They've earned it."

"Hate, though?" I prompted. "What's that for, then?"

"Not them." Nina shuddered, as if she was fighting the emotion welling up, like a volcano trying to fight its explosion. "I…oh, *God*, Matthew. I hate…I hate…"

She bent forward, pressing her face into her hands. "Everyone else in there. Those men—"

"Those 'men,' if you can call them that, were straight-up douchebags, Nina. They don't deserve your hate. They don't deserve anything."

"Even so. I do. I *hate* them. All of them, the ones just like them. So… so much. They don't care about Eric or Jane. They don't care about her school or dreams or anything else but their own stupid lives, their own ridiculous reputations. I hate all of it. This world. This life."

Nina sighed, slumping against the railing. We stood there for a moment. She shivered, and I reached out and pulled my jacket closed across her body, then kept my hands locked in place, as much for proximity as to keep her warm. Nina blinked, her eyes wet. They still hadn't lost that haze of fury. Not completely.

God, she really was magnificent. Enough to make me forget about the cold December weather. I was happy to be here, free again to look at her.

"What about me?" I asked cautiously. "Do you hate me too, doll?"

The air around us stilled as she looked up. Our eyes locked, green to gray. It was slightly uncomfortable—there was this feeling that this woman could see straight into the depths of my sad, sorry soul.

But even so, I'd never look away from her. I couldn't. And I no longer cared what it cost me.

"No," she said. "I could never hate you, Matthew."

What about love? I wanted to ask. But I held my tongue, sensing that would push her too far over an already precarious ledge.

Instead, with my grip on the jacket, I pulled her a little closer, off the rail so that our chests were only an inch or so apart.

"How about forgiveness?" I asked, searching her face for a change. "Do you forgive me yet? Maybe a little?"

She examined me for a moment, and I thought she might say no. I thought she might say she could never get past my betrayal, my refusal to believe her in her worst moment, my insistence on believing the worst when I was presented with the truth. I wasn't sure *I* would ever forgive myself for that.

But if she could, I'd find a way.

But instead of answering, she did something else entirely. She stood up straight again, looked me in the eye, and kissed me.

CHAPTER EIGHT

Nina

His lips were soft, and his hands were warm. With his jacket around my shoulders, I was enveloped at last in that familiar scent that comforted me in my dreams, though never so much as when I was curled on that rotting mattress at Rosie's.

No, I didn't want to go there. Not like I did most nights as I tried and failed to sleep in the plush comforts of Eric and Jane's guest room. Just as I'd let myself go, allow my mind to drift toward sleep, suddenly I'd be back in that cell, swathed in the absurdly thin blankets, scratching at bites left by bedbugs, trying not to hear the sounds of wails and jeers from the dormitory down the hall. Praying those intrusive hands wouldn't return that night or any other.

It hadn't been long. Fifteen days was all. But it was long enough to stick with me. I was beginning to think it always would.

I inhaled deeply, allowing the sting of the cold air to penetrate those memories, keep them at bay. Matthew's scent flooded me instead: the heady wool of his jacket, the light cologne he preferred, the overtones of soap, ink. Perhaps a tinge of cigarette smoke too? And now champagne.

It was all delicious. Intoxicating. I wanted to taste him forever.

My skin prickled with warning. I didn't deserve this. And I was too angry for him to deserve it either. He had already proven that he was no refuge, no port in the storm when I needed him most.

But that didn't mean I didn't want him to be. Because he smelled good, and he felt good, and even more than everything else, he felt like *home*.

Below us, the city erupted with muted shouts of sirens and car horns. There were nights, even here in Eric's stronghold townhouse, when I felt like the darkness that threaded through the city of my birth threatened to crash through my very windows and eat me alive. I was only just now beginning to realize how fear had eroded the core of me my entire life.

And now…with him…even though I shouldn't, I felt so, so safe.

His tongue touched mine, begged to twist together, to dive into the taste of me. I groaned as my hands grabbed that silky soft hair and yanked. A pang of desire shot between my legs, where I was suddenly and disturbingly aware there was absolutely *nothing* guarding me from him.

Maybe not so safe after all.

Maybe a little bit dangerous. In the best possible way.

And maybe, I realized…right now…that was for the best.

For all his warmth, Matthew was really just a blazing fire. He had burned me once, and he would burn me again if I let him.

If *I* let him.

The choice, in the end, was mine.

Somehow, without even thinking about it, I managed to tear myself away. His heavy breathing sent feathery plumes of white into the night air while he gazed at me, taking in my dress, my legs, my heaving chest. He had spent long enough examining the lace of my dress that he was perfectly aware it wasn't lined.

Had I chosen it precisely to see the expression on his face when he figured that out?

Perhaps.

But now, I wasn't so sure I wanted to be viewed that way. I turned around, content to remain in his arms, but facing my back toward him so I could look out to the city and reassemble my good senses.

Just below, cars raced up and down Central Park West, one of the few thoroughfares in Manhattan with two-way traffic. It was a behemoth that stretched down to Lincoln Center, only fifteen or so blocks south, an explosion of light and color marking the beginning of Central Park's chasm of darkness in the night.

As Matthew's hands tightened at my waist and his lips feathered kisses up and down my neck, I gripped the railing and remembered those moments—twice—that I had run into that darkness with this man at my heels. Reckless, skittering into the park at night. But he had said he would chase me anywhere. Until, of course, he wouldn't.

His teeth found my ear and sank down softly before the warm slip of his tongue curled around my lobe.

I shivered with desire as one of his hands cupped my breast. Brazen as always.

Though he had tried to respect my need for discretion, Matthew had never really cared where we were when it came to demonstrating his desire for me. The family's seats at the opera, for crying out loud. He had taken some part of me wherever and whenever he wanted.

You're no different, a small voice pointed out in the back of my mind as he found my other breast, pinching and toying with my nipples through the thin silk while he continued that delicious torture of my ear.

"Ah!" I gasped, as much at the sudden bite below my jaw as the memory of sinking to my knees for him in the middle of the park, pulling down the top of my dress, and forcing him to take his pleasure out all over my skin.

No, I had never really cared where we were either.

"Please," Matthew whispered, his smooth, deep voice croaking slightly; from cold or want, I couldn't say.

His right hand left my breast, and then I heard the telltale clink and zip of his belt and pants zipper. Then both hands dropped, and my skirt was pulled up my legs, crinkling around my waist so I was bared to him from behind.

In front of me the city glimmered. I closed my eyes, wanting nothing else than to feel his body close.

Matthew slid between my legs, and the slick welcome there might have told him everything he needed to know. Still, he remained poised at the entrance, waiting for my consent.

"Please, Nina." His voice rumbled at the base of my neck, his stubble scraping over my skin. He wanted me to turn. Wanted me to kiss him. But he was waiting for me to choose. "Say you forgive me, baby. I'm begging you."

I arched my neck as he sucked deeply over my pulse, like he was eager to take any sign of life from me. Honoring each beat of my heart that was for him.

But the words he wanted...I wasn't capable of them. Not yet. Maybe not ever.

How could I explain to him the betrayal I still felt? I loved him, yes. I was fairly sure at this point I would love this man always. But in my moment of need...he had failed me. He had believed the other side. Searched for the worst in me instead of taking my best.

But that didn't mean I didn't want him. It didn't mean that right now, on this rooftop, I didn't need him. In fact, I had never needed anything more.

I reached around and grabbed his hand, then pulled up my dress in the front so he could feel me on both sides. His fingers followed my lead, slipping around to find the bare skin and sleek, groomed remnant of hair, then pressing deeper to find that concentration of pleasure I could almost swear was made for his touch alone.

My clit. Yes, my *clit*, I thought to myself. No more euphemisms. No more veiled language. I didn't want to be afraid of my own body anymore, of my own pleasure. Matthew's fingers were on my clit, and they were rubbing and pinching and moving in that rhythm that I had thought at one time only he could find, but now I knew I could find on my own too, maybe teach someone else, another man, someone worthy of me, someone who loved me, someone who would never hurt me...

The idea sliced. I groaned. No, I couldn't think about that. Right here, right now, there was only Matthew, and how badly I needed *his* touch, even if I couldn't accept his love.

"Do you feel that?" he asked. "Do you feel how badly I need you, Nina?"

His *cock* slipped between my thighs, back out, and in again. Another word I whispered silently to myself, embracing the crass, carnal beauty of what we were doing, what we were about to do.

Cock.

Pussy.

Ass.

Clit.

I wanted them all. I wanted him to take them all. I wanted all of *him*, and I wanted him everywhere.

And so I straightened my arms against the railing, pressing myself back into him, allowing him to take a solid grab of my hips with both hands and slowly, slowly, to press his considerable length deep inside me.

"Matthew!" I choked as he filled me completely.

He was not a small man, and it always took a moment to adjust. He waited patiently, bending over my upper body to whisper dirty nothings into my ear, hum lightly, let me feel his warmth through my back, my legs, arms, all parts he touched.

And then he stood straight again and really began to move.

"Oh!" Each moan erupted from me in time with his unforgiving, deliciously harsh thrusts.

"Does that feel good?" he asked as he urged me to brace myself against the rails. Then he took my hand and guided it back around his neck, urging my fingernails to dig into his skin. Matthew loved a little punishment. He loved a little pain when he took me.

When he *fucked* me, I corrected myself.

I raked down the side of his neck. He hissed, then stood up, and suddenly, his palm met my ass with a slap that echoed off the sides of the buildings behind us and across the street.

I jerked forward, shocked by the sudden arrows of desire that shot through me with each harsh blow.

"Is that what you want?" he demanded as he pummeled forward. He spanked me again. "Just like that?"

"Uhhhh, *yesssss!*" I hissed back.

But he didn't give me more. Instead, he fell over me again, insistent on proximity as he pounded into me. His grunts were animalistic, his teeth on my neck carnivorous. Matthew devoured me with every harsh thrust, and I took it, I cried out for it, I shook through every deep, penetrative motion.

My orgasm overtook me with a jolt, forcing my mouth open in a long silent scream as I spasmed in his arms. Matthew slipped an arm around my waist and hauled me up to his chest so I was sheltered over the railing in his arms while we both shook together.

"Oh God," he muttered over and over again. "Oh God, oh *God.*"

He started murmuring something else into the back of my hair, something unintelligible, peppered occasionally with words like "grace" and "sinners." Before I could stop them, tears welled up and just as quickly slipped down my face.

Our bodies seized together as we fell apart completely. And then, maybe a few minutes later, maybe hours, they eventually softened into nothing.

I collapsed against the railing, and Matthew fell too, catching himself only on his arms on either side of me as he slipped out. My skirt fell, no doubt a wrinkled mess. His jacket had long fallen from my shoulders to the ground, but it wasn't until he stooped to pick it up again that I felt truly cold.

"I need—I need to go," I stuttered as I stepped away, doing my best to smooth my skirt back into place. Suddenly I felt terrible. This wasn't me. Or maybe it was—and perhaps that was even worse.

Matthew looked up from where he was trying to redo his tie and vest. When had I torn *those* off? At some point, I realized vaguely, it had happened. But I had no memory of anything other than my desire.

And now my shame.

My eyes were bleary. His were sharp, yet unfocused.

"What?" he asked as he struggled with a few buttons. "Nina, just wait a goddamn minute, all right?"

But I couldn't. I shook my head, letting my newly shorn hair tousle around my face like a limp curtain. Heat was rising, an uncomfortable, humiliated flush chasing away all the beautiful pleasure that had been there before.

"No," I whispered as I backed quickly toward the door. "I'm sorry. I can't."

CHAPTER NINE

Matthew

The sound of the door slamming behind her jerked me out of the trance I didn't even know I was in. Two seconds ago I had been whispering Hail Marys just because I had never felt so equally blessed and damned at the same time. Now I was alone under the night sky, my dick all but hanging out in the freezing cold wind. And all from loving and wanting and fucking this woman.

And now, once *again*, she was running away.

"Not this fucking time," I growled.

I yanked up my zipper and trotted toward the door, no longer caring that my vest was flapping open or that my shirt was only half tucked in and probably missing a few buttons. Those rich pricks downstairs could see my bare ass for all I cared. I wasn't letting Nina de Vries get away.

I sprinted back to the main floor, but instead of a party full of New York's elite, I found the catering staff busy cleaning up. Frankie was gone, along with Xavier and the other hundred or so people who had crowded themselves into the townhouse.

Jesus. How long had we been on the roof?

"A woman," I said to a girl carrying a tray full of empty glasses. "Just came running down here. Tall, blonde, stunning, in a black and white dress. Did she leave?"

"Ummm…"

The waitress faltered, though through her confusion she still managed to eye my undone shirt and tie. Interest sparked. I huffed and rolled my eyes. *Move it along, sweetheart. This ain't for you.*

"She's downstairs with Eric and Jane," Tony spoke up behind me. One brow rose as he took in my appearance.

I was too busy to notice. Finally, a break. "Thanks, man."

He nodded as I dashed around him toward the stairs.

The bottom floor of the townhouse was the last space of the building that hadn't fully been remodeled. What was once one of the great Gilded Age houses of New York had served as an apartment building for years. Eric and Jane had initially bought the top floor until Eric purchased the rest of it late last spring. At first I'd been surprised they even wanted to stay here after everything that happened—after all, when you shoot the man who's persecuted your family for years and he bleeds out on your living room floor, maybe you don't want to stay there anymore. But more and more, I understood. You can't really run away from your ghosts and demons. You have to exorcise them instead. Eric had just done it with drywall instead of a priest.

So maybe it was fitting that in the last empty space of the house, my own personal demon was standing by the window waiting for me.

Alone.

"What the fuck, Nina," I spluttered as I toppled into the room. "Are we really back to this again? We finally get somewhere, and you just take off? *Really?*"

But she didn't answer, just continued to gaze through the back windows that looked out to a small garden behind the townhouse— tiny by most standards, but a massive luxury on the Upper West Side. Nothing says wealth like a backyard in Manhattan.

"Just look at them," Nina murmured, pulling aside the gauzy curtain.

Through the window, Jane and Eric were standing together, arms wrapped around each other as they gazed at a fountain in the middle of the garden, clearly enjoying a moment of solitude after the evening's reverie. Every so often, Eric would kiss his wife tenderly on top of her head, and she would nuzzle against his shoulder.

My chest ached at the sight.

"Nina," I started again, but she kept talking.

"We are such fools, Matthew. We can't stay away from each other, but together we are miserable, aren't we?"

"Speak for yourself, duchess," I said, unable to curb the acidity in my voice. I couldn't lie. Her words stung. Suddenly I made her miserable? How could that be when touching her made me feel like I was God himself?

"I do," she said. "Because no matter how much we might want it, we are never going to be that. And it really is torture."

I frowned. It took me a moment to figure out why her words bothered me so much. After all, it had been months since that night in Boston when we had stared at each other in the dark, equally convinced the other was lying. Fewer still since I'd divulged the particulars of our relationship to my boss and accepted leave before watching Nina's disappointment in me clang like a hammer to a bell. I'd lived with the separation. Tended bar. Moved through this city like a ghost. I had been mourning my own life like it was already over.

But as I looked at her now, I knew that deep down in my gut, I hadn't confessed to my boss like he was my priest because I was trying to keep my job. I was doing it because loving her, even when I hated her, was more essential to me than any career. This wasn't the afterlife —it was limbo until I realized what was really going to happen. Leave or no leave, I'd known the second I stepped into Cardozo's office that morning that my career at the Brooklyn district attorney's office was over.

And that one day, after the dust had settled, Nina and I would find our way back to each other. Because we had to. There was no other way.

How could she not know that?

"You're just scared," I said bitterly. "Like you always are. We dance around each other like wildcats, but when we finally do what our bodies and minds are screaming for, you run off like a scared little bunny who can't face the music."

Nina whirled around, tossing my jacket to the floor. Tracks of tears streamed down her porcelain cheeks.

"I am *not* scared!" she snapped. "And kindly fuck you for saying so!"

I was stunned—I'd never heard her talk like that before. But my shock didn't last long.

"Fuck me?" I retorted. "How about fuck *you* for running off for, what, the fifteenth time since we met? You once accused me of using you, but I'm starting to think it's the other way around. Think you'll *ever* stick around after I make you scream my name, sweetheart? You might be surprised by what happens."

"Why?" In wild, jerky movements, she swiped a few more angry tears off her cheek. "So you can accuse me of more heinous crimes? Spy on me for another secret investigation?"

"Don't do that," I said. "I swear to God, Nina, I was *always* on your side. I was just confused for one fucking minute when I saw that video."

"Confused? You mistook another woman for me! You actually believed I was capable of forcing children into prostitution, Matthew!"

"It was a mistake!" I shouted. "And believe me, baby, I am paying for it. Every fuckin' day, I am paying for it. I have plenty of regrets in my life, Nina, but none so much as not taking a second look at that clip. Just...please!"

"Please what? What do you *want* from me?"

"EVERYTHING!" I roared.

I sucked in breath like I'd just run a marathon. Nina stood with her back flat against the window, eyes wide, left hand pressed to her heart. For a moment, I saw the ring that used to gleam on that hand. Gaudy and big, flashing in the tiniest of lights. And then I saw another, the one buried deep in my bureau at home. The one *Nonna* had given me the day after my grandfather's funeral. The one I knew I'd never be able to give to anyone else but the woman standing in front of me.

This was it. *She* was it for me.

But she'd lost hope in that future, just like I had once. Somehow, some way, I had to make her believe again.

I took a jagged step toward her, then another, and another until finally I was standing just inches from her complete and utter majesty. Even post-coital, wrinkled, and tear-stained, she really was a queen. How anyone could do anything besides worship her, I'd never fucking understand.

And so, more out of instinct than anything else, I sank to my knees. It fit. It really did.

Loving this woman was the greatest sacrament I'd ever known.

Loving her was holy.

Leaving her was the real sin.

"Everything," I repeated as I pressed my face into her thigh, inhaling the scent of silk and flowers and sex and *us* as I did. "I want the fucking world with you, Nina. I want you always and forever. A—"

I paused. Was that really the way to end it? Deep down, though, I realized I was saying this prayer every day. Begging God to grant me mercy through this woman's love.

"Amen," I whispered with finality, squeezing my eyes shut.

Her hand slipped into my hair, threading fingers so gently through the strands, I nearly started to cry right along with her.

"Oh, Matthew," Nina said in that sweet, sad tone that broke my heart every time.

Because she only said it when she was sorry. She only said it when she had nothing else to say.

"Please," I whispered fiercely as I found my way back to my feet. Gently, I placed my palms to her cheeks, cradling her face with reverence. "Please forgive me, Nina. I belong to you. I will *never* forsake you again. I promise."

She opened her rose-petal mouth, and for a moment, I considered plundering it. Crushing those petals between my lips, forcing her to succumb the way she always would.

But you can't force love back to you. It has to come of its own accord.

This I'd finally learned.

And so, I waited. Let the uncomfortable silence settle over us like a cape. I'd wait all night if that's what she needed. Hell, I'd wait forever.

Nina opened her mouth. But before she could answer, there was a cautious tap on the glass. I cursed. Nina jumped back. Together we turned to find Jane and Eric peering through the windows, waiting for us to step aside so they could come in.

I sighed and swiped my jacket off the floor while Nina opened the door.

"Everything okay?" Jane asked as Eric shut the door behind them.

Nina drifted further away. I fought the urge to grab her hand and pull her close again. I had nothing to hide. Not anymore.

"Hey," I said, trying and failing to act as if Nina and I hadn't just been staring at each other like Rhett and Scarlett. "I, ah, hear congratulations are in order."

Eric slung an arm around Jane and grinned down at her. "For now. Jane's kind of mad I told everyone."

"Because I literally just got the letter!" she protested weakly. The glow on her face said she wasn't too angry. "It's just grad school. Not the Nobel Prize."

Eric just shrugged and kept grinning at her. I didn't think I'd ever seen the guy smile this much, he was so damn proud of her. He looked looney. And it was catching.

I glanced at Nina with a smile of my own, expecting her to be watching them with the same kind of fondness. But she was turned toward the windows again, staring out to the backyard patio with her back to everyone else.

"So...is everyone friends again?" Jane asked hopefully, looking between me and Nina.

Eric's smile disappeared, his mouth pressed into a firm line at the question. I got the feeling he preferred to hear about his cousin's romantic life on a need-to-know basis.

"I hope so," I said, still watching Nina like a hawk.

But instead of returning my gaze, she turned around with firmly crossed arms and faced Eric and Jane.

"Actually," she said. "I have some news. This is goodbye for a bit, I'm afraid."

And just like that, a vise closed around my chest all over again. Goodbye?

Jane's brow crinkled in confusion. "But you just got here."

"Olivia and I are planning to spend the holidays with Mother on Long Island," Nina said calmly. As if she didn't have a half-torn skirt or blackish tearstains drying on her cheeks. "Tomorrow I'm driving to Andover to get her. We'll stay the night with Skylar and Brandon so she can see Jenny and the others. After that, we'll go straight to the Hamptons. You and Eric are welcome to visit, of course, but I assumed you'd be with your own family. Once Olivia goes back to school, I'll be leaving. For Italy. I don't know for how long."

My head couldn't have jerked any harder if it were on a spring. "You're *what?*"

Nina sighed, but still didn't look at me. It was as though I wasn't even there.

"I've decided to tell Olivia about her father," she said to Jane and Eric. "Her *real* father. Giu—" She gulped on the name. "Giuseppe."

Eric studied me, then her. "That's his name? The professor?"

Nina nodded. "It's going to be very hard. But she deserves to know the truth. Whether or not she'll want anything to do with me after is another story."

"She will," Eric replied, more kindly than I'd ever heard him. "Kids forgive their parents for just about anything, cos. It might take a bit, but you're doing the right thing."

"Yes. Well."

Nina wiped at a few more tears that had escaped, then accepted a handkerchief Eric took out of his pocket. I scowled. Why hadn't I thought to offer her my own?

"First things first," she said. "I need to find Giuseppe's surviving family and tell them about Olivia. He had two daughters from his first marriage. Olivia will want to contact them, I'm sure, and I don't want them to be surprised." She shook her head with obvious dread. "It won't be easy, introducing myself as their father's former mistress."

Jane reached out to pat her shoulder. "They might be surprised, but it's been a long time. I doubt they'll take it out on Olivia, however they feel about you."

Nina shrugged. "Perhaps."

I swallowed. I really couldn't deal with the idea of her facing this alone. I was the first person she had told all those months ago. Well before Jane and Eric knew. When the only other person who knew was her good-for-nothing husband. It seemed wrong that she would return to this part of her life without me.

I opened my mouth to volunteer to go with her, but found I couldn't. Because the reality was, I didn't have the freedom. Not like these people with their endless bank accounts. I had a mortgage to pay. Bills to cover. A sister and a niece who depended on me. I couldn't leave them hanging without any kind of income for however many weeks.

"Anyway." Nina cleared her throat, then handed Eric back his handkerchief. "It's been a long evening, and I have to get up early. I think I'll turn in." She walked to the door. "It was a lovely party. If I don't see you, merry Christmas, Jane. Merry Christmas, Eric."

Both Eric and Jane repeated her sentiments in oddly distant, maybe even shocked voices.

She turned to leave.

"Nina," I called out, unable to stop my voice from cracking slightly. What was I going to say?

Wait.

Don't go.

I love you.

Marry me.

"Merry—merry Christmas, doll," I settled, knowing she wouldn't appreciate my desperate pleas for devotion in front of Jane and Eric.

Still, I couldn't help the last word. It just slipped out.

Nina paused for a moment in the doorframe, biting her lip. I could feel Jane and Eric watching us intently, but I didn't dare check them. I knew if I did, when I looked back, Nina would be gone.

Then she looked up, her silver eyes practically ablaze in the moonlight streaming through the windows from the garden.

"Good night, Matthew," Nina said quietly and left.

I stared at the empty doorway long after her footsteps had faded up the stairs.

"Zola."

At the sound of my name floating softly on the night air, I turned. Jane was watching me with pure pity. Eric with something more skeptical.

"Hey," I said, suddenly conscious again of my disheveled clothes. Jesus, I probably looked like I'd been fucking one of the caterers in their coat closet. "I, ah, I should go."

"Well, before you do. I just thought of something." Jane stepped away from Eric with a knowing glance. "Nina. Italy. It's been a long time for her, hasn't it?"

I nodded, massaging my neck. Everything suddenly hurt. "Yeah. Eleven years, I think."

God, my chest hurt. Just the thought of her being there without me made me want to throw myself into oncoming traffic, mortal sin or not. Being without her was purgatory anyway.

"She's met your family, right?"

I nodded. "The one time."

Jane cocked her head. "Your grandmother speaks Italian, doesn't she?"

"She does, yeah. So did my grandfather. They, um, came over when they were teenagers."

"How about you?"

I shrugged. "I speak it all right. Not like a native, but I grew up hearing it a lot, especially when I lived with them. And then I was stationed in Sicily long enough to become pretty fluent. Why?"

Jane rolled her eyes at Eric, who just snorted and shook his head.

"I'm going upstairs to have a nightcap with Nina." He dropped a quick kiss atop Jane's head. "Catch him up quick, pretty girl. He's kind of slow on the uptake."

I frowned at him as he left. "What the hell was that supposed to mean?"

"Zola," she said gently. "You need a better job than tending bar. And Nina...well, on top of the fact that she shouldn't be going anywhere alone with Calvin's trial about to start...she's also going to need an interpreter, don't you think? I know she speaks some Italian, but..."

"She's not fluent," I finished for her. Finally, what she was saying clicked. My eyes popped open.

Jane smiled, a mischievous grin that was almost childlike with glee. "What do you say? Want to surprise our girl?"

INTERLUDE I

"Page Six"
New York Post
December 19, 2018

Friend or faux? Socialite indicted for fraud

Socialite and three-time divorcée Caitlyn Calvert (age 30) has been indicted on charges of fraud and identity theft related to the human trafficking case against New York real estate financier Calvin Gardner, estranged husband of Nina de Vries. Ms. Calvert, who was until this October known briefly as Mrs. Kyle Shaw, was charged with impersonating Ms. de Vries in order to use her name and connections to associate Ms. de Vries with a shell corporation that funneled money for Mr. Gardner's trafficking operations. Ms. Calvert also faces civil charges in a suit filed by Ms. de Vries herself.

Ms. Calvert has a strong connection to Calvin Gardner, who was charged with masterminding a ring that trafficked underage Eastern European girls into prostitution in the Northeast in return for falsified immigration documents. His trial date was delayed again following the sentencing of his wife for accessory. A new date for the trial has been set for March.

"There's even speculation that Caitlyn Calvert isn't her real name!" said an anonymous source close to Ms. Calvert's circle. A *Post* investigation revealed no records of a Caitlyn Calvert born anywhere in the Paterson, New Jersey, area, from which Ms. Calvert claims to hail.

Could Calvert be yet another pseudonym? Perhaps Calvertovsky might be more fitting!

————

The Village Voice
December 28, 2018

Trafficking ring mastermind files for bankruptcy

While awaiting trial on charges of fraud, money laundering, and human trafficking, Calvin Gardner's company, Gardner Investments, filed for Chapter 11 bankruptcy Friday afternoon. This can't be good news for the scandal-plagued investor, whose ongoing divorce from socialite Nina de Vries has been widely publicized, particularly following his estranged wife's guilty plea to aiding and abetting a human trafficking scheme allegedly masterminded by Gardner himself.

"Gardner Investments has been in trouble for a while now," vouched a source from inside the company who spoke only on the condition of anonymity. "Mr. Gardner has always wanted to be considered one of the top investors in the city, but the truth is, he was always more like a little kid trying to play baseball in the majors."

Though reports have confirmed that Mr. Gardner still retains his residence at the couple's Upper East Side penthouse (despite the fact that it is owned by Ms. de Vries's family), it's clear that Gardner's funds have quickly been drying up, as both his and his estranged wife's personal assets have been frozen and under review during the divorce. He is reportedly doing everything he can to have the will of Celeste de Vries, Ms. de Vries's grandmother and the former CEO and chairwoman of DVS Industries, overturned in probate.

"He's been making the rounds trying to get loans and credit," said another source from a competitive firm. "But people are just shutting him out. The truth is, without the de Vries name behind him, he's nothing. Maybe he always knew it from the start. Honestly, his best chance at staying afloat in this town is through his wife either way."

———

New Year's Eve, 2018

Calvin Gardner sat at a rusted card table in the basement of an old building in Harlem, drumming his thick fingers on the torn plastic surface. He was starting to feel like he might be running out of air. The room had no windows, only cinderblock walls, and every few feet large green pipes curled in and out of the concrete like the coils of a great snake.

Gardner shuddered. He hated snakes. He hated most animals, but snakes in particular made him feel queasy.

There was also a leak somewhere in the building. He had been listening to the drip since he'd arrived an hour ago, and by now it was practically a jackhammer.

Drip. *Drop.*

"You know what?" he said suddenly to the empty room in the slightly roughened English that hadn't born any trace of Hungarian since he was twenty-two, maybe twenty-three. "Fuck this. And fuck *them.*"

He stood with a screech of his chair, his belly pressing uncomfortably against the metal edge of the table. Yeah, he would leave. And who was going to stop him? What the fuck was this, the Skull and Bones? Janus was a joke now, and everyone knew it.

He ignored the way his palms grew sweaty at just the thought of challenging the most prominent—and deadly—secret organization in America. No, he was going to do this. He wasn't going to sit around to be made a fool of. Not now, not ever.

But just as he turned toward the door, it opened.

Immediately, Gardner collapsed into his folding chair, which creaked from the force. A dead giveaway.

Two men entered the room. Michael Faber, sometimes known as Finn, was heir to a wine conglomerate that owned half of Napa. He was tall and thin and dressed in the kind of suit Gardner had commissioned at least five times over the years but which had never looked that classy on his short, squat frame.

The other was much more casual, a muscular man in a black t-shirt and jeans. He took a military stance against the wall next to the door, hands folded at his belt, legs a shoulder-length stance apart. Security, obviously.

Gardner gritted his teeth. He would have brought security too, but he couldn't afford them anymore. To complete his humiliation, he'd had to fire the entire staff at the penthouse, where he now squatted free of charge but completely alone, thanks to the freezing of the accounts. So for now, his security was gone, his driver, his secretary, even the investigator he'd hired for a bit to follow Nina on her infernally boring walks to and from the gym.

He knew they should have fought the freeze, though his lawyers initially thought it was a good idea. Nina's cousin Eric would have never let her go hungry—the fucking de Vrieses might have been cold as ice, but their family loyalty ran deeper than anyone knew. Gardner knew, though. Oh, did he know. He'd been trying to chip that fucking block for almost eleven years now. And for what? An empty penthouse?

A fucking pittance. The memories of all his humiliations at the hands of the family made his blood boil all over again. They'd pay. One day, they'd all pay.

In the meantime, there was still the Pantheon money, sitting pretty in the Caymans. But if he put a toe over there, the fucking IRS would be breathing down his neck in a second. Which is why he needed Faber's help. Why he was crawling back to Janus one last time.

"What the fuck is wrong with you?"

Gardner's head snapped up at the sound of Faber's voice, and he realized he'd been daydreaming again. He started to sweat—he couldn't help it around these people.

"Nothing," he said. "I'm fine. Nice of you to show up. Thank you."

He had to pay homage. He couldn't afford to piss off this guy. Even if he was looking at him like he was a bug on the bottom of his shoe.

Gardner didn't like Michael Faber, but he was one of the only four men he *knew* were a part of the Janus society. He wasn't supposed to know—no one was. And the fact that he did know would either be what protected him or killed him.

"Let's not beat around the bush," Faber said. "Letour is going down. His trial is next week, and the society is letting him hang. I'm sorry, but we're out."

Which meant only one thing. They were going to let Pantheon and the whole fucking operation land on him. And keep all the money to themselves.

"No!" Gardner sputtered. "You can't! After everything—I demand an explanation. I've been a loyal assistant to this organization for a decade. Did everything you asked of me. *Everything.*"

"And it was appreciated," Faber said coolly. "By the old order, for sure. But probably not the new."

Gardner frowned. "What do you mean...the new? Is someone replacing Carson?"

The taller man just looked down his very long nose. "You didn't know?"

It was a joke, of course. Gardner wouldn't have known. He wasn't a member, despite the fact that he had tried for *years* to become an exception to the rule of Ivy League initiation. He was so close, before de Vries showed up.

He hated being made to look like a fool. These people always looked at him like he was clueless, and it fucking infuriated him.

Faber chuckled toward his guard, who grinned back.

"Jesus Christ." He shook his head. "Once, you almost had me, you know. You were *almost* like one of us. But Jude really didn't tell you anything, did he?"

"Tell me what?" Gardner gritted through his teeth. It hurt. He probably had a cavity in one of his molars.

"Eric de Vries is going to be voted in as caesar," Faber stated plainly. "It'll take place after the new year. And if I were you, I'd get out of town. Out of the country, if you can. Even if de Vries doesn't do you in, it's completely possible someone else will out of fealty. There are plenty who'll be eager to prove their loyalty to the new man in charge. Especially considering how he's coming to power."

"What—what do you mean?" Gardner asked, a prickle traveling up his spine like a spider.

"What do you mean, 'what do you mean?'" Faber replied lazily. "It's his birthright. What did you think was going to happen?"

"I—what? Birthright? I thought that Janus was democratic. What is this, a coup?"

Faber laughed, an all-out guffaw that echoed around the tiny room. "Good God, Letour really kept you in the dark." Faber studied his nails, like he wasn't sure whether he should tell him much either. He almost seemed to be enjoying the other man's obvious ignorance.

Gardner's eyes narrowed. He wouldn't beg. He would not.

"De Vries didn't stage a coup," Faber said almost lazily. "Carson did. And he was successful for the last twenty-odd years or so. But before him, Eric's father was the caesar. And his father before that. And so on, since the beginning of the society itself." He shrugged again. "Now the prince shot the usurper dead. Dethroned the fraud. What's the saying? 'The king is dead. Long live the king.'"

The prickle turned into an all-out icicle. Gardner felt as though he couldn't breathe. Oh God. Oh fucking *God*. Eric de Vries was now the head of the most powerful underground organization in the country? Janus, through its previous leader, had essentially sponsored nearly *all* of Gardner's illegal activities for the past ten years. It had all been in exchange for the promise of membership—what Gardner had desired more than anything in the world. To be truly special. Elite.

And now...those dreams were slipping away along with his

company, his marriage, everything he had claimed as his over the past ten years.

"He wouldn't," Gardner argued. "There's no way Eric will accept the position. Jude said he was done with it."

"Jude is going away for the next twenty years because of his part in the abduction of de Vries's little wife," Faber replied. "He doesn't matter to any of us anymore. He's out."

"But Eric's a black sheep," Gardner tried again. "And soon he won't have the company anymore either. I'm fighting the will in probate, you know—"

"You'll lose," Faber informed him. "Do you really think there is a single judge in New York, or even the country, who will rule against the de Vries bank accounts? Not to mention the old lady had those assets locked up tighter than her wrinkly old arse."

Gardner frowned in distaste. He had always, *always* hated Celeste de Vries more than any of them. The old hag had treated him like a common thief, watching him at family dinners like he was going to steal her precious silver and Limoges.

"Still," Gardner said, more weakly now. "Eric hates the society. I can't believe he'll want to lead it now."

Faber shrugged. "Eric is more like his family than he thinks he is. When I informed him of the society's plans, his response was something along the lines of, 'keep your friends close and your enemies closer.' And if that makes me his enemy…well, I'll be working harder now to be his friend again. And so will everyone else."

That might have been the exact moment when Gardner's blood ran cold.

"So, what?" he demanded, spitting onto the table before he could help it. "Did you call me to this fucking cell to tell me I have to kiss Eric's ass now?"

"Oh, I think that time has passed, don't you?" Faber replied. "I just called you here to see you squirm. And to tell you that as of today, to you, the Janus society does not exist. The accounts in the Caymans have been transferred to Deutsche Bank under a different name. The properties in New England will still belong to you under Pantheon— until the IRS seizes them, I assume—but we will have no more dealings with you, your company, or any of your known associates, including Ms. Calvert."

Shaw, Gardner thought. That must have been why the old codger had dropped Caitlyn the second she was implicated in the trial. She might as well go back to using Csaszar, if she could even remember how to say it.

Faber slapped his palm on the table, startling Gardner and yanking him out of his own thoughts.

"This is your only warning," Faber said. "As of now, you're on your own. If you contact me or any member using the society name again, it may be the last thing you ever do."

He stood back up with a terrible, chilling smile. One that Gardner had wished he could give to his own enemies, once upon a time.

"Goodbye, Gardner. I'd say good luck, but I'm not sure I mean it." Faber cocked his head. "To be honest, I'm sort of hoping Eric still has a taste for vengeance. It'll make this year a lot more fun if he does."

The door slammed behind him, and Gardner waited another full twenty minutes, until his heart rate dropped to half normal, until there were no longer telltale drops of perspiration across his brow. Then he stood up and climbed the stairs to the lobby to exit the building himself.

Once outside, the blare of New York shouted at him from all around. He pulled out his cell phone as he turned in the direction of the subway—*the fucking subway*—and dialed the first name on his recent contacts.

"Bleeker and Levy."

"Isaac Levy," Gardner barked, ignoring the loud cry of a taxi horn when he almost stumbled into the street.

"One moment, please."

He had finally reached the subway top, but he would wait here to have his conversation. He wasn't interested in the cretins down below overhearing his private business. After the fucking *Village Voice* article, you never knew who was looking in on you these days.

The hold music switched off and was replaced by the bored tones of his erstwhile attorney.

"Mr. Gardner," said Levy. "I don't know what this is about, but—"

"Levy, you have to push through the probate fight. I need that money! As soon as you get it, you'll get paid, I promise."

"Mr. Gardner, as I've told you several times, the likelihood now of winning your challenge of Celeste de Vries's will decreased substantially when you were indicted. It would be wiser now for you to take the money from your bankruptcy filing and move on from your fight with the de Vrieses."

"I don't fucking care about a fight!" Gardner hissed. "I just want to take them down. It's what they deserve! They will *not* win this one, not after ten years!"

There was a long sigh, audible even on the busy street.

"Mr. Gardner, you haven't paid your last bill. I'm sorry, but until the bankruptcy goes through, I'm afraid I cannot do any more on your behalf in this trial *or* your divorce, nor will I. And if you do not secure representation or respond to Ms. de Vries by the end of March, she may be able to petition for divorce on grounds of abandonment. I don't think I need to tell you that would be *very* bad for your case."

Gardner swore. He had known from the start that tactic was never going to work. Nina had the might of Eric's money behind her. And now that rat bastard was going to be caesar?

He, on the other hand, had jack shit.

"Fucking *fine*," he snapped before cutting off the call. But instead of putting his phone away and descending into the train tunnel, first Gardner pulled up a web browser and typed in a search.

"There's more than one way to skin a cat," Gardner muttered to himself as he looked through the results. "If Nina thinks she's bested me now, she's got another thing coming."

II

SECONDI

CHAPTER TEN

JANUARY 2019

Matthew

The train was late. That in itself wasn't particularly surprising.

But the train was late when I had double parked the black Ferrari (Eric's assistant had gone a little overboard with the rental—not that I was complaining) outside at the curb after bribing a station agent to watch it for twenty minutes.

I pulled on the brim of my fedora and checked my watch. We were at eighteen now.

I had originally planned to pick her up right after she landed, but had scrapped that as soon as I'd arrived two days prior and discovered how fucking big Fiumicino Airport was. Sifting through international arrivals for Nina would have been like finding a needle in a haystack, beautiful blonde needle or not.

Jane had informed me, however, that Nina wanted to travel a bit more modestly on this trip, despite Eric's offers otherwise. She had insisted on flying commercial and taking public transportation to Florence. Like she was still a nineteen-year-old student and not a thirty-year-old heiress. She wasn't even taking security, now that news had gotten out about Calvin Gardner's bankruptcy. Her argument was that the paparazzi wouldn't recognize her here, nor would there be an investigator, so why worry?

———

"I GET IT," Jane said after Eric and I had both voiced our doubts about her plans.

"Why?" I demanded. "You guys have more money than God. If I had access to a company plane or a charter that cost me the equivalent of a bagel for most people, I'd never deal with TSA again."

"Exactly," Eric said. "What is the point?"

"It's about independence," Jane said. "The first time Nina went to Italy, it was to find herself. My guess is, she's not just doing this for Olivia. I think she's going back there to get a taste of herself again, too. And when you're nineteen, that starts with getting around on your own."

———

"IL LEONARDO EXPRESS dall'Aeroporto di Fiumicino è ora in arrivo al binario quarantadue."

The announcement of the train's arrival blared almost unintelligibly over the intercom, and I held up a hand to block the sun as I watched the train from Fiumicino slow as it approached, its red-painted nose pointed where I stood. I tried to wait patiently as the train stopped, and people began to pour out of its exits, luggage in tow, all of them eager to stand up and get moving.

No blondes, though. No tall ones anyway. With exquisite bone structure. And legs that stretched for miles.

I searched and searched until most of the train seemed to have emptied. Shit. Had she missed it? Had I written down the wrong one? Or she decided to hell with the whole remembering-her-student-past thing and gotten a car instead?

So much for a good surprise. Calling up to her hotel room wasn't nearly as romantic.

"This way, um, per favore."

Down at the end of the platform, I finally caught a familiar sight:

Nina, caught in a ray of sun that lit up her chin-length hair like a halo. Immediately, I started jogging toward her. She, however, was too busy to notice, trying in broken Italian to direct the porters carrying her four giant suitcases.

"*Per favore portami a*—shoot, how do you say 'just bring it to a taxi'?"

"*Scusi, signorina*," I said, ignoring the fact that she was married to use the more playful "miss." "Can I be of some assistance?"

At the sound of my voice, Nina whirled around with a squeak.

"Matthew?" She glanced around like she thought the boogie man might jump out from behind me. "Matthew, what—how—what are you doing here?"

The look on her face was almost as adorable as the way she was stuttering. And by adorable, I mean uncertain and perfect and completely fucking kissable.

I hadn't seen Nina since the night of Jane and Eric's party, and since then, I'd been spending my time taking every shift I could at Envy, tying up odds and ends for my family back home, attending Mass with *Nonna* five separate times over another chaotic Zola family holiday season. All while anticipating this exact moment.

This right here—this was my real merry Christmas.

Or in this case, a happy New Year.

"Hey, doll."

I slipped a stealthy hand around her waist and delivered a quick kiss to her cheek, getting a brief whiff of roses as I did. God, she smelled good. It had been nearly a month since the party—a solid month of unanswered calls and terse text replies.

I'm not ready, she kept saying every time I tried to contact her. *I need time.*

Well, time was up. I had a job to do in more ways than one.

She looked a bit more like herself, though. Gone was the dark eye makeup and the body-baring dress. The hair had grown out close to an inch, and Nina was back in shades of white and gray—a lacy sweater on top of tailored gray pants, over which she wore her favorite heather gray cashmere coat.

Her lips, though. Those were bright red again.

She sucked in a breath as I released her. Maybe I shouldn't have—she was wobbly for a moment, even in flats.

"What are you doing here?" she asked again.

"Would you believe me if I said it was fate?"

Nina only tipped her head, not even bothering with a reply.

"Jane and Eric didn't like the idea of you going alone. Come on, do you really blame them?" I asked when Nina opened her mouth to protest.

She closed it, then opened it again. "I...well, I suppose not. But—"

"I know you didn't think we were done talking after the party, duchess."

She blinked. "Well, you never came back, did you?"

"I called. I texted. Accepted your one-word answers. And then the holidays, you know. I do have a family of my own. Anyway, I figured this was a pretty good way to show you."

Her brows wrinkled, revealing that cute little furrow between them that I wanted to kiss. "A good way to show me what?"

"That you mean the fucking world to me." I reached up a hand and gestured toward the porters clearly looking at Nina as their target. "Plus, I'm pretty sure if Jane suggested it that night, you would have said no. We agreed a surprise was a better tactic."

"Matthew, this really isn't necess—"

"*Per favore, porta i suoi bagagli alla Ferrari nera fuori,*" I interrupted her to give the porters instructions about where to take her bags and handed one of them twenty euros.

They nodded, one of them with an impressed whistle at the mention of my car, and ducked around us. Nina was still watching me with a little irritation and a lot more shock.

"You were saying?" I said.

She just folded her arms and snorted adorably.

"All right, duchess," I said. "Tell you what, I'll go if you can tell me what I just said."

She opened her mouth, then closed it, opened it again, closed it again until that furrow had appeared once more. Picture-perfect frustration. Her lips, however, were twitching at the corner.

"Fine," she said. "It *was* a little fast for me. But it will come back, you know. I just need to practice."

I grinned. "Well, I think we can both agree that you need an interpreter until then. Lucky for you, I'm available."

"Fine," she said. "Then you can start by telling me where you just sent all my things."

———

THE LITTLE BLACK coupe dipped and dived around the traffic on the congested Via Giovanni Giolitti with ease. I didn't mind driving in Italy as much as I remembered. For all their reputations as crazy drivers, Italians weren't any worse than the average New York cabbie. I was used to this kind of frenetic pace.

"Do you even know where I'm going?" Nina called over the roar of the road and the traffic. It was hard not to watch her enjoying the sun. It was an unseasonably warm day for January in Rome with temperature topping seventy, so we drove with the windows down, listening to the cacophony of the city. Thank you, global warming.

Nina, however, was dressed for it, having shucked her coat and sweater to make herself more comfortable in the thin cotton tank top that showed off a distracting amount of her neck and collarbone. With a silk scarf wrapped around her head and a pair of white, cat-eyed frames guarding her eyes, she looked more like a silver screen film starlet than ever.

"Jane sent me your itinerary," I called back as I swerved around a delivery truck that made a sudden stop. "I changed it for a better one. I hope you don't mind."

Nina pulled off her glasses to stare at me. "You didn't."

"It might have been five stars, but that hotel was full of tourists and stiffs," I said. "I thought you wanted to work on your Italian, baby."

When she worked her face into a tight little scowl, I had to laugh again.

"Don't worry," I said. "I found a great *pensione*, owned by the same family for five generations. Right in the middle of Trastevere, with house-made *cacio e pepe* to die for. I promise, you'll love the beds too."

"Matthew!"

I almost held my hands up in surrender, but reminded myself to keep both on the wheel.

"In separate rooms, of course," I amended.

Was it my imagination, or did she look a little disappointed when I said that? I just laughed and shifted gears. The Ferrari shot forward, and the streets of Rome flew by.

———

I PARKED the car in a small garage a few blocks from the *pensione*, but only after depositing Nina and her monogrammed Louis Vuitton trunks near the entrance to wait for me.

"Did you bring your entire wardrobe with you, doll?" I asked when I returned to find her still standing outside the closed front door.

She snorted. "Hardly. But I had to pack heavy. I don't know how long I'm staying."

"You do know they have laundry services in Italy, don't you?"

She ignored me as the door opened after I knocked, and a kindly-looking landlady greeted us.

"*Salve, signora.*" I tipped my hat toward her, then asked about our reservation and whether or not they had a bellhop. I prayed to God they did. Otherwise I'd be stuck dragging these mini ship containers up four flights of stairs.

"*Sì, ce l'abbiamo,*" she replied before instructing me to leave them inside the door.

Thank Christ.

The landlady smiled and stepped back to let us into the inner court-yard at the center of the U-shaped building common to this part of the city. I heaved the trunks to the place where she pointed and checked us in while Nina wandered around the courtyard, looking around with an expression somewhere between familiarity and awe.

The building had a gray baroque facade made of stone, but its inner peristyle and the colonnades surrounding the lower level indicated that, like so much of Roman architecture, it had probably been erected over a much older foundation stemming from ancient times. The joke in Rome, I'd heard, was that no one could build anywhere because every time you dug for the foundation, you'd find something else that needed to be preserved. It was true, too. In a single city block, it wasn't uncommon to spot a two-thousand-year-old ruin, a medieval church, a Renaissance-era villa, and a jumble of baroque and neoclassical apartments.

Nina weaved her way around the columned floor, sometimes fingering the leafy vegetation and what looked like a few dormant grape vines for good measure. A fountain sang in the center, surrounded by a few bistro tables and an in-house bar at the far end. Balconies ringed the courtyard four stories up, at the top of which I could just see the remains of a much larger balustrade around the penthouse suite. Our suite. Containing two rooms. For us to sleep in. Separately.

I was frowning by the time I looked down again.

"It's very lovely," Nina admitted when she returned to where I stood.

"Just something I happened to find."

I didn't mention that Jane and Eric had actually put me up in the very hotel Nina booked—some five-star swank fest where even the bellhops wore tuxedos. I decided to cancel the reservation before I even made it to the front desk to check in. Nina had enough sterile glamour. This was a trip for family. For rediscovery. She needed intimacy and warmth. Places that felt a little like home.

And so, over the last two days, I'd been scouring every corner of Rome looking for something that would produce that exact expression of shy pleasure. Worth every damn minute.

"*Signore.*"

I turned as the landlady approached and gestured toward the balconies.

"Do you want to take dinner in your room later?" she asked in Italian. "We serve directly to the penthouse. It's very beautiful to watch the sunset with *aperitivos* and then to eat."

Beside me, Nina stifled a yawn. I glanced at my watch. It was closing in on five—laughably early for dinner by Italian standards, but pretty damn late for Nina, who looked like she was about to fall over from jet lag.

"If the kitchen's open, we'll take dinner in thirty minutes," I replied with a glance at the menu drawn on a chalkboard by the bar. "Two of the daily specials, every course. And a bottle of your best white wine."

The landlady's brow rose with that curious look people get when they smell money. "The best?"

I nodded. "The very best."

———

TWO HOURS LATER, Nina and I were lounging on the rooftop deck, bellies full of pasta and wine just as the sun was finishing its sojourn below the horizon. Nina's long legs were splayed out in front of her while she stared up at the sky, looking for stars. I hated to tell her that we probably wouldn't see any more here than we would in New York. But I supposed she could always hope.

"Ten years," she groaned sleepily. "It has been more than *ten years* since I had a meal that good." She stretched both arms overhead, then forced herself to sit back up. "Thank you for finding this place. It really is so much better than overpriced room service."

"Anything for you, doll," I said just as lazily as I swirled the last of the white Montepulciano around in my glass.

I'd gotten over my jet lag yesterday, but right now, under the haze of wine and food, I was feeling it a little more. I wanted to collapse into a bed. Preferably with Nina. But since there was no way she would let me, I was content to not stargaze a little longer.

I tossed back the rest of the wine, allowed it to sit on my tongue for a moment. Then, without thinking, I pulled a pack of cigarettes and a lighter out of my jacket pocket and flipped one into my mouth.

"What is that?"

I froze at the sudden sharpness in Nina's voice. "What's what?"

"That." She pointed a slender finger at my mouth.

I took the cigarette out and looked at it as if I hadn't realized it was there. "Oh. This."

Nina was sitting up straight now. "When did you start smoking? I've never seen you do that before."

For a second, I wanted to retort that there were a lot of things she'd never seen me do. Things she'd never let me do because we were too busy sniping at each other or trying to keep me a dirty secret. Things like kiss her or hold her hand in public. Things like sleep with her more than one night in a row or keep her from running the fuck away when I pissed her off.

But instead, I looked down at the cigarette. "I...I guess I hadn't for a long time when we met. Not since I was on tour."

"You smoked in Iraq?"

And just like that, the rest of the evening's levity disappeared, replaced by the black cloud of anyone mentioning that hellhole.

I put the cigarette back between my lips and lit it, then took a deep pull and exhaled away from the table.

"You'd be surprised what men do to cope with being over there," I said. "A smoke here and there was the lesser of a lot of evils, believe me."

Nina watched me a bit longer, her full mouth twisted in displeasure. I didn't like it. I didn't like the pity—and mild disgust—in her eyes either.

"So, why now?" she asked after I was halfway through.

I took another deep inhale, watching the end of the cigarette turn to ash, the paper burn away. "Honestly. It just seemed necessary. After you—after you turned yourself in."

Her forehead crinkled with confusion. "Why would that make you do it?"

"Probably because not being able to save someone I love is a giant fucking trigger," I said, a hell of a lot more calmly than I felt whenever I thought of Nina sleeping in a prison cell. "I loved my men too, Nina. And losing them...well, I won't say it wasn't as bad as when I had to watch that footage of you being taken to jail. But you were a close second. Especially thinking that maybe I could have prevented it."

She stayed quiet while I finished my cigarette. I used it to light the end of a second, then put the butt out in the ashtray at the center of the table. Great, now I was chain smoking.

"Give me that," Nina said.

Before I could stop her, she had plucked the cigarette out of my mouth and put it to her own. Her cheeks hollowed as she sucked on the end, then exhaled through pursed lips. I stared, hypnotized. Watching Nina de Vries smoke was like watching a swan do back flips.

"Okay, okay," I said. "Give it back. You shouldn't be doing that."

She took another pull on the end. "Why?"

"Because it's going to give you fucking cancer, Nina, that's why. I don't want you smoking, and that's it."

"Well, I don't want you smoking either for the same reasons. How does that sound?"

I scowled. "What does that matter?"

Didn't she understand how hard this was going to be? Didn't she understand that I needed *something* to keep me from grabbing her, from loving her, from doing the only other thing in this godforsaken life that made me feel even a little bit at ease with myself? Cigarettes were a poor substitute for the calm I found in worshipping Nina de Vries. But right now, they were all I had.

"Because," she said as she held the cigarette up and watched the ash slowly forming at its tip. "I don't like to see people I care about hurting themselves either." She tipped her head to one side, as if daring me to take it. "So. I'll stop. If you stop. Do we have a deal?"

We stared at each other hard across the table. Suddenly this felt like a test. And as soon as I realized that, I also realized there was only one right answer.

People she cared about. Which meant she still cared about me.

Well, then.

"You little minx," I muttered, as I took the cigarette out of her hand and stabbed it in the ashtray. "Yeah, all right, duchess. We have a deal."

And just like that, Nina grinned. And I grinned back with the triumph of passing yet another test with flying colors.

CHAPTER ELEVEN

Nina

W e left bright and early for Florence. I had fallen asleep
sometime just after nine o'clock, though I was woken twice in
the night by loud thumps on the wall next to me, and once more by an
unintelligible shout. That time I crept out to investigate.

"Matthew?" I had called cautiously through the door.

For a while, I thought he was asleep. Perhaps I had imagined that
shout, or else he really was just dreaming.

But then, he answered.

"I'm fine, doll," came his groggy voice.

I had paused. "Are you—are you sure?"

Was it my imagination, or did he sigh?

"Yeah, baby, I'm fine. Go back to bed."

So I did, hard as it was. Because something had changed the night
before when I stole his cigarette. It had been automatic—watching him
do something that he knew was self-harming produced a protectiveness I couldn't hold back. So now, I could no longer pretend I didn't
care about Matthew. It was ingrained.

But the next morning, I couldn't help noticing the dark circles under his beautiful green eyes, though the rest of him was as gorgeous as ever in a pair of fitted black pants, a bright white shirt, and a brown leather jacket. Casual, yes. But with his ever-present fedora, Matthew managed to be as effortlessly debonair as ever while he sipped his morning espresso in the courtyard, waiting for me to finish my own coffee and *sfogliatella* before we checked out.

How one person could make something as simple as a white Oxford shirt look so good was beyond me. Was it the contrast of the color with his inky dark hair and the two-day stubble outlining his sculpture-worthy jaw? Maybe it's the way it matched the flash of his teeth in a crooked smile that made my stomach turn not once, but twice?

Luckily, I seemed to have a similar effect on him. I had chosen a form-fitting gray skirt, and yes, it was partially to enjoy the way his eyes dilated whenever I recrossed my legs and exposed my left thigh through the slit that reached well past my knee. He couldn't *quite* keep himself from leering whenever I stretched my arms and thrust my chest outward. And I particularly enjoyed his expression when he noticed the three-inch silver heels I'd chosen to go with this outfit.

"You all right over there, doll?" he asked when he caught me staring at him instead of the flaky pastry.

I looked up. "Hmmm?"

His gaze managed to be both sympathetic and slightly dangerous beneath the brim of his hat

"You looked a little lost in thought," he replied before pushing my plate toward me. "You need to eat, duchess. We have a long drive ahead of us."

Yes, I was aware. Three and a half hours or so to another *pensione* Matthew had found in Florence, where I would mentally prepare myself for the first step on my agenda: finding Giuseppe's wife and revealing our affair. I sighed, not because of the impending drive, but because I did feel a little lost.

I was here. In Italy. A place I hadn't visited in more than ten years—not because I couldn't have or didn't want to, but because I was terrified of the ghosts I might confront. For more than a decade I had kept the memories of this country at bay, blindly trying to forge ahead with the lies that were supposed to protect my daughter and me, but instead they ended up nearly strangling us.

Now I was cutting us free—but was the truth just as dangerous? Other shadows were cast by the sunlight shining through the bougainvillea. They hid in the lilt of the language, in the cracks of the limestone facades.

They were even evident in the Roman nose and burnished skin of the man sitting in front of me.

Every desire I had ever felt in my life was here. There was no running away now.

So yes, I was a bit overwhelmed.

"I'm all right," I said instead, picking up the cream-filled pastry and taking a generous bite.

I was going to gain ten pounds at the rate I'd been indulging, but found I didn't really care. Not when Matthew watched me lick a stray bit of the orange-flavored cream from my lip like it was the most fascinating thing he ever saw.

The Ferrari purred on our way up the boot, and might have made for good conversation if we had had any. Instead, we just kept alternately leering at each other and daydreaming, like we were each waiting for the other to make the first move. After an hour of watching his forearms flex every time he gripped the steering wheel, I was having a hard time not asking him to pull over so I could jump into his lap like a crazed teenager. What was the matter with me? I was still so angry at him.

Wasn't I?

Matthew cleared his throat as a road sign informed us we were entering Tuscany.

"So," he said a bit awkwardly. "Did you get to see much more of the area when you were in school here?"

I looked up from where I had been staring nakedly at his Adam's apple. *Why* was the muscle on that part of his neck so bloody sexy?

"What? Oh, um, a little. Mostly Rome, Venice, and a few of the other big tourist hubs. I went to Milan for the couture shows and fittings, but otherwise, I only saw a little outside Florence and a few school-organized tours. Giuseppe took me to Siena once—it's close to the farm. That was very pretty."

Matthew glowered at the mention of Giuseppe. "Well, maybe we don't have to go to that town this time."

"What about you?" I prodded, ignoring his obvious jealousy. "Do you know the area well? You were stationed in Sicily, weren't you?"

He nodded. "I was, yeah. But Sicily is a bit different than the rest of Italy. I tried to explore whenever I had leave. Went to Naples to visit family on weekends, some other parts of the country on longer liberty. I came up here once to see the *Cinque Terre* after a few people told me it was one of the prettiest places in Italy."

"And is it?" I asked. "I never went there, but I heard nice things too."

Matthew smiled. My heart gave an extra thump.

"It is. There are no cars allowed into the towns, you know, because they're all carved into the cliffs. No big chains or resorts allowed either —almost everything is local. You have to either hike down or take the train in, which runs through these tunnels. And then you can hike between the five towns. Or pick your favorite and just stay there."

"Which is yours?" I wondered. I loved hearing him talk like this about things he so clearly enjoyed.

"Well, everyone likes Vernazza because of the church and the castle," he said. "And the pretty photo-ops. It is nice, the way it curls around this little marina. Some people vote for Monterosso because it has the best beach and an actual resort. But my favorite was the fifth town, Riomaggiore. It's quieter than the others. When I went, I stayed in this hostel that was actually owned by a woman from the Bronx, if you can believe that. Her father was from Riomaggiore, and she decided to move back and take over his business when he died."

I couldn't help but smile with him at the recollection. Everywhere he went, Matthew seemed to find a connection with someone. "That sounds like a nice inheritance."

"Bit of work, but yeah. It was nice, so far as hostels go." He side-eyed me. "Have you actually stayed in a hostel, duchess? Packed in with all the other poor students?"

I reddened, unsure exactly why. "No," I admitted. "I haven't."

"Eh, you're not missing much. Maybe smashing into a room with ten other eighteen-year-olds is fun when you're young and stupid, but it gets old fast when you're a twenty-six-year-old officer and tired of barracks. At this one, though, I only had to share a room with two other guys. And it had a really nice rooftop deck, just a few houses up from the sea. Made for a good place to eat. Alone."

"What did you have?" I genuinely wanted to know. Matthew's face lit up when he described food. And I wanted him to keep talking.

"Nothing fancy. I didn't have much money, so I went across the street to the little deli. Picked up a half a loaf of bread, a carafe of wine, a couple slices of prosciutto, and a little container of the pesto they made fresh every day. They're famous for it in Liguria, you know."

"I didn't know," I murmured, waiting for him to continue. He really was a good storyteller.

"I took it back to the hostel, climbed the five flights of rickety stairs up to the roof. And on the little deck that was maybe ten by ten square feet, I ate my pesto and bread and prosciutto and wine and watched the sun set over the Mediterranean." His brow wrinkled as he recalled the memory. "That was my last leave before we were deployed to Iraq, actually. Funny."

He was quiet for a few minutes afterward, brooding on some other unspoken memory that he clearly didn't want to share.

"Sorry," he said. "I didn't mean to monopolize the conversation."

"You didn't. It just makes me want to see it with you."

"It's not much. Food and a view, that's all. Maybe one day I'll show you."

"Show me now," I said without thinking.

I couldn't help it. It was Sunday. Florence could wait a few more hours if this sense of ease could continue.

Matthew looked at me and grinned. "All right, doll. I will."

———

AFTER PARKING at the top of Riomaggiore, we changed into more appropriate walking attire and then scrambled down the steep streets of the tiny city until we reached the deli from Matthew's recollections.

("It's still here!" he hooted in triumph.) We bought the exact same meal he described and enjoyed it atop one of the huge slanted rocks jutting out over the water. It wasn't exactly the balmy summer sunset from his last trip, as the wind forced us to bundle up in our coats. But my belly was warm with food and something else by the end of it. Something that seemed quietly like happiness.

We decided to walk the main trail along the cliffs to the next few towns over, exploring first Manarola and Corniglia. We found ourselves in Vernazza after the path popped us into the town center next to a jumble of brightly painted fishing boats and a church just after they had let out the afternoon Mass.

"Do you mind?" Matthew asked, nodding toward the open doors. "I won't be long. It is Sunday."

"I'll come with you," I said and followed him into the small medieval basilica.

Our footsteps echoed on the stone floors. Matthew dipped his fingers into water in the font by the entrance and crossed himself, then quickly found a row about halfway to the altar, touched his right knee to the ground, then slid into the pew. I followed, but by the time we were both seated, he had already arranged himself on the kneeler and folded his hands in prayer over the top of the pew in front of us. His lips moved wordlessly, but otherwise he was still, head bowed, eyes closed.

I sat back, content to look around like the other tourists who had ventured in while parishioners were still praying or lighting candles on a stand near a small wood confessional box. It was a relatively simple church compared to some of the much more ornate cathedrals in Europe—a traditional basilica in the shape of a cross, where the seating was arranged between rows of thick columns of crooked lime-stone bricks that matched the walls, upon which hung small carved pieces of Catholic iconography, the largest of which was a prominent and bloody crucifix.

And still, for all its humble appearance, there was something quite beautiful about the place. As I watched dust swirl in a stream of light shining through one of the small arched windows, I was struck with awe. There was something sacred about this place and others like it that people erected for nothing more than a spirit they believed in. Whether or not I thought that spirit, that God was real, I did believe their faith—Matthew's faith—was worth honoring.

Beside me, Matthew crossed himself again, then sat back on the pew with me.

"Better now?" I whispered.

He flashed another heart-stopping grin. "Much. Thanks for humoring me, doll."

"What do you say when you pray?" I wondered quietly when he relaxed against the hard wooden back. I had never done it myself, unless you counted the services I'd been forced to endure a handful of times at First Presbyterian Church.

"Oh, the usual stuff," he said, watching a clergy member walk around the church, nodding to a few people, speaking quietly to others. "If I'm doing penance, then there are the standard Hail Marys, Our Fathers, Glory Bes and all that. But when I'm on my own, I pray for my grandfather's soul, and for my father's too. For *Nonna*, my sisters and their families; for my friends, some of them. And I pray for my mother and the grace to forgive her."

I opened my mouth to ask more about that. Matthew never really talked about his mother, who had essentially left him and his sisters after the car crash that had taken their father. But I knew those wounds ran deep. And I could understand that. I too had a parent who had abandoned me as a child. I knew what it was like to have someone who was supposed to love you the most leave you to the wolves.

"I prayed for you too, just now," he said almost casually, as if he were letting me know he had picked up my mail or something equally benign. "You and Olivia."

"A prayer for me?" I tipped my head, not quite sure why my heart thrummed in response. "What did I do to deserve that?"

"Well, I pray for you a lot. But this was one extra."

"What was it for?"

Matthew shrugged. "I just asked Him to help us out tomorrow. I know it won't be easy for you, talking to this woman about her dead husband. So, I asked Him for some mercy on your behalf."

I wasn't sure what I thought of it, this praying business. I honestly wasn't sure I was worth the trouble.

But in the end, I found that I liked it. For more reasons than just myself.

"Olivia is Catholic," I said as we stared up at the great beams that held up the church.

Matthew turned. "Come again?"

I sighed and turned back to him. "I still don't know why I did it, but I asked for her to be baptized just after she was born. To give her a little something of her father, I suppose, something she could access in New York, when the time came. I'm not Catholic, of course, so they fought me a bit. But her godmother—Caitlyn—was. Is, I think. And Giuseppe was, even if he wasn't particularly pious. I never saw him pray or anything. Not—not like you."

Matthew offered a crooked smile. Something half-guilty, half-boyish, and completely endearing. "Ah, well. Some might say that's just the mark of a man who knows who he is already, sinner or not. It's those of us who actually worry about our mortal souls that you probably have to be wary of."

He was trying to be light, but as soon as he said it, a heaviness settled atop his broad shoulders. I was reminded once more of just how hard he was on himself. That for all his accomplishments, all the good he had done in the world, Matthew really did think worse of himself than just about anyone.

Another thought occurred to me.

"Did you confess?" I asked after a moment. "After—after that night in September? When you—when you came to see me at the station?"

He was quiet for a while before answering, staring down at his clasped hands like he thought they might hold the answer there. He almost looked like he might start praying again.

"I did," he said finally. "And then I didn't go to Mass for a while because I didn't think I was, um, clean enough to receive the sacrament, if you want to know the truth. I didn't think I'd served my penance, no matter what the priest said. It was—" He sighed. "It was the worst when you were sentenced. When the papers reported that you were in Rikers. I about lost my mind when that happened, Nina.

Especially knowing that if I came anywhere near you, I'd make things so much worse for both of us. It killed me."

My heart twisted, imagining him in that state. So riddled with guilt over us that he couldn't even manage his most essential functions. Turning himself into a chimney of all things just to cope.

Well, I had been in a state myself too.

"So, then what did you do?" I asked. "Besides smoking, of course?"

If he heard the joke in my voice, he ignored it.

"I just...prayed," he said simply. "And maybe tried to drown my sorrows in a bit too much liquor. But mostly I just prayed to God to forgive me for what I'd done. He gave me a woman to love, and I betrayed her. It's the greatest blasphemy."

I bit my lip. "You sound like a priest when you talk like that."

That crooked smile returned. "There's no other word for it that I can think of. I look at you, and I know it's true. Real love is holy. Sacred."

We stared at each other for a long moment.

"Would you—would you have asked me to convert?" The question toppled out of my mouth like rocks thrown off a bridge, clumsy and harsh. "If we had ever..."

I trailed off. For some reason I really didn't like talking about the dreams we had once shared. Especially if they could never be. The idea of myself in an off-white dress, placing a ring on Matthew's hand, him sliding one onto mine. In a place like this, it was a little too potent.

Matthew watched me carefully. I held my breath. I was nervous. The truth is, despite having baptized Olivia Catholic, I had never had any intention of joining the church myself. I wasn't even sure I believed in God.

But what if Matthew said yes? What then?

"I won't lie," he said. "If I had gotten married before, it probably would have been in a church. Maybe one like this. But then again, I never really saw myself getting married in the first place."

My heart sank.

"Before I met you, that is."

I tried and failed to ignore the great thump in my chest.

"To be honest..." Matthew reached out tentatively to take my hand

and cradled it in his much larger ones. "I doubt God really cares about where we get married. I think He just cares if we honor the gifts He gives us. Do our best to be worthy of them. One day," he said in a voice that was suddenly haggard. "If you'll let me. I'll be worthy of you again, Nina. I promise you that."

But you already are, I wanted to say and discovered I believed it.

As if he could hear me, Matthew looked up. His dark green eyes were large and open, as if inviting me to search for any trace of deceit. There was none. Nothing but love. And hope.

And in my heart, I found that I had forgiven him at last. A great weight lifted from my shoulders that I hadn't even known I was carrying, and my chest felt full of light, as if the rays through the windows were penetrating the darkest parts of me and illuminating me with this man's love.

"Matthew," I whispered. "Do you think your God would be angry if I kissed you? Right here in this church?"

The crooked smile returned, then morphed quickly into a full grin. He slipped his fingers around my neck and pulled me close, touching his forehead to mine. I inhaled his lovely, masculine scent.

"Probably not," he said as our lips hovered only a breath apart. "Considering I just asked Him for exactly that."

"You did not."

"I swear on His name, I did, baby. And who am I to turn away His gifts?"

And then he kissed me, tame and quick, lips meeting softly, yet with enough vigor that I sighed with relief. His mouth curled into a smile against mine at the sound.

"Finally," he concurred. "The priest, though, probably isn't too happy with us."

"Oh!" I tried to break away, all too aware now of a soutane-clad man lurking around the altar, casting disapproving looks through a pair of smudged glasses.

But Matthew turned my face back to his.

"Hold on there, duchess," he murmured before stealing another kiss. "Sure, the priest might not like it. But you know, I'm not sure I care."

CHAPTER TWELVE

Matthew

We meandered through the towns for the rest of the day, taking our time to get back to Riomaggiore despite the chilly winds sweeping off the sea. I got the feeling Nina didn't want to leave. Fair enough—neither did I.

But even if it didn't feel like we were stealing time, in a way we were. There were other things waiting for us in Florence, and then back in New York once we were done. And a few kisses didn't make a life, much as I might have wanted them to.

When we had finally checked into our *pensione* in Florence after enjoying a simple cliffside dinner in Manarola and then hiking back to the car, it was nearly midnight. Nina was yawning every few seconds as we walked the stairs to the rooms I'd booked side by side.

"Well, this is you," I said, handing her one of the keys when we came to a stop.

She looked down at it for a moment, then back up at me. "We're not staying in the same suite?"

"It's a smaller place. They didn't have suites with multiple bedrooms."

She blinked. "Does it...does that matter?"

I paused. Was she saying what I thought she was saying? Could it really be that easy?

"Well, I know you let me kiss you and all, but I didn't want to presume that means we're going to bed together, doll," I replied easily. "But I'm not going to argue if that's what you want."

If I sounded too eager, I really couldn't help it. Ever since that kiss, innocent as it was, I'd wanted to show her how badly I'd missed her in every other way. Still, I had the sense she was a bit like a deer at the moment. One false move and she'd take off in the opposite direction.

She worried her bottom lip for a moment.

"Hey," I said, reaching out to take her fingers. "What is it? You can tell me."

She looked at our hands, connected. "What would you think if... Matthew, do you think you could bear it if we *only* slept together? For now?"

I knew what she meant. That she couldn't handle another frenzied, almost violent coupling in the dark of night. At the party, there had been a sense that if we didn't find our way together there on the rooftop, we might have killed each other instead. We were two champagne bottles, shaken and ready to burst with need. Selfish, only willing to take what we needed without thought for the other.

I hadn't been able to give her what she needed then. But I was sure I could do it now.

"Of course," I said.

Her shoulders sank in relief.

"But I'm going to keep the other room for now," I continued. "In case—in case you need some space from me, all right?"

Nina frowned, and for a moment I thought she might tell me to return the key. Maybe I'd get what I *really* prayed for in that church, and she would throw her arms around my neck and tell me she loved me again and that I was crazy for thinking she'd ever want to be apart from me.

But instead, she nodded. "Good thinking."

We went into the room, then awkwardly took turns in the bathroom, waiting for each other to change into pajamas like we were hostel roommates, not people who knew every inch of each other's bodies intimately. It felt wrong. Stiff.

But it was what she said she wanted.

"Is this all right?" I asked her when I emerged in a pair of boxer briefs but no shirt. Usually I didn't sleep in anything at all, so I figured this was a compromise. The idea of sleeping fully clothed honestly made my skin crawl.

And yeah, I'd be lying if I said I wasn't at least trying a *little* for the hungry expression I saw then. Nina's gaze devoured down my bare chest, lingering over the muscles of my stomach that I kept up like a carefully tuned machine.

"Um, yes," she said like she had something stuck in her throat. "I'll just get changed myself."

While she got ready for bed, I decided to make us a couple of nightcaps. It was late, but I was a little worried, if I was being perfectly honest, about sharing a bed with her. She didn't know about my occasional nightmares—or the fact that they had been returning since September. Maybe if we knocked ourselves out a little harder than usual, they wouldn't come tonight.

I turned the small radio on the nightstand to the first station that had something decently relaxing, then poured a couple of fingers of the grappa I'd purchased in Riomaggiore into the water glasses on the bureau. But when the bathroom door opened, I stopped what I was doing. I couldn't see anything but her.

Her hair was mussed, her face scrubbed pink and free of makeup. She wore only a thin, white silk nightdress that reached to mid-thigh and curved along her small breasts and delicate waist like a ribbon wrapped around a package. She looked beautiful. Simple. Perfect.

"Dance?"

Nina's mouth opened slightly in surprise as she looked at my now-extended hand. "I...really?"

Doubt was written clearly across her face, warring with the desire that was undoubtedly written across mine.

"It's just a dance, doll. No harm, no foul."

"So you say. But you're shirtless, and I'm in my underwear."

Her thin blonde brow arched. *There's my girl*, I thought to myself. I couldn't help it. I loved bringing this side out of her.

She shook her head in that same way *Nonna* did whenever I was teasing her about serving day-old *amaretti*. *Scamp*, she'd call me. And she was right.

Nina knew it too.

But instead of shooing me away, she called my bluff and took my hand. And there was that electric spark, the one that never failed to skip through our fingers when we touched. We had tried and failed to ignore it so many times. But I was done.

Nina approached with the grace of a trained debutante, looking for all the world like she wasn't in her nightgown and bare feet, but a gown and tiara. And I guided her to the center of the room like it wasn't just a simple room, but a ballroom of a royal court. Like maybe I could be her prince. A worthy consort to this undeniable queen.

"You'd better be careful," she said. "I've been taking lessons since I was three. Do you even know how to dance properly?"

In response, I pulled her tight so she was flush against me and I could catch her waist with my other hand.

"Oh!" Nina gasped.

"No more questions, beautiful," I ordered. "Just let me lead."

A waltz picked up on the radio, and I started to whirl her around the room as best I could.

To her credit, Nina was actually a really good dancer. She probably *had* been taking lessons since she was three, since she could clearly keep up with me and then some. *Nonna's* simple instruction to Frank Sinatra standards was no match for Nina's teachers. Still, by the end, we were both shouting with laughter and delight, out of breath and clinging to each other once the music ended.

"Oh!" Nina cried as I dipped her again. "Oh, that was fun. Matthew, I'm shocked—you can actually waltz!"

I grinned down at her. "And foxtrot and jitterbug and swing dance, if you're up for it."

"Oh, I *love* to foxtrot!" she said, holding up her arms for another round like Sofia begging for a piggyback ride. "Eric was always terrible at it, but it was my favorite step. He was my practice partner, you know."

I chuckled. "No, I didn't know that. But I'm definitely going to give him some shit for it."

I was about to take her on another gallop around the room, but the music shifted, and a different, much slower tune filled the air. Pavarotti's rendering of *Turandot*, it sounded like. Its most famous aria, "Nessun Dorma."

Just like that, I was transported back to the Met. Sitting with Nina in that warm, red box at Lincoln Center. Whispering lyrics of passion into her ear while I brought her another kind between her legs.

"Do you remember this?" I asked as I pulled her close once more. I pressed my nose to her neck, inhaling her sweet scent. "Do you remember that night?"

"Of—of course," she stuttered, even as her arms encircled my neck, and one hand automatically began playing with my hair. "I could never forget that night. The good...and the bad."

I swallowed. Of course. I remembered the best parts of that night and had done my best to block out the worst. The way she'd discovered my previous fling with one Caitlyn Calvert Shaw. The way she'd run into Central Park only to throw herself to her knees and forced me to take the pleasure she thought I wanted from her body. Used her like she thought I had used others.

And I did it. Fuck me, I did it. Because at that point, I would have taken her any way I could get her. Angry, happy, sad, delighted. Nina was Nina to me, back then. Whatever form she took.

But now...now I could see what that selfishness had brought me. She had never fully trusted me. And just when she was finally thinking about it...I'd thrown it all away.

"But do you know what it's really about?" I asked her as we began to sway gently back and forth to Pavarotti's vibrato. "The song, I mean."

"I remember the lyrics you whispered," she said. "'None shall sleep.' After he claims the right to marry her, she begs for a way to get out. So they come to a new agreement, correct? If she can discover his name before sunrise, he'll die. And so...none shall sleep while she searches for the means to her freedom." Nina pressed her nose into my neck, as if the idea of freedom was too much for her. "A bit blood-thirsty, isn't she?"

I held her all the more tightly, enjoying the way the curve of her slim waist fit perfectly to my palm. "I think most people would kill to be free. They'd do just about anything."

She didn't respond.

"My sympathies are more with Calaf, though."

She lifted her head. "The beggar who wants to marry her? Why? All he does is trick her."

I shrugged. "Only to show her the farce of the whole system. And remember, at the end of the night, when she realizes she's doomed to marry him...he gives up his name of his own accord. He'd rather die anyway than entrap the woman he loves. He would do anything to make her happy." I stroked her hair, gently. "I understand how he feels."

She stopped swaying, pressed her hands to my chest, framing the cross and San Gennaro token that dangled between her fingers.

"Oh, Matthew," she said softly. "But he's wrong. Don't you know that? He's completely wrong."

"How do you figure?" Opera was the language of love, wasn't it? If Puccini didn't get it, what hope was there for anyone else?

"I didn't understand this until I met you, but love isn't about sacri-fice. It's not about clipping your own wings so your partner can fly, hoping desperately they'll carry you with them. It's about..." She chewed on her bottom lip a moment, trying to sort it out. "It's about making it safe to soar together."

My heart thumped like a drum at the truth in her voice. Oh God. Oh my fucking *God*. She was so damn right it hurt.

"And do I?" I asked, my heart now stuck in my throat as I tried not to hold her too close. "Nina, do I make you feel safe? I want to, baby. I want to so fucking badly."

She touched her nose to mine, her eyes squeezed tightly shut.

"You did once," she whispered. "I believe you will again." When she opened her eyes, they were shining. She hiccupped slightly. "I have faith, you know?"

It melted my cold, scarred heart.

"God, do I ever," I murmured, then captured her lips with mine.

We swayed together a bit longer, body pressed to body, mouth brushing mouth, tongue occasionally even touching tongue, until the music finally ended. Nina laid her head on my shoulder, clearly exhausted, whether from the last few days' travel or the intensity of the conversation.

"Come on, baby," I told her, and then, before she could say anything, I bent down and swept her into my arms, holding her to my chest. Precious cargo. The most.

"Let me put you to bed," I told her as I carried her there.

Her hand remained clenched into the back of my hair, even as I laid her on the bed.

"Shh," I told her as she nuzzled into my chest.

"Don't go," she murmured, pulling me close. "Please stay with me."

I brought her knuckles to my lips and pressed kisses to her empty left ring finger. "I'm here."

There was the urge to do more, of course. I knew in my soul that I'd want this woman carnally until the day I died, and there was a good chance she'd let me have my way, too. I could sink her into the linens, cage her under my body. And she'd give, because in her own way, Nina had never been more vulnerable.

But for once, I was in no hurry to take her. Because for once, the sun rising the next day wasn't a threat, but a blessing. We weren't limited to a few short hours to get what we needed from each other's bodies, maybe our hearts if we could. Tonight, we had a little bit more. We had tomorrow, and the next day, and maybe the next day, too.

That night, my dreams didn't haunt me. My mind stayed blank, my thoughts at peace. Because all I had ever wanted was safe in my arms. And for once, I was safe in hers.

CHAPTER THIRTEEN

Nina

"We could go to the Uffizi. Or see the *David* since you've never gone. The lines are much smaller this time of year, so I'm sure we could get in quickly."

Matthew gave me a look as he picked up his cappuccino from the top of a bar just off the Piazza Santa Croce. "Come on, doll. There's no use putting off the inevitable."

I sighed. It was nine thirty in the morning, and Matthew and I had been up for hours. After spending the night wrapped together in our own perfect cocoon, the fact that I was still on New York time prevented us from sleeping in any later than six. We'd gone for a chilly run along the Arno River, watched the sun rise over the terracotta roofs from Piazzale Michelangelo, then meandered back through the old town to clean up at our *pensione*. Eventually, we wandered toward the Piazza Santa Croce and nodded politely to the shop owners at the *mercato* as they prepared to open for the day until we found a place to get some coffee and a few *cornetti* for breakfast.

Matthew licked a few errant crumbs off his bottom lip, and I inhaled sharply. This torture had been going on all morning too. Like last night, getting ready for the day required a bit of musical chairs. Matthew showered first, and when he emerged, it was impossible not to be a little hypnotized by the way the drape of his towel revealed the elegant curvature of muscle and bone at his hips and abdominals. A few stray droplets clung to his amber skin, then slipped over his left pectoral. I had watched as though in a trance, then looked up to find him watching me back, one brow perked as if daring me to do more than just look.

I considered it, truly. But in the end I edged around him, clothes in hand, and contented myself with a fairly cold shower and more time than necessary to get myself dressed and ready for the day.

It wasn't that I didn't want to feel his soft skin under my fingers and bury myself in his fresh water scent, particularly after having spent the night completely surrounded by his warm, solid body. It was that I wanted it perhaps too much. And I just wasn't quite ready to be overwhelmed by him all over again. Not yet.

Much good it did me. I was still salivating, and it wasn't because of the half-eaten pastry on my plate. With the collar of his black wool coat popped up and his favorite gray fedora tilted to one side, Matthew looked more like a private eye than usual. The kind who generally seduced the lady in distress.

"You came to Florence to do something," he pointed out. "Might as well get it over with. Then, if you want, we can climb the Duomo or check out some Botticelli."

My heart skipped again, but this time with dread. In my purse was a small piece of paper bearing an address. Eric had contacted a local investigator before Christmas, who had tracked down Giuseppe's wife. My first point of contact.

"You're right," I said bleakly, then tipped back the remains of my cappuccino. I wasn't finishing the *cornetto*. Not with the knots in my stomach. "We should go."

"Wait, doll. I have something for you."

Matthew pulled from his pocket a small brown cardboard box the size of a pack of cards and set it tentatively on the bar, next to my empty cup.

"What's this?" I wondered.

"One year ago today," he said, "I walked into a bar and met you. And my life changed completely. I know it's not an anniversary, per se —though one day, God willing, maybe we can celebrate one of those too. But for now, we have this."

For a moment, I couldn't breathe. An entire year. Had it really been that long since I had stumbled into that bar on a cold winter's night?

Matthew nudged the box toward me. "It's not much. I can't really afford a lot of fancy jewelry these days anyway."

"Well, I have enough of that regardless." I picked up the box. "What is it?"

"I saw it at a shop by the Vatican the day before you arrived."

I lifted the top. Inside, nestled in a bit of blue silk, was a gold coin-shaped medallion not unlike the one Matthew wore bearing the like-ness of San Gennaro. This one, though, had a delicate engraving of a woman inside a circle of writing that said "St. Anna" along the top of the pendant and the initials "O.P.N." at the bottom.

"What does that stand for?" I asked, pointing to the engraving.

"*Ora pro nobis*. It means 'pray for us' in Latin. Saint Ann is the patron saint of mothers. And equestrians."

I looked up in time to see his mouth quirk in a slight smile. "Horses?"

"It seemed to fit." Matthew reached across the table and closed his hand on top of mine and the necklace. "Don't worry, I don't expect you to wear it—that's why I didn't get a chain too. But I thought maybe you could keep it in your pocket sometimes if you want, for good luck. Or, you know, in the back of your closet, if you'd rather."

He shrugged, like what I did with the trinket was of no conse-quence, but the way his eyes darted, avoiding my gaze, told me differ-ently. He needn't have worried.

I took the pendant out of the box and wrapped it securely in the blue silk. True, it did feel a little strange to think of wearing the iconog-raphy of a religion that wasn't my own. But that didn't mean I couldn't keep it close. I pulled out my wallet and tucked the silk-wrapped disc into the empty coin purse. Once it was zipped, a circular outline was evident through the leather. It would spoil the Chanel, but I couldn't have cared less. It would only do more to remind of this moment.

"I'll treasure it," I said. "Thank you, Matthew."

His green eyes shone with pleasure. "Anytime, doll."

"I'm really glad you're here," I told him honestly. "I don't know that I would have had the courage to go through with this if you hadn't gotten it in your head to follow me. Thank you."

"I'm sure you would have done fine. But…" He gave me a funny look, then sighed. "I should tell you something."

I frowned, and my stomach clenched a bit tighter. "What is it?"

He paused, looking entirely too guilty for my comfort.

"I didn't just come of my own accord," he said as he turned his saucer back and forth on the bar top. "I wanted to, but I, ah, couldn't afford it. My administrative leave is unpaid, see, and I couldn't just take off and leave Frankie with all the bills, so…well, Jane and Eric, um, technically, they hired me. To meet you here. Paid for the car, the hotels. All of it."

I swallowed. My skin felt like it was prickling all over. Was it September all over? Matthew suddenly encouraging our relationship again when in fact he had an ulterior motive?

I did love you, he had insisted only a few weeks ago.

I had been too angry, too confused to believe it then.

But now? Had I meant it when I said I had forgiven him?

I looked up. "So, you're getting paid to be here?"

Matthew nodded uncertainly. "That's right. I had to take it if I wanted to come. Frankie can't pay the mortgage by herself. And she and Sofia, they depend on me, you know…"

I nodded, though I felt quite ashamed. Of course. How could I have been so selfish not to consider the very real things this relationship had cost him? Or this trip, for that matter? But I had never had those kinds of responsibilities, had I? Even now, when I was technically dependent on Eric, I never questioned that he or anyone else in my family would lend me enough—more than enough—to live on. I had never had to work for a single thing. Not really.

"Are you mad?"

I blinked as I retrieved my phone from my purse. "Mad? No. I'm not sure what I think about Eric hiring a babysitter for me, but I'm not mad that you accepted an offer to replace the job I cost you."

Quickly, I pulled up a contact and pressed the call button.

"What are you doing?"

"Hush," I said. "It's ringing."

Matthew's mouth dropped, but curiously, he obeyed.

"Bridget McAvoy," answered Eric's personal assistant in a dignified, if sleepy voice.

"Hello, Bridget, this is Nina de Vries," I said, then flushed as I realized what time it was in New York. "I'm so sorry to wake you. I'll call back—"

"No, no, no, Ms. de Vries. I was up, I promise."

I smiled. Matthew's brows crinkled in amusement.

"Well, if you're sure…"

"Yes, Ms. de Vries. Mr. de Vries said you were top priority during your trip. Is everything all right? Something you need?" The poor woman sounded confused that I was calling her at all.

"I need you to pass a message on to Eric, please. I'll send him a text too. It's come to my attention that he hired Mr. Zola to accompany me here as a translator."

"Oh…yes…you see, Mr. de Vries simply offered Mr. Zola the equivalent of his former salary at the district attorney's office." Bridget spoke quickly, clearly concerned that I was upset over the arrangement. "It's only enough to pay his bills, ma'am."

"No, no, Bridget, you misunderstand," I said. "It's not enough."

"Not—not enough, ma'am?"

Matthew was frowning even more adorably now. By this point, the street around us was humming with activity as people finished their morning commutes. He could obviously only hear my side of the conversation.

"Not nearly," I said. "Bridget, please run a check on Mr. Zola's accounts, and then tell Eric that I am requesting funds from my trust to pay the balance on the remainder of Mr. Zola's debts, including his student loans and mortgage."

Matthew's elbow slipped off the bar.

"Nina," he sputtered. "What—*what*?"

"And I would like whatever wage he is receiving for this trip doubled," I finished with a wry smile. "Eric won't argue, and if he does, tell him to take it up with Jane. Or call me, if he must."

"Very well," Bridget said, still somewhat bleary. "Will there be anything else, Ms. de Vries?"

"No, Bridget. Go back to sleep. Thank you."

I placed my phone on the bar top carefully. Matthew looked like he was having a hard time speaking.

"What…what did you just do?" he asked hoarsely.

I sighed. "Please tell me you can accept a simple gift."

"Nina, you just—if you did what I think you did—you—that's not exactly a simple gift!" He gestured toward the now empty box on the table, as if to demonstrate the difference.

"Matthew." I quieted him by setting my hand on top of his. I had never felt so sure about, well, anything. "Did you mean what you said last night? About wanting me to feel safe?"

"Of course, but—"

"Well, I want the same for you." I inhaled. I hadn't really understood how true that was until I said it out loud. "Did you ever consider that? I can't do much for you, but my money can. Eric might be holding the purse strings, but some of the money in that bag belongs to *me*, not him. And I'll use it as I like."

"Still—"

"It's already done. You don't owe me anything else." I brushed my thumb over the top of his hand.

Finally, he stopped sputtering. "Owe you anything else? What's that supposed to mean?" He pulled off his hat and rubbed his face. "The whiplash, Nina. It's real. A month ago you wanted nothing to do with me. Now you're feeling guilty yourself?"

I sighed, and turned to look over the *piazza*, now bright with sunlight, the white marble facade of the Basilica di Santa Croce gleaming brightest of all at the far end.

"Look at us," I said. "Look at *this*. We are in one of the most beautiful places on earth, and for the first time, I can stand next to you in broad daylight. I can look at you and not have to hide my expression for concern of who might see. Kiss you without fear of being discovered."

Slowly, Matthew smiled, casting a dimple on the left side of his cheek. But I wasn't through.

"But there is still a mess waiting for me back in New York. Another just a few minutes away. I've already cost you your job. I suspect continued involvement with me may cost you more than that."

Matthew looked uneasy, but he didn't argue.

"Just as I thought," I said, though the knot in my stomach tightened.

"I cost myself my job, Nina. I should have turned over the case from the beginning."

"Either way, I won't blame you if you don't want to deal with me anymore. So...you don't have to."

Just like that, his frown reappeared. "Come again?"

I swallowed. "You're not beholden to Eric because this money will come from *my* inheritance, not his. So forget whatever he is or isn't paying you for. *I'm* the one doing that. And I'm saying...if you don't really want to be here, you can go."

I'd told him last night that love was about keeping the other safe enough to fly together. Now I was putting my money where my mouth was, so to speak. Without a tether, a duty to Eric...would Matthew fly away again now that his wings were no longer clipped?

Essentially, I was asking if he was here for the money, or if he had really meant what he said about wanting to repair what had been broken between us. If he really would do whatever it took.

Matthew replaced his hat and examined me for a few long minutes. I stared at my empty coffee cup, wishing there was a bit more to drink for want of something to do. The brittle *cornetto* seemed like it would stick in my throat.

But then he cracked another sly half-smile. "In broad daylight, you say?"

I looked up and flushed under the sudden heat of his gaze. "Well, yes. It is nearly ten."

With a simple, graceful movement that never failed to catch me off guard, Matthew slipped a hand under the folds of my coat to grab my waist and pulled us both to standing. And then his lips were on mine, sweetened with espresso and cream, lush and open as only Matthew could be.

I opened right back, to a chorus of whistles from passersby, even a clap from the barman who had served us. When Matthew finally released me, I was completely out of breath.

"I don't know what to say about you buying me off your cousin," he said. "But I'll never say no to kissing you in the open, duchess. Not when I've been dreaming about it for an entire year."

"You're not the only one who can take care of the people you love, you know," I reprimanded him, even as I took his collar with both hands and pulled him close again.

He pressed his forehead to mine. "Love?"

I closed my eyes, trying to ignore the fear knotted in my stomach right alongside the joy when he looked at me like this. "It's looking that way again, isn't it?"

I could feel his smile curve against my lips.

"I'll hold you to that, Ms. de Vries," he said, and then kissed me again.

CHAPTER FOURTEEN

Matthew

After I spent a few more minutes making out with Nina in the middle of the street like we were sixteen-year-olds on spring break instead of thirtysomethings on a somber mission, we finally left the *piazza* and started making our way toward Gavinana, a residential neighborhood in the southeast part of Florence.

A weight had been lifted. Not entirely. Not all the way. There were a lot of questions still, and I could feel New York and the burdens of home waiting for us like a dark cloud ready to burst. I also wasn't sure what to make of the sudden generosity that would change my life in more ways than I could count—or if I'd even accept it once we were home.

But I understood what she was trying to do. Nina valued freedom more than anything else, I was discovering. And why not—she had lived in one gilded cage or another her entire life. The fact that she loved me enough to, in her mind, set me free? I'd take it. The rest—all the questions and complications waiting for us in New York like a storm brewing on the horizon—would be solved eventually. They had to be.

It was a nice, if slightly cold day, so we decided to walk the forty or so minutes to Gavinana, meandering across the Ponte San Niccolò to Lungarno Francesco Ferrucci, a street that afforded us glimpses of the river every so often. Nina was dressed in some of the most casual clothes I'd ever seen her in. Under her cashmere coat, she had traded her typical designer dresses for a pair of tight, dark jeans and equestrian-style riding boots that were putting some less-than-innocent thoughts in my head. With her hair tied back and cheeks pinked from the breeze and (I hoped) a bit of happiness, Nina looked like she could have been a student again. But still, as ever, a perfect lady.

Eventually we turned off the main thoroughfare and came to a stop outside a nondescript apartment building a few blocks south of the river. The quaint restaurants and artisan shops of the central part of Florence had long turned into more practical places like hardware stores and supermarkets. Fewer of the charmingly crowded and semi-ancient Renaissance and neoclassical buildings; more newer structures made of brick or concrete that had more in common with my family's house back home than the churches and converted *palazzi* that comprised so much of Florence's older district.

"She's on the third floor," Nina murmured as we stared up at the U-shaped apartment building on Via delle Nazioni Unite.

I grabbed Nina's hand, squeezed, then let it go. She needed to do this herself, not with me forcing her.

"I'm here," I said. "You lead the way."

We climbed the stairs at the far end of the courtyard to the apartment number scribbled on the scrap of paper Nina had been clutching for the last thirty minutes.

"You can do this," she murmured to herself as she stared at the plain white door. Then she stood to her full height, straightened her chin, and knocked.

Footsteps shuffled immediately on the other side, and then the door opened. A pretty, slight woman with deep-set eyes and dark hair threaded with silver at the temples appeared, dressed casually but nicely in a pair of tailored brown pants and a simple blue sweater. She was holding a small orange dishtowel, as if she had come from cleaning the kitchen.

I swallowed. She could have been anyone from back home, any of the village who had raised me or my sisters in Belmont, who had shouted familiarly from across the street or shared Mass with us on Sundays. She could have been anyone in my family.

"*Salve. Chi siete?*" she asked, her sharp eyes flickering with inquiry as she looked us over.

Nina took a deep breath, her brow furrowed. "Um, hello. I mean, *ciao*, um, *pronto. Siete* Vilma Ros-Ross—"

I cringed at her poor, stuttering Italian. I wasn't a perfectly native speaker by any means, but it was still painful to hear Nina crippled so badly out of nerves. She could manage a few phrases better than this.

"*Buongiorno, signora,*" I inserted myself quickly, continuing in Italian. "My name is Matthew Zola. We're visitors from the United States. My friend would like to speak with you, please. Is there any chance you speak English?"

The woman nodded. "Yes, I speak English." Her eyes darted suspiciously between us before settling back on Nina. "Who are you?"

I turned to Nina and tipped my head. She inhaled once more. *Come on, baby,* I thought. *You can do this.*

"Hello, *Signora* Bianchi—"

"Marradi," the woman interrupted curtly. "Dr. Bianchi, he died almost ten years past. I remarried."

Nina swallowed, then nodded, almost looking like she was in pain at the mention of her former lover. I did my best to ignore the twinge of jealousy in my gut—it had to be a sin to be envious of a dead guy, but here I was. I would probably always envy anyone who got those parts of Nina's heart before I did. Especially when he didn't deserve her.

"I apologize. *Signora* Marradi," Nina corrected herself awkwardly. "My name is Nina de Vries. I knew your late husband, Dr. Bianchi. He —he was my professor when I was a student here. I, um, I wondered if you might have a moment to talk. About...about him."

Something in *Signora* Marradi's face stiffened when Nina said her name, and by the time she was done speaking, the woman's entire body was straight as a board. It was obvious she had at least some idea of who Nina was to her deceased husband. I wondered how many other "students" of his had shown up at her door over the years.

"*E tu?*" She turned to me suddenly. "*Anche tu conoscevi mio marito? O solo questa ragazza americana?*"

So, she was back to Italian, clearly to alienate Nina. Well, I wasn't having that.

"No, I didn't know your husband, *Signora* Marradi," I said in English. "I'm just a friend of Nina's. But I promise you, what she has to say is important. Will you listen, please? We'll only take a moment, or else we can return another time that is better for you."

Signora Marradi's jaw tightened visibly, and she looked like she wanted to tell us to leave. But finally, she stepped aside for us to enter her flat.

"Please come in," she said, gesturing toward the small sitting area just inside the front door. "I will make us a coffee. And then we can…"—she trailed off as her gaze raked up and down Nina's trembling form—"talk."

———

"So that's it," Nina said sometime later as she finished the story of her involvement with Giuseppe Bianchi. "Olivia is ten now."

Signora Marradi sat thin-lipped in a Victorian-style chair, holding her cup of now-cold espresso following Nina's description of how she had met Giuseppe Bianchi, had an affair with him over the course of several months, and then departed home only to find she was pregnant shortly after.

Yet again, I was struggling with déjà vu. Like the hard-eyed expression on *Signora* Marradi's face, this place was all too familiar. The crucifix hanging near the door, the thin lace doily covering the coffee table, the dark, old-fashioned furniture scattered around the apartment. It was different than home, yeah, but there was enough in common with this place, between this woman and the one who raised me, that I was having a hard time feeling anything but sympathy for her. I couldn't help wondering how it would be if this were *Nonna* and some broad showed up telling her that her husband had fathered another kid with someone else before he died. I'd probably show her the door before she could say another word.

But this wasn't some broad. This was Nina. And unlike some stranger, I knew her side of the story. I knew she wanted only the best for Olivia. I knew she wanted to free herself from the chains of the past, not bind them. And that she had more than made up for her mistakes.

Nina picked up her cup and saucer, finally able to take a drink herself. I'd been the only one making use of the refreshments *Signora* Marradi had prepared. But there was still no response by the time Nina had replaced her espresso, recrossed her ankles primly under the chair, and placed her hands in her lap.

For the first time, she was more patient than I was. I was used to interrogating witnesses, to waiting out the answers I knew were coming. But right now, the tension was just about killing me.

"*Signora* Marradi," I said finally. "I know it's a lot to take. Perhaps we should come back—"

"No," she replied curtly, then set down her cup hard enough that some of the coffee splashed over the side to the saucer. "No, not yet." She sighed. "You are...well, you are not the only *woman*"—disdain dripped from the word, making it clear she might have preferred another word completely—"Giuseppe had when he was a professor."

Nina's face didn't move, but she couldn't manage to look up either. "Oh," she said quietly. "Yes, I...I see."

"And you all think it is okay? Taking up with another woman's husband?"

Signora Marradi's voice was openly bitter, but I didn't think it was just to do with us. We all knew the stereotypes, of course—that men called their girlfriends and wives names like "sweetheart" and "doll" so they could avoid mixing up names in the heat of the moment. Somehow, my grandfather made it something different when he called every other woman by their Christian names and turned the endearment into something special for his one and only. *Nonna* would flush because she knew she was the only doll he had. He took something crass and made it a gift.

Nina, to her credit, just shook her head solemnly. "No, *Signora*

Marradi, I do not think it's okay. I'm not asking for your forgiveness, because I know I don't deserve it."

"So, what do you want?" asked the woman. "Money? We are not rich. I work in an office only a few days each week, and my husband, he only owns a, how do you call it, *negozio di ferramenta*."

"Hardware store," I supplied, finally feeling useful. "He runs a hardware store, doll."

Nina blinked back at *Signora* Marradi. "Oh, no, no, you misunderstand. I don't need money. But if you—"

She cut herself off as she caught the quick jerk of my head. I didn't know *Signora* Marradi well, but something told me she wouldn't take kindly to her husband's former mistress offering charity. I knew it was coming from a good place, but now wasn't the time.

"No," Nina said, this time more firmly. "No, I don't want money or anything like that, *Signora* Marradi. I only wanted to come because, well, my daughter. She doesn't know, you see. She couldn't, until now, for reasons I won't bore you with. But I plan to tell her soon about her father because, well, I think she deserves to know. For a long time, especially after Giuseppe passed, I believed it was in her best interests not to. But now..."

She shuddered, clearly thinking of Calvin. I reached over and took her hand. She squeezed lightly and let it go, letting me know she was all right.

"Now, I know that was another terrible mistake," Nina continued. "My daughter needs to know where she comes from. And if you're willing, I would like her to know her family too. You and Giuseppe had two daughters, is that correct?"

Signora Marradi's eyes flashed. She had just been about to take another sip of espresso, but Nina's question stopped her again. "Yes."

She did not elaborate. Nina waited again.

Signora Marradi set down her cup. "Do you have a picture? Of the little girl?"

Nina nodded. "I do. One moment, please." She rummaged through her purse to find her phone, then quickly pulled up a picture of Olivia and turned it toward *Signora* Marradi. "This is her just a few weeks ago before Christmas. She had just come in from riding her horse."

I craned my head to look with them. Olivia was standing outside the barn at the Long Island estate, looking a damn sight like her mother in riding clothes, smiling shyly at the camera while she held her helmet in one hand and the reins attached to a big black horse in another.

"Damn, she's getting big," I murmured.

"Ten now," Nina said, mostly to me. "We celebrated her birthday late, when she was home for the holidays."

Signora Marradi studied the picture for a few minutes.

"She looks like Giuseppe," she admitted. "She has his eyes." But then she pushed the phone back to Nina. "No. I don't think so. Your daughter, she looks very nice. But she is not a part of my family. Tell her that her father is dead. But we do not need to know her. Or you."

Nina's mouth dropped in pure disappointment. "But—"

"He wanted to leave us for you," *Signora* Marradi said curtly. "Just before he died. He had others, you see. I always ignored them because they did not matter. But you—you wrote him letters. I found them, you see. He said he told you to let him go, but just before he died, he wanted to go to New York. He must have wanted to find his new family."

Her anger was palpable despite the low tenor of her voice.

Nina closed her eyes for a moment. "I never asked him to do that," she almost whispered. "I wanted him to meet Olivia. But he didn't know about her. I was—I was planning to tell him when I came. But he didn't know about that plan either. I—my last letter was taken. It was thrown away."

The two women stared at each other, both torn with grief and anger over a man who had clearly never been good enough for either of them. I wondered if either of them could see it.

"I think," said *Signora* Marradi, "that you must go."

"But—" Nina tried.

"No," said the other woman. She shook her head, causing small wisps of gray and black hair to feather around her shadowed features. Suddenly, she looked quite tired. "You have done enough. Please leave."

Nina opened her mouth like she wanted to argue again. But there was nothing else to say. Several awkward seconds ticked by before I realized I needed to do something.

"Come on, doll," I murmured, holding out a hand to Nina, who was still paralyzed in her chair. "Let's go."

This time, she allowed me to pull her up and take her to the door, leaving the numbed *Signora* Marradi staring at her espresso.

"Thank you for the coffee," I called before the door shut behind us.

There was no reply.

Nina walked as if in a trance as I guided her down the stairs, out of the courtyard, and to the sidewalk that would take us back to town.

And it was there, finally, that she stopped again.

"Well," she said softly as she turned to me, eyes glistening. "I suppose that's it, isn't it? I don't know what I was thinking, coming here."

I stroked her cheek softly, wiping a few stray tears with my thumb. "You thought you were doing the right thing, baby. You did the best you could."

"Which accomplished nothing," she said bitterly, then pressed her face into her hands. "Oh God, what if that's all I'm really capable of? Just...*nothing?*"

"Ah, Ms. de Vries!"

We turned to find *Signora* Marradi walking swiftly down the sidewalk while shoving her arms into a worn trench coat to guard from the cold that she was otherwise underdressed for.

"Here," she said crisply as she came to a stop and thrust a piece of paper at us like it was a weapon.

Nina was upset enough that I took it for her.

"What's this?" I asked.

Nina wiped under her eyes. When she was finished, she wore a strange smile that made her look like a sad doll. An *actual* doll.

"An address," said *Signora* Marradi. "For Giuseppe's olive farm near Siena. Do you know it?"

She searched Nina's face. The underlying question was clear too: had she known it with *him*?

But my girl, to her credit, didn't look away, despite the fact that her deep gray eyes still welled as recollections clearly washed over her.

Instead she lifted her chin, looked straight into *Signora* Marradi's eyes, and nodded.

"Yes," she said. "I know it."

Signora Marradi didn't look away either. Anger, then under-standing flashed through her dark eyes as well.

"The farm, we have to sell it," she said. "My daughters, they are there now to prepare."

Nina started in obvious surprise. "Sell it? But I thought Peppe did that before…"

She trailed off as *Signora* Marradi shook her head.

"No," she said. "He wanted to, but the girls were so upset, he kept it."

She shrugged, if to say, *that was that*. Then she glanced sadly back at Nina's purse, as if she still saw the picture of Olivia laughing across the black screen on her phone.

"I think they would like to know about their sister," she admitted. "You should go there and tell them. Giuseppe is dead. I will not keep his secrets anymore."

CHAPTER FIFTEEN

Nina

S *ecrets.*

The word rang inside me like a gong as we drove out of Florence.

"You're very quiet," Matthew said. "More than usual. What's on your mind, doll?"

He switched gears and sped forward as traffic disappeared on the highway, away from the city. He hadn't said it, but I rather thought he was enjoying the Ferrari more than he let on. Normally I might have enjoyed his obvious pleasure. Right now I barely noticed.

"I was thinking about Giuseppe." I turned to him, suddenly uncertain. "Do you really want to hear this?"

Relief washed over me when Matthew simply shrugged. "I mean, I'm not surprised, given what we're doing. And we all have our pasts, baby. You wouldn't be you without yours." He flashed a brilliant, slightly sharkish smile at me. "I want to know all of it. Even if it does make me want to punch a dead man."

I bit back a smile. His humor was perhaps a bit ghoulish, but I preferred joking to jealousy. So much better than the brutal possessiveness I'd endured from my husband.

But Calvin had never really been a husband at all, had he? Maybe that was part of why.

"I was thinking of what his wife said," I answered as the hills of Tuscany ebbed and flowed around us. "About his secrets. It made me wonder how many she had to keep."

"I think that probably depends on what they were. You, for one. But it doesn't sound like you were much of an anomaly in his life."

"No," I said shortly. "It doesn't."

I felt like a fool. I shouldn't have been angry, of course. A twenty-year-old girl getting involved with her forty-two-year-old married professor? It was beyond cliché. Tragic, really. Pathetic. Even more, perhaps, if he really had intended to leave his family for me, as his wife said.

"But you know, everyone has secrets," Matthew interrupted my thoughts. "Just because you have some doesn't make you a liar."

"Doesn't it?" I asked softly.

He cast me a meaningful look before changing lanes to pass a truck. I kept my eyes firmly forward.

"I don't think so. I mean…" He shrugged. "I can't pretend it didn't sting that you didn't tell me sooner about Olivia. Or about your involvement in Calvin's business. But today I thought, why would you? What did I do to deserve that kind of honesty?"

"Oh, Matthew, don't be so hard on yourself."

"I'm not," he said shortly. "I just think that's an unfair assumption most people make. They think secrets are something that should be freely offered. But secrets are precious. They're earned. That's how you know someone really loves you, I think. They confide the things they wouldn't have told anyone else." His mouth, so beautiful and full, twisted into a sardonic half-smile. "I like to think that's when you knew you loved me, Nina. You had to tell your honest-to-God truth. Otherwise, how do you know the person really loves you back?"

I sat there quietly, ruminating on his words. I looked down at my hands, folded in my lap, and for a moment, saw a ring of bruises play around my wrist.

I hadn't told him everything. I wasn't sure I ever would. For one, there was a part of me that worried about what he would do if he knew every side of my marriage. Matthew had a protective side. More than protective, really. Matthew looked at me like I was whole. There was no pity in his eyes, the way the people who knew even bits and pieces of what Calvin did—my housekeepers, my assistant, Caitlyn—looked at me, like I was a wounded animal who would be better put down than forced to live. I couldn't bear it if he thought of me like that. Like I was ruined.

Even so, if what he said was true... If my secrets were a gift, why wouldn't I want him to have them all? Perhaps he was right. Perhaps I'd never know he truly loved me until he knew them all.

"Will you tell me one of yours?" I said. "Something you've never told anyone else. A trade, if you will?"

Matthew glanced at me. "I've told you secrets. Like Iraq, remember?"

His gaze darkened. I didn't press. The memory of him on his knees, sucking blood from my finger after I had pricked myself on the sharp pin on his Navy Cross, would stay with me always. I had listened to him tell a story that was less about the valor for which he had been honored, and more about the deep guilt he carried from the horrors of that day.

Was that when he began to love me too?

"Well, that's one," I said. "But you have two of mine, or you did before I gave one to your boss. You owe me another."

He shot me a quick, green gaze, then turned back to the road. "What if it's something you don't like?"

"It's fair to assume I won't. That's why we keep them, isn't it?"

"I don't know. Maybe sometimes it's to protect others, not ourselves."

He looked at me again, and this time, we were both thinking of Olivia. Of my family. Again, the ghosts of bruises throbbed on my wrist. And my jaw. My ribs.

Sometimes I wondered if I would ever know how to let go of them completely.

Well. I was trying, wasn't I?

"I haven't spoken to my mother in over twelve years," Mathew said after he passed a slow-moving Fiat. "Not since I got back from Iraq."

"That's a long time." I knew that Matthew was estranged from his mother, but I didn't realize it had been over a decade.

"Some scars really are permanent." His hands squeezed the steering wheel. "I was just getting out of class, on my way to Envy. I had just started law school, working nights at Jamie's bar like I am now. And I got a call from Joni. She was trying to live with Mom at the time—during one of her sober periods. Joni's the baby, you remember?"

I nodded. Joni, Matthew's effervescent youngest sister was full of life and naïveté that even the city hadn't beaten out of her yet. She was easily the most effusive of all his family members. I had liked her at once.

"She always had a soft spot for our mom," Matthew continued.

"The baby of the family usually does," I concurred.

He grunted. "Anyway, it was seven o'clock at night, and Joni was stuck at this high school in Trenton after a soccer tournament or something. Mom was supposed to pick her up, but she didn't show. So poor Joni, this eleven-year-old kid, is alone in a terrible neighborhood, scared as fuck and without any train fare." He scoffed, like he still couldn't believe it. "She just fuckin' forgot about her. Fell off the wagon for maybe the third or fourth time." He shuddered. "I hate to think what would have happened had she actually tried to go to Trenton."

"Why is that?" I wondered.

"Because she was the one driving when my dad died. Not that it mattered. They were both lousy drunks, so it could have been either of them who crashed the car. I told you that too." He looked at me as if to point out that he didn't actually *have* to be telling me a secret at all. He didn't owe me confidences.

"Yes," I agreed. "You did."

"Anyway, I went to pick Joni up. And by the time we got back to Belmont, I was fuckin' livid. Because I get home, and Tino, a family friend, calls us from his restaurant. Mom's at the bar, singing 'All

Night Long' with the jukebox before she passes out across a couple of stools." He shook his head with disgust. "That was it. I couldn't do it anymore. I felt like *I* was the one who was eleven, not Joni. Forced to be the grown-up, getting ready to take it on the chin from my old man while my mom just watched, half passed out on the couch."

At the thought of it, I found my own hands balling up, ready to do their own damage to anyone who had hurt this beautiful man. Yes, I understood his protectiveness very well. There was more to love than just secrets.

"I wish I was more forgiving," he said. "But I'm really not. Not to those who hurt the people I love, Nina. And she did that. Again and again and again, she did that. So I wasn't going to stand by and watch her do it to my sisters like she did to me. I didn't care if she got back on the wagon or stayed there. She was out of luck."

"So what—what did you do?" I wondered.

"Told her if she contacted me or the younger girls again—Joni, Marie, and Lea were all still minors at that point—I'd file for a restraining order. I said I was done, and I meant it."

We sat there for a moment, thinking about the story. Matthew wished he was more forgiving? Until now, I had really considered him the soul of mercy. Now I wasn't so sure.

"My sisters don't know any of this," he said. "They know Mom and I don't speak, but not why. And not about the legal threats. Frankie doesn't talk to her either for her own reasons, but the younger ones do now that they're grown. And because supposedly Mom is sober. Lea sees her on birthdays and holidays. Sometimes Marie and Joni tag along. Things like that. Lea knows the whole damn family on that side."

"Your mother is Puerto Rican, isn't she?"

Matthew nodded. "Half, yeah. Her dad was from Santiago, but he went back before I was born. My grandmother died when I was a kid, so I didn't know either of them, and they only had the one child, my mom. But sometimes we'd see distant cousins and stuff."

I thought of the day at the Cloisters, when we had run into one of the cousins from that side and his wife. A whole side of his family that Matthew had given up because of this anger. I almost argued that enough time had passed. That if she was sober and trying, didn't she deserve a second chance just like anyone else? If his sisters could do it, why couldn't he?

But there was a steely resolve in Matthew's eye that was utterly unwavering. And considering that I had hardly spoken to my own father in years, I wasn't in a position to argue.

"Everyone wants to believe in unconditional love," he said. "But you know...you're right about one thing, baby. Love as sacrifice ain't real love. We all have to have our limits. Our parents are supposed to teach them to us, but when they don't, we have to find them for ourselves." He sighed, clutching the steering wheel hard. "She crossed the line. There was no going back after that."

He didn't want to talk about it anymore, and I let him be, content to remain lost in my own thoughts as the Tuscan countryside sped by, blurring my past along with the winter farmland.

But my thoughts kept circling back to one constant refrain. I was glad that Matthew had worked so hard to assert his own safety in a world that damaged so many. Knowing him, witnessing that strength, had given me the courage to draw my own line in the sand. To say enough was enough, and take back freedom and dignity that I knew I deserved.

I just hoped that by the time this trip was over, I wouldn't have crossed Matthew's line myself. I didn't think I could bear it if he ever looked at me and, after all the things I had done, all the secrets I'd kept, decided that in the end, I wasn't worth his mercy.

CHAPTER SIXTEEN

Nina

The farm was not exactly how I recalled, a fact that confused me until I remembered it was the middle of winter. Giuseppe had brought me here in full bloom of spring, when the olive trees were thick with buds, and flowers and dew shone on the gnarled branches like a layer of glistening gold.

"Holy shit," Matthew murmured as he steered up the drive. "What happened here?"

"What do you mean?" I asked.

"The trees. They're completely bare." He shook his head. "I'm no olive farmer, but I remember the ones in Sicily having leaves year-round. I don't think they're supposed to look like that."

Immediately, I knew he was right. I had explored Tuscany several times as a student—and never had I seen its famed olive orchards like this: row upon row of desiccated, barren trees, ancient and bent as if recovering from some invisible war.

Matthew pulled to a stop in front of the farmhouse, where another small white car was parked in the dirt drive. We got out and pulled on our coats, Matthew his hat. Then we faced the stone villa.

Stout and square, its construction was similar to most of the farmhouses around the region. Its walls were a mosaic of sandstone and brick, topped with a terracotta roof. The entrance was shaded by a small porch covered in vines now twisted and bare in winter, but which I remembered flush with bright green leaves and the tiny buds that would eventually become sweet green grapes.

"Has it changed much?" Matthew wondered.

"Not like the trees," I said, only now noticing the bits of stonework crumbling here and there, the roof shingles that needed to be replaced, and the wood fencing surrounding the house that split here and there from weathering. It went far beyond "rustic."

Giuseppe had loved this farm. It was his family's birthright, a place they had owned for more than four hundred years, he had told me. He would have hated seeing it like this. The disrepair, like the trees, was tragic.

The front door swung open, and a young, willowy woman who couldn't have been older than twenty appeared. She had long brown hair and eyes to match that were deeply set above high cheekbones, a slightly hooked nose, and full lips caught in a scowl.

She looked like Giuseppe, yes, with perhaps a passing resemblance to the woman I had met only this morning. But instantly, even with the darker complexion, I felt like I was seeing an older version of my own daughter, Olivia. For a moment, I couldn't breathe.

"Jesus," Matthew whispered, clearly seeing the resemblance too.

"*Salve*," called the girl as she approached, then rattled off a few questions in rapid Italian that I couldn't follow.

Matthew tipped his hat and answered in kind. Yet again, I was impressed by how quickly he had adapted to the language here. He said he wasn't completely fluent, but he seemed to communicate with ease. All I caught was our names as he gestured to himself and then to me.

"I see," said the girl in English. "You are Americans." She sighed, as if the very thought exhausted her. "Well, I am Lucrezia Bianchi, one of the owners. My sister, Rosina, she is inside. If you want, we can show you around. The realtor is lazy—he won't be back until tomorrow."

"Maybe you need a new realtor," Matthew joked.

The girl's mouth quirked, but there was too much bitterness there for a full smile to emerge. "Follow me. There's some mess in the kitchen from the work, okay?"

I glanced at Matthew, who shrugged, as if to say, "What else can you do?" And so, we followed the girl into the house with the acute sense of people expecting ghosts to pop out behind every corner. And why not? Memories could be nearly as frightening.

Like a lot of houses of its kind, it looked larger than it was. The thick stone walls took up more space than one might expect, and the fact that there were so few windows meant that most of the house was cast in perpetual shadow, dependent on sconces, a few dusty chandeliers, and the occasional sunlight reflecting off the warm stucco walls.

Most of the interior was still the way I remembered it—the plain, sturdy furniture, the smooth wooden sink, the beaten tile floors. I started when I spotted the old stone fireplace at the far end, complete with the rug where Giuseppe had lain me bare in the firelight. The memories were so far away—he was nothing but a ghost. But they were powerful, nonetheless. That was, of course, the spot where my daughter had likely been conceived.

Matthew took my hand as we walked into the living room. This time, I didn't shake it away. I wanted his solid strength close.

"When was this place built?" Matthew wondered.

Lucrezia shrugged. "It's not *so* old. Only three hundred years, I think. They had to rebuild after a fire."

Matthew gave me a sly wink. I knew what he was thinking—this was such a difference between the United States and nearly everywhere else in the world. We had such a truncated view of history, so evident in things like architecture. A hundred-year-old house in the United States would be exceedingly rare and considered absolutely ancient.

"It was profitable until a few years ago," continued the girl. "We made olive oil. We had enough to pay the caretakers, and a good yield that we sold at the markets. But then the trees got sick. More than half of them are dead now."

"It's a shame," Matthew murmured as he looked around. "It's a beautiful place."

"Rosina!" hollered Lucrezia from the bottom of the stairs. "*Dobbiamo mostrare la casa a degli americani.*"

There was a clattering of footsteps, and another girl appeared who resembled Giuseppe even more strongly than her sister.

"*Perché?*" she demanded. "*Quali americani?*"

Beside me, Matthew cleared his throat. "That would be us," he said, in English for my benefit before repeating himself in Italian.

"Oh!" said the girl. "Hello."

"This is my sister, Rosina," said Lucrezia. "I'm sorry she is rude. She loves the farm very much. We both do."

The younger girl broke into a sudden spat of angry Italian, and Lucrezia immediately started snapping back at her. I couldn't follow most of it, but it was clear they were mostly fighting about selling the house.

"Excuse me," I broke in suddenly. "But there's been a misunderstanding. As much as I'd love a tour of the grounds, I'm not here for the house. I'm here to meet, well, the two of you."

The girls immediately stopped squabbling to stare at me.

"Us?" repeated Rosina, shoving a messy lock of brown hair out of her face. "Why are you here to meet us?"

"Your mother sent me," I said. "She—I met her this morning. I, well. I knew your father, Giuseppe, a long time ago. My name is Nina de Vries."

Their expressions didn't change, but something else, something much more subtle did. A tiny shift in posture, a slight movement of chins. Whatever it was, it was palpable and frosty. And told me that, like their mother, they understood exactly my connection to Giuseppe Bianchi.

"Our father?" Lucrezia asked. "When did you know him? He died almost ten years ago."

I nodded. "Yes, I know. I was very sorry to hear it. I was a student of his at the university the year before his death."

The frost turned to ice.

"*Lo sapevo,*" Rosina muttered to her sister, which I did understand as "I knew it."

I took a step forward, hands held out as I reluctantly dropped Matthew's. "I know what you must be thinking."

"That we're surprised our father had an American lover?" snapped Rosina. "No, not such a surprise. Four of you came to his funeral. And you all looked like whores."

"Rosina!" snapped Lucrezia.

I swallowed. "No, it's all right. I—it's all right."

"Well," said Lucrezia, who was, like her mother, a bit slower to speak but maybe more intimidating than her sharp-tongued sister. "What do you want, then? A keepsake? Forgiveness? We don't have either. *Babbo* left us nothing but this old farm, and now it isn't worth anything. With so many dead trees, it can't even earn enough to pay the taxes."

Once again, Rosina burst into a torrent of Italian and looked like she might cry. It only lasted a few seconds until she remembered she had an audience. Then she stomped over to the mauve-colored sofa and flopped down, arms crossed.

Lucrezia sighed, then turned back to me. "Well?"

I swallowed, then pulled out my phone. "I wanted to show you this. I..." I glanced nervously between the girls. "You're not wrong about the nature of your father's and my relationship. And I apologize for any pain I may have caused. But I can't say I regret it completely, because if I hadn't known him, I never would have had my daughter. Olivia."

I held out the phone, and Lucrezia took it. She looked like she wanted to throw it back to me until she got a good look at Olivia's school picture from this year. All resentment was replaced by complete and utter shock.

"*Cavolo,*" she whispered to herself. "Rosina. *Vieni qui.* You need to look at this."

Rosina pushed herself from the couch, muttering grumpily in Italian.

"What? What did she have to—*figlio di puttana!*" she snapped when she saw the photograph.

Matthew snorted beside me. "Technically, it should be *figlia*, no? Daughter of a bitch would make more sense."

Both girls looked up from the phone.

"Ha!" Rosina barked a terse laugh.

Lucrezia handed the phone back to me, looking from me to the screen, then back at her sister. "She looks just like Rosina. Just with blonde hair."

I nodded. "She resembles both of you quite strongly, I think."

The girls both nodded, but then awkwardness descended again.

"Look," I told them, ignoring the way my heart was racing now. "I realize it's a lot to take, learning you have a half sister on the other side of the ocean. She doesn't know about you, but she will, soon. Which is why I'm telling you about her first. Because I know my daughter. She will want to meet you. And I thought if you had some time to think about it...maybe you would consider meeting her too. One day."

The girls were quiet for a long time. Seconds passed. Then minutes. Matthew shuffled next to me, rubbing his fingers together, and vaguely, I wondered if nervous anticipation was making him want a cigarette again. I certainly felt like it might help.

Finally, Lucrezia spoke. "It *is* a lot," she agreed. "I think my sister and I, we need to talk about it. Perhaps...maybe we could take your phone number?"

"Would you let me take yours too?" I asked.

With a quick glance at Rosina, Lucrezia nodded. "Yes. Okay."

Relief washed over me as the girl took out her phone and we traded contact information. It wasn't much. But it was also better, maybe, than I had anticipated.

Afterward, the girls walked Matthew and me both outside. They were clearly eager for us to leave—ready to discuss the bombshell I'd just dropped in their laps, beyond the prying eyes and ears of strangers. But I felt, well, if not good, then at least somewhat hopeful.

"It's just a thought," I said as I stood at the open passenger door, peering back at the farm. "But if you need some help with the taxes, perhaps I can be of service. You wouldn't have to sell. Not immediately, anyway."

"Oh, no," Lucrezia began. "We could not accept—"

"Oh, please," I pushed. "It's the least I can do, and it would be no trouble. You can have some time to decide what you really want to do with the place. And perhaps if I bring Olivia to Florence—if you're willing, of course—you could meet her here. I think she would like it, meeting her sisters on the farm your shared family has owned for so long."

The girls glanced at each other. Rosina didn't bother to hide her pleading eyes.

Lucrezia turned back, looking defeated, but also a bit relieved. "Okay. We would appreciate that. Very much."

I smiled. "I'll be in touch."

The girls waved goodbye, and Matthew and I got into the car.

"You're going to buy that villa for them, aren't you?" he asked as the girls went back inside.

"I don't need to buy it for them," I replied. "It's already theirs. But if they are willing, I might be interested in going into the olive oil production business. Help them replant, if they like, or rehabilitate the land so it's at least sustainable."

Matthew glanced back at the farm. Something remarkably close to jealousy sparked in his eyes. "So you want to keep coming back here, don't you?"

I softened, then slowly reached out and turned his chin back so he was looking at me again. Vulnerability shone through those deep green eyes. I wanted to kiss it all away.

"I don't want the farm for me," I said. "My time here was fleeting. Beautiful for a girl of twenty, but I don't need those memories anymore. I have new ones. Much better ones now."

The jealousy flickered, but it was a flame that was going out.

"I want it for Olivia," I said softly. "So that when she is ready, she will have a place to see her family's history. To meet her sisters, if they want. To know her father in the only way she can. She'll need that, don't you think?"

Matthew was quiet for a moment. Then he lifted my hand and pressed his lips to my knuckles.

"You are a wonderful mother, Nina," he said. "It's one of the many reasons I love you."

The simple words lifted my heart. They truly made me fly.

Once again delightfully uncaring of who might be watching, I placed my hands on either side of his beautiful face and pulled him in for a kiss—delicate at first, but one that eventually spoke of the longing that both of us had for closeness. Matthew's tongue twisted around mine, and I opened to the kiss, suddenly needing to be closer than I had ever been before.

With no small effort, I broke the kiss, pecked one more on the tip of his slightly crooked nose, and smiled.

"I love you too," I whispered. "Now, please. Take me away from my past. From here on, I only want my future."

Matthew grinned and started the car. "With pleasure, baby."

But before we could leave, there was a quick rap on my window. I jumped, and we turned back to find Rosina standing there, gesturing for me to roll it down.

"Hello," I said. "Is everything okay?"

She looked unsure, harried, as if she had run out without telling Lucrezia.

"There is something more...I think you should know," she said. "Lucrezia doesn't want me to say, but she is wrong."

I frowned. "What is it? You can tell me."

"My father. Do you know how he died?"

A sharp ripple of something etched up my spine. "I—it was heart failure, wasn't it?"

Rosina nodded. "That is what the doctors said. I was only eleven, so I only knew from my mother. But when I got older...well, I am in medical school now. I looked at the autopsy report." She sighed. "And there were significant amounts of poison in his system. Not enough to be an overdose immediately, but later, to mimic a heart failure. No one would have known if my mother had not insisted on the autopsy."

I pressed a hand to my chest. "I hadn't known that. My God."

"My mother, she told me later. There was an investigation. The university said a man visited him in his office. But they never found him. And...there was an alibi for him, I think."

Beside me, tension radiated off Matthew's entire body. I could hardly breathe.

"What happened with it?" Matthew asked. "Is the investigation closed?"

The girl shrugged. "Unsolved, they said. My mother said we should move on, that *Babbo* was maybe just an addict. Maybe she thought one of *you* gave him this drug. But I never stopped thinking about it. I was young...but I don't think my father was an addict. I wondered if maybe you knew."

She looked directly at me, her dark gaze unwavering. The question was clear: Had I known about her father's drug problem? Was I, the impetuous student with apparently no moral compass, perhaps responsible for it?

I cleared my throat. "I—no, Rosina. I never knew Giuseppe to do any sort of illegal substance."

She gave me a hard stare for a moment more, then finally stood up, seemingly satisfied.

"That's what I thought," she said. "And that's all I know." Then she glanced over the car, noticing for the first time its expensive make. It's apparent wealth. "Goodbye, Nina."

I raised a hand in farewell, startled at the sound of my name issuing from her mouth. Maybe because she looked so much like her father. It felt like Giuseppe himself was the one wishing me farewell.

"Goodbye, Rosina," I said. "And good luck with the farm."

CHAPTER SEVENTEEN

Matthew

Nina was quiet for the entire drive back to Florence. This time, I didn't press her to talk, sensing she needed a minute to process. It's not every day you introduce yourself to the daughters of your married former lover. Most people would rather jump off a moving train.

I was proud of her. I was. She looked her mistakes in the eye and took it on the chin like a champ. But I couldn't lie to myself either. Seeing that farm and the way Nina's gaze traced lovingly over its worn interior and admittedly picturesque grounds, sick trees and all? Listening to her all but offer to buy the damn place, to keep that part of her life forever? It was hard. More than hard.

I had my own relationship with this country. With Naples, and parts of Rome, where my grandmother was from, and Sicily, where I was stationed. Before today, I'd dreamed countless times of visiting the land of my ancestors with the woman I loved, sharing in its culture and history with her, making the kinds of bonds that last a lifetime, all swimming in what Italians called *la dolce vita*: the sweet life.

But today made me want to get the hell out of Italy. Take Nina someplace else. But not back to New York either. Somewhere we could start fresh. Where we could maybe lose the ghosts of our pasts and get a real chance at a future together.

Jobs. Family. Secrets. None of that seemed to matter to me anymore. All I wanted was freedom. For her. For me. For us, together.

But here she wanted to anchor herself to those ghosts for Olivia's sake.

Or maybe her own?

I shook off the idea. It was jealousy, plain and simple. Nothing more.

Still. She was the one who brought up secrets on the way to the farm and asked for mine without offering any of hers. And while I still believed everyone had rights to their own, it did make me wonder what she might be hiding. I wanted to believe the time for secrets between Nina and me had passed, but I wasn't a fool. I'd hurt her. She had plenty of reason to hold things back.

So it wasn't a huge surprise when we reached the *pensione*, and Nina dawdled a minute outside the two rooms we had paid for—one of them still completely unused. Then she asked quietly if she could have some time to herself.

I tipped my head. "You sure, doll? You don't have to be alone if you don't want."

Nina nodded. "I'm sure."

She fingered the edges of my jacket for a moment like she was considering pulling me close. But then she released them.

Part of me wanted to fight it. Wanted to wrap my arms around her and make her accept that she had a partner whether she wanted one or not. But that's not partnership. That's force. I'd decided back in December that I would do whatever I could to show Nina I wasn't going anywhere. That if she needed a champion, she had me. On her terms, not just mine.

And right now, Nina needed some space. Well, that was all right. I had some questions of my own that needed answering.

"I'm going to walk, then," I said as I delivered a quick kiss to her cheek. "Stretch my legs. I'll be back in time for dinner around eight."

"Don't hurry," she answered, then slipped into the room and closed the door.

———

"*Mattia Zola?*"

"*Sono io.*" I stood from the small chair as the door to the office of Silvana Ruggeri opened.

Ruggeri, a chief prosecutor in Florence, was an attractive, if slightly intimidating woman that reminded me a lot of the female Marines I had known in the service. Unflinching.

"You're very persistent," she said as she locked her office door. "The secretary said you were waiting for the last hour and a half." She turned and looked me over. "You look like your cousin when I knew him. Yes, I can see the resemblance."

I tipped my hat. "I'll take that as a compliment."

But Ruggeri wasn't flirting. The opposite in fact: this woman was hard as nails.

As soon as I'd left the hotel, I'd called my cousin Marcello, a detective with the *polizia di stato* in Naples, about Giuseppe Bianchi's death. If the girls were right and some kind of investigation happened, there should be a record of it. It had been a pure stroke of luck that the investigator assigned to the case still worked in Florence—and happened to be a friend of the family.

"Zola told me you wanted to know about the Bianchi case?" she asked, referring to my cousin much the same as people did me back home—by our shared last name.

I followed her into the main stairwell of the old building. Our footsteps echoed down the steps.

"I know it's a long shot, but I'm only here a few more days. I spoke with his daughters today, and they had some interesting things to say. I wondered if you could corroborate."

She eyed me curiously. "Zola said you're a prosecutor in America?"

I nodded. "I was, yeah. On leave right now. Law enforcement runs in the family, I guess."

"Why do you care, though? That case has been closed for years. There is no hope of solving it."

We exited onto the street, where a rush of people filled the sidewalk of the busy street in the San Lorenzo district, forcing us to stand a little closer than necessary.

I paused, wondering just how much I should give away. Fuck it. Marcello had vouched for Ruggeri, and Nina's secret was out in the open. I had nothing to lose by asking.

"I'm here with a friend," I said. "An American woman who had an affair with Giuseppe Bianchi a year before he died. When she went back to New York, she was pregnant, and she had the baby. She was on her way to tell Bianchi when he died."

Ruggeri's face remained stoic, but her eyes flashed with interest. Yeah, she saw the potential connection there as much as I did.

"And you think she might have something to do with Bianchi's death?" she asked finally.

I shrugged. I wasn't planning on giving anything away myself. "Seems a little strange, don't you think?" I held up my hands. "I just have a couple of questions. I don't want to stir up trouble."

Her sharp black gaze raked over me, as intense and critical as any inspection I'd ever endured in boot camp. I half expected her to fine me for the scuff on one of my shoes.

But instead, she checked her watch.

"I have an hour for a drink. There's a cafe around the corner. I'll tell you what I can."

I tipped my hat again. "I'll take whatever you have to offer. And drinks are on me."

——————

THE STORY RUGGERI told me over a couple of *aperitivi* was at first similar to other unsolved homicides I'd encountered back home. Rosina's story was true: after the autopsy, foul play was suspected due to traces of toxins found in Bianchi's system.

"We spoke to his wife, his friends, many others. Searched his office too. There was no sign of any drug use. And his behavior was not consistent with an addict," Ruggeri said before taking a sip of a Negroni. "Not that it mattered, since what was found turned out *not* to be any kind of narcotic. So I don't know why the girl thought that. Maybe her mother gave her another story."

"Then what was it?"

Ruggeri studied me for a moment. "Did you say that your friend, she tried to contact Bianchi just before his death?"

Okay, evasion. She was trying to see if I was the real deal. Well, I had nothing to hide.

I nodded. "She wrote him a letter, but her family intercepted the reply. As far as I know, Bianchi never knew about the baby."

Ruggeri twisted her mouth around. "I see. Hmm."

"So, any suspects, then?" I prodded gently.

Ruggeri examined me again, then relaxed, seeming to decide I was either harmless or maybe helpful. "One, in fact. There was a man who was checked into Bianchi's office building by security approximately four hours before he died. Not an Italian. But too old to be a student."

That didn't necessarily mean anything. There were loads of expats and tourists in Florence at any given moment.

"His name wasn't Calvin Gardner, was it?" I asked, just on a hunch.

"No, it wasn't American."

I slumped as Ruggeri took another drink.

"It was Hungarian," she finished.

I sat up straight. "Any chance you remember what it was?"

Ruggeri gave me a dry look that said "Are you kidding?" more clearly than if she had spoken the words. "It was ten years ago, Mr. Zola." But even so, she screwed up her brows in thought. "Although maybe..." She snapped her fingers again and again, as if it would conjure the name by magic.

A bolt of steel scampered up my spine. I edged forward slightly in my seat.

"I only remember because the name, it was catchy. Something like Carol..."

"Károly Kertész?" I supplied.

She snapped loudly and pointed at me. "*Yes*! That's it." Then she frowned. "How did you know?"

I held up my glass, almost as in salute. "I'll tell you when you're finished. Please go on."

"Well," she said as she clinked her wedding ring against her glass. Ruggeri was a fidgeter. It was her only tell. "In the end, we had two problems: the first was that it took several days for the labs to confirm that the cause of death wasn't simply heart failure, but a rare nerve agent that is difficult to detect. You are familiar with Novichok?"

I tipped my hat up in surprise. "The chemical agent the Soviets used against their spies in England last year?"

Ruggeri nodded in satisfaction. "Yes, that's it. Very powerful. A delayed release, though if it was strong enough to kill Bianchi within an hour, we still don't know how he was exposed. Perhaps his espresso, but we think if he drank it concentrated like that, he would not have made it home." "Maybe he didn't drink it until he was home," I said. "Maybe it was slipped in a water bottle or something. Or another product he had with him. There was the British agent that was killed when it was put into a perfume bottle. It killed someone else too who handled it."

Ruggeri's eyes flashed. "Yes, there was. Interesting."

I set my empty glass back on the table. "Very."

She shrugged. "Well, it won't do us any good now. The other problem was that Kertész left the country immediately after. Interpol put us in contact with the police in Budapest, but because of the Novichok agent, it ended up with Hungarian intelligence—I don't know how to say their name, so I won't. But that, of course, got AISE involved too. Everyone was convinced the Russians were behind it. That maybe Bianchi was one of Putin's agents."

I whistled, legitimately impressed. It was a solid red herring, to the point where I wondered if Calvin had really masterminded it. Use a potent black market agent notoriously created by the Russians to kill their own compromised assets, tie the whole thing up in international affairs, and slip away undetected.

Essentially, what started as a potential run-of-the-mill homicide ended up garnering the interests of both the Hungarian and Italian versions of the CIA—all spooks, all secretive, and all suspicious as fuck. These were people more interested in intelligence assets than solving crimes. A dead professor wasn't going to motivate them to do shit.

"Did any of them ever get back to you about it?" I wondered. "The intelligence wonks, I mean."

"No. I only asked because an AISE pig made a grab for my ass when they came to take it over. So I wasn't going to just let him take my case, too. I followed up with the Hungarians myself."

I smirked. I liked Ruggeri. She reminded me of my sisters—Lea in particular. Wouldn't take shit from anyone.

"So what did they say?" I asked. "Anything good?"

"Eh. Hungarians…" She shrugged, but didn't finish as she took another sip of her cocktail, as if mere mention of the Hungarians was enough to complete the thought.

I wasn't following, however. "They didn't care?" I tried.

"Maybe? I don't know. They said there was no record of this Kertész entering the country any time close to the death. But who knows? They could be lying. They might think we were lying too. Or they might have been protecting their own. We don't know that Giuseppe Bianchi was a spy. But we don't *not* know that."

I frowned. I was picking up a lot of strange things surrounding the death of Nina's professor and the actions of her husband, but spy games wasn't one of them. If Calvin Gardner was a Hungarian or Russian asset, I was the Pope. More likely was the fact that he got the agent on the black market with the help of all his own low-life associates in Eastern Europe. And that people working in intelligence assumed there was an ulterior motive, even if there wasn't. It seemed Calvin had anticipated that too.

"Anyway, the case, it is closed. Unsolved, though we did not inform Bianchi's family of the investigation, only that nothing was found, and Professor Bianchi died of perhaps an overdose." Ruggeri shrugged.

"And now?" I asked. "What about now?"

Ruggeri squinted. "I don't see what's different."

"What if…if I could tell you where Károly Kertész is right now?"

Ruggeri stared at me. "How would you know that? And how would you know it's the same man?"

"I'd bet my life savings it's the same man," I replied dryly. "It's a long story. But I'll give it to you if you want."

She did. And so, I laid out the rest of the details she was missing from the plot. The fact that Károly Kertész was Hungarian, yes, but had repatriated long ago as a U.S. citizen under a new name: Calvin Gardner. My guess was that by 2009, Gardner had used a fraudulent passport based on his old papers when he came to Italy for the purpose of murdering his wife's lover so he could keep his mitts on her fortune, and in doing so kept the paper trail that would lead back to him almost perfectly clean.

"Károly Kertész is a gold-digging son of a bitch whose lifetime achievement has been extorting an heiress and running one of the largest human trafficking operations in the American Northeast," I finished. "From what my team and I gathered, he's been funneling women from all over Europe into prostitution rings for a decade or more. What's a little murder on top of that?"

Ruggeri had listened to the story with a quiet satisfaction that people got when they were immersed in a really good novel. "Hmm. Very interesting. *Very* interesting."

"Interesting enough that you might want to reopen the investigation? Or call your friends at AISE to see if they'd like to help?" I leaned closer. "Any chance your contact at Hungarian intelligence might remember you?"

Ruggeri smile, her red lips spreading with cool, competent knowledge. "Oh, yes. He liked me very much. My husband was not so much a fan."

I smirked. Ruggeri was hard, but she wasn't ugly. Yeah, I could see her using her looks to her advantage when it suited her.

"Well, then," I said when I sat back in my seat. "I've got some friends at the CIA who might be curious about this as well."

I removed a card and placed it on the table, then hastily scribbled my cell phone number on the back and scratched out my office phone.

"It's better to reach me here," I said as I slid it toward Ruggeri.

She examined the card, then tucked it away in her purse before pulling out one of her own and writing her own cell phone number too.

"I think I will be in touch, Mr. Zola," she said. "Thank you for the drinks. It has been most...illuminating. Tell Marcello I said hello."

I picked my hat off the table and leaned in to trade farewell kisses to the cheek as I stood. "And you as well, Ms. Ruggeri. I appreciate it more than you know. *Ciao.*"

CHAPTER EIGHTEEN

Matthew

I arrived back at the hotel with a skip in my step, eager to relay the news to Nina and hopefully find her waiting for me. In bed. I wanted to celebrate.

We had a little hope at last. I wasn't entirely sure what to do with the information Ruggeri had provided, but it was all worth knowing. That at one point, multiple governments had been on the lookout for Calvin Gardner under his other name. It was a big fuckin' deal to be using a Russian chemical agent as a murder weapon. Maybe big enough that it wasn't something his previous alliances with the Janus society would allow him to pay off. Everyone's influence had a limit. Maybe this would crack the dam.

Now I had only one thing left on my agenda: use our last night here in Florence to make things right between Nina and me once and for all. We were close. So close.

"You ready for dinner, doll?" I asked as I unlocked the door to the room we'd been sharing. "The landlord said there's a fantastic *trattoria* close to the river we can try if—Jesus."

I found Nina standing in the middle of the room in nothing but a slip, throwing clothes into her trunks like she was a kid throwing rocks into a river.

"Whoa, whoa, whoa," I said, holding out my hands like I was approaching a wild animal. The door closed behind me, and I tossed the room key and my hat onto the desk. "What's going on here?"

Nina hurled a pair of shoes into a trunk with a loud thunk. "Get *out*."

"Come again?"

The carnage wasn't limited to her clothes. There was a broken vase in the corner, and it looked like someone had gone to war with one of the pillows. Feathers were everywhere.

I pulled off my jacket, sensing we were going to stay a while. "Nina, are you okay? What the hell happened here?"

"*You* happened!" She whirled around, a twister of silk, blonde hair, and fury. Her face was streaked with tears. "I saw you. With *her*."

"What? What are you talking about?"

"Maybe fifteen minutes ago. I took a short nap, and then woke up and went for a walk through the city to clear my head. Then I rounded the corner, and I *saw* you, Matthew! Sitting on the fucking sidewalk, enjoying your drinks, smiling at her with that infuriating smirk of yours!"

I jerked, as much for hearing the word "fuck" come out of Nina's mouth as for what she was implying. The last time I'd heard her swear like this, she was losing it on Eric and Jane's rooftop.

"Wait, what?" I asked. "You saw me…oh! Nina, no. That's not what you think. That was Silvana Ruggeri, she's a—"

"I don't want to know her *name*!" Nina spat like a wildcat. She struggled with a blouse, then threw it backward on the bed with the mess of feathers. "Fuck it. I hate that shirt anyway. It can rot in this godforsaken city with the rest of this mess."

I took a cautious step forward. It was the day. The stresses of the trip. She was tired and scared—that's all this was. Right?

"Nina," I tried again. "I don't know what you think you saw, baby, but I swear to God, I was just trying to—"

"You *kissed* her!" she shouted as she turned around and threw another piece of clothing straight at me. It fell to the ground impotently. "Don't bother denying it, Matthew. I *saw* it. I saw the entire fucking thing!"

"I kissed her? What the fuck are you talking about?" I was finally losing my patience.

"God, you won't even admit it? You'll just lie straight to my face?"

I rubbed a hand over my face. "Jesus fucking Christ, Nina. Emotional is one thing, but this is fuckin' nuts."

"Don't do that. Don't make me out to be crazy when I *know* what I saw." She turned back to her packing in a huff, and picked up another pair of heels to toss into another trunk like hand grenades. "You kissed her, Matthew!"

I frowned. "Are you talking about when we said goodbye? We're in Europe, doll. That's what everyone does."

"Oh, that's a fine excuse!"

The second heel clocked me straight in the forehead.

"Jesus!" I batted the thing to the ground. Fuck this gentle shit. "What the hell has gotten into you?"

"You!" she shouted through mounting tears, even as I charged across the room through a hail of silk and leather. "You're no different than all of them!"

"Nina. Goddammit, Nina, will you fucking *stop?*"

I parried a sleek white handbag and managed to grab her arms before she could snatch another round of ammunition off the bed. She was sobbing by this point, pearl-shaped tears welling from her silver eyes, fury etched over her brow.

"Why?" she cried. "Why couldn't you have been different? I believed in you again, Matthew. I believed you weren't like the others!"

Keeping hold of one of her shoulders with one hand, I fumbled in my pocket, took out Ruggeri's card and pressed it into her palm. Her chest heaved as she sucked in labored breaths. But eventually, she managed to look at it.

"What is this?" she croaked.

"The business card of the woman you saw," I said, releasing her only when I was sure I wouldn't get smacked. "Her name is Silvana Ruggeri. She's a prosecutor here in Florence, and she was the one who looked into Giuseppe's death. I traded kisses with her on the *cheek* when I said goodbye. So I could come find *you* and tell you what I found."

Nina swallowed. "So she…you didn't know her before? When you were here, I mean?"

I sucked in another impatient breath. "After Rosina's story, I figured I'd look into it a little while you took a rest. As it happens, my cousin knows Ruggeri, put us in touch, and we talked about the case over a cocktail, all right? It was nothing, Nina, I swear." Cautiously, I slipped a finger under her chin, asking her to look up at me. "Tell me you believe me."

She swallowed thickly. "I—" She closed her eyes, heavy with shame. "Yes, I believe you."

I let out a breath I hadn't known I was holding. "Good. Now sit down and tell me what else is really bothering you. Because I know it wasn't catching me having a harmless drink and a polite farewell."

She sighed and sank to the edge of the mattress. I pushed aside more of her clothes so I could sit next to her. I wanted to take her hand, but sensed she didn't want the contact. Not yet.

"I felt sick on the way back from the farm," she said. "I kept thinking the same thing again and again. The girls knew. Their mother knew. I was the only one who didn't know."

"Didn't know what?" I asked as gently as I could.

"That I wasn't special to him," she whispered, looking down at her hands, which were splayed over her knees. "I thought I was. I really, truly did, Matthew. But instead, he used me, just like he used other women too." She looked up. "And when I saw you with that woman… all I could think about was that night at the opera when we saw Caitlyn. How I felt then. Like I wasn't special to you either."

Ah. So that was it. I knew something was bothering her on the way back from Siena, but I had thought it was just the shock of meeting Olivia's half sisters and confronting her own guilt. This was something else entirely. This time the shame was mine. Not just for how Nina had felt that night, misguided though it was. And not for Caitlyn either—not after the things she had done.

Right now I felt for every woman I had treated poorly over the course of my sad, pathetic life. Maybe they had used me back, but that didn't really matter now. If my past with any one of them could make Nina feel like she was less than everything to me...I'd take it all back in a heartbeat.

"I thought he loved me," Nina said softly. "And it cost him his life." When she looked up, her beautiful gray eyes were as wide as a cloudy sky. "I know you don't want to hear about this. You don't want to hear about when I loved another man."

She was right. I didn't. But I cared a whole lot more about her than my own stupid pride.

"You have to let it out," I said. "I'm not going to hold your first love against you, doll. And what he did...it's not your fault either. Any more than it's your fault that Calvin talked you into going along with his businesses and everything else."

She stilled. "How does that work? I was an adult."

"You were nineteen, twenty. An adult at that age in the eyes of law, sure. But you weren't completely grown either. These men saw that. They saw your vulnerability and groomed you to fit their agendas."

I shook my head to myself. I'd seen enough tabloid pictures of Nina around that age to know just how young she had really been. Doe-eyed, innocent, completely untouched.

Did she need to hear this right now?

Shame curved her body into a crescent.

Yeah, she definitely needed to hear it.

"You were too young," I said to her. "Barely more than a child. There are people who look for women like that. Young enough to mold them into whatever they want. Vulnerable enough that they'll never say no. Maybe your Giuseppe was like that, maybe he wasn't. But the next one definitely was. Calvin manipulated you and coerced you for ten years, baby. But now you're free. Do you understand? With me, you'll *always* be free."

She looked at me for a long time, like she was digesting my words one at a time. Then with a slow curving fall, like a birch tree felled by a storm, she collapsed onto my shoulder and buried her face in my shirt with exhaustion.

"How could he?" she mumbled into my shoulder. "How could he do that to those girls? How could he do that to me?"

I didn't have to ask what she meant. Giuseppe Bianchi had been dead for ten years, but the scars from his actions still remained. Nina didn't just see his ghost in his older daughters, but in her own too. Her guilt was eating her up. It was making her crazy.

"Hey," I said as I stroked her hair. "When you calm down, I need to say something else. I think it's my turn."

She huffed and shuddered again, but eventually, she lifted her head to look at me. "Okay."

"Do you really think I would do that to you?" I asked, looking straight on. "I know I'm not an angel, Nina, but do you really think I would do that to *you* of all people? To my own daughters, if I ever have them, God willing?"

She sniffed. "So many do."

"I'm no saint, baby, but I'd like to think I'm not 'many' people either. Especially when it comes to you."

Her eyes shone like soft gray stars in the outer stretches of the universe. The remnants of her tears clung to her lashes like diamonds. "No," she said softly. "You're definitely not."

"Well, then. How about a little trust now? I think it's time."

"I'm so scared," she whispered. "*Signora* Marradi, Matthew. Did you see her? So hard. So *empty*. If you…if you ever did to me what he did to her…it would ruin me, don't you see? And yet, every moment I spend with you, I just fall that much more in love. You own me, Matthew. You t-truly do."

With that, she started to cry all over again. The confession hurt her more than she wanted to show.

I pulled her close again, hushing her sobs, letting her shake into my arms.

"I don't own you, Nina," I said as I stroked her hair. "And I never will. But we belong to each other just the same. Remember what you said? About making each other soar? That's all I want, Nina. That's all I've ever wanted since I met you."

"How do I know?" she whimpered. "How do I know that's really true?"

Her hair was silk under my rough hands. I could have held her like this forever. But instead, I gently nudged her up so I could cradle her face, splotched though it was with tearstains and emotion, between my hands.

"You don't," I admitted. "Until I can show you, every day until our lives are done. That's why it's called faith, baby. You have to believe."

She closed her eyes, like she was praying herself. And then, slowly, she nodded.

"Okay," she said. "I understand."

Slowly, I leaned forward and kissed her. It was a slow kiss. Gentle. And it was possible I needed it more than she did. But she opened to me like the petals of a flower, and we took solace from each other's touch for several long minutes until she had stopped shaking and I could no longer feel repressed sobs vibrating through her body.

I sat back, still cradling her face between my hands. "Better?"

Shyly, she nodded. "Yes. Better." She bit her lip and shifted slightly as her eyes dropped to my mouth.

Suddenly, I was very conscious of the fact that she was sitting in front of me in just a flimsy piece of silk. And, if the temperature of the room was any indicator, nothing more than that.

With both hands, I traced the path of her cheekbones from nose to temple, then drifted my hands over her jaw, down her neck and to her waist. Then, with a sudden move, I pulled her firmly onto my lap so she was straddling me with her long legs, giving me clear access to her graceful neck and smooth chest. God, she was magnificent, even in barely more than scraps. More regal than she could possibly know.

I licked the side of her neck, eager to taste her perfection. Nina shivered, her hands digging into my shoulders, but keeping me close.

"How about," I said after I did it again, "you let me show you how true it is, Nina? Let me show you how I feel."

She shivered again as my teeth grazed her skin.

"And then?" she asked. "When you're gone again, and I'm overtaken with worry and fear? What will you do then?"

"The same thing," I said as I continued my progression of licks and nips over her shoulder so I could push aside the flimsy strap with my nose. "Again and again, Nina. Don't *you* understand, baby?" I sat up straight so I could look her in the eye. "I'll never stop wanting to love you. I'll show you again and again, for the rest of my life if you let me."

CHAPTER NINETEEN

Nina

And there it was. The promise he had made before, the one that hung in the air, suspended like particles of dust, turned golden not by the setting sun but by the rich hue of promise.

Even the light in this country seemed different. In New York, everything was so cold, blue and gray the way the light bounced off skyscraper and sidewalk. But here, with only the warm stone and terracotta to reflect the world around us, even the air seemed cast in gold.

For the rest of my life. And, he seemed to infer, for the rest of mine. If that's what I wanted.

Reluctantly, I pressed my hands to his chest.

"Wait," I whispered. "Wait, Matthew. Please. Stop."

His mouth paused, hovering just above the fabric guarding my breast. A muscle in his jaw ticced, but he straightened, worry flashing through the desire in his deep green eyes. He wanted me, yes. It was evident in the way his hands couldn't quite let go of my slip, the way his breathing was just a bit labored. But the truth was clear.

I'm no saint, he had insisted. I almost smiled. How wrong he was. When it really mattered, Matthew was as patient as a saint.

"What is it?" he asked, his voice hoarse with want. "Still too...too soon?" He almost sounded afraid of the answer.

I pushed back a stray lock of his silky dark hair. "No, it's not that. I..."

I could feel his need pressed against me and wondered if he felt it pulsing through my entire body as well. Wondered if he could feel my own and the way it made me tremble in front of him.

But something else was still between us.

That word again.

The *secrets* that drove every fear I had.

I wanted them gone. I wanted him to help me chase it away forever.

"Please," Matthew interrupted my brooding. "I can't take this anymore."

"Can't take what?" I asked.

"This fear. I know you feel like you can't trust me, Nina. I know I fucked up last summer. But I swear to God, my job, my house, it doesn't fucking matter if we're not together. This is *all* I want. *You* are all I want."

My stomach twisted. So many women fantasized about moments like these, when a man would give up the world just to be with them. But I found I didn't want to cost Matthew the world. I hated that I had cost him anything at all.

"Oh, no, that's not—Matthew, I—"

"I have something for you," he said suddenly. "Don't move."

I watched as he went to his shoulder bag and rooted around for a moment. He returned with something cradled in his palm.

"This isn't the way I wanted to do this," he said quietly, almost to himself.

I frowned. "Do what?"

For a moment, he only blinked at me, his eyes large, green pools of love and apprehension.

"Matthew," I tried again, more gently this time. "Do what?"

"I imagined bringing you up to the top of the Empire State Building. Like we were Cary Grant and Deborah Kerr, but we actually made it up there in the end."

I smiled. His sisters were really right about him—their brother had a terrible romance with old movies. I had never told him how many of them I had watched alone in my room, not because I was particularly fond of black-and-white cinema or the stunted dialogue, but because they made me feel closer to him during all those months when I never believed I could be.

Deborah Kerr and Cary Grant...it was a reference to *An Affair to Remember*. A film I had actually seen. One where the two characters, both involved with others, meet on a steamer on its way to New York. And at the end of their journey, they promise to meet at the top of the Empire State Building to start their lives together. In six months, they said, if they still felt the same, if they could make themselves worthy of each other, there they would go.

In the movie, of course, they were temporarily thwarted when the heroine got into a terrible accident at the bottom of the building. But the hero's intention was clear. If she had managed to meet him up there, their real lives together, an eternity, would have started at the top of the New York institution.

Which meant...

This time, I really couldn't breathe. I didn't even want to think about what might be happening right now for fear that it wouldn't.

"I was going to take you up there at dawn," Matthew said as he took my hand in his. "Not at sunset like everyone else. But in the morning, when we could be alone and watch the sun rise over New York. And I was going to tell you that even if I couldn't lay the world at your feet, I'd never stop trying. I was going to show you the city and promise you that one day, we'd make it ours again. We'd cover every damn inch of it with *our* love, Nina, not the shadows of our pasts."

The raw vulnerability in those deep green eyes had me shaking. Was he...no, he wasn't. He couldn't. Matthew wouldn't.

"Matthew," I whispered. "What are you saying?"

A shy smile spread across his face like jam on toast. Perfect and impossibly sweet.

"I'm saying I don't need a fancy building to show you I love you, doll. I don't need to wait for the perfect moment, because every moment with you is perfect. For the last year, I've been living for those moments—every second I get with you."

I melted toward him. "Oh, Matthew. I've lived for those moments too. I have."

"But the thing is, living for the moment isn't enough for me anymore. I want the next moments too. I want tomorrow, Nina. I want forever."

I watched with awe as Matthew sank to one knee in the middle of the mess I'd made, the mess that somehow matched the two of us perfectly. I was in nothing but my undergarments, Matthew wore only his street clothes. All our pretenses stripped, the world around us in shambles. And yet, just beyond our window, the beauty of Florence glowed in the golden light of the future. And Matthew's eyes still shone with pure, miraculous love. For me. For us.

"I know it won't be easy," he said solemnly. "I know we've got a hell of a fight ahead of us. I want to fight with you. I want to do everything with you and for the rest of our lives, Nina. All I want to do is show you how much I love you. And it starts here. It starts now."

He held up his other hand and, with his thumb, opened a small blue velvet box, then turned it toward me.

I couldn't breathe.

It was a ring. Nestled in its velvet slot, the white gold of an intricately filigreed band sparkled in the sun, curving around an exquisite cushion-cut diamond. Two carats, at least. Antique. It had to be. I couldn't imagine how Matthew could afford something so precious, so unique otherwise.

Matthew's voice was low, almost a whisper. But strong. Certain. "Will you marry me?"

"I..."

I could only stare at it. It was so beautiful. *He* was so beautiful.

And I didn't deserve any of it.

"But, Matthew," I said unable to keep the sudden tears at bay. "I'm still married. How could you want—how could you ever—"

He shot to his feet, tossing the ring to the mattress in order to grab my wrists and hold me steady. I pulled, but he wouldn't let me go.

"Shh, shh," he crooned. "It's all right. It's just a question. That's all it is."

I looked at the ring, gleaming in its box on the bed. That was much more than a simple question.

"And I didn't say we're going straight to a church."

Matthew brushed a loose strand of hair away from my face. The simple gesture brought my focus back to him.

"It's a promise, Nina. It's simple. I want the future with you. I want forever with you. Do you want it with me too?"

I hiccupped. "I—It's not that. I—Matthew, what will we do? How can you want to marry me when I've cost you so much? When I'm still tied to someone else?"

"Well, I know we can't skip over to city hall when we get back, doll," he said. "But it doesn't mean the intent isn't there. Nina, you have me. I don't know how else to prove it to you. If this isn't enough..." He shook his head, shoulders slumping with sadness and regret.

"It's enough," I said quickly, suddenly choked. "Oh, Matthew, it's more than enough. Please believe me, it's *all* I want."

He looked up again, eyes reignited with hope. "Then I'm going to ask again, and I want a straight answer. Nina Evelyn Astor de Vries, when all this is over, one day, when you're free like I know you will be, will you be my wife? Will you let me be your husband? Woman, will you please fucking marry me?"

We blinked at each other like owls, stunned by the candor of our own emotions. And then, because I couldn't stop myself, I threw my arms around his neck and closed the distance between us.

"Yes," I whispered against his soft lips. "My answer is yes."

He was still for a moment, as if he wasn't sure he had heard me correctly. "I...I'm going to need to hear that one more time. Just—just to be sure you actually said it."

A smile played over my lips. "Yes, I'll marry you, Matthew Luca Zola. As soon as humanly possible, I'll marry you."

His eyes closed, and he mumbled something unintelligible.

"What was that?" I murmured.

They opened again, and a sly half-smile appeared. "Just a quick prayer. Something along the lines of 'Thank fucking God.'"

I giggled. I couldn't help it.

But the humor in Matthew's eyes disappeared as quickly as it had come. Instead, along with the love that simply always seemed to shine there when he looked at me, some fierce undercurrent rippled to the surface. That animal edge my beautiful man could never quite tame.

His hands slid up and down my back, the angst of the day melted off. That was Matthew's magic. Most of my life, I had been a glacier. He melted that wall and suddenly I was as volatile as a river.

He slipped my straps off my shoulders, and the top of my slip fell to my waist, baring my breasts and allowing him to bury his face between them.

"Do you feel it?" he asked as he pressed a kiss to one side, then another. "Do you feel how much I love you, Nina?"

I weaved my fingers into his hair, enjoying its lush, silky texture. I wasn't sure that anyone who had been hurt like we had could ever fully trust another to love them. But maybe that was part of the bargain. Because I did love this man, more than I could really fathom for myself.

And maybe he felt the same about me.

"I do feel it," I whispered, hardly able to keep my voice from shaking with want. "Please, Matthew. Show me."

"I want us to show each other." His tongue slipped between his full lips and touched the very end of my strained nipple. "Nina." His voice shook slightly. "Please, I...please tell me we can—"

I pulled him back to me.

"Take me," I said. "Please, take everything away. I want *nothing* between us."

"Your wish is my command," he growled, and with a sudden rip, my slip fell away from my shoulders in two shredded pieces of silk, joining the mess of clothes and feathers and wreckage on the floor.

Before I could argue, I was suddenly swept up and tossed onto the bed. I recovered just in time to find Matthew shucking the rest of his clothes. In his hurry, he abandoned his usual fastidiousness, kicking his shoes and tailored wool pants into the rest of the mess, affording

me only a few seconds to admire the genuine beauty of his form—
broad shoulders, narrow hips, the step-laddered sculpture of muscle
and smooth golden skin that soon covered me on the bed.

He took a handful of hair and twisted it tightly behind my head.
"*Fuck.*"

It wasn't poetry. But I had never wanted that. Matthew's sometimes
coarse beauty was balm to my soul, accustomed as it was to the pristine polish of my family, my entire life. Who cared for a veneer when
everything beneath it was broken? Matthew's face was scarred from
actual battles. His language was rough, sometimes unfinished, his
clothes, while tailored, always slightly worn and frayed. And yet, I
wouldn't have changed a single thing about him. I loved him, not in
spite of the imperfections, but because of them.

His tongue twisted in mad, frenzied circles down my neck,
followed by his teeth, his lips, sucking hard, leaving their own marks.
The spot over my left breast throbbed, the place where I had encouraged the remnants of such bruises for months when we were apart. As
if those reminders of him could help me ignore the other bruises I had
never chosen.

Then he sat up on his knees, spread my legs, and surveyed my
naked body like a mercenary pirate examining the splendor of his
conquest. Or no, perhaps not a pirate after all. In this light, this country, this room...Matthew was no longer stealing another man's wife.
Here, he was only taking what was rightfully his. Not a pirate, then. A
prince.

"Let me see it." He picked up the ring box from where it was
buried in the linens and removed the piece of jewelry. "Give me your
hand."

Obediently, I held up my left hand. In September, I had removed
the gaudy rings that had felt more like shackles for ten years. Sold
them, in fact, before leaving an anonymous donation at a women's
shelter only a few blocks from the jeweler in Kip's Bay. I watched with
awe as Matthew pressed a kiss to my bare finger, then held up the ring.
And as he slipped it down to my knuckle, he slid inside me as well,
deeper than he ever had before.

"And there we are," he murmured as he dropped my hand and fell forward to cage me between his arms. His lips found mine, and our tongues began a delicious grapple.

"There we are," I gasped. "Oh, Matthew, *please*."

"Please, what, baby? What do you need?" He pressed in deeper, willing me to take all of his considerable size.

"I—I—" I couldn't speak as I arched against the bed and wrapped my legs around his waist.

He pulled out, then slid back in. And did it again as he sucked reverentially on my lower lip. His movements were slow, but almost harsh as he located the depths of me, trapped me against the linens, dared me to throw him off.

But I didn't want to. Matthew wasn't scared of the fight. I knew that now. Tenacious and valiant, he would fight for those he loved with every fiber of his being. His friends. His family. And me.

I arched as an arrow of need shot through me, violent and true. Matthew slipped a hand around my neck and urged me up to wrap my legs around his waist as he sat back on his knees. Then, with a sudden thrust, I was backed against the wall, my head smacking the plaster as Matthew buried himself even deeper.

"This," he mumbled into my neck. "You. Me. Oh, *God*, Nina. You don't even know."

"Don't know what?" I whimpered, squeezing my eyes shut as he thrust harder, taking a punishing pace that still somehow set me free. "Tell me."

"How much—how much I love you. How much I need you, Nina. With fucking *everything* I am."

His eyes squeezed shut with anguish, though he continued to move. I threaded my hands into his hair and pulled, urging him to look at me again. When they opened, his eyes were wells of love and fear.

"Yes, I do," I told him honestly, my voice barely more than a whisper. "Yes, I do, my love. My all. I know because I feel the same. You are my heart, Matthew. You are my everything."

He groaned, the animal sound visceral and vibrating through us both. His hands gripped the flesh of my thighs hard enough to bruise, but the pain was delicious. His mouth found my breast, bit lightly into the soft flesh. I screamed. With love. With joy. With every unnamable emotion I had ever felt for this man. For everything I ever would.

CHAPTER TWENTY

Matthew

L ater, after the sun had fallen beyond the hills and the sky outside our window was black with night, I held Nina in my arms. The room was a mess and our stomachs were empty, but I still wasn't sure if this was real. I was a damn sinner, and I was pretty sure I was ending up in purgatory, if not hell when I finally croaked.

But if there was a heaven, this would be it, wouldn't it?

"You're still awake," she murmured, her voice huskier than normal. *From all the screaming,* I thought with a smirk.

Yeah, yeah. I could still get it done when I had to.

I looked down at where her left hand lay on my chest, idly playing over my skin. *Nonna's* ring gleamed in the moonlight. Holy shit.

I didn't know why I'd brought the thing until that moment when Nina had looked at me with fear that tore a hole through my chest. She had been trembling, like a baby deer caught in a wolf's gaze. I wanted her to know I wasn't the wolf. Or maybe I was, but she would never be my prey. I'd protect her with every animalistic urge I had. I was *hers* body and soul.

I wasn't stupid. She still belonged to another man in the eyes of the law. Just like we'd have to face the mess of clothes and broken lamps in this room in the morning, we'd have the rest of our mess waiting for us still in New York. But those days would come to an end eventually, and then Nina and I would be free. Really, truly free. We couldn't run forever. But we could still return together. I hoped.

"I'm still awake," I confirmed after a minute.

"Thinking of what?"

"Of us," I said honestly. "About tomorrow."

I picked up her hand and examined it in the dim light. I hadn't actually expected the ring to fit, given the fact that there was a solid eight-inch difference between Nina and my grandmother. But for all her height, Nina's bones were delicate. The ring looked perfect on her long, slender finger.

"Tomorrow," she echoed faintly. But I didn't tense. That wasn't doubt in her voice, I didn't think. Fear, maybe, but not doubt.

"It's not the ring, is it?" I asked.

Nina's tastes were at least as particular as mine. I'd be disappointed, maybe, if she didn't want *Nonna's* ring. But it wouldn't be the end of the world. I wanted her to be happy more than anything. Even if it meant I had to take out a second mortgage to pay for the one she wanted.

"Absolutely not," she said, holding it up to examine it. "It's perfect."

Relief washed over me. "Well, that's good. I wasn't sure. It's an antique, that ring."

"More than an antique," Nina said. "This is an heirloom, Matthew. Vintage Damiani. Art deco."

I frowned down at her. "How did you know that?"

She smiled up at me, preening proudly. "I do know a *bit* about fine jewelry, you know."

I raised a brow. She was good, but was she that good? I hadn't seen much in the way of antiques on Nina's person.

"All right," she admitted. "I looked at the marking on the inside when you were in the bathroom."

I snorted. "I see. Connoisseur, clearly."

"Did you find it in town?" she wanted to know.

"Ah, no. It was…" I didn't know why I was so damn nervous to tell her this. "It was *Nonna's*. She gave it to me after *Nonno* died. To give to the woman I was going to marry." I picked up her hand again and passed my thumb over the familiar stone. "I've had it ever since. Never thought about giving it to anyone until I met you. Not even Sherry."

Nina was quiet for a long time at the sound of my ex's name. I didn't talk about her much—you tend not to when the story involves her fucking around while you're on the other side of the world getting shot at. But Nina knew about her. She knew what it meant.

"I'm…I'm honored," she said at last. "Truly I am." She blinked against my chest, her eyelashes tickling my skin. "What about your grandfather? Do you know how he got it?"

I relaxed against my pillow and told her the fable of how my grandparents met on the subway platform only a few months after *Nonno* got off the boat from Naples. How *Nonno* had seen the girl who turned out to live only a few blocks from him and proceeded to escort her to her catering job, waited hours until she was finished, then took her right back home, safe and sound.

"Well, you're right about the heirloom. It's been in the family for a while. The story goes, the day after he met *Nonna*, he booked a ticket right back to Naples. But not to stay—to get his mother's ring. He was only seventeen, but he knew the moment he saw her that she was the one he was going to marry."

"I suppose when you know, you know," Nina said as she gazed at the ring.

"Yeah, you do," I said, though I was looking at her. "Which is why the night after we met, I pulled it out of my sock drawer. And I've been carrying it around ever since."

We lay there for a long time, her looking at the ring, me looking at her. It was perfect. Peaceful. I could have stayed in that room forever.

But forever can't exist in a room. It has to include the rest of the world too.

"Matthew," Nina said. "We have to talk."

"Don't even think about giving that back, duchess. You took it. It's a binding agreement."

She smiled. "That's not what I was going to say."

"Then what?" I was trying hard to stay playful, but it wasn't easy. "Baby, you're looking at me like you're going to kill my puppy."

Nina sighed with something suspiciously like regret. Goddammit.

"It's all right," I said quickly. "I know you can't wear it when we get back. Maybe you can put it on a chain or something. Keep it close to your heart or whatever until he finally signs the paper..."

I trailed off, unable to keep the bitterness from my voice. I was trying to be fair, but it was going to be damn hard to return to New York and not be able to shout from the rooftops that Nina de Vries was going to be my wife. Goddammit. What had I done?

Nina was quiet for a long time.

"I'm sorry," I said. "I'm ruining the moment."

"No, you're not," she replied. "I was just thinking about something else."

"Oh? What's that?" She was trying to save my feelings, I was sure of it.

Nina sat up, her dark blonde hair falling to one side, just an inch or so from her shoulder. She took a deep breath. "You said everyone is allowed their secrets. But I don't want to keep them from you. Not if— not if I'm going to be your wife. Your *real* wife, Matthew."

I understood what she meant. After living in a farce of a marriage for years, Nina was being explicit. Nothing about us would ever be for show. If I hadn't already done it three other times, I would have made love to her right there just for saying so.

But.

"More secrets, duchess?" I asked softly. My heart ached, but not because I was scared of what she would say. It could be anything, but I'd never leave this room without her with me. It hurt because of the fear I saw mirrored in her silvery eyes.

We stared at each other for several minutes, a deadlock.

"Not right now," she lied.

I knew she was lying. Just like I knew I couldn't press her. Because I had said it myself: secrets had to be earned, not expected. As badly as I wanted to know I'd earned every secret she had, it wasn't my place to say that for her. Not now. Not ever.

"All right," I said. "One day, then. I can wait. It doesn't matter now. Not when I have everything I need."

"Everything?" she ventured doubtfully. "Do you really think I believe you'll be content as a house husband? Or a bartender?" She rubbed my arm. "I know you miss your work."

I swallowed bitterly. "Maybe. But not as much as I missed you. Maybe I don't need to be a lawyer anymore."

Yeah. Even I couldn't convince myself of that one.

Nina knew it too. "You don't really mean that. You love your job. It's who you are."

I frowned. Something about that bothered me. "Who I am is not a job, doll." I sighed. "One thing's for sure, though. When we get back to New York, I probably need to find a lawyer of my own." Fuck. That was going to be expensive.

Nina frowned. "What? Why?"

"You didn't think I was just going to head back to the shadows after this, did you? You think your husband's going to be happy that you're shacking up with his former prosecutor? I guarantee he's going to try to have my license revoked. But I don't plan on letting him, no matter how much it costs."

At that, she sat up and looked down at me, apparently forgetting that she was naked. "I will *not* have you ruin your life for me. I will not have it, Matthew. Absolutely not."

I frowned. "I wouldn't be ruining my life. In case you didn't notice, I've been pretty fucking miserable without you. That's not going to change if I end up getting my job back, which is looking more and more unlikely these days."

Cardozo had been dodging my calls for weeks. Gardner's trial wasn't for another couple of months, but I figured that by now, my boss would at least have a plan for bringing me back unnoticed.

Unless he didn't.

"So, what will you do instead? Tend bar?"

I cringed. I wasn't going to admit it, but I hated working at Jamie's. Nina was right. I missed...well, not the office, per se. But I missed my work. Investigating a case. Putting together an argument. I liked the puzzle work of the law as much as the satisfaction that I was doing some good with it. I missed knowing every day that I wasn't a total waste of space on this planet.

My reaction was clearly all over my face.

"What if I could ask Eric to give you—" Nina began gingerly.

"Don't even think about it," I cut her off sharply. "If you even *think* the word allowance or trust or imagine for a second that we are getting married without an ironclad prenup, you don't know me for shit, Nina. I am not marrying you for your money, and I won't have a single person even thinking it. No arguments."

"But if it's because I cost you your job—"

"For the last time, you didn't cost me my job," I barked. "*I* cost me my job, Nina. And I'm getting a little tired of saying over and over that I'd do it again in a heartbeat. I made my choice. I'll take the slap on the wrist, maybe get fired, and move on. And I'd do it again in a heartbeat if it still meant falling in love with you, so just drop it, all right?"

She had the decency to look contrite—so much that I felt a little sorry myself for snapping at her.

"Look," I said, turning to cup her face. "It's going to be all right. It's a job, not my life. Besides, now we don't have to hide, right? That's done with now. It's over."

But for some reason, that gleam didn't return to her eyes.

"Nina. Isn't it?"

"Matthew," she said quietly. "You don't know him like I do. He's vindictive. More than you can possibly imagine."

I almost asked her why she thought that, but decided against it. I wanted to know where she was going with this.

"Think about what he's already done," she said. "Matthew, he forced his cousin to pretend to be *me* for ten years to get what he wants, and it can't have only been because using my name got him what he wanted for his business. He wanted to ruin me in the end, at whatever cost to himself. Calvin is…"

"An uncouth, egomaniacal, sociopathic motherfucker," I finished heavily as I reached the same conclusion. "Who is unfortunately not as stupid as I thought. And the second he knows that we're together, much less engaged, he's going to fuck things up for me permanently. That's what you're saying, right?"

"I can't imagine he won't try," Nina said.

I chewed on my lip. As much as I wanted to believe that Calvin's potential threats had no teeth, I knew the truth. It was one thing to admit I had fallen for a defendant's wife and allow myself to be put on administrative leave. It was another to be splashed across the New York tabloids and have every detail of our relationship picked apart by the press, even if I managed not to lose my license. Calvin and Nina were national news, and I couldn't afford to be blacklisted in every state and county.

The truth was, if I didn't have the ability to do my job in any capacity, I didn't really have much of anything beyond the woman next to me. And as much as I wanted to say that being her husband would be enough...she and I both knew the truth. It wouldn't be. That's not who I was.

"Fine," I agreed irritably. "You're right. But I have to see you. Nina, we *have* to see each other still."

"Of course," she said, capturing my face between her hands and kissing me.

I slipped a hand around her waist and pulled her close, kissing her for a good long time, more than was really necessary just now. But Nina gave as good as she got. We were both feeling that desperation.

But when we broke apart, she continued speaking.

"Matthew, tell me you understand. Until I am fully divorced and Calvin's trial is finished...no one in New York can know about us. Not even Jane and Eric. You know Jane. She can't keep a secret to save her life."

Slowly, I nodded, hating myself more every second. "No one can know."

Nina pressed her forehead to mine. "We have to be quiet. We have to be careful."

I inhaled her scent of roses, feeling that heady high of love, not fear. That's what would keep me going for the next several months. The promise of this scent. The knowledge of this night.

"We keep it quiet," I repeated, every word tasting like lead. "Until the trials are over. No one will know a thing."

INTERLUDE II

New York Sun
April 14, 2019

Gardner trial verdict pending

After months of delays, the explosive three-week trial of New York financier Calvin Gardner finished this week at Kings County Criminal Court, with all parties eagerly awaiting a verdict.

In what's been called an extension of the largest human trafficking case in New York State history, Gardner, 49, was charged with sex trafficking, fraud, and identity theft in relation to a Brooklyn-based real estate scam tied to munitions magnate Jonathan Carson, who was killed in De Vries Shipping CEO Eric de Vries's apartment in May of last year.

"The Brooklyn DA lost its primary target when John Carson died last year, and now he's looking to put a feather in his cap at any cost," said Craig Moroney in a statement outside the Kings County courthouse. "He tossed around accusations like spaghetti at a wall. Except not a single one stuck."

Prosecutor Greg Cardozo had a different perspective. "It's simple," Cardozo told reporters. "Calvin Gardner and others like him believe they are above the law. They believe they can buy their way out of trouble when they're caught. But the Brooklyn district attorney's office is here for one reason only: to get criminals like him off the street."

Cardozo argued in court that similar investigations were ongoing across the region. None of the prosecutors' offices in New Jersey or Connecticut could confirm.

The trial reached its pinnacle on Monday with the testimony of Gardner's estranged wife, Nina de Vries, 31, who filed for divorce last fall after pleading guilty to misdemeanor charges of permitting prostitution in conjunction with Gardner's schemes. Ms. de Vries served as the signatory on nearly every property through which Gardner and the shell corporation, Pantheon LLC, allegedly funneled young women from a variety of Eastern European countries.

The prosecution successfully argued for Ms. de Vries's testimony to be admitted as evidence as an exception to spousal privilege because of her involvement with Mr. Gardner's alleged crimes.

On Monday and Tuesday, Ms. de Vries was questioned extensively by both the prosecution and the defense. She described finding false documents in her husband's study, discovering Hungarian strangers in her property in Newton, MA, who appeared to be prostitutes, and dropped the bombshell that her husband had hidden his own Hungarian name and identity from her for the duration of their marriage.

"It's the reason I immediately changed my name back to de Vries," she told the jury. "For ten years I believed I was married to someone named Calvin Gardner. Imagine my shock when I discovered his real name was Károly Kertész."

Gardner's defense, however, was quick to rebut, objecting to Ms. de

Vries's commentary as speculation, and then argued there was nothing inherently wrong with changing one's name and that the majority of Ms. de Vries's testimony amounted to little more than hearsay.

"Immigrants have been changing their names upon arriving in this country from its beginning," said Mr. Gardner's attorney in a statement. "It's about as American as apple pie. Mr. Gardner has done nothing but support his wife and family for more than a decade. Perhaps Ms. de Vries's discomfort with Mr. Gardner's original name reveals more about her own bigotry than anything he has supposedly done to her. Or perhaps this is simply the remnant of Ms. de Vries's grievances against her husband that she intends to air during their divorce."

Whether that is the case or not is ultimately up to the jury. A verdict is expected sometime next week.

———

April 2019

"And have you reached a verdict?"

"We have, Your Honor."

Calvin Gardner edged forward on his seat, ignoring the way the back of his khaki gabardine pants stuck to his thighs with sweat or the way the hard wood chair dug into his hamstrings. His palms were clammy as he wiped them together in anticipation, and the brass buttons on his navy blazer clinked on the edge of the table.

According to his lawyers—overpriced hacks who had taken over the case only after he had promised to bring his divorce case to the firm as well—they had a good chance. But the deliberation, at seven full days, had been longer than usual. Nina, goddamn her, was a sympathetic witness, even if the sharks next to him had seemed to tear apart every word she said. Still, he couldn't deny the way his heart thumped when she described Ben perfectly. He knew he shouldn't have given them the Brookline house. It was easily his worst move, catching her attention when nothing else had. Plus, everyone liked blondes. Especially ones that looked like her.

Unable to help himself, Gardner stole a look over his shoulder. There she was in the third row, patiently waiting with her hands clasped in her lap, the only sign of nerves the way her lip was clenched between her teeth.

She was dressed nearly devoid of color again. An ice-gray coat with a high collar that, along with her hair, tended to give her an angel-like appearance, but were fitting in other ways. Devoid of personality, yet too pure to spoil. "Suffragette white, of course," his lawyer had joked when she had taken the stand last week. Gardner hadn't found it funny. The idea that she had been silently protesting him for years made Gardner want to jump over the desk and throttle her there and then.

When she realized that he was looking at her, Nina startled like she was one of her damn horses on Long Island.

Gardner leered. She looked away. Bitch.

"We the jury, in the case of The City of New York versus Calvin Gardner, find the defendant…"

Gardner leaned forward, causing his chair to creak loudly through the courtroom.

"…not guilty of the charge of human trafficking in the first degree."

There was a minor thrill of voices through the gallery. Behind him, Gardner heard his wife gasp: "*What?*"

He smiled, feeling his entire chest balloon with relief and pride.

And so they went on, down the list of charges, one after another. Gardner did his best to maintain a placid expression, but inside, he howled with victory. He had won. He had *won*, in spite of those fucking threats from Janus and the clout that Eric de Vries thought he had over this goddamn city. Blackmailing the judge had been a last-minute effort, but it had paid off in the end when he had tossed out more than half the prosecution's evidence. Certain types of men couldn't say no to underage pussy, and this one was no different. It had been a risk—a *huge* risk.

"Congratulations," said Clyde, turning to Gardner with an outstretched hand.

Of course the smug fucker was happy. He'd practically bankrupted Gardner in the process of this trial. But freedom was better than jail, even with nothing to his name. For now.

"And the restraining order?" Puffed with satisfaction, Gardner watched his wife stand, white-faced.

Clyde smiled, revealing a row of stained, horsey teeth. "She was only able to have it extended through the trial. As of now, you're a free man."

"Not free yet. Now you need to get me my money."

"*Our* money," said Clyde. "There's the matter of that settlement de Vries offered, too. We need to talk about that. Harvey doesn't think you'll get any more. And I don't have to remind you of your bill, Mr. Gardner."

"Yeah, yeah, yeah," Gardner said distractedly as he watched Nina making her escape. Beyond the doors was a hoard of photographers, already shouting her name. New York's *princess*, foiled again.

He squinted his eyes and stood. He had a few things to say to her. Things he'd been saving up over the past few months. Things that no longer had to wait.

"I'll meet him back at the office in an hour," he told Clyde. "Thanks again. Really."

Abandoning the lawyer's proffered hand, he shoved his way out of the courtroom and tracked Nina down the hall, shoving his way through the throng of reporters who all shouted his name too.

"Mr. Gardner!"

"Calvin!"

"How do you feel about the verdict!"

"Will this affect your divorce with Mrs. Gardner?"

"Get the hell out of my way," he snapped, shoving the closest photographer hard enough that he nearly fell down the steps. The rest fell back. Typical. Shove one, the rest fall, like bowling pins. Sheep.

He spotted her across the street, purchasing some iced tea from a street cart vendor. As soon as she spotted him, her large eyes widened even more, and she shoved a bill at the vendor and darted away. Was she—was she really headed toward the *subway* in her pristine white coat? *His* wife? *Nina*?

"Nina!" he shouted after her. "You might as well turn around, princess. You know I won't give up."

Goddammit it, he really hated to run. Thankfully, she stopped, whirling around with sudden fury.

"And what is *that* supposed to mean?" she snapped.

"Hello, princess," he said. "Nice to see you, too."

"You are not supposed to talk to me. Go away, Calvin, before you get into more trouble."

She glanced around nervously. Gardner tried not to smile, then decided not to bother. He always did enjoy the way he made her scare like this.

"I'm not doing anything wrong. Your little restraining order expired at the end of the trial. That's today, in case you missed it. Which means I'm free to see you as much as I want. *And* Olivia, come to think of it," he added, unable to help himself.

He really did love seeing her squirm whenever he mentioned her waifish daughter. Honestly, the kid always gave him the creeps, with those huge dark eyes of hers that seemed to see right through him.

But she didn't squirm. Instead, she straightened to her full, irritatingly tall height. Gardner was thankful he had worn lifts today, but that still put him an inch or two below her when she was in heels. Fuck.

"I don't think so," she said. "You'll leave Olivia and me alone, Calvin. You won't have a reason to see her anymore anyway."

"And why's that?" he asked. "She is my daughter, after all."

Again, to his disappointment, she didn't squirm. If anything, his normally demure wife looked about ready to hit him. God, what had she been doing the last six months?

"She absolutely is not," Nina said much more calmly than she looked. "And as of last week, she knows it too."

It took a moment for Gardner to process what she had said. His face grew hot, like a kettle about to boil over. She *knew?* Which meant…others likely knew too?

"And, Calvin?"

He remained frozen as Nina leaned forward, causing her necklace to dangle down toward the ground.

"What?" he gritted through his teeth.

She was still beautiful, even if she was over the hill at thirty-one. But he had never wanted to mess up that beauty more than now.

"I know about Giuseppe," she said in a voice that was cold as ice. "I know what you did."

She knew about... He couldn't even finish the thought before he took a step back and immediately hated himself for it. Nina was as thin as a mannequin—how could she manage to intimidate *him*?

"What's that?" he demanded suddenly, shoving a meaty finger toward the piece of jewelry dangling from her neck. Some ugly medallion and something else that flashed in the light.

Nina captured it before he could identify anything.

"Nothing," she said quickly. "A good luck charm I borrowed from Jane for the trial."

Gardner snorted. "That's cute. Who would want any of that whore's luck?"

A mistake. Nina's silver eyes blazed. And then, before he could stop her, she had overturned her entire cup onto his white shirt, covering it

"What the *fuck*!" Gardner screeched as the iced tea splattered down the front of his shirt and pants. He danced on the sidewalk, and irritably noticed the sound of cameras clicking behind him. "What in the *fuck*, Nina?"

"You may have won this battle," Nina told him bitterly, even haughtily despite the fact that *he* had just been fully acquitted in this damn trial. "But the war is far from over. You would do best to stay out of my way and respect those I hold dear."

"Is that a challenge, princess?" he sneered even as he was picking the wet fabric off his skin. "What do you think you're going to do? Snub me to death?"

But she didn't speak, only crossed her arms and looked him over. The revelations she had just made throbbed in the back of his mind, stunting his speech long enough that she didn't even deign him with a response. Instead, she turned on her heel and continued down the street.

As she walked, Gardner was filled with fury despite the victory of the day. She was infuriating. A bitch. Self-righteous when she had no fucking right to be. She had always thought she was better than him.

And now she was embarrassing him again, revealing the rest of their secrets to the world, threatening him with charges of what, murder? Of her beloved professor more than ten years ago?

It was laughable. Which had to be the point, he realized. It was all just a game, like she had been doing for years every time she pointed out a stain on his shirt or crumbs on his mouth. That didn't even touch the early days, when he actually tried to be nice, but she rebuffed his attempts to claim his rights as a husband as if he had suggested she jump into a vat of boiling oil.

All she had ever done was humiliate him. And for that, he wanted to kill her... No, not kill her. No, death would be too easy.

He wanted to make her pay. Make her understand, once and for all, that he wasn't a man to be trifled with.

And that was just what he would do.

III

DOLCI

CHAPTER TWENTY-ONE

APRIL 2019

Matthew

"I don't know how to tell you this, Zola. But you're out."

I slumped in the chair next to my former investigative partner, Derek Kingston, while we faced Greg Cardozo, an executive assistant DA and head of the Bureau of Organized Crime and Racketeering. And my—now former—boss.

It killed me that I hadn't been able to attend the verdict with Nina or be there on the days she was put on the stand. Eric and Jane had shown up, of course, but I'd been confined to my house, staring at my cell phone like a desperate teenage girl, waiting for text updates while I refreshed the *Post* coverage of the trial again and again.

Today, though, Cardozo had been nice enough to invite me to his office to go over the verdict. Out of respect, he said, since Derek and I had been the ones who spent nearly a year building the damn thing— more if you included the case against John Carson and our successful prosecution of Jude Letour. I appreciated it, too. It wasn't Cardozo's fault the jury had swung toward Gardner, who had clearly greased the wheels at some point—how, I wasn't sure, but these assholes seemed to collect the secrets of the judiciary like pennies on the subway. I'd seen it time and time again. The second I heard there was a new judge on the case, I knew they would lose.

"I'm *out*?" I asked. "Are you kidding me?"

On some level, I'd expected it, of course. But after months of silence, a small part of me had hoped that with my careful discretion, the whole thing had blown over. Gardner was free, yes, but the DA was now absolved of a conflict of interest when it came to his prosecution.

And yeah, it's one thing to expect. Another to hear it out loud.

"Greg, come on," Derek put in. "He's paid his due. It's been almost eight months since de Vries confessed. She pled and served. It should have been done a while ago. Do you really think people will care?"

"Ramirez seems to think so," Cardozo replied. "Considering he was voted back in by the skin of his teeth, I think his exact words were 'the last thing I need is a goddamn sex scandal.'"

"Really?" Derek replied. "Didn't that public defender sleep with his own damn client? He got, what, a month off, and then he was right back to work."

"That's the Bronx," Cardozo said like he was referring to a cockroach. "Not Brooklyn. We got different standards here."

"So it's not enough the fucker somehow bought the judge and won?" I cut in. Usually I was happy to get into a pissing match over the differences between boroughs, but right now, I didn't give a shit. "He has to get me fired too?"

"Give us a little credit, Zola. This isn't coming from that bastard Gardner," Cardozo said. "It's from Ramirez. I'm sorry, but someone told him about you and Ms. de Vries. He got a call from someone in Italy, I think, checking on your credentials. Woman named Ruggeri. She mentioned your girlfriend."

I slumped further down into my chair. Fuck. "She's not my girlfriend," I said. Technically I wasn't lying.

"What were you doing in Italy with Gardner's wife, Zola?" Cardozo pressed.

"I—her cousin hired me as an interpreter. I went with her to Florence to…interpret."

Derek's mouth dropped. Cardozo looked like he wasn't sure whether to sock me or congratulate me.

"Not your girlfriend, huh?" was all he said in the end.

I ground my teeth. "Well, if I'm fired, does it really matter if she is?"

Cardozo rubbed his chin thoughtfully. "I think I'm supposed to say it would look really unprofessional and we certainly don't condone it," he said evenly. "But I've heard of worse, like Derek said. I mean, we aren't the Bronx, but we aren't perfect either."

I snorted. "Give me a break."

Greg reached across the desk and offered me his hand. "Done. You're a good man, Zola. And a damn good attorney. You'll land on your feet. And I'll provide any reference you want. That's a promise."

———

I SLEEPWALKED out of the building, but only after I was given the other bad news: that in six months, I'd be losing my exemption license to carry as well. Under New York's strict gun laws very few people were allowed firearms outside their homes, but prosecutors could have them, depending on the DA. I'd taken my military-issue Beretta with me to and from work for seven years, having heard too many stories of guys jumped by former defendants or their associates in a madcap vendetta.

Jesus, Ramirez must have been really mad. Why didn't he just chop off my balls while he was at it?

Outside, the sky darkened with the threat of thunder. Usually I liked the spring storms. They pooled in the sky and opened up with a deluge of water to wash away the city's sins, give it another chance to start over.

But today it felt like nothing could wash away the filth of the last year. For the first time in my life, New York didn't feel like a problem I was meant to solve. It felt like a damn trap. And I was a mouse, caught in the cage.

"Zola! Zo!"

I turned to find Derek jogging down the street after me.

"Hey," he said. "You all right?"

"I just lost my job and my gun. Would you be all right?" I said.

Derek had the decency to look contrite. "It's a low blow, man. It really is."

"It's not even an election year," I rattled on. "And do you know how many ADAs fuck around with each other? Half of 350 Jay has, and the other half is just waiting to."

"Yeah, I was, ah, aware of that." The look on Derek's face told me he was most likely part of that particular population.

"It's fucking bullshit," I said. "I recused myself. I went on leave. I've been pouring drinks and moping around this city for eight fuckin' months, and for what? So I could get canned after giving them everything I had for the last eight years? *Fuck!*"

I kicked a stray can and considered pummeling a mailbox nearby. I had never wanted to hit something so badly.

"Sorry," I said once I had cooled down. "I just needed to get that off my chest."

"It's no problem," Derek said. "I don't blame you. It is bullshit, plain and simple. You're the best man they have. Cardozo said it himself. Now you'll just be the best man somewhere else. They'll be sorry once they have to face you in court."

I grimaced. Was that where I was headed? I still couldn't totally imagine myself defending shitheads like Calvin Gardner for a living.

"I, uh, I meant to ask you," Derek said. "Have you heard from Frankie lately?"

I frowned. "Have I heard from my sister whom I live with?"

Derek shifted on his soles. "I just tried to call her a few times in the past couple months, and I haven't heard from her. I was wondering if…well, is she seeing anyone?'

I sighed. Originally, I thought Derek and Frankie would be good for each other, but my sister had been acting funny for months now. Ever since running into Sofia's dad, actually. She staunchly refused to tell me *anything* about that interaction—only that the guy was not in Sofia's life and never would be.

But she had disappeared that night at Jane and Eric's well before I left. And I never did find out if she left in the company of the big Brit, who for some reason called her "Francesca."

"I don't know, man," I said truthfully. "I don't think so."

"Oh, um. Good, I guess." Derek toed his sneaker into the pavement. "So, you and the heiress, huh?"

I sighed. "Don't act like you didn't know."

"Well, knowing and suspecting isn't the same thing." Derek shoved his thumbs into his pockets.

"Was she worth it?"

I didn't have to ask what he meant. But I still didn't like it.

"I can't answer that. It's like asking whether you prefer life without air or water. You need them whether you want to or not."

Derek looked taken aback. "Need, huh? That's deep, man."

I sighed. I wasn't feeling particularly deep. I was feeling pissed off. And frustrated. And kind of lost.

But underneath all that was a fact that hadn't been there a year and a half ago.

I could lose my job. I could lose my house, my car, whatever else the world decided to take away from me. But I wouldn't lose the fact that I was completely in love with Nina de Vries and always would be.

Like the air. Like the water.

"Yeah," I agreed with Derek. "It runs *real* deep."

He nodded, almost as if in awe. "Not a total loss, then."

"No," I said. "Definitely not."

He gave me a sharp slap on the shoulder. "Don't be a stranger, you hear?"

I nodded. "Thanks, man. You too."

———

I DROPPED my briefcase on the floor with a smack when I returned home, half-inclined to kick it clear across the floor.

"Shoes off, *Zio!*" called Sofia from the living room, where she was happily ensconced on the sofa watching TV while she chattered to a couple of dolls. It was the tail end of Frankie's spring break, and she and Sofia had been enjoying a week-long "staycation." Which also meant I hadn't seen Nina in just as long.

"Hey," Frankie said as she looked up with surprise from the kitchen, where she was making coffee. "That was quick. How'd it go?"

I slumped onto a barstool and scowled. "They found out about Italy."

Frankie grimaced, though it wasn't with much surprise. When I had told her my plans to be an interpreter for Nina de Vries, my sister had tried to talk me out of it for over a month. It wasn't until I threatened to tell Sofia the name "Xavier" that she finally shut up about it.

"Ah, Mattie. I…"

"I swear to God, Frankie, if you say I told you so, I will strangle you with that apron you're wearing."

My sister just rolled her eyes, and went about pouring herself a cup of coffee. She held up the pot. I nodded, and she poured me a mug.

"So, what does that mean?" she asked tentatively as she doctored hers up, then handed me mine black.

"It means I'm officially a career bartender until I get some interviews lined up." I shrugged. "Cardozo said he'd give me a reference, even if the DA won't. I don't know. I'll check the public defender's office. Maybe there's something there, if not at Legal Aid."

"Will that…will that be enough?" Frankie asked tentatively. "To cover everything, I mean?"

I stared into the bitter black liquid. Right now, I sort of wanted to drown in it. I hated that she even had to ask me this, that she couldn't just trust me to take care of her and Sof like I always had. Right now I was a failure in more ways than one.

"I don't know," I admitted. "I guess we'll find out."

"Well, I have to ask, though," Frankie said. "Are you going to learn from this?"

I looked up. "What's that supposed to mean?"

She walked around the kitchen counter to sit with me at the bar.

"It means…" She sighed. "It means have you finally figured out that this girl is nothing but trouble? I mean, I hoped you had, considering you haven't seen her at all for the last couple of months, right?"

I opened my mouth to tell her that there was nothing going on, that she didn't need to ask that question, and that I was doing just fine on my own. But found I couldn't say any of it. I hadn't been lying to my sister for the last three months, exactly, but I certainly hadn't told her that Nina and I were engaged either. Maybe it was even a little exciting, at first, waiting until Frankie had left for the day while Nina waited at a cafe around the block. Ten minutes later, a knock at my door, and Nina and I were consecrating our to-be marriage all over my damn house. Yeah, it was fun sneaking around. Sometimes.

But most days were heavier. Every time I saw Frankie or anyone else in my family, the news of my engagement was on my tongue. I had to endure strange looks when I protested a little too loudly at the idea of being set up with another friend's daughter or told Frankie I was staying the night at Quinn's (instead of the Grace). I didn't like lying to my family. Even when I was sleeping my way around New York City, they still knew about it, to some extent. Now I had someone in my life who would be my wife, and God willing, the mother of my children at some point. And I couldn't tell a soul.

Suddenly I was full of action. I needed to get out of this house. I needed to get out of this city. More than anything, I needed to see the one person with whom I could be completely honest, even if it was just to sit next to her and pretend I was nothing but a family friend.

"I'm leaving," I told Frankie. "Give Sofie a kiss for me."

"Where are you going?" she called. "We never get to see you!"

"Job hunting," I lied yet again, hating myself even more. "Don't wait up."

CHAPTER TWENTY-TWO

Nina

"Oh, Jane, it's marvelous. It truly is."

I examined myself in the floor-to-ceiling mirrors Jane had installed on one side of the room, making the space look more like a dance studio than a place for clothing design. The mannequins scattered around the perimeter were the giveaways, along with the enormous table, sewing machine, various bolts of fabric, and stacks of sketches and designs that Jane had been working on for the last several months. Since receiving her admittance into the Fashion Institute of Technology MFA program in March, my cousin-in-law had thrown herself headfirst into her new career.

"All these other fashion twinkies will have spent the last few years as elves in some workshop or another," she told me when I had found her sketching furiously. "Me, I've got a useless law degree and a closet full of homemade clothes. I need to catch up."

As it happened, I was thrilled for her. Since her abduction last year and the loss of her and Eric's baby, I had watched them both cycle through multiple stages of grief and frustration, particularly as Calvin's involvement in John Carson's schemes became more evident.

The fact that they had also been trying for a baby for months without any success made things that much more difficult.

So, when Jane announced her intention to apply to FIT last fall, Eric and I had both encouraged her, culminating with Eric's announcement of her early acceptance at the Christmas party. It was the most animated I'd seen her since she lost the baby, and it was obvious that Eric was equally thrilled with her progress as she threw herself into her new work.

She also had genuine talent. To the point where I had asked her to design my dress for the MET gala instead of going through one of the couture houses as I would normally. Though Jane alone was serving on the planning committee this year, the family had received its customary invitations, largely because of the donation Eric had made in our grandmother's name (at my suggestion). This provided an endowment large enough to fund an entire new wing of the Costume Institute, Celeste's favorite part of the Metropolitan Museum. It had only been possible after the will was finalized with the state and the executor had fully transferred all assets into everyone's names.

I might have been more satisfied that Calvin had lost his battle in probate court if I had seen a penny of my inheritance. Unfortunately, it seemed another addendum was in the will that had *not* been read aloud in her office.

"I'M SO SORRY, Ms. de Vries," said Thomas Clark, the lawyer who had been appointed the executor of Celeste's estate and will. "I simply didn't think it was important at the time given the fact that you and Mr. Gardner were still married."

I sat in the middle of the office where my family had just gathered to accept their assorted documents and deeds containing their apportioned shares and inheritances from Celeste's estate. It was heady business, dividing up a seventeen-billion-dollar empire. The majority of it went to Eric, of course, in his role as the family heir and CEO of De Vries Shipping, as well as primary trustee over the various accounts designated for maintaining the properties Grandmother had bequeathed to other family members.

I, however, had asked to stay behind. Because there was a problem with my own inheritance.

"*So, what does it say?*" I asked. "*That I lose everything in the event of a divorce?*"

I was struggling not to shake. Or throw my purse across the room. Just when I believed I was mistaken about all the wrongs I thought Grandmother had committed, this confirmed my worst nightmare—that she really did prefer I stay in a loveless and abusive marriage just to protect the family legacy.

"*There's nothing in here about divorce,*" Clark said uneasily. "*But there is a stipulation about a legal separation. You were to receive one bequest if you were married to Mr. Gardner. The seventy-five million and your apartment on Lexington Avenue. But there was fine print here that if you and Mr. Gardner separated during probate, your inheritance was to be frozen until your relationship was resolved.*"

"*And...if we divorced?*" I couldn't believe this. I could not believe this.

The lawyer shook his head. "*This document says nothing about divorce. Which in this case has been interpreted by the court to mean...you may receive nothing at all. I'm sorry, Ms. de Vries.*"

The shaking increased. I was right. I was right the entire time.

"*So you're saying I'm effectively broke?*" I asked. "*You do realize that the rest of my personal assets have been frozen as a result of this divorce, do you not? I am currently living on an allowance from my cousin, and the majority of my trust will probably end up going to my ex-husband. I will have nothing if this is true.*"

"*Mr. de Vries seems to be a generous sort,*" said Clark uneasily. "*Perhaps you might take this up to him, considering he sits on the board of your trust as well. He may loan you money against it.*"

"*So I'm supposed to live the rest of my life begging as a poor relation?*" I asked. "*I cannot believe that is truly what she wanted!*"

"*Either that, or perhaps you may consider seeking employment.*"

"*Excuse me?*" I asked.

The lawyer tilted his head. It was almost as if he were enjoying this.

"*In layman's terms, perhaps your grandmother wanted you to get a job.*"

———

"I just don't know."

Jane's voice pulled me out of my daydream—or day-*mare*, as it were. I couldn't get the lawyer's voice out of my mind. Or the despair I felt whenever I thought of the conversation that had taken place last week. Perhaps I wouldn't have minded if I weren't qualified for so little. I doubted I could even get a job as a waitress if I wanted. I really did have nothing.

Jane walked in half circles around me, clutching a pincushion in one hand, a notebook in the other, and a pencil in her mouth as she examined me. This year's theme of "Athens" was somewhat less complex than last year, in my opinion. I expected to see a lot of versions of what I was wearing—toga-like gowns meant to evoke the classic sculptures of Aphrodite and Athena. Mine was ice-blue silk, but Jane had done some truly ingenious embroidery around the hem and over my shoulder with silver thread that sparkled as I moved.

"Hey," she said. "Cheer up. You know Eric and I aren't going to let you go hungry."

The pity on her face was sweet, but it didn't help.

"I've been taking advantage of the two of you for months now," I said. "It's becoming embarrassing. Olivia comes home in a month. What are we going to do? Live in your basement?"

"Well, I was thinking more the guest rooms on the third floor, but whatever you want." Jane crouched to the floor and started fussing with the hem of the dress. "If you really want to be on your own, Eric will get you an apartment."

"Yes. I'll think about it. But honestly, if we need space, we can just stay at Mother's. She'll be at the Hamptons all summer anyway."

I didn't add that in either arrangement, I would still be dependent on the generosity of my family. And for the first time in my life, I found the idea extremely distasteful. Just a few months ago, I had plans to return to school, but I couldn't even do that. According to my lawyers and Eric, it apparently made more sense now for me to stay close to Olivia's primary residence in order to avoid charges of abandonment (despite the fact that I would have literally been closer in Boston).

I hated every minute of it. I wanted to strike out on my own so badly I could taste it. Matthew really was rubbing off on me.

"Well, maybe Calvin will agree to the terms of the latest settlement next week and you'll be free," Jane said as she stood again.

"Wouldn't that be nice?" I muttered.

So far, every one of Eric's increasingly bloated offers to Calvin on my behalf had been shut down. My husband hadn't moved on his demands, which he argued were all the more reasonable given the fact that the judge presiding over our divorce had indeed sided with his claims that he had signed our prenuptial agreement under duress.

"Hey," Jane said, taking my wrist and shaking it slightly. "Snap out of it. You're literally going to a ball in about four days. Isn't that supposed to be what most girls dream of?"

I sighed and went behind the privacy screen in the corner where I could change but talk at the same time.

"Sometimes I feel like the balls are the prison," I said as I carefully pulled off the gown, then handed it over the screen to Jane. "I'm locked in a beautiful house of mirrors."

"Every house has its exit, though."

Jane looked like she understood. And she did, a little. But she had only been in this family for a few years. I had been trying to find that exit my entire life.

"They do," I agreed as I stepped into my shift dress. "But every time I think I've found a way out, it's just another mirror. And then somehow it smashes."

Jane looked like she wanted to say something else, but before she could, there was a knock on the door. We turned to find Eric entering just as I was stepping out from behind the screens.

"Are you two about done?" he asked. "Because look who showed up. I invited him for lunch."

He stepped aside to reveal Matthew stepping into the room.

"Zola!" Jane cried as she immediately engulfed him in a hug. "We haven't seen you for months. How are you? Is everything all right?"

Matthew returned her embrace, but his eyes darted immediately to me. Full of warmth, and love, and…sadness?

Oh, dear.

"I'm good, Jane. I'm all right."

She released him, and he rubbed the back of his neck. It was then I noticed he was dressed in a suit instead of the more casual fare I'd grown accustomed to over the last several months. This one was a beautiful gray-blue gabardine, with a navy tie and a crisp white shirt. A far cry from the dull black pants he typically wore to the bar, or the less formal chinos and sweaters he wore when we were able to sneak away to see each other during the day. He had gone somewhere important today.

"Nina," he greeted me with a nod. "Nice to see you again."

Jane looked eagerly between us with that same expression she'd worn since we had returned from Italy. We hadn't told anyone of our engagement—or even that we were involved, thinking it would be best not to risk it for everyone's sake during the trial. But now it was over. Wasn't it?

"It's nice to see you too, Matthew," I said. "Jane, would you mind zipping me up?"

"I'll do it."

Matthew quickly crossed the room and turned me around, his hands firm at my waist. His fingers danced up my back ever-so-briefly before he pulled my zipper closed.

"There," he murmured as his fingers drifted down my shoulders. "You're perfect."

"Looks like someone has a crush," Jane murmured to Eric, who just shook his head at her.

"Mind your business, pretty girl."

As Jane and Eric became absorbed in their own repartee, I turned to find Matthew looking at me with the ever-present love and heat that never seemed to fade no matter how often we managed to slip away to the Grace or his house in Brooklyn when his sister was gone.

His gaze flickered down to my bare neck.

"It's in my purse," I murmured so only he could hear, knowing he was wondering where my chain—and its ring—was. "I had to take it off for the fitting."

He nodded briefly, then turned around so we were facing Jane and Eric and standing a solid three feet apart.

"So, you're staying for lunch?" Jane said, her cheeks slightly reddened from whatever Eric had whispered in her ear.

Matthew nodded. "If you don't mind me crashing. I was in the neighborhood…"

"Of course, of course!" Jane said. "You don't even have to ask, Zola, really."

"It's fine," Eric concurred, though a bit less excitedly. "We're having chicken. One of Jane's mom's recipes, I think."

"Eric! Is Jane down there?"

Eric popped his head out of the room toward the stairs. "Yeah, what's up, Tony?"

"There's a couple of guys here with a truck full of boxes for Jane. Can she come verify? I don't want to have them brought in until she says. It's a lot."

"Oh!" Jane erupted and clapped her hands like a small child. "*Yes!* That's the new fabric from Paris! Eric, *wait* until you see this. I have big plans for your next suit!"

Eric rolled his eyes at me, as if playing dress-up for his wife was just about humoring her. But the glimmer in his eyes and quirk of a smile at the corner of his lips told me he was more than happy to be her mannequin.

The two of them tromped up the stairs to look at the new shipment, leaving Matthew and me alone in the room. As soon as they were gone, Matthew slipped a hand around my waist and crushed me against his chest. He didn't kiss me, just held me tight. My arms wound around his neck, and I found myself wanting to be as close as I could. Immediately, a sense of safety and homecoming coursed through me. This was where I belonged. I never felt quite at home except for these scant minutes I was with him.

After several long breaths, he released me and brushed a few errant hairs back from my face.

"Hello," I said as I stroked his cheek.

Then he did kiss me, slow and sweet before offering a melancholy smile. "Hi, beautiful."

"What are you doing here today? I wasn't expecting to see you until tomorrow." I was supposed to be coming to his house just after nine, after his sister was gone for the day.

He pressed his forehead to mine and exhaled, sounding as weary as I felt. "I just really needed to see you. I hope that's all right."

"Of course it's all right. But what happened? You look like you've been run over by a taxi."

He sighed again, then dropped to the loveseat behind us and scrubbed his face with his hands. "I was fired today, baby."

"What?" I sank beside him. "Oh, Matthew, that's terrible."

"Cardozo called me in to discuss the verdict. Hence the suit." He gestured at himself. "Like an idiot, I thought it might mean I was going back to work, so I dressed for the occasion. Just, the opposite, though."

"Well, for what it's worth, you look very dashing."

The corner of Matthew's mouth tugged upward, but no smile emerged.

"What happened, then?" I pressed. "Calvin knows nothing, I'm sure of it. He would have said."

"It was Ruggeri, that prosecutor I met in Florence. I don't know why, but apparently she called the DA to make sure I was legit. Except he didn't know why I had taken leave. And he wasn't too happy to find out that I had gone with you to Italy."

Guilt lodged in the pit of my stomach. It must have been all over my face, because Matthew immediately wrapped an arm around my shoulders.

"Hey, hey, shh," he comforted me, pulled me in to his chest. "It's not your fault. I put myself on that damn plane, Nina. I didn't have a choice."

It didn't help. Would there ever be a day when my presence in his life wasn't completely destructive? He didn't have a choice? Was he just willingly throwing himself onto the fire?

"I just don't know what I'm going to do," he continued. "I can't keep working at the bar. To start, I just don't earn enough. I'm barely making ends meet right now, but the idea of begging for a job with some nasty criminal defense firm makes my skin crawl."

"Not everyone who needs a defense lawyer is terrible," I told him. "I needed one, didn't I?"

He looked up. "That's different. You also have a habit of martyring yourself for the people you love."

"And you don't? Who's the one who works day and night at that terrible bar so he can take care of his sister and niece?"

We blinked at each other. This, I supposed, was what they called a stalemate.

"Maybe," he said. "But it's not just that. I've spent my career fighting the rest of those assholes, and I can promise you, baby, they aren't exactly as altruistic as you are."

"So what will you do?" I asked. He must have had a plan.

"I don't know. I really don't. An attorney with my experience at Legal Aid earns about half what I earned before. There's not a snowball's chance in hell I can get a position at one of the other New York DA offices, considering how they all know each other, but even if I did, it wouldn't be the same. Ramirez is one of the good ones—the others are beyond corrupt. It's why I thought your family could trust him to begin with."

I didn't say anything more. Matthew's despair was palpable, his longing thick. Part of me wanted to march all the way to Brooklyn and demand a meeting with this Ramirez to tell him exactly what he was losing out on. That he had terminated the most honorable man in the city. What a loss for the people of New York.

"Sometimes I wonder if it would be better to leave," he said, now leaning back on the couch and staring vacantly up at the crown molding on the ceiling. "Get the hell out of New York and start fresh."

"Would—would you?"

I hadn't honestly imagined it before now, with the exception of a few moments when we were at my house in Newton. Matthew was so, well, New York. Much more than me, despite the fact that we were both born and raised here.

To my disappointment, he only shrugged.

"I don't want to leave Frankie in the lurch, but I also know she doesn't want a roommate with Sofia living there. Even if I sold the house, there isn't enough equity in it to split with Frankie so she could afford something for the two of them." He shook his head. "It's just a pipe dream, really. I'm just angry today."

"You know, this wouldn't be a problem if you had let me—" I started gently, but Matthew cut me off quickly.

"Nina, we've been over this about a thousand times. You don't even like accepting your cousin's guest room despite the fact that you have as much of a right to the family fortune as he does. Why would you think I would want to accept any handouts at all from a family I'm not even a part of?"

After several weeks and several fights, Matthew had decided to refuse all my attempts to pay off his debts out of my trust—or allow Eric to do so on my behalf. Upon our arrival home, he had called every loan officer to request the money's return to Eric's accounts. I didn't really understand it. Perhaps I didn't have any money to call my own, but Matthew had to know that the value of his home really was a paltry sum compared to my family's total holdings. It wasn't much more of a gift than paying a parking ticket. Or a few nice dinners.

But Matthew wouldn't be Matthew without his pride, infuriating though it was.

"Yet," I corrected him softly. "Not a part of...yet."

He looked at me then with such utter longing I thought my heart might break in half.

"Yet," he murmured as he took my left hand and stroked the finger where his ring should really be.

"Do we really have to keep a secret anymore, doll?"

I glanced in the direction Eric and Jane had gone. Part of me desperately wanted to tell them. And I did think I could trust them. But at the same time, I didn't want to implicate them in anything to do with the divorce. They were trying to make a new life for themselves. I understood why they would want to escape the drama.

"There is another meeting with the lawyers next week, after the gala," I said. "I think if we hold off until the papers are signed, it would be better."

"Better for you or for him?"

I pulled my hand away and stroked his face, delighting in the rough stubble under my fingertips. "For me and for *you*." I considered the look on Calvin's face after he had seen me at the courthouse. Should I tell Matthew what he had said?

His expression told me I should not. Better to keep my head down, get these papers signed as soon as possible. Then we really would be free. After just a bit longer.

"Come on, my love." I stood up and tugged on his arm to follow. "Let's get us both a glass of wine and pretend we're just two people over for luncheon. I think a little food will do us both some good."

CHAPTER TWENTY-THREE

Nina

We found Jane and Eric setting the table in their dining room for a lunch of roasted chicken and salad along with a bottle of Sancerre. Over the last several months, I'd only just gotten used to the fact that Jane and Eric preferred to take turns cooking rather than employ a chef. With only a housekeeper and their security, their staff was quite minimal compared to what I had grown up with. Not much of a cook myself, I had at least learned to do dishes particularly well.

"Eric always overcooks the chicken, so I'd recommend the dark meat," Jane said as she set a serving dish of carved pieces on the large table that took up most of their dining room.

"I think you'll find this is perfectly basted," Eric countered as everyone took their seats. He poured out the wine as Matthew served me some salad, then took some for himself.

"You always say that too," Jane said.

"Just try it, pretty girl."

Jane blushed and looked down at her food without answering. Beside me, Matthew chuckled to himself. Though on the outside Jane and Eric appeared to bicker constantly, those who knew them well could see it for what it was: their remarkable chemistry that really never seemed to fade.

"This looks great," Matthew said.

"It's not much, but we've been missing meals a bit," Jane said. "Nina's only been home, what, twice this week?" She winked at me, then looked knowingly at Matthew. "My theory is that she's seeing someone on the sly. She was gone with Olivia for ten days on Long Island, and then all this week, she kept sneaking out."

"Is that so?" Matthew asked. "Who's the lucky guy, huh?"

I stared resolutely at my plate, knowing that if I looked at him, I'd lose my battle against the rising flush in my face. "No one," I muttered and took a drink of wine.

Eric, who was a bigger fan of privacy than all of us, just shook his head at Jane.

"You should come for dinner this weekend, Zola," he said instead. "We're having a couple of investors over. One of them is Karl Kramer."

"We've met before. In court." Matthew didn't look as if he had enjoyed the experience.

"Who is Karl Kramer?" Jane asked.

"He's one of the top defense attorneys in the city," Eric said before taking a bit of chicken breast. By the look on his face, it seemed Jane was correct—it was overcooked. He chewed it anyway.

"And one of the biggest scumbags too," Matthew said.

"Yeah, well. Contacts are contacts, aren't they?"

I nudged him on the shoulder. "Perhaps it might be good for you to meet him in this kind of setting."

Matthew put his fork and knife down on his plate and turned. "Is that what you think I should do?"

I sighed. "Given the circumstances—"

"What circumstances?" asked Jane. "What's going on?"

Matthew grimaced at me, then took a long drink of wine before speaking. "As I told Nina downstairs, I was fired today. The DA found out about my trip to Italy with Nina, and he viewed it as a pretty bad conflict of interest. They made my leave permanent. I am no longer an assistant district attorney for the Brooklyn DA, and probably won't be for any other DA in New York."

"Are you serious?" Eric demanded. "After the check I just wrote?"

Matthew frowned. "What do you mean?"

"Oh, nothing," Jane said. "Just that he thought this might happen and tried to encourage the DA to keep you on with a fat campaign contribution."

Matthew's face turned white. "Oh, fuck. Eric, you didn't." He rubbed a heavy hand over his face. "Shit, no wonder he was suspicious. Ruggeri's call was just the nail in the coffin."

"Petri dish, you're getting corrupt in your old age," Jane said sadly. "Not everyone can be bought." She turned to Matthew sympathetically. "That really, really sucks, Zola. I'm so sorry."

"Shit, man," Eric said. "I'm sorry too." He looked at him more carefully. "But look. Since we're at least partly responsible here, the least we could do is hook you up with contacts for a new job. I heard Kramer's firm bills a *lot*. Hell, I'm sure there's a spot in the DVS legal team if you want to work for me."

"Associates start at five hundred an hour at Kramer," Matthew confirmed, not terribly enthusiastically. I noticed he didn't even reply to the offer of working for DVS. "But I didn't get into law to make money, per se. A little coin is nice, but I wanted to get these guys off the streets, not work for them. Like I told Nina, I wanted to do some good." He shook his head. "After seven years with the DA, I can't really see myself just switching sides like that, Eric."

But it was me he looked to with regret. Like he thought he was disappointing me or something.

"Nor should you," I said. "Ever."

I was dying to touch his shoulder, his knee—anything to demonstrate that I cared. He didn't actually *need* to work anywhere he didn't want to. At some point, he and his family would want for nothing, once I was unraveled from this terrible mess. Didn't he know that?

The sharp green look that flashed my way told me he did know that. Very well. And did not particularly appreciate the insinuation.

I kept my hand in my lap. Matthew sighed.

Eric cleared his throat as Jane raised her eyebrows at him over her wineglass.

"That reminds me, Nina," Eric said. "With the trial and everything, I forgot to ask you how it went with Liv. How did she take the news?"

Every eye in the room turned on me. Beside me, Matthew's entire body tensed. He already knew this story, of course, and had offered to be with me when I told her. He thought it might make things easier, given the fact that she liked him and that he could support my story as someone who had been in Italy with me.

But this was a matter between Olivia and me. Matthew couldn't save me from that, no matter how much he would have liked.

I had chosen to wait until her April break to tell Olivia the news of her true parentage. February had been too soon—for one, her sisters in Florence were still reticent when it came to talking to me, and when Olivia begged to go with her friends on a ski trip to Vermont for the week, I had acceded. I wanted my darling girl to have as much happiness as she could these days. I didn't like the shadows I had seen under her eyes too often when she was home.

The week before the trial, I had chosen to take Olivia to Southampton for a week of riding and vacation instead of staying with Eric and Jane in the city. By way of helicopter directly to and from Boston, we had managed to escape the local press entirely, and so it was in the warm, hay-filled barn, after a day of riding our horses on the beach, that I had told my daughter the truth of where she had come from.

———

Olivia sat down on one of the worn wooden stools in the tack room and pulled a felt rag tight between her hands.

"Does this mean Daddy isn't actually...my daddy?" she asked finally.

For a moment, I wondered if I should say no. Children love their parents no matter what. Thinking of my own absent father, I knew that as well as any. I could, in fact, tell her the same thing other adopted children heard: that while they had one parent by birth, they had another by love. That her father was her father no matter what. I could allow her to have a relationship with him even when I could not and allow her to negotiate it on her own terms as she got older.

But I was done lying. She deserved the truth, and the truth was that Calvin had never loved her or shown any interest whatsoever in being her father. The sooner she stopped clinging to that as a possibility, the better. For her own safety, if nothing else.

"No, darling. He is not."

Olivia was quiet for a bit more, the only evidence of her internal strife being the way she continued to wring the tack cloth beyond an inch of its life.

"Good," she said finally, then looked up with an expression more tired than any ten-year-old girl ought to be.

"Good?" I repeated.

"Yes. He doesn't act like a father. He's never given me hugs or said he loved me or done anything with me at all. Not like my friends' fathers do when they get them from school sometimes. Or your friends. Like Mr. Sterling, remember?"

Ah. So that weekend in Boston had made quite the impression on her. My heart warmed at the clear memory of one afternoon when Skylar, Jane, and I had entered the house to find Matthew and Brandon, Skylar's husband, asleep on a sofa, each with a small girl curled up on their chests—Brandon nestled with his daughter, Jenny. And Matthew's arm wrapped securely around Olivia.

"Yes," I agreed softly. "I do remember."

"And, Mama...you were scared of him. Weren't you? I saw you. That one time."

I almost told her everything right then. It would have been so easy to make the man she had grown up with into a villain for her as well as me. And maybe one day I would divulge everything that had gone on in our lives. But for now, this one trauma seemed enough.

"It doesn't matter now," I said. "But yes, I was sometimes. And that's why I'm doing everything I can to keep him out of our lives. I'm so sorry I lied to you, my love. I should never have done it. But from now on, it's you and me in this world. And I promise, I'll never keep secrets from you again."

She quieted once more, digesting each word like a separate bite. But she didn't wring the tack cloth quite so tightly.

When she spoken again, it wasn't with the questions I expected. She didn't wonder where we would live or what would happen to Calvin or any of those basic questions I would have expected.

Instead, she asked, "Do you have pictures of the farm? And of Lucrezia and...Rose...Rosi..."

"Rosina?" I completed for her as surprised relief flooded through me. "Yes, I do."

I gave her my phone, and she didn't ask me anything more, just wandered outside to a bench near the paddocks. And there she sat, looking at all the pictures Giuseppe's daughters had sent over the past few months after I had helped them pay their farm's taxes, and then with some help from Eric, invested a bit in the replanting of olive trees. Olivia kept looking at one in particular—the two older girls in front of a row of saplings. Their arms were draped over each other's shoulders, and they were toppling over, open-mouthed and bent forward mid-laugh. Their joy sprang off the screen, and Olivia whispered their names to herself again and again. Sometime later, I heard "my sisters" float on the wind out to sea, like she was sending a message to them herself.

————

"It went as well as it could have," I said after describing the basic events. "It was never going to be easy, breaking my own daughter's heart."

The table was silent as I finished the story. Jane sighed and looked at Eric, who was tight-lipped, brow furrowed. They all cared about Olivia, and I was glad for it. But it would be a long time before my sweet girl learned to trust me or anyone else again. I was under no illusions otherwise.

This time, Matthew didn't hold back. He reached into my lap and took my hand purposefully, daring me to pull away. I did not. And when Jane and Eric changed the subject to something more neutral, I let him keep it there until we were finished eating and both of us stood to clear the dishes.

"Walk me out?" he asked after we had finished, and Jane and Eric were making their excuses to go upstairs for a "nap." In her defense, Jane did look particularly tired.

I followed Matthew out to the street, but when he leaned in for a kiss, I stepped back as I caught a ruffle in the curtains by the door.

"I adore Jane," I said, nodding at the house. "But remember, she's not particularly discreet."

Matthew snorted as he looked back at the window himself. "That she is not. Somehow Jane missed the stage of life where everyone else got a filter." He sighed heavily and rubbed a rough hand over his face. "I hate this."

"I know," I said, dying to reach out and brush a stray lock of hair from his forehead. "But we have to wait."

"Sure, duchess. We have to wait." He exhaled heavily. "I'll call you when I'm home, all right? I love you."

Before I could answer, he turned in the direction of the subway, where a train would whisk him downtown to work, and then on home to Brooklyn in the wee hours of the morning. But suddenly, he turned back.

"I don't want to wait with everyone," he said suddenly.

I frowned. "Matthew, I thought we talked about this."

"We did. I understand why we can't tell your family yet. But I want to tell mine." He rubbed the back of his neck, a sign of frustration I was beginning to recognize. It usually appeared when he was putting together words but couldn't come up with the perfect execution. "I want to tell my grandmother, Nina. My sisters. When you get engaged to someone, they're supposed to meet your family. They're supposed to get to know them. Mine has only met you once. Even Frankie doesn't know you've been coming around."

His eyes looked pained, and it was then I realized this was such a key difference between us. For me, family was less of a buttress to my life and more of a cage. They were supportive monetarily, but for the most part my family were obstacles to overcome, people who thwarted my dreams more often than they helped. For Matthew, his family was the corner-stone of life, its stability hard won and even more thoroughly defended. The relationship he had with his sisters and grandmother was truly his *raison d'être*. Which meant that until they knew what we were to one another, my place in his life wouldn't be real. Not to him. Or really, to me.

With another glance at the window to make sure Jane wasn't watching, I reached out and squeezed Matthew's hand. "All right."

After all, with any luck, I'd be out of this marriage within a week or two.

Matthew blinked. "All right?"

I nodded, grinning at the sudden light that shone from his hand-some face. "When would you like to do it?"

"How about Sunday?"

"Sunday?" Sunday was only a few days away. And the day after that was the gala. Things were moving faster than I thought.

Matthew nodded. "We'll join them for midday Mass and then go to my grandmother's for dinner. We can tell them then."

My palms felt clammy. This was new. Calvin had never had family to impress, and even then, the stakes were so much different. Would Matthew's family be accepting of me and all my terrible flaws?

But his grin was blinding, and even through my trepidation, I knew this was the right thing to do.

"All right," I said. "Sunday."

CHAPTER TWENTY-FOUR

Matthew

"Stop humming," Frankie said from the backseat as I turned off the West Side Highway.

"Stop snapping," I said, but did as she asked instead of continuing my rendition of "I've Got the World on a String." "I got a little song in my heart, Frankie. What's so wrong with that?"

"Yeah, Mama. What's so wrong with that?"

I chuckled at the drawn-out vowels in my niece's pronunciation of "wrong." Despite Frankie's best intentions, Sofia was sounding more and more like a character from *Goodfellas*.

"You should have her audition for *A Bronx Tale*, Frankie," I said. "She'd fit right in."

Frankie made a rude gesture that I could see through the rearview mirror, then went back to messing with Sofia's hair.

"I don't know what you have to be so chipper about. You only woke up a half an hour ago." She looked me over irritably through the rearview mirror. "God, I hate men. All you need is ten minutes and you can walk out the door looking like a GQ model."

I turned up Tenth Avenue and tipped my hat to one side. "If it makes you feel better, it took me closer to fifteen. I had to shave."

I'd even picked out my clothes the night before, like I was a ten-year-old kid getting ready for school pictures. Gray tweed suit, *Nonno's* felt fedora, my favorite red tie that had more than a few memories attached to it by now.

"Today's a big day for me," I added. "Bringing a girl to church and all."

Frankie snorted, but there wasn't much humor in her eyes. Just like last night before I'd left for work, when I'd told her we needed to pick up Nina on the way to Belmont. I knew that look because I gave it to her often enough myself, and it felt like I'd seen it nonstop for the last year. She hadn't stopped looking at me that way since I'd told her that Nina was coming today. She didn't know why, but my sister wasn't stupid. Maybe she was in the dark about the engagement, but no one was going to believe that Nina was just a friend.

And despite my sister's obvious disapproval, the fact couldn't have made me happier.

Frankie glanced down at Sofia, then covered her ears. "I still don't think you should bring her home until she's not married anymore."

"Mama!" Sofia wiggled out of Frankie's hands, mussing up her hair again.

"Sofia! I just finished tying that! Now, hold still."

So I chose to ignore Frankie's worries as I turned onto Seventy-Fourth Street, then drove up Central Park West and around the block so I could pull up directly in front of the townhouse. Nina stood outside in the sun, dressed to the nines in a light blue coat over a cream-colored dress, with matching lace gloves. A small cluster of feathers and silk was pinned to her glossy, golden hair, a fishnet veil dropped just over one side of her brow. More than ever, she looked like a classic film star, plucked out of my dreams for this fine spring day. A perfectly put-together lady, whom I would take great pleasure in dirtying up later on.

"She looks like a princess!" Sofia squealed.

"She looks like something," Frankie muttered.

I turned around and pointed at her. "Be nice."

Frankie held up her hands in mock surrender while I got out.

"Hiya, doll," I greeted her with a quick kiss on the cheek. "You look like a million bucks. I like that hat."

Nina flushed as she touched the netting. "It's a fascinator, actually—my grandmother's, once upon a time. It's not too much, is it?"

I smiled. She looked so uncertain despite the fact that she was so damn perfect. "It's church, baby. It's never too much. *Nonna* still wears a veil, if you can believe that."

There was a knock on the window—Frankie, gesturing that we needed to get a move on. I checked my watch. Shit, it *was* past ten.

"All right, all right," I said as I opened the passenger door for her. "Get in, baby. The Lord waits for no one."

WE MANAGED to slip into one of the family's usual pews at Christ Our Redeemer just before the big wood doors were shut and the organs and choir *really* started in earnest. It was the typical array of locals who still attended the Italian Mass in Belmont—a smaller group now than when *Nonna* was a girl, but Father Deflorio had his faithful flock who had been showing up every Sunday at eleven for the last forty years.

"Nice of you to show up," hissed Lea from the pew in front of us, where she was busy wrangling her youngest in her arms while her husband, Mike, was doing his level best to shut the older ones up as the procession of ministers and the priest passed waving incense.

"Please. They're just starting," I retorted as I removed my hat and laid my coat over the back of the bench.

Nina followed suit, nodding politely at the row of sharply curious Zola sisters who were craning their necks around in front of us to examine her like she was a cut of meat at the butcher.

"Eyes front, ladies," I told them. "God hates a gossip, you know."

"Hush!" Lea hissed as the procession passed our row.

Father Deflorio nodded amiably toward us as if Lea hadn't just scolded me like I was one of her kids.

"Yeah, hush, *Zio*!" Tommy, my oldest nephew, said, prompting echoes of "Hush! Hush!" from Pete and Sofia.

"Psst!" *Nonna* leaned over from where she stood near the end, scowling furiously at all of us, veil and all.

"See what you did?" I said to Lea.

Beside me, Nina chuckled. I grinned. Lea just scowled and turned back to help her husband quiet their kids, but not before glancing sharply at Nina again, who was now looking around curiously at the church's ornate Romanesque interior.

"You good, baby?" I murmured to her, touching the outside of her hand, but not daring to do more than that in the church. Not with my sisters apparently watching our every move. Not knowing how nervous Nina was today about our news.

"I'm fine. But it seems like you need to behave," she said with a nod toward my family.

I frowned. It was a little strange, the way they were acting. It wasn't as though they had never met Nina before, even if it had been more than a year since she had seen most of them. There was something about the way all of them kept turning back to check her out like they were preparing for a knife fight in the alley. Or the way my grandmother hadn't even said hello. I wasn't sure what was going on, but I faced the front of the church, hoping the awkwardness would calm down over the next hour.

Things went relatively smoothly. Nina stood when we stood, sat when we sat, and kneeled when we kneeled, only really looking like an outsider when she remained in her seat while the rest of us shuffled forward to receive communion. She particularly seemed to enjoy the second reading from the book of Daniel, which was the basis for today's sermon.

"'Daniel answered, "May the king live forever! My God sent his angel, and he shut the mouths of the lions."'"

"Lionesses, I bet," I whispered to her. "All of them."

Nina elbowed me in the ribs, but her smile was genuine.

And so it wasn't until the end, when the procession had completely gone and the doors were flung open again that Lea whirled around to me with a finger pointed straight at us.

"What is *she* doing here?" she demanded.

I recoiled, automatically putting my arm in front of Nina, as if I could shield her from my sister's wrath. "What the hell, Lea?"

"Matthew!" hissed *Nonna*, gesturing toward the altar and the giant crucifix hanging in the apse. A sort of "Shut the fuck up, Jesus is watching, and we're in a church, Matthew" reminder to clean up my mouth.

"Sorry," I said quickly. "But seriously, Lea, what the hell?"

"*Zio!*" Not one to be outdone by her aunties, Sofia chastised me this time.

"Dad!" said Tommy. "*Zio* said 'hell' in church, so why can't I?"

"Hell!" chirped Pete. "Hell, hell, *hell*."

"Lea, come on," Mike cajoled wearily as he grabbed Pete by the collar of his shirt and Tommy by the sleeve. "Let's not do this here, huh?"

"Take the boys back to the house with Sofia," Lea said as she handed the baby off to her husband. "And for God's sake, don't let Father Deflorio hear them talking like that on your way out."

"I told you this wasn't a good idea," Frankie murmured as Mike followed his wife's orders.

"Stop," I said sharply.

Nina shrank into my side, clearly uncertain where all Lea's vitriol had come from. "Hello, *Signora* Zola," she said with a wave at *Nonna*. "It's nice to see you again."

My grandmother continued to act as though neither of us existed, gesturing to Joni and Marie to start moving so they could all exit.

What. The. Hell?

Kate leaned across Frankie and touched Nina's hand to get her attention. "I love your fascinator, by the way. *Very* Jackie-O."

I exhaled with a bit of relief. Okay, so not everyone was going to be a giant bitch today.

Nina smiled gratefully. "Thank you."

"Doesn't make it all right for you to be here, though. Not after everything you've done to my brother."

"Yo!" I snapped as Nina's face practically fell to the floor.

"Matthew, perhaps I should go," she said.

Without even thinking this time, I grabbed her hand. "What? No. I asked you here. I didn't know the vultures would descend the second we showed up. In a *church* for God's sake."

"Why? Wasn't she married in one?"

It was Lea who said it, of course. Right now she was staring at Nina's and my joined hands like we were about to torch the entire church.

"Aw, give her a break, Lea," Joni broke in from *Nonna's* other side. "I read in the *Post* that her husband is a real jerk and won't let her go. Like I said last night, it's not *all* her fault."

So, that was it. The harpies hadn't said a word to me about Nina over the last year or more since most of them had seen her last, but that didn't mean they weren't gossiping about us behind my back, especially since *someone* obviously told them she was coming today. And since everyone (especially Frankie) knew Nina was still married, they also apparently knew the shitty press version of the events. Fan-fuckin'-tastic.

I turned to question Frankie, who was messing with her bracelet, which looked perfectly fine. When she finally looked up, it was with a casual shrug, as if to say, "What did you expect?"

And with that, guilt punched me in the gut.

I should have known better than to do it like this. I should have prepared them first. I should have prepared *her*. I was just so damn starstruck, blown over by the fact that Nina de Vries had actually agreed to be my wife one day, and that she was finally ready to make it real. I'd stupidly believed my sisters and grandmother would be equally happy once they knew.

But somehow I had forgotten that at any sign of a threat, my family went from puppies to a pack of Dobermans, all snapping at the slight hint of a threat to the family sanctuary. When Joni and Marie started dating, Lea had been known to interview their boyfriends, and had actually asked one of Marie's for a resume. Hell, I'd casually threatened more than once to pass some of my sisters' boyfriends' names on to my contact with the NYPD—and that was tame compared to some of the shakedowns I'd delivered as a mouthy teenager with an anger problem.

Once again, the pack mentality was out in full, right here in the middle of the church. It had just been a while—a really *long* while—since I'd been with anyone on the receiving end of it.

"I'm sorry," Nina spoke up. "I don't understand. Did I do something—"

"Yes, you did something wrong," Lea snapped, apparently not caring at all that other parishioners were watching us curiously, or that her voice was echoing around the marble columns. "You took my brother for a ride. You wrapped him around that little lacy finger of yours and made him fall in love with you. And then you ruined his life. He lost his job because of you, did you know that?"

I turned around to glare at Frankie. This time she lifted her chin right back at me. Yeah, she wasn't happy about any of this either. That little brat organized this entire coup.

"So, he lost his whole career, everything he cared about, not to mention you wrecked him for other women who could *actually* make him happy," Marie counted out methodically on her fingers.

"And every time he thinks he's rid of you, somehow you come waltzing back to stick your claws into him all over again," finished Joni.

"I think that about covers it, don't you?" Kate asked sweetly.

"I—I—" Nina looked at me helplessly. "Matthew, I—"

"It's not just that," Frankie said. "He's been moping around this city for almost a year at this point, pining for a woman he can't have."

"No offense, Nina. You're fabulous and everything, but you shouldn't be here," Joni said.

"Ever," Kate added.

In the middle of all of them, *Nonna* crossed her arms, presiding over them like a hen over her chicks while they pecked the hell out of a corncob. What did that make me? Used fuckin' corn?

I snatched my hat and jacket off the pew. "That's how you feel? Fine, then. We're going. We don't need this."

I started towing Nina toward the aisle, ignoring the resistance on her end.

"Matthew, wait, I—"

"No," I said sharply, glaring over her shoulder at my family members, who all wore matching expressions of disdain and worry. "I brought you here to see my family, but all that showed up were a pack of feral cats. You don't need to put up with this, baby. And neither do I."

"But, Matthew," Nina protested gently. "They're your family. You have to—"

"No," I interrupted stubbornly. "I don't."

"Mattie?"

The voice behind me, plus the five identical expressions of shock and disgust facing me meant this was really, *really* not my day.

Because I knew the owner of that voice. That tone. I hadn't heard it in close to ten years, nor had I wanted to. But some things you never forget.

Instead of closing my eyes and acting like I hadn't heard, I put my hat back on and turned to face the proverbial music.

"Ah, hey, Sherry," I said. "Long time."

Nina's fingers around my hand tightened. Yeah, she recognized that name.

It was one of those moments where time felt really, really heavy. When you reach your late thirties, some people haven't changed at all. And others have aged a lot.

Sherry was the former. She was thirty-four now, but time had been kind to my ex-girlfriend, who was still petite, dark-haired and dark-eyed. She had a body shaped like a Coke bottle and a come-hither smile that once made her the object of both boys' and men's fantasies for about a twenty-block radius, and made me the envy of most of my friends, even after I left for Iraq.

Once, she'd broken my heart; fuckin' smashed it all over this neighborhood. Right now, though, I was wondering what the hell I'd ever seen in her compared to the woman next to me.

Sherry didn't seem to pick up on that vibe, though. Instead, her mouth curved to one side with the knowledge of a woman who knew she could wrap most men around her finger without even trying.

"I see you still like those old-fashioned hats," she said. "Some things never change, huh?"

Sherry winked. Nina's hand gripped mine so hard I thought she might break it clean off.

"I thought you moved out to Jersey," I said. "You got married, right?"

She nodded. "I did, yeah. But, um, it didn't work out. I'm back home for a bit now." She gestured with pink-tipped fingernails toward a couple I recognized as her parents, who were chatting up Father Deflorio near the exit.

"Who's this?" she asked, nodding toward Nina, who had dropped my hand and was standing quietly as she removed her gloves. "Your girlfriend?" The last word dripped with disdain.

"Hello," Nina said loud enough that everyone could hear her. "It's lovely to meet you. I'm Nina de Vries."

She offered a handshake, and when Sherry took it, Nina closed her left hand over both of theirs, as if to give an extra grip. But no one paid attention to that. Not when we were practically blinded by a flash when a stream of light caught on a diamond that was no longer hanging from her neck, but in its rightful place on her ring finger.

Sherry's mouth dropped as Nina pulled back her hands. "Is that— is that your grandmother's ring?"

I pressed my lips together, trying and failing to hold back a giant fuckin' grin. Suddenly, I felt giddy. "Yeah. Yeah, it is."

"I'm not his girlfriend," Nina confirmed. "I'm his fiancée."

"What?" Sherry blinked furiously as she glanced between Nina and me. "I—you're—"

"Engaged," Nina said. "That's correct."

Sherry frowned. "I was talking to Matthew, actually. Not you. It's been a long time. We have some things to resolve, fiancée or not."

I frowned. "Sherry, we don't need to do this. It's fine. Really. I'm over it. I moved on a long time ago."

"Maybe you're fine, Matthew, but I'm not."

Nina took a subtle step forward. It was a small movement, but it put her squarely between Sherry and me, and I watched in surprise as my generally calm, reserved heiress became every bit the lioness as the women standing behind us.

"I know who you are," Nina said evenly, in a voice that wasn't loud or sharp, but was somehow as ominous and heavy as the stone around us. "And I know what you did."

"What I did...*excuse* me?" Sherry flailed. "Listen, I don't know who you are, but you don't know me—"

"I know you're the kind of woman who cheats on the best possible man there is. I know you're the kind of woman who lets her lover go to war and cheapens his sacrifice by opening your legs to any other man who comes your way."

"Oh, listen, now," Kate murmured behind us.

"Mattie—" Lea started.

"*Hush,*" Frankie's voice came clear, quieting the rest so that Nina could continue.

"But," Nina said as she drew her terrifyingly icy gaze up and down Sherry, who practically shivered in response. "I also know you're the kind of woman who regrets it. So I'll say this to you nicely the first time, but next, the gloves will *really* come off. You don't deserve him. Now, in case you've forgotten, he also has an entire family of fierce women who don't take kindly to people who hurt him. Nor do I. Like Matthew, I come from a family who will do absolutely anything to protect the people they love. And I do mean anything."

She took another step forward, forcing Sherry to look up at her, which, given the difference of nearly a foot between them, meant that Nina pretty much towered over my ex-girlfriend.

"I suggest you don't test me on that point," she said, her voice low and menacing.

Sherry, though, was no slouch. Her fingers clenched and unclenched repeatedly, and her eyes squinted with fight. For a moment, I thought they might literally come to blows in the middle of the church.

But then she stepped back, flickering glances at me and the rest of my family, who remained perfectly silent.

"I see," she said. "Well, I'll be going. Mattie, I'll um, see you around, I guess."

I tipped my hat at her. "You have a nice day, Sherry."

We all watched her leave, shoulders slumped in defeat. When Nina and I turned around, we found the rest of my family staring at her, expressions torn between irritation, shock, and respect.

"You're *engaged?*" Lea's loud voice finally interrupted the awkward silence.

Nina's hand found mine again and I squeezed it tight. "This wasn't really the way we were planning to tell you, but yeah, Lea. I asked Nina to marry me. And she said yes."

"*Signora* Zola," Nina said as she returned to my side. "I realize it's a surprise, but I would very much appreciate the chance to…explain everything. Please." She glanced at me, but even in that split second, her deep gray eyes were full of so much love, I thought my heart might burst in the middle of the church.

Right back at you, baby.

"Please, *Nonna*," I said. "Just give her a chance to say her piece. Fair's fair."

Everyone waited for what seemed like the length of the entire Mass we had just sat through while my grandmother looked us both over.

"Yes," *Nonna* said, breaking her silence at last. "I think so. We need to talk. With Matthew *and* you."

Nina nodded, and to my surprise, none of my sisters argued. Instead, they filed out of the church, following *Nonna* obediently. Her word, apparently, settled the issue.

I turned to Nina with awe. "Where did that come from?"

"When you're faced with lions, you can be eaten or learn to tame them. I choose the latter." She shrugged.

I had to smile. She really had been listening throughout the whole sermon, which had, in fact, been on the famous parable of Daniel and the lion's den.

"You're not in the clear, though. You should have told me they would be angry."

I turned with a hand on Nina's back. "I'm mad at myself, doll. I should have predicted this, and I didn't. You sure you want to go? We can still make our escape."

But Nina just shook her head. "No, there's no going back now. And I wouldn't want to anyway."

I took her hand and kissed her fingers, lingering over the ring that still gleamed in the sun. "Well, I hope you can channel that lion-taming for another few hours, baby. The pride is heading back to the house now."

"Into the lion's den we go?" she murmured playfully.

"Good God, I hope not. But if the claws are out, you can handle it. That's for damn sure."

CHAPTER TWENTY-FIVE

Nina

I wasn't sure I had ever been so nervous as when I followed
Matthew, his five sisters, and his grandmother into the ramshackle
house just a few blocks from the church. Not when I told Grandmother
I was getting married. Or when I was pregnant with Olivia. Not even
when I prepared to ask Calvin for a divorce.

In that moment, nothing was more terrifying than facing that
formidable clan of women who loved Matthew more than anything. I
could only cling to the fact that we had that in common. I was fairly
certain it was the reason why I was being invited to their home in the
first place.

I wasn't sure what had happened in the church, exactly. One
moment Matthew and I were being attacked by his sisters, and the
next, I was ready to rip a stranger's eyes out just for *looking* at Matthew
wrong. I did know that my beloved walked with a renewed bounce in
his step all the way to his grandmother's house, and I was somehow
buoyed by the exchange as well. For the first time, it felt as though we
were really and truly a team of sorts. Or at least on the way to
becoming one.

And I liked it very much.

I understood his family's concerns. From their perspective, I was just another girl, like Sherry, who had already broken their beloved Matthew's heart. But I wasn't. More than anything, I wanted to protect and love him, just like they did. Maybe, if it were possible, even more.

I just had to prove it.

"Where are the children?" I wondered as Matthew took my coat and hung it on the rack near the door amidst the shuffle of his sisters shucking their own coats. The last time I had been here, the sounds of children's feet running up and down the stairs had sounded like hail on a tin roof.

"Mike took them back to our house," Lea said shortly. "So we wouldn't be interrupted."

She didn't wait for my response, just followed her grandmother and the rest of her sisters into the dining room at the end of the narrow hall that ran the length of the house.

Matthew hung his hat and jacket alongside mine, then dropped a kiss on my cheek.

"It'll be fine," he told me. "Once they get over the shock, they'll be pussycats, I promise."

"*If* they get over it," I grumbled.

But my beautiful man could only grin. "We're here, aren't we? Baby steps, beautiful. We'll take them together."

He took my hand and guided me to the back of the house. The lightness I had detected outside of the church only seemed to persist the closer we came to his grandmother's home. Similar to when he had kissed me on the street in Florence, it was clear that Matthew was thrilled to be open with his family about his life. About me.

I took it as the compliment it was.

"Can I help with anything?" I asked Lea as I found her walking into the kitchen with a large empty platter.

The last time I was here, Lea had been enormously pregnant. Now she was as petite as her grandmother, but more solid somehow, with her sleeves rolled up and her hair pulled back in the no-nonsense bun of an infant's mother.

Her mouth tightened. "No, that's fine. We're just putting some antipasti together. And then we can all…talk."

Matthew tugged me over to the table, where we took our seats as his other sisters remained clustered near the back window, talking amongst themselves. Frankie turned and faced us.

"Thanks for ratting me out, by the way," Matthew said, as if he were talking about spilled milk. "It's not like I would have wanted to talk to them myself about losing my job, Frankie."

"I don't know, would you?" Frankie said. "You're about as proud as it gets, Mattie. It took you weeks to even tell me when you started taking shifts at Envy last fall."

He scowled. "Still. How would you like it if I dropped the bomb that you ran into Xavier a few months back and didn't tell anyone, huh?"

"Xavier?" Kate's head popped out of the kitchen as she shuffled in carrying several wineglasses, followed by Lea with a tray of appetizers.

"Thanks a lot," Frankie said.

"Wait, wait, wait," Joni broke in. "Isn't Sofia's dad named Xavier?"

"Brilliant," Marie said. "She really cracked it this time!"

"Shut up, Marie," Joni snapped.

"It's really *none* of your business," Frankie informed all of them.

The other four immediately burst into argument.

"Jesus Christ," Matthew muttered.

"Who is Xavier?" I asked him, taking advantage of the temporary commotion. "Other than Sofia's father, I mean. I gathered that."

"He charmed Frankie's socks off before leaving her high and dry with a kid on the way and no one to contact," Lea said from behind us. "He's the kind of man who leaves people in the lurch. Sound familiar, Nina?"

I couldn't help but flinch. Was that really what they thought of me? I wasn't sure I could fault them.

"Hey," Matthew snapped at her. "For real, should we just go? I told you in the church, Lea, I got no problem walking out of here."

Lea just grumbled, then went back to the kitchen to help her grandmother.

"Xavier was at Jane and Eric's Christmas party," Matthew said as he turned back to me. "Tall guy. British. Black hair. Deep voice." He shrugged, clearly unable to recall much more. "To be honest, doll, I was more focused on finding you that night."

I, however, stared at him wide-eyed. "You don't mean Xavier Parker, do you?"

On my other side, where she was being interrogated by her three younger sisters, Frankie stiffened.

Matthew frowned. "Why, do you know him?"

"Not well, but we've met a few times," I replied. "He lives in London, but our social circles are fairly small. He went to school with Eric."

Matthew glanced at his jabbering sisters. "What's his story? Frankie's always been a damn mute about the guy."

I drummed my nails on the tabletop, trying to remember. "He caused a bit of a scandal, from what I recall. He's the illegitimate son of an earl or maybe a marquess. At any rate, his father didn't have other children, and then surprised everyone by naming Xavier as his heir instead of letting the estate pass to his cousin or nephew or whatever. Grandmother's butler, Garrett, was English, and had a lot to say about the whole ordeal. It was this big to-do when a boy from East London was named presumptive heir to this title, apparently."

"Then what happened?" Matthew wondered curiously.

I tapped my chin. "I honestly don't know much. Just that Garrett thought he was an ungrateful, rebellious brat. Attending Dartmouth, for instance, instead of Oxford or Cambridge like everyone else in his class. That's where he met Eric, who brought him home a few times when he was at school. Nice boy. Tall, like you said. After that, I heard he went to culinary school, of all things, and started several restaurants until his father died maybe three or four years ago…"

By the time I was finished talking, the room had gone silent. All five of Matthew's sisters were silent and listening intently, the rest of their arguments apparently forgotten. Even his grandmother had stilled in the door, holding a platter of antipasti.

I blinked. "It isn't the same Xavier, is it?" I asked as I looked around. "Sometimes he uses the name Sato. His mother is half-

Japanese, I believe, and that's her maiden name. Is that—it's not the same person, is it?"

But by the look on Frankie's face, he plainly was. And not only that, a fair amount of the story was news to her.

"Wait a second," Joni said. "Are you saying that Sofia...*our* baby Sofia...could be *royalty*?"

"She didn't say her dad's Prince William, you idiot," Marie said, earning a jab in the gut from Joni.

Frankie still hadn't spoken, though her dark green eyes, so like her brother's, were large and pleading.

"Did you know, Fran?" Matthew asked gently as he reached across me to clasp his sister's hand. "About this title, or whatever it is?"

Matthew had been the self-appointed caretaker of his sister and her daughter for several years now. He had always told me that Sofia's father didn't want anything to do with them. His impression was that the man was some kind of derelict—a criminal, maybe, or just someone passing through New York on a lark.

Clearly, that wasn't the case.

"I..." Frankie shook her head, and her eyes watered as she looked around. "I knew about his restaurants. And his mother. The rest, though..." She inhaled deeply as she buried her face in her hands. "I never knew," she mumbled into her palms. When she looked up, her eyes were red and rimmed with tears. "I have to...can you all just give me a minute, please?"

There was an awkward silence around the table. The rest of Matthew's sisters found their seats. Wine was poured, plates were filled, and finally, once the clink of silverware had started, Matthew's grandmother finally took her seat at the head of the table.

"So," said Mrs. Zola. "You want to get married." Her sharp gaze flickered between me and Matthew, then down to my hand. "How did this happen?"

"I, ah, asked her in Florence," Matthew said.

"*Florence?*" Frankie's voice echoed. "Mattie, that was *months* ago."

"We have had to stay discreet because of my...issues...with the press," I admitted, rather uncomfortably.

His sisters did not look impressed.

"Three months ago. Three days ago. It doesn't matter, Fran. The truth is that I knew the second I met Nina that she was the one." He shrugged adorably as he looked at me. "What can I say? It was love at first sight. I couldn't look away."

"Well, we know that, fool," Lea snarked. "You were making ga-ga eyes at each other the whole time she was here last time. But that's not necessarily love. In your case, more like lust."

"If it's not love, then you don't know a thing about your brother," I snapped, unable to help myself.

Lea opened her mouth like she wanted to yell back at me, but was stopped when her grandmother put a hand on her wrist. Matthew took my hand in encouragement.

"I want you to be happy, Matthew," said Mrs. Zola. "But..." She tapped a manicured nail on the glossy wood tabletop. Then, apparently deciding to take a different tack, she turned to me. "Nina. You're a very nice girl. Strong. Smart. You been through a lot. And I don't want to blame you for it, but there are problems, you see. Problems for my Matthew."

I nodded. "No one here will argue that, Mrs. Zola."

"The worst, you're still married," she started. "How are you gonna be engaged to my Matthew when you belong to another man?"

Matthew's grip tightened.

"I do not *belong* to my ex-husband," I said, perhaps more vehemently than necessary. Just the suggestion of it made my skin crawl.

"*Nonna*, they've been separated for months," Matthew added. "It's the issue of the money that's holding up the divorce. That's it. Well, that and he's a damn criminal."

"Yes, there is *that*," Mrs. Zola replied. "And from what the papers say, so is she." She jabbed a finger in my direction. "These crimes, they cost my boy his job, no? He worked for many years for this job. He loved being a lawyer, didn't you, Matthew? And we were all so proud of him. People, they call their pasts baggage. We all got it. But yours, it's a weapon. It hurt my Matthew. How much more will he have to take, eh?"

Matthew opened his mouth to argue, but I set a hand on his arm to stop him. All around the table, I saw his grandmother's concern reflected in his sisters' eyes. The anger that was there this morning had disappeared, but worry and fear were still present.

"It's fine," I said softly to Matthew. "After all, I can't really be a part of this family if they don't know everything, right? They've earned my secrets, Matthew. Just like you."

And then I turned, and for the next hour, while everyone else snacked on olives and prosciutto and cantaloupe and all the other delicacies Mrs. Zola had provided, I proceeded to tell Matthew's sisters and grandmother everything about myself I could think of. I started from the beginning. From my childhood on the Upper East Side and my father's abandonment. The year I spent abroad and how I met Giuseppe. And then everything that mattered.

"That rat!" Joni squealed when I was finished. "First he tricks you into doing everything for his shitty business, then gets you to take the rap for it, and now he wants to steal your fortune too!" She covered her mouth with both hands. "I would *die*. I really would."

I smiled. "I appreciate that, but it's not really the point. I just want you to know that in part, I gave myself up for this crime to save Matthew. To put my husband away. It didn't work, but it was my only chance to do what was *right*."

"These girls," Mrs. Zola said. "The daughters of your lover. In *Firenze*. What happened with them?"

I cringed. For the first time, the idea of Giuseppe as my lover made me physically ill. Maybe it was the fact that I knew his daughters and mother, had seen the pain I'd caused directly. But even more so, I suspected it was because the idea of giving myself in any way to a man other than Matthew seemed so completely *wrong*.

"We're going back to see them this summer," Matthew said. "To see the progress with the farm, the one Nina bought for them."

I squeezed his hand. "Maybe, with any luck, to pick a wedding venue too?"

Matthew's eyes shone before he turned back to his grandmother. "And we're bringing Olivia. She deserves a family, *Nonna*. And I hope that one day, you'll all let her be a part of this one."

Matthew's grandmother glanced between us, her dark eyes flicking back and forth with the speed of a pinball. It was clear now where

Matthew and his sisters got their penetrative green eyes from. He said he took after his grandfather and his father, but the heart of this family was in the woman sitting at the head of the table.

And so, I tried again. "Mrs. Zola, I know it's messy. I know my situation isn't what you would have chosen for your grandson. We could have kept it a secret from you, just like we have to do with my family because I can't trust them to be discreet. Not the way Matthew trusts you. But your grandson bleeds loyalty to this family. Nothing is truly real in his life if he can't share it with you. That's why we're here. Out of respect and love for you and the other amazing women in this house."

"*Nonna*, we're not here to ask your blessing," Matthew added. "We'd like it, but if we have to, we'll do without it."

"But, Matthew, how do you know she's not just using you?" protested Lea, shutting up only when her grandmother held up her hand, her gold bracelets clinking as they fell down her wrist.

Matthew shook his head with frustration. "You think Nina is trying to get everything she can from me, but what you don't know is everything she's done to make my life better. Don't tell me you don't remember who I was before we met. I was a lost man, Lea. I was wandering, angry. Spent most of my time knocking on married women's doors only to leave them the next morning. I'm sorry, *Nonna*, but it's the truth."

His grandmother, to her credit, didn't look particularly surprised at this revelation. Nor proud, either.

"How is that *any* different than what you're doing now?" Lea pointed out.

"It's worlds different," Matthew protested. "It took me one drink with Nina to feel like I'd found my center. Like I'd found the one person on the planet who could learn the worst about me and still see the best." He glanced at me again, and tipped my chin with one finger. "Who could earn every secret I had and still love me for them."

My insides warmed. Oh, how right he was.

"I..." Matthew sputtered for a moment when he turned back to the six frowning women watching us. "Look, you want something more? She even tried to pay off my debt. My mortgage, credit card debts, my student loans, all of it! I wouldn't let her, because I'm just as proud and stubborn as every other person at this table. But she still tried. Because the truth is, she wants to take care of me, take care of *us* just as much as I want to take care of her."

Frankie turned to me in shock. "Is that true?"

I shrugged. "It was my first attempt. I can't guarantee there won't be others, but for now I'm biding my time."

"Well, since he's unemployed now, I'd say the time is right," she replied dryly.

"Can it, Frankie," Matthew snapped. "Otherwise, I'll toss you out of the house myself, and you can have Mike babysit you with the other kids."

His sister just smirked over her wine.

"There's a saying between two people who love each other," I told him sweetly. "'What's mine is yours.' Ever heard of it?"

Matthew's mouth opened. I took the opportunity to kiss him on the cheek. A few of his sisters chuckled.

"She got you there, Mattie," Kate said warmly, followed by a chorus of agreement from the others.

It was a good sign. The room was warming. All except for the one distinctly cold attitude.

"Mrs. Zola," I said. "Let me put this as clearly as I can."

I took a deep breath, which seemed to be mimicked by my audience. But I found I was no longer nervous. I had been preparing for this moment, perhaps from the time I met the man sitting next to me. Like a horse finding her way home, every step I took was true.

"I could not love anyone more than I love this man. His kindness. His intelligence. His incredible compassion. He may not always be so generous with himself, but I know the truth just like you do. I see him for the genuinely *good* man he is—the very best man there is. All I want to do is cherish him and treat him the way I know he deserves. Give him all the love that he provides you and these wonderful women with every day. Because that's who he is. And that's who I am when I'm with him."

Matthew's hand slipped into my lap and picked up my left hand, which he raised gently to his mouth. Our eyes met over the sparkle of the ring, and for a moment our audience disappeared.

"I love you too," he said in front of his entire family, but in a tone meant only for me.

My heart felt like it would burst from happiness as he pressed a tame, but passionate kiss to my lips.

Eventually, though, we turned back to the head of the table, where Mrs. Zola was still watching us carefully over the rim of her glass.

"I see. And Matthew, you feel the same about her?"

"I'm just doing what *Nonno* told me."

"Oh? And what was that?"

Matthew smiled, and the warmth on his face lit me from inside as he caressed my cheek. "He said one day God would give me a good woman to love, and when I found her, I better love her well." His thumb brushed over my lips. "Who am I to turn down a gift from God? Especially when she makes me feel like this?"

On the other side of the table, Joni, Marie, and Kate sighed in unison. Frankie's and Lea's expressions were both still concerned, but had softened considerably with something else that looked like love for their brother, yes, but also understanding.

Sofia Annamaria Zola dropped her hands to her lap, appearing to have come to a decision.

"Well," she said. "We're just gonna have to do something about this *cattivo*, aren't we?"

Matthew and his sisters all grumbled their agreement. And in that moment, I wasn't sure how, but the two-person team I was on grew just a little bit bigger.

"Welcome to the family, Nina," said Frankie as she gave me a kiss on the cheek. "But I gotta warn you. Once you're a Zola, there's no going back."

This time, I really couldn't help but grin. "I really hope so. I can't wait."

CHAPTER TWENTY-SIX

MAY 2019

Matthew

Three…two…one…*home*.

I came to a stop outside my house after finishing my run home from the gym. Breathing heavily, I checked my watch.

"Shit," I muttered. Time to get my ass in gear. I could not be late. Not tonight.

"Mattie? Is that you?" Frankie called from the kitchen as I entered the house.

"Shower!" I called back as I made for the stairs.

A minute later, I was in my room stretching when there was a knock on the door.

"You decent?" Frankie asked.

"Yeah, come in." I stood up and pulled off my sweat-soaked shirt, then lay on the floor and started my sit-up regimen.

Frankie crept in, carrying a large bouquet of Easter lilies.

"Aw, that's sweet, Fran, but I'm more of a red rose kind of guy, you know."

"Oh, shut up," she said. "I'm having a personal issue and I need your advice."

I raised a brow. "If you don't like him, send them back. And if you *really* don't like him, send me." I started a round of Russian twists. "So who's the new guy?"

"Not new. Old. More than four years old, if you know what I mean."

I paused, twisted toward her. "Xavier?"

Frankie hadn't said much more about her baby daddy since the minor explosion at *Nonna's*, only because I wasn't one to push. Our sisters, on the other hand, definitely were, so I was pretty sure they knew every damn detail there was.

"Lea told me to call him. So I sent an email to his office."

At that, I paused and sat up. "Whatever happened at the Christmas party?"

Frankie shook her head. "We, um, talked."

"Not about Sofia, I take it?"

She shook her head. "More the, um, 'alone' kind of talking. And then I left. I'll spare you the details."

I made a face. "I appreciate that. And you haven't talked to him since?"

She shrugged. "He doesn't have my number. He sent a few emails to my work address, but I didn't answer. I didn't know what to say. Until now, apparently."

"Are you thinking you're going to tell him about Sof?"

Frankie shook her head. "I don't know. I barely know him, Mattie. We had a fling almost five years ago now, and he was with someone else at the time, and then..." She shook her head. "Anyway, I just said it was nice to see him again. That was it. That was this morning. These arrived while you were out. Plus this."

She handed me a card, which I opened and read out loud.

LIKE A RIPPLE *that chases*
    The slightest caress of a breeze,
    Is that how you want me to follow you?

. . .

Xavi

I WHISTLED. "NOT SUBTLE, IS HE?"

"He didn't write it or anything. It's a famous Japanese poem. I looked it up."

I handed her back the card. "I don't know how I feel about reading my little sister's love letters, Fran."

"Don't be a jerk. What does it mean, though?"

"Seems pretty clear to me. He's asking what you want."

"Which is…"

I shrugged and turned over to hold a plank. "Do you really need me to tell you that?"

"I do when I don't know!"

This wasn't like my sister. She wasn't usually the indecisive type. "You messaged him, Frankie. Seems like you want to talk to him."

"And say what? Hey, don't know if you remember me, but thanks for the two one-night stands, they were super fun. Oh, and by the way, that first time, I got pregnant that night and had your baby and never told you." Frankie sighed and sat down on my bed.

I started moving back and forth between my hands and forearms, grunting with effort before settling on my forearms for good. "It seems like he a lot more than remembers you. And he sure as shit seemed to remember you at Christmas."

"You don't want to know."

I grimaced with effort. Two more minutes. "I thought you were going to have mercy on me with that."

"I can't go there again," she continued. "It was bad enough back then. He was engaged, you know."

"Mmph." I *really* didn't want to think about my sister getting involved with anyone, much less someone else's fiancé. Even if it did make me a damn hypocrite. "What about now?"

"Well, in December, he said he was single." Frankie lay back on the bed and sighed heavily at the ceiling. "I wanted to tell him. But I just kept thinking of…"

"Thinking of what?"

"Mom."

I frowned, then pushed myself up to sit. "What about her?"

Frankie sat back up and pulled at a lock of hair hanging down from her ponytail. "The way she left after Dad died. I mean, it's all right that Lea and them are making peace with her. But I remember too. I remember how it feels to have your own parent walk away from you. Like you're nothing." She looked up at me. "I think you were right, you know, staying away from her. It's why I don't let her near Sofia. I don't want her to break her heart."

"Yeah, but Sofia doesn't know Xavier. You don't really either."

I got up from the ground and moved to sit next to Frankie. Nina's face when she talked to Giuseppe Bianchi's widow flashed through my mind. The humility in her when she introduced herself to his daughters.

"You know, I'm wondering if we shouldn't at least *try* to say hi to Mom next time she calls," I said.

Frankie's mouth dropped. "You're kidding. *You* want to talk to Mom?"

I massaged the back of my neck, feeling uncomfortable. "I don't know if I *want* to, per se. But if there's anything I've learned over the last year, it's that people can change. And something she did ten, twenty years ago…well, it might not be the person she is now. I'm not saying we have to invite her in, or anyone else you don't want for your own sake and Sofia's. But, you know, when it comes to Sofia's dad, maybe you can answer the door. Maybe you can talk on the porch. Have a conversation. You know what I'm saying?"

Frankie rubbed her lips together in thought for a bit, then nodded. "Yeah. Yeah, I see. Something to think about anyway."

"All right. I wish I had more brotherly advice for you. But I'm tapped out, and now I have to get ready."

She hopped up from the bed. "Say no more. Hey, Mattie?"

"Yeah?"

"You know, I thought about it, and I think it's a good thing, you and Nina, after all. She loves you. Anyone can see that."

I turned. "You finally coming around, little sister?"

"I think it's good for you, too," she said as she walked toward the door. "I see how you love her. How you talk about her daughter. Soon you'll have a real family to protect. Not just me and the others. We're all grown. You need a family of your own. I'm glad you're getting one."

The idea of Nina and Olivia as *my* family made my chest warm. I smiled. "Thanks, Fran."

"Have fun at the ball, Cinderella," she teased as she left.

———

TEN MINUTES LATER, I was showered and in my room drying off when my phone buzzed on my bureau.

"Perfect timing," I said. "I just got out of the shower."

"And so you decided to tease me with that image?" Nina's voice, slightly husky, purred through the speaker.

I turned, examining myself in the mirror with a towel wrapped around my waist. Not too bad for thirty-seven. I was fit. Could still make out the individual muscles of a solid six-pack. If anything, since meeting Nina, I had more of a reason to look good, just to hear her sound like that.

"Could be," I said, turning away from my reflection. "Since you're being stubborn and wouldn't let me get ready with you uptown. Should I send you a picture? Let you know what you're missing?"

"Matthew..."

"I'm just kidding. For now. Anyway, I'm getting dressed, so I won't be late, if that's what you're worried about."

"No, that's not it. Actually, well, there's someone at the door for you, and no one has answered the door, so she called me..."

"Matthew!" Frankie's voice shouted before I could ask Nina what she meant. "Get down here!"

"Hold on, doll."

Keeping Nina on the line, I jogged downstairs to find my sister signing for some kind of garment bag and a shoebox. A young woman who looked a little too buttoned up for the typical bike messenger bristled as she handed me the bag and shoes, but her gaze drew over me a little too slowly for formality.

"Oh, for crying out loud, Matthew," Frankie said. "I didn't mean come down in your towel."

On the phone, Nina chuckled. "Perhaps I do want that picture after all."

"Yeah, yeah, yeah," I told them all.

I glanced down at my naked torso, which the messenger seemed to be enjoying. *Eat your heart out, lady. This ain't for you.*

"Thanks," I told her, then fished a crumpled five-dollar bill from the key bowl, shoved it into her hand, and shut the door. I carried the packages upstairs, Nina still on the phone tucked under my ear.

"Did you just shut the door in that poor woman's face?"

"I gave her a tip," I said as I hooked the garment bag over my closet door. "What did you want me to do, chitchat with her in my towel? I have things to do. Anyway, what's all this?" I asked as I hooked the garment bag on my closet door.

"A gift. Something for you to wear tonight."

I frowned. "What? I have a tux."

I glanced at the 1980s Armani hanging from the back of my door, freshly dry-cleaned and pressed for tonight's party. Nina had seen it before—exactly one year ago, in fact, when we had tried to say goodbye to each other at the last gala. Of course, that evening hadn't exactly panned out the way we thought. Eric ended up killing a man, and I'd spent a sleepless night trying to understand what happened until Nina showed up on my doorstep the next morning.

"Darling, I'm going to tell you something, and I don't want you to be angry."

I frowned suspiciously as I wiped a few drops of water off my chest. "What's that?"

"Relatively soon, you may have to attend a lot of these things, and not just as a family friend. There will be certain…expectations of you. I don't think I need to tell you that some of the attendees can be rather unforgiving."

"You're saying I don't fit in with all the muckety-mucks on the Upper East Side? Duchess, I already knew that. I just didn't think you cared."

I tried to ignore the pain I felt at the idea that maybe she did care after all.

"Oh, *my* reputation is ruined beyond rescue. But I do care about you. And these events aren't easy for anyone, much less outsiders. It will be easier for you to navigate if you have the right...costume."

I turned around like she was standing behind me, not talking on the phone. "What are you saying, my wardrobe is rags?"

I was trying to be light, but to be honest, I was more than a little offended. Every vintage suit in my closet was chosen with love.

Nina chuckled. "My love, I *adore* your style. You know that. No one makes a fedora or a pair of suspenders look better than you do."

"I'm sensing a 'but' here."

"As impeccable as your taste is, it's not always...how shall we say...*à la mode*."

"Topped with ice cream?"

"It's French for 'of the moment.'"

I pulled on a pair of underwear and hung my towel from a hook over my door. "I know what it means, Nina. But I like my clothes. They're vintage, so they aren't supposed to be '*à la mode*.' They're supposed to be classic. Plus, I chose all of them from Kate's shop, and every last piece was tailored to fit *me*. What is this, some off-the-rack crap? You don't even wear that."

"Give me a little credit. Just open it before you say no."

I turned to the garment bag, tempted to throw the damn thing out the window instead. I didn't like this feeling. Like she was ashamed of me. Like I was some doll who needed to be fixed.

"Listen," I started.

"Matthew, will you please put your ridiculous pride aside and listen for one moment?" Nina's tone turned sharp.

I paused.

"Matthew?"

"I'm listening."

There was a sigh. "Did it ever occur to you that I appreciate the way you fill out certain garments as much as you so openly do of me?"

I grimaced. "That's nice of you to say."

"Please. This is a gift. I'm not trying to hide you, nor am I trying to dress you up and make you something you're not. Just open it. And if you don't like it, I'll donate it or something."

"Donate it?" I asked. "You can't just send it back?"

"Well, couture isn't really something you can 'send back,' my love. Especially since I would prefer *not* to be banned from Ricardo's atelier. I love Givenchy too much."

"Couture?" Intrigued, I unzipped the bag and nearly dropped what was inside from shock alone.

"This is cut to fit you as well," she said. "Kate already had your measurements, but I had her send one of your old suits that was bound for donation to Paris."

I nearly choked. "To *Paris*?"

"Just look at it, my love. Please."

So I did. And when I took the whole thing out of the bag, I had a hard time breathing for a moment. It was a simple tuxedo, so dark blue it was almost black, paired with a sleek white shirt and a matching white tie. The differences in the stitches, the lines, the fabric and any number of uncountable things between this and the clothes hanging in my closet were too many, too subtle to count. Platinum gold buttons instead of plastic, each engraved. But the sum was definitely more than the whole of its parts. This tux *did* make my collection look like house rags.

It was a piece of art. There was no other way to describe it.

"Okay. It's legit. But, baby, this is too—"

"Stop," she interrupted. "I already said I can't send it back. So please do me a favor and just try it on. Hang up and FaceTime me, please."

I signed, then I did as she asked.

"All right," I said once she answered the call. "Here it is."

She didn't speak at first, although I definitely enjoy the way her gaze turned hungry as I backed away from where my phone was propped on the bureau and put on the clothes.

"Well?" I asked once I had everything on except for the tie. My shirt cuffs were still open too—I'd pick out a pair of cuff links later.

But when I turned to the mirror, I didn't need her to answer. The damn thing fit like a glove. I looked like a million—no, a billion —dollars.

"I think...I think I need to see it in person," she said breathlessly. "Matthew, it looks *wonderful*."

I turned from side to side, peacocking left and right. "I think it looks all right," I conceded.

"More than all right."

I took off the jacket and hung it carefully before returning to talk to her. "I still don't understand why you went through all this trouble. It's not like I can even escort you properly tonight."

"I did it because, oh, Matthew, it's finally happening! I didn't want to say until I knew for sure, but the lawyers called today and said not only did we win in probate court, but also that Calvin is finally willing to sign the papers this week. Tomorrow, in fact!"

"Are you serious?" I asked. "Tomorrow, you're going to be a free woman?"

"Yes!" she said. "So I want to celebrate tonight. A little, if you don't mind." She crowded the screen like an excited little girl, her face shining with eager happiness. It was contagious.

"I want to tell *everyone*," she said. "We can make our announcement later this week, but tonight, Matthew, once we're inside, we don't have to hide anymore! It's a closed event. No photographers. They'll even collect cell phones inside the ballroom. We can dance all night if we want to, not just for one song..." She smiled sweetly to herself, clearly caught up in the same memory I'd had. "I wanted to celebrate. This is just one token of my gratitude to you. For all you give me. For how much you love me. Please say you'll accept it."

"Deal," I said, unable to keep the stupid grin off my own face. I couldn't lie. I'd do just about anything to make her happy. "Now what, duchess?"

"Now," she said. "Will you please let that poor seamstress back into the house to do the final adjustments? She's probably getting cold on your front porch."

I blinked. "You mean the messenger?"

"Who is actually one of the seamstresses who brought the suit all the way from Paris, yes. Please go downstairs and let her do her job." Nina preened prettily for the camera. "And then I want you to come straight here when you're done, please. So I can show you in person just how handsome I think my fiancé looks."

CHAPTER TWENTY-SEVEN

Nina

"My dress was designed by Jane Lee," I said for what had to be the twentieth time since I'd exited the limo that had dropped me and Eric outside the event.

We were some of the earliest arrivals, being lower-profile guests and attracting less fanfare than some of the true celebrities the museum and *Vogue* had courted for this year's event. As instructed, I was using Jane's Korean name, which she was trying out as a potential designer label. Eric hadn't looked particularly happy when she had informed us of her decision, but I understood. There would be enough remarks about her fledgling career being propped up by the de Vries name without actually using it in her brand.

"What about your jewelry?" asked the reporter, a sassy young girl in a sleek white column gown and questionable accessories.

"Oh, it's my own," I said, touching the small medallion of St. Anna I was actually wearing on a gold chain, just over my breastbone. "A gift from a friend in Rome."

"Ooh, *Rome*!" cooed the girl.

Other than the diamond studs in my ears and the pounded metal cuff on my wrist, Matthew's necklace was the only other piece I was wearing amid a crowd of Harry Winston wreaths and Bvlgari crowns. I had chosen to let the luster of the dress speak for itself, styling it with a sleek updo that matched the draped effect of Jane's toga-styled design. It was the crystal beading that really made it special, each piece sewn individually throughout the gorgeous fabric Jane ordered. I had requested the family's stylist do very little in the way of makeup—just a few brushes of white-glittering highlights over my cheekbones and on my chest that gleamed in the right lights, like I was a statue in Greece.

As I spoke, I looked over the reporter's shoulder toward the top of the steps. Matthew was supposed to be meeting me inside after gaining access via the security entrance on the side of the building like last year. As much as I had wanted to walk the red carpet hand in hand with him, we both admitted it would be better to wait for our official debut. After all, the papers still weren't signed.

"Thank you," I told her, and decided that I was done speaking to the rest. Jane and Eric were busy on the other side of the steps chatting away with a reporter from the *Village Voice*, so I took the opportunity to make my escape and find the man I *really* wanted to see tonight.

The museum was lit up, just as magical as ever for the gala. Cora had really outdone herself this year, having wrapped the museum's massive neoclassical colonnades completely with glittering lights and flowers, and actually reconstructing a ceiling-high Trojan horse out of white hydrangeas that towered in the main lobby.

I followed the trickle of people into the exhibit, glancing left and right. Where could he be?

"Looking for something?"

I jumped as his deep voice wrapped around me, then turned to find Matthew standing next to an exhibit of gorgeous Roman paintings suspended over a water bath.

He looked positively regal in his new midnight blue tuxedo, which fit him even more perfectly than I'd imagined, managing to render his shoulders sleek and broad at the same time, tucking exquisitely at his trim waist, extending down through his long, muscular legs. In typical Matthew fashion, he had added a few twists of his own—a white silk pocket square in the front and antique sterling cuff links that looked to be engraved with his grandfather's—and therefore Matthew's—initials. He was breathtaking.

At the time I placed the order, right after we returned from Italy, I couldn't really explain why I had felt such an urge to get it for him, particularly when we were forced to come to this event separately, covertly. But as he stood there, surrounded by the literal works of art, I knew exactly what it was. Matthew, just as much, or perhaps more than any of the rich museum benefactors, loved beauty. He took more pride in his appearance, in enjoying the good things in life where he could get them, than anyone else I knew. Yes, I had grown up with luxury my entire life, but I didn't think I had truly started to appreciate what made certain things so fine, expensive or not, until I met Matthew.

And so I bought the tuxedo, because I could. Because I knew he would appreciate the craftsmanship, the perfection more than anyone. Because he genuinely deserved it more than most and I wanted him to have one thing of his own that he could call art. And because very soon, it might be the last chance I ever had to afford something like this for him, and I wanted him to *feel* like the work of art I knew him to be.

"Oh, Matthew, you look..." I genuinely couldn't get the words out. "Matthew, you look incredible."

He nodded his head, as if he were tipping an invisible fedora instead of his absurdly thick head of inky dark hair. "Thanks, doll. It was a little weird accepting it, but I have to admit, I don't feel like as much of a stranger as I did last time." He slipped an arm around my waist and pulled me close. "And you too, duchess. I mean, wow. You said Jane did a good job, but, Jesus and Mary, Nina. I can barely breathe looking at you."

His eyes dropped to my lips, and I arched toward him as naturally as breathing.

"We shouldn't, right?" he murmured.

I shrugged. "I don't know. We're inside now. They collect everyone's devices and so forth at the door."

"Well, I mostly don't want to mess up your makeup," he said. "You really do look like a goddess tonight. Aphrodite herself. Or maybe Helen of Troy."

"Then I suppose that makes you Paris," I said coyly. "Fighting to steal another man's wife, right?"

"The one killed in action? Nah. Tonight, I'm the guy that gets the girl. Happy endings for all."

He touched his nose to mine, and then we both looked around at the guests filtering around us. Many were actors, musicians, and other people far more recognizable from the tabloids than I was. Their clothes were equally as fantastic. One well-known singer passed by in a completely sheer, skin-colored gown that put nearly every part of her anatomy on display. By her styling, it was clear that she was supposed to resemble a naked Greek statue. I couldn't decide whether or not she was pulling it off.

"Well," I said as she passed. "That's one way to interpret the evening."

Matthew hadn't even taken a second look. "I don't know, baby. She can do what she likes, but if she's looking for attention, she sort of gave the game away, don't you think?"

"What do you mean?"

"I'd rather spend the evening wondering what a woman's got on under her finery, you know?" He drifted a finger over my collarbone, tugging lightly on the silk twisted over my shoulder. "Makes it that much sweeter when I get to unwrap the package."

His touch heated me to my core as I imagined just how Matthew might unwrap *me*.

"You need to stop looking at me like that, duchess," he murmured, though the knowing smirk told me he was quite enjoying it.

"Then you need to stop making such suggestive comments."

"Never."

I leaned closer so that our noses were only a hair's breadth apart. "Promise?"

Matthew's eyes swept closed, then opened again with a new intensity. "With every bone in my body."

We stared, caught in each other's thrall for several long seconds. It occurred to me then that this might truly never disappear. Matthew and I had known each other for well over a year now. True, we had never come to that place where the mundane, everyday facts of life threatened to overtake passion. But there was a spark between us that wouldn't ever really fade, no matter how many events we attended, how many mornings we were blessed to wake up together. The ember it came from was too hot. A fire everlasting.

"Come on, doll," Matthew said as he pulled at his collar, looking as though it were physically painful not to kiss me. "You promised me a dance or ten."

"Um, all right," I said. "But I need to use the powder room first. I'll meet you at our table?"

"Sounds good. I'll get us some drinks."

Matthew took off, blending perfectly into a crowd of couture and some of the most avant-garde fashion in the world. I sighed, and once I had lost sight of him, turned the corner to find the bathroom. But when I reemerged, I ran directly into the last person I wanted to see tonight. Or ever.

My husband.

"Whoa!" Calvin neighed like he was actually the horse he sounded like he was directing, steadying himself by grabbing and nearly knocking over one of the posts demarcating where guests could and could not go.

"Calvin? What are you doing here?"

I hadn't seen him this close for so long, and he looked quite different. He hadn't lost weight exactly, but everything about him seemed to have sagged in the last several months so that his tuxedo billowed a bit, as though it had been tailored for another body. His skin, always with a sheen of sweat, now looked pallid and blotchy, the red tip of his nose having spread to other parts. His eyes also had the same glaze as the nights when he would turn to me in a bourbon-soaked rage.

I shied toward the wall. "You need to go. You shouldn't be here."

"Oh, princess. Is that what you think?" he said. "Live somewhere else and you can just tell me what to do? I have some things to say to you. And I'm not leaving until you *listen*."

I scowled, but glanced nervously at the other guests, who were looking at us curiously.

"Please," I asked, trying for a bit more courtesy and ignoring the pounding of my heart. Every single part of me was screaming *run.* "I promise. I'll call you tomorrow."

"Ha. I've heard that before," Calvin sneered.

I looked around for a security guard or one of the personnel, but then my phone buzzed with a text.

MATTHEW: You coming? I'm about to go in.

I SWALLOWED. Oh, dear. What would Matthew do if he saw Calvin? What would Calvin do if he saw Matthew? Hastily, I tucked the phone back into my clutch, but not before Calvin grabbed my arm and turned me back to face him.

"Who was that?"

I wriggled my hand out of his sweaty grasp. "Don't *touch* me."

"Was that him? I saw the name. Marcus or Matthew or something like that. Are you seeing someone?!"

His voice was erratic, wavering over the words. He sounded desperate and looked even worse.

"Keep it down," I pleaded. "I don't know what you're doing here, Calvin, but you need to go. Now."

"I came because we need to talk!" Calvin snapped. "Without the damn lawyers. Just you and me."

"*What* makes you think I would ever want to be in a room with you alone?" I shouldn't have argued back, but suddenly I couldn't help it. "Honestly. The restraining order might have expired, but my distaste for you has not. I don't know why you decided to come here tonight, but it was a mistake. We are all but finished with each other. It's *over.*"

Before he could say another word, I turned on my heel and made my escape down the hall. I needed to find Matthew and warn him. And then we needed to leave. Immediately.

"Nina! Nina, come back here!" Calvin shouted.

I ignored him, looking for the entrance to the ballroom. The hall was filling up, and so thankfully I was able to slip between other guests and avoid the attendant collecting everyone's phones. At the far end, I spotted a familiar girl holding a clipboard and a walkie-talkie and quickly crossed the room.

"Angela?" I said, tapping her on the shoulder. "You're Cora's assistant, aren't you?"

She turned. "Um, yes, Ms. de Vries, right?"

I nodded. Good, she knew me. "Yes. I just wanted to ask why my husband is here. Calvin Gardner. I did not request an invite for him." I glanced over my shoulder. No Calvin. I lowered my voice. "We are estranged, you see."

The girl colored. "Oh—I—oh, no, that's my fault. P-please don't mention it to Cora. She would be so furious. She expects us to know these sorts of things."

I softened, but only just. "Can I ask how, exactly, he got a ticket to the most exclusive party in the world without Cora's okay?"

"He, um, called earlier this week, asking for his ticket to be sent to him directly because he was away on business," said the girl. "I didn't think you would mind considering he was your husband and all. I'm so sorry, Ms. de Vries. I just assumed he was your plus-one!"

I gritted my teeth. Stupid girl. For once, I actually wanted someone to know my sordid tabloid history, and she was oblivious.

"Okay," I said, thinking fast as I caught Calvin shoving his way through the crowd, eyes on me and murder all over his face. If he saw Matthew, that would be it. "You can make it up to me. There's a man in the ballroom in a blue Givenchy tuxedo. He has black hair, green eyes, a few inches taller than me, and his name is Matthew. Look for a young Cary Grant."

"Who?"

I sighed impatiently. "He's very, *very* handsome, all right?"

The girl nodded, though her cheeks pinked with excitement. "Hot guy in a blue suit. Got it."

"I need you to find him and tell him to meet me by the Greek statues downstairs. Tell him we need to leave immediately."

"Got it. Okay."

The girl hurried off in the direction of the ballroom. I spotted Jane and Eric near one of the exhibits in the new hall, canoodling openly without a care for their potential audience, and decided that would be a better way to distract my errant husband.

"Eric! Jane!" I called out, waving so they would see me. I hated to interrupt such a heated moment, but this was important. Lord, I really should have told them everything.

"Oh my God," Jane said as I approached. "Nina, you look amazing. And so *tall!*"

"Hey!" I looked down at myself and then back up. As a member of the planning committee, Jane had elected to get ready here much earlier, and so while she had seen my dress, of course, she had not seen the full effect of my stylist's work. My strappy silver heels were a bit taller than the ones I usually wore, I supposed, lending to the more statuesque look.

"Thank you," I started to say, but my other announcement was ruined when both Jane and Eric's faces dropped at what could only be one thing.

Calvin.

"Nina!" he barked at me, huffing as he shoved aside several people, ignoring the others who followed the commotion. "We weren't done. I want to know who the hell has been texting you, and I want to know *now.*"

I turned around, straightening to my full height. In these shoes, I had at least six inches over the man, and for the first time, I truly didn't care. For years he had put me in kitten heels, even flats whenever we took part in social engagements together, balancing our height difference with preposterous lifts in his own shoes. Now I wanted nothing more than to intimidate him as he had done to me for so long.

"Calvin, don't," I said sharply. "This is not the time nor the place. I beg of you, just let it go. It's only a friend. I promise."

He clearly didn't believe me—and neither did Jane and Eric, if their raised brows were any indication.

"Just a friend," Calvin sneered. "It's that Italian who showed up at the house, isn't it? What was his name? Mark? Michael?"

"Matthew. His name was Matthew," I said before I could stop myself.

Then I felt like my breath was caught in my ribs. Matthew had been going to the house? Or was he talking about last year, when I would occasionally see him lurking around the corner, checking on me? Did Calvin know about that too?

Oh *God*, I hoped the girl had found him in time and convinced him to leave. My voice was so quiet I could barely hear it, but the intensity —almost longing?—ingrained in each syllable of Zola's given name sent a shiver up my spine.

Beside us, Jane and Eric exchanged puzzled glances.

"You think you're going to get away with this," Calvin growled. "Well, *you're not*. I'll—"

"Calvin." Eric's voice finally piped up when I somehow couldn't. "Let it go." He glanced at me as if to ask if I was all right.

Calvin was barely able to hide a sneer. Eric didn't look away, and I watched with some amount of awe, as they engaged in a stare-off that seemed to last a full five minutes.

And then, finally, Calvin turned away.

I sighed to Jane, like I was merely irritated with Calvin's presence. "I need a cocktail."

Calvin scowled. "Now, just wait a minute."

"No," I snapped and took off through the crowd, though behind me, I could hear Eric telling Jane he was coming with to make sure Calvin didn't cause a scene.

Do not get them involved, I told myself. This was Jane's big night. Her debut as a designer. I didn't need to ruin that with my ongoing marital crises. I darted around a few tables, eager to lose both my soon-to-be ex-husband and my cousin. *Where* was security when I needed it?

"Nina," Calvin chased after me. "I'm not going to leave until you talk to me!"

I glanced into the ballroom. Matthew was nowhere to be seen. From the other side of the room, the girl with the clipboard gave me a thumbs-up. I breathed with relief and hurried inside.

"Senator Wick," I said, running into a familiar face in front of whom I knew Calvin wouldn't make a scene. "How lovely to see you again."

And so it went—me frantically trying to escape Calvin's grasp, latching myself on to various donors and people he wouldn't want to lose face in front of, and Calvin tailing me in and out of the party for more than thirty minutes.

Eventually, and partly because I knew that Matthew would come looking for me soon, I ducked out of the ballroom and into a stairwell, where we were still close to the party, but wouldn't be overheard.

"*What?*" I demanded when I turned around to find Calvin lumbering after me. "What is it that you want that the lawyers can't deal with? If the final agreement isn't to your liking, we can look at it again."

"Lawyers?" he hissed. "You have ruined me, do you know that?"

"I rather think we ruined each other." I bristled. "You weren't the one who ended up spending two weeks in prison, Calvin."

He cackled lightly to himself.

I squinted. "You're drunk. Go home. The penthouse is yours. You have everything you want."

"I will *not* be embarrassed by you, you fucking bitch!"

I tried to brush past. "I'm getting security."

"The hell you are," he said, lunging for me again. "You don't know what you've done. Millions. I owe millions and millions. Can't you understand that? All I wanted was enough to start over."

"All you wanted was everything I have!" I yelped as I scampered away. "Your bad investments are *not* my problem anymore. Honestly, it's not my fault that you're such an embarrassing failure!"

"I am not!"

"You've lost!" I snapped at him. "I don't understand why you won't accept it and let me go!"

"Because why the fuck should I?" he demanded. "I put ten years into this. I should walk away with more than a few lousy million. I should be right on par with you and your goddamn arrogant-as-fuck cousin!"

Suddenly, he grabbed me and shoved me hard against the wall.

"You think you can just walk away," he sneered. "Did you forget, princess? Did you forget that there is a price to pay for making a fool out of me?"

"Get off me!" I shrieked, trying to escape his iron-tight grip.

But he wouldn't let go. Faced with the choice of toppling down the stairs or staying in one piece, I followed him until we reached the empty bottom floor. Calvin threw me to the ground, then tripped on his own feet and fell on top of me.

"There's those legs I remember," he leered when my dress pooled around my hips. "A little long for my taste, if you want to know the truth, but everyone else always said you were a catch. Who was I to argue, huh?"

His erection pressed between my legs as he fumbled with his zipper. Every one of his stinking smells embraced me in a sickening hug. Alcohol, sweat, cheap men's deodorant. Some kind of decay that only belonged to him.

"Do you like that, princess?" he asked. "I think you secretly want it just like you always did. Should I do it here? How about in the elevator again, huh?"

The effect was like tinder. Suddenly, the small fire that had been burning inside me all night—no, for the last eighteen months, really—burst into a massive pyre.

"NO!" I shrieked. "YOU WILL NOT DO THIS TO ME ANYMORE!"

I kicked and punched and beat with all my might, wishing I had done more than Pilates and spinning classes that would help me throw off this monster.

And suddenly, he was gone. It took me a second to realize it, but when I finally opened my eyes again, I sat up to find Calvin pinned squarely against the opposite wall, eyes bulging as he looked at his captor. My savior.

Matthew.

CHAPTER TWENTY-EIGHT

Matthew

C alvin Gardner's throat gave easily under my fingers, with the pasty color and texture of bread dough just after it was done rising, and with the same faint yeasty odor too, thanks to the amount of beer he had consumed. I barely noticed. It took every ounce of self-control I had right now not to strangle the man in his socks and leave him to melt all over the marble.

I'd been wandering back and forth between the ballroom and the Greco Roman exhibit since that twitchy assistant had approached me with Nina's message. Everywhere I looked, she had just been, leading me on a merry chase around the event. The reason why only became apparent when I had decided to take another route to the bottom floor and heard Nina's scream echo up the stairwell before it was swallowed by the live music at the party.

Now one word clanged through my ears like a fire alarm, blocking out the sound of Gardner's frantic wheezing.

"'Again'?" My voice shook from the effort it took not to crush the man's windpipe. "Nina, what the fuck did he mean by 'again'?"

"What do you think?" Gardner's glossy eyes bugged as he spoke hoarsely between his teeth. "She was my wife. She still is. Not just some dirty wop's whore."

"Was I *fuckin'* talking to you?" I slammed him into the wall again with a satisfying thwack.

"Matthew!" Nina cried out from where she was still crumpled on the floor, her dress torn up one thigh, makeup smeared across her beautiful face.

I had at least six inches on Gardner, and even if I didn't outweigh him, I was definitely packing a bit more heat, muscle for muscle, pound for pound. But adrenaline does funny things. In Gardner's case, it allowed him to stomp on my foot when Nina called my name, pushing me off guard long enough to wriggle out of my grasp. But not for long.

I whipped around and wrangled him just as quickly into a half-nelson, smashing him face-first into another one of the massive marble columns in the hall, just before I whipped out the switchblade I had in my breast pocket and pressed the steel edge into his wobbling jowls.

"There ain't a DA in New York City who doesn't walk around with some kind of protection, you slimy sack of shit," I growled. "Now, you say one more *word* about her, and I will slit your turkey neck from ear to fuckin' ear. You got that?"

"Matthew."

I looked up and found Nina watching me with a curious expression. Some horror, yes, which was morphing quickly into shock. Some disgust. And maybe a little desire.

"Maybe I should give the knife to you, baby," I told her. "You can stick him like the dirty fuckin' pig he is, huh?" I pressed the blade deeper into Gardner's neck, and the loose skin oozed over it.

"P-please," Gardner wheezed. "Please, she's—a—"

"She's *what*, you rotting can of shit-eating worms?"

Gardner swallowed heavily, but mumbled low enough that I couldn't make out what he was saying.

I shoved him against the column again. Hard. "What was that?"

"I said," he croaked between harsh, labored gasps, "that she's a *whore*. And this…just…proves it."

I couldn't help it. I dropped the knife, whipped Gardner around, and delivered a harsh right hook straight to hit jaw that had him dropping to the ground like a heavy sack of wheat.

His head echoed down the corridor as it smacked the marble floor. I squatted down and checked his pulse, wondering if I should feel guilty that I was even wondering if the man was dead. I did not. I felt nothing but rage.

Slow, but steady, Calvin Gardner's heartbeat thumped under my fingers. But he was out. For now.

I retrieved my knife, then joined Nina on the ground. "Nina. What was he talking about?"

She was crumpled to the floor in her finery, shoulders shaking like we were in the middle of the damn arctic.

"Come here," I said. God, I wanted to fuckin' *kill* him for touching her like that. Instead, I pulled out my phone to call Derek.

"No, don't," Nina said, stopping me with a gentle hand on mine. "It will r-ruin the event."

"Who cares if it ruins the event? This asshole just stalked you here and assaulted you. And I'm pretty fucking sure at this point it isn't the first time, is it? He's not going to stop, baby. He needs to be locked the fuck up!"

She bit her lip hard enough that it turned white around her tooth. "Please, Matthew. It's Jane's big night. I—I don't want to be—"

"Be what?" I demanded, wanting to shake it out of her myself. "You don't want to be what?"

"A burden!" she burst out, practically a scream that echoed down the hall and through my damn chest.

Three syllables, but it was enough to make her look like she'd run a marathon, red-cheeked, wild-eyed, and exhausted.

"That's all I've ever been," she said fiercely. "And what he did. What he's done. I refuse to be defined by it, Matthew. I re*fuse!*"

I swallowed, wanting to fight back. I wanted to protest, to tell her that she was being ridiculous. But her words struck a chord I understood better than I wanted to admit.

I knew what it was like to be treated like I was nothing by the people who were supposed to love me. For the first fourteen years of my life, I had two parents who chose the bottle over me and their five young daughters. I had a father who was more willing to punch his son in the face than admit when he was wrong, and a mother who would have rather hidden from her kids than face her short-comings and be the mother they needed. If it hadn't been for my grandparents, I would have been even more angry and bitter than I was as an adolescent, with a safe home, yes, but always with the knowledge that in a perfect world, I shouldn't have been there in the first place. That my sisters and I, while still loved, were burdens as well.

You live your live long enough that way…you come to believe it. You come to hate yourself for it.

But my girl had never even had a *Nonno* or a *Nonna* to give her the encouragement when she needed it. She had a heartless grandmother and a flighty mother. And then traded them for an unavailable profes-sor, followed by an abusive husband. You could grow up with all the money in the world, but it couldn't do shit to replace the core needs that every human deserves. Love. Pure. Unconditional. From at least one damn person.

Well. That could be me, couldn't it?

We really were a pair. Which was why I knew that the only real way to save a person like that was to love them anyway. It's what she had done with me. I could do the same for her. I always would.

"Fine," I said as gently as I could manage. "I won't call. Yet. But, Nina…you need to tell me exactly what happened in the elevator. Not because you're a burden. You won't be. But you deserve truth, baby. I will love you. No matter what. Do you understand that?"

She blinked, tears caught in the generous sweep of her eyelashes. "I —yes. I do."

I pressed my forehead to hers. "Good. Now tell me the truth, Nina. What did he mean, 'again'?"

Nina slumped into my shoulder. "Matthew, you don't want to know."

I tipped her chin up, forcing her to look at me once more. "I really do. And you really need to tell me. Nina, I love you, and you love me. I'm going to marry you, no matter what you say. I think I've earned your secrets. Haven't I?"

Her eyes welled again, and her lower lip trembled. "Yes," she whispered. "Oh, my love, yes, you have."

"Then tell me, Nina. Tell me everything."

Slowly, she pushed my hand off her chin, then leaned back against the wall. With a quick glance at Calvin, she took a deep breath, and started.

"It was my first time organizing the gala," she said, speaking more toward her hands, now clasped in her lap. "Olivia was four. I was twenty-four. It was the first time I had anything resembling a job or anything close to it since she was born." She shook her head. "Calvin... he didn't like it."

I stayed quiet, keeping my eye on the slumbering giant in question. Above us, the party raged out of sight, quieted by the heavy steel doors at the top of the stairs. We were still alone. For now.

"It happened about a month before the gala," she said. "I was working late a lot, and he didn't like it. It made me...unavailable. In those days, he liked having me around, you see. Sometimes he would bring people back to our apartment just to show me off. To men he was trying to impress. Business investors or people he was trying to start some business with. You can imagine."

I could, yeah. Way too clearly. Nina, at twenty-four, tall and queenly, young and bright—relegated to being literal arm candy for a bunch of slobbering, middle-aged hacks.

I swallowed. Maybe I needed to pray again.

"One night, he was throwing an impromptu salon, you might call it. Several investors were there—I honestly don't know who. But I couldn't come, because we were busy here. And he was so embarrassed—you remember how he gets about being embarrassed. I don't know, maybe something else happened that day..."

"Hey," I said gently. "Don't justify it. Whatever that motherfucker did is on him. I don't even have to know what it is to know it's inexcusable."

Nina inhaled deeply, then exhaled again. "Perhaps."

I hated that she could even doubt it.

"Then what happened?" I prodded.

She sighed. "He came here to find me and bring me home. He was waiting for me at the elevators when I came out of the institute. It was late, around eight, but we still weren't finished. He said I had to come home. I said no. And when I was going up to the exhibit to go over some things, he followed me into the elevator. And just like that day with you, it got stuck. And I was trapped there. With him."

She shivered, wrapping her arms around herself.

"Usually he would wait until he we were home," she whispered. "Until we were behind closed doors. But that night...oh, God, Matthew, he was *so* angry."

She leaned forward and buried her face in her knees, unable to say anything more. I could easily imagine what had happened, though I wasn't sure it was entirely accurate.

"Nina," I said carefully. "I need to know the truth. I understand if you can't talk about it, but, baby, just nod your head, yes or no. So there is absolutely no misunderstanding. That day in the elevator...did your husband hit you?"

She bit her lip, then slowly, she nodded.

"Multiple times?"

Another slow nod.

I inhaled deeply and exhaled through my nose. Don't kill him. *Don't* kill him. Yet.

"Did he..." I shook my head as I reached down and fingered the rip in her dress. God, I could hardly think it, let alone say it out loud. But I had to. I had to in order to do what needed to happen next. "Did he rape you?"

She bit her lip. Two more tears fell down her porcelain cheeks. And then, so slowly it followed the crack in my heart, she nodded one last time.

"So it wasn't claustrophobia that day, was it? That's—that's why you're afraid of elevators. Because of what he did to you in one."

It made sense, now. She wasn't afraid of any other confined spaces. Cars, planes, trains. Crowded rooms, balconies. None of them made a difference. But it was elevators—especially *that* elevator, I realized—that made her jump into a terror because of this.

"I couldn't get out," she whispered. "Matthew, I couldn't get out!"

It was then I finally pulled her under my arm, stroked her hair until she started to calm again.

"Was that the only time?" I asked. I had to.

Her face buried in my shoulder, she shook her head silently.

"And was it...was that the first time?"

She paused. And again, shook her head.

"The last?"

Another pause. One more shake, side to side.

"Usually...I would just let him take what he wanted. After a while, it was easier than fighting him. Except for the times I just had to." She touched her wrist with one hand.

"And after you and I started—"

"*No,*" she interrupted vehemently, sitting up in a fury. "Oh, Matthew, please believe me. I never cheated on you—"

"Cheated?" I said with disbelief. "Do you really think that if your husband raped you, I'd consider it cheating? As if I, the other fucking man, even had a right to say it anyway?"

"You have a right," Nina said, sniffing. "You have a right to what belongs to you. As have I, do I not?"

I closed my eyes and concentrated on breathing even though my blood was boiling. Sure, there was a part of me that wanted to agree with her, say she belonged to me.

But it wasn't quite right.

"I don't make that choice, doll. You do."

"Well, I did," she said, her voice floating sweetly through the air. "Every day since I met you, my love."

"And when you did fight him?" I asked, even though I already knew.

Every bruise I had ever seen on her beautiful body was flashing through my mind. The shadows on her delicate wrists. The fading marks on her thighs or neck.

I closed my eyes, not wanting her to see the strong urge to murder I knew must have been reflected in them. The anger I felt toward myself for not knowing, and yet somehow knowing. And never really acting on it.

It would be so easy. It scared me how easy it would be, and how attractive. Haul him out on the premise of a citizen's arrest. Bring him into the park and shove him in the trunk of my car. Wait until it was dark, then take a drive out to East New York. Maybe to The Hole, where we had first found his fall-down properties. Or nearby Betts Creek, right behind the water processing plant.

A couple of cable ties at the wrists. Dunk his feet in a pair of concrete boots. Down he'd go, into the mud and sludge with the rest of the leeches to rot. One call to Derek, or even Eric, and the evidence would be swallowed forever. No one would ever fucking ask what happened to Károly Kertész or Calvin Gardner, because the world all knew it would exponentially be better off without this piece of slime in it.

But.

Nonno's face flashed before my eyes. His bid for me to do him proud. To be better than the rest. Not to sink to the lowest denominator, give in to every one of my base instincts, even when they screamed at me to find vengeance.

Yeah, it would be easy, for sure. But that didn't make it right.

So instead I prayed, harder than I had ever done in my life. I prayed for forgiveness. I prayed for grace. I prayed for the strength to keep my weapons in my pocket and not turn them on the enemy who deserved them more than any man I had ever known.

Holy father, grant me the strength to forgive. Grant me the strength to walk away. Grant me the strength to be worthy of the gifts you have given me. Especially the love of this woman in her hour of need…

"Matthew?"

Nina's voice, clear as a birdsong, brought me out of my trance.

"Who else knows?" I asked.

She blinked. "N-no one."

I shook my head. "Someone knows. Your staff, maybe? A cook, a nanny? Did anyone ever say anything?"

She looked incredibly uncomfortable. "I—well, perhaps my old assistant, Moira. And maybe our cook, Marguerite. But they never saw anything."

"Anyone else?" I prodded. I needed more, for her sake.

Nina swallowed. "And…C-Caitlyn."

That genuinely surprised me. "Caitlyn? Your best friend? The one who literally tried to *be* you for ten straight years?"

Sadly, she nodded, allowed me to pull her back into my chest. "Ironic, isn't it? The one person I trusted with my secrets was the one who had the most to hide from me."

"Nina," I said as I stroked her hair. "Baby, why didn't you tell me? Fuck, I could have helped."

"I wanted to protect you," she whispered. "You, Eric, Jane, Olivia. Oh God, but I couldn't even do that, could I? You heard him, Matthew, he's not going to stop. And he'll take Olivia, and he'll take her like he took all those girls, and he'll s-sell her, I know he will, and—"

"Shhhhh," I said, wrapping both arms around her now. "He's going to do nothing of the sort."

But she pushed me away, suddenly full of action. "I can do more. I must do more. I can't keep these secrets—look at them, look at the way they hurt people! I don't want to hide anymore. I'll refile on grounds of abuse. The lawyers said if I did it that way, it will be messy, but would be maybe harder for him to fight in the end...even if it is just my word against his..."

As she babbled on about her divorce plans, I examined Gardner's swollen carcass, which was now snoring.

"Nina," I interrupted suddenly. "That's not necessary. But did you mean what you said about not hiding anymore?"

Beautiful and tear soaked, she nodded. "Y-yes."

My girl. So brave. So damn valiant in ways I was only starting to understand. Ways I'd spend the rest of my life trying to understand if she would let me.

I pulled out my phone and scrolled until I found the contact I wanted.

"Zola!" Derek answered at once. "What's up, man, it's been a minute. How are you?"

"Hey. You at work?"

"Yeah. Actually, I'm at the station right now catching up on some paperwork. What's going on?"

"Two things. I'm at the Met with Nina. I'm sitting here on a citizen's arrest of Calvin Gardner."

"Zola..." I could hear the disappointment in his voice. The same kind of tone men took when they saw a friend go too far down the rabbit hole with a girl who was no good. I knew what they all thought. That I'd thrown away my life.

"This is different, King," I said a little too sharply. "Look, we have evidence of sexual assault against his wife, all right? I need you to send a squad car here ASAP to pick him up."

"Sexual assault? Zola, come on. He's not breaking the law by going to a party, is he? And do you really even know that—"

"Yes, I fuckin' do, Derek!" I broke out. "I saw it myself!"

Derek was quiet a minute. "Okay. Okay, sorry, man. Anything else?"

"Yeah. Call Jenny Kester in the domestic crimes unit in Manhattan. You have her home number?"

"Um, yeah..."

"No one will take my calls right now, King. you know that. But Jenny's a good egg. We went to law school together." I rubbed my face, wishing there were more I could do. But this was the right thing to do. "Tell her this is coming from me and that you need an emergency subpoena for the Metropolitan Museum of Art."

"Zola, come on. Do you really want to involve another DA in your obsession with this girl? It's over, man. She lost."

"It's *not* over," I said, looking up at the cameras that hung from the corners of the room, and which I knew for a fact were installed in every elevator. "These are new charges. Rape in the first degree. And we have video proof."

Nina's mouth fell open with dread. "We—we do?"

"The Met has had twenty-four-seven surveillance cameras in every exhibit and elevator since 2004," I told both her and Derek. "I know because of...well, some things that happened here last year." I didn't want to say to Derek that I had gone into the security room and personally deleted the evidence of Nina's and my tryst in the elevator last year after learning that it recorded remotely even when it was offline. "Unless that elevators just 'happened' to be out of order that day, there is a recording somewhere of what he did to you, Nina. Irrefutable evidence."

Nina blanched. "I...oh..."

The look on her face stopped me from rattling off more orders to Derek. Instead, I put my hand over the receiver. "Do you want to let him go?"

"I...I..."

My heart thumped with her. "Yes or no, Nina."

She blinked, and then her face hardened. "No. I want him in jail." She shook her head and straightened. "Let them release the tape if they want. I'm done hiding his secrets too."

"That's my girl." I kissed her on the cheek. "All right, Derek. You're asking for the security footage from the elevator bank that goes to the Costume Institute, March and April of 2013."

"All right. And who am I looking for here?"

I paused. I almost didn't want to say, because I knew Nina wouldn't like it.

But Derek was good. I knew he wouldn't joy-watch any of that shit, although whoever ended up prosecuting the case would, and so would the others. I'd seen footage of shit like that before. It wasn't easy for anyone to look at that sort of thing. It made any decent human being sick to their stomach.

"The perp is Calvin Gardner. And the victim..."

I turned and found Nina watching me, her gray eyes turned to steel. She was crying and wild, but I was so fuckin' proud to say she had never looked less like a victim. She nodded slowly. *Do it*, she seemed to say.

"The victim is Nina de Vries."

Derek swore softly to himself. "You *really* don't know how to stay out of trouble with this girl, do you?"

I looked at Nina again and touched my finger to her face. "Good trouble, though."

She smiled, then placed a soft kiss on my lips.

"Thank you," she whispered.

"It'll be there, King, I promise. We'll wait here with Gardner for the patrol unit. First floor. The Greek room."

"And I thought I was going to have a quiet night at home," Derek said. "Wait there. I'll be there too."

He hung up. Nina and I sat there for a moment, still digesting everything for a few moments. Then, finally, I managed to push myself up from the ground.

"Duchess, I'm going to need that sash around your waist," I said, even as I started stripping off my own white bow tie. It was a shame to be ruining any part of the suit Nina had bought, but it had to be done.

She handed me the garment, and then I crossed the hall to where Gardner lay. I bound his hands firmly behind his back, then sat his sloppy ass up so that he was sitting against a balustrade leading down to another floor, and tied his hands to the balustrade behind him.

Then I sat back on my heels, and without any mercy, reached back and slapped him across the face as hard as I could.

"Wake up, you stupid son of a bitch."

Gardner blinked, groggy and his eyes fixed on me, and then he registered where he was and what had happened.

"I—what? What the fuck!"

"Calvin Gardner," I said. "Károly Kertész. Whatever the fuck your name is. In about ten minutes, you'll be under arrest for rape in the first degree. That's a class B felony, punishable by up to twenty-five years in prison. And I don't care how many judges you think you can bribe in this city—I know more. And now I will personally make sure your sloppy ass lands behind bars if it's the last thing I do."

POSTLUDE

New York Star
August 4, 2018

Disgraced investor sentenced for first degree rape of socialite wife

Setting a landmark precedent for marital rape, Calvin Gardner, originally known as Károly Kertész before changing his name in 2004, was sentenced today for twenty-five years in a maximum-security prison for several counts of physical assault and rape of his estranged wife, New York socialite Nina de Vries. The case first burst on the scene when a 2013 video recording of Ms. de Vries being assaulted by her husband in an elevator at the Metropolitan Museum of Art was leaked and went viral.

Gardner has faced nothing but legal woes over the last few years, but managed to elude them until last month, when former Brooklyn prosecutor Matthew Zola uncovered long term extortion of local judges and law enforcement officials. Mr. Zola was originally an attorney with the bureau pursuing the trafficking charges that Mr. Gardner eluded late last year.

"Even though I was off the case, something wasn't right," he said. "As a friend of the family, I couldn't let it slide. So I did some digging, and it was pretty obvious what was going on."

As a result of his work, six separate judges in the New York City districts have been indicted with child rape and corruption charges. Additionally, the Brooklyn DA has filed an appeal in the original sex trafficking case against Mr. Gardner, for which the disgraced businessman could face an additional fifty years if convicted. Additionally, the Italian government recently made a public extradition request for Mr. Gardner to stand trial for the murder of Giuseppe Bianchi, a literature and arts professor in Florence.

Ms. de Vries was not present at the sentencing and could not be reached for comment, but many speculate she may be present next week for the final hearing of her divorce proceedings against Mr. Gardner, which she refiled on grounds of abuse. Ms. de Vries is asking for full custody of their daughter, whom she has revealed is not even biologically related to Mr. Gardner, but a product of Ms. de Vries's affair with Professor Bianchi when she was an exchange student abroad.

EPILOGUE
SEPTEMBER 2018

Matthew

"Darling, I really don't think it should go there. Wouldn't you like that big, heavy bookshelf in your own private office?"

Brandon and I turned from where we had just set one of my bookshelves on the far side of the living room. Brandon straightened and wiped his brow, which shone with sweat, and I pulled at the collar of my grime-stained t-shirt. We both turned to find Nina leaning against the wall, dishtowel in hand, looking a dead ringer for Grace Kelly in a light blue skirt, a thin white tank top, and her hair tied back in a ponytail at the base of her neck.

"You know," Brandon said, "there are these people. Called movers. And you can actually pay them to move things that might break your back. You know, like bookshelves?"

"Nina and I like to do things ourselves," I said with a wink at my fiancée. "Ain't that right, doll?"

Nina flashed a smile brighter than the rays of sunshine dappling the room through the windows. "Indeed, my love. But to come back to the question of your lovely shelf…"

After a summer of sitting on pins and needles in New York, it was officially move-in week for Nina and me—and one I never thought I'd make too. As of today, we were officially Massachusetts State residents, living in the little white craftsman Nina purchased at just twenty-one for a future she barely allowed herself to imagine. Today we were finally taking real, solid steps toward the happy ending we'd almost had to steal.

It hadn't been an easy summer. Four solid months of keeping things quiet while the Manhattan DA built their case against Calvin. Then six weeks ago we caught a break when Caitlyn Calvert turned out to be a better friend than Nina thought. After she quietly pled guilty to charges of conspiracy, trafficking, and identity theft, Calvin also provided the Manhattan ADA overseeing Nina's rape charge with a shocking amount of evidence that Calvin Gardner had been stalking Nina for years before they met and had essentially conned her into marrying him with the intent to embezzle as many assets as he could. Tapes, emails, text messages, letters. Caitlyn had been documenting Calvin's every move for more than fifteen years.

As a result, the terms of Nina's prenuptial agreement were still overturned, but in her favor, not in Calvin's. Which meant that overnight, she became the sole owner of the Lexington Avenue penthouse, the house in Newton, what little was left in their savings account, and sole guardian of her daughter, Olivia, while the government seized the rest of the more illicit holdings of Pantheon and Calvin got a jail cell where he could rot.

Nina had decided to drop her own suit against her former friend. I thought she was being too nice, but she insisted retribution wasn't her style.

"You know," I had told her the day she made her decision. "Catholics don't believe in karma."

Nina had used part of the summer to convert to Catholicism in anticipation of our wedding the next year, and we spent a surprising amount of time debating what Nina found to be the more questionable parts of the faith.

"No, we don't," she replied thoughtfully. "But we do believe in grace."

Well, she had me there.

At any rate, it was looking more and more like God has his own agenda when it came to vengeance against the sins of Calvin Gardner. Caitlyn's revelations had turned into something of a domino effect. As she came forward, so did many of the women Calvin had trafficked and abused over the years. And they, in turn, pointed fingers at a number of prominent men whom Calvin had successfully blackmailed—including several U.S. attorneys and the judge originally presiding over his case. The trafficking ring case was reopened, this time as a federal investigation that could potentially land Nina's ex transferred to federal prison for the rest of his life. Nina's entrapment was also shedding a new light on things, and I'd already moved for a new trial of her case as well. We had high hopes for an acquittal—Cardozo had already told me he wouldn't stand in the way.

But it wasn't until Calvin was finally locked up for good that I saw my girl really relax for the first time since I'd known her. The Nina I knew had always been graceful and gorgeous, but she was buttoned up tighter than one of my vests at Thanksgiving. I had seen glimpses of someone else more carefree and chased that woman for more than a year trying to tease her out.

Now that chase was over. She ran straight into my arms on a daily basis.

"I know what you're doing," I said as I drummed my fingers on the side of the wood.

Nina blinked innocently, though her gray eyes sparkled with humor. "Oh?"

"Oh?" I mimicked. "Do you really think that batting those eyelashes at me is going to get me to shove all my furniture into the one room in this house you've designated as mine, duchess?"

Her sweet, soft mouth curved into a suggestive smile. "I don't know. Is it working?"

I slipped a hand around her neck and brushed her jaw with my thumb. Her scent of roses washed over me, along with the sweet taste of her breakfast—espresso and chocolate—along with the promise of something even sweeter sometime later.

"How about now?" she murmured, her lips only a hair's breadth from mine. Then she leaned in and whispered in my ear: "I promise I'll thank you properly tonight. Or maybe this afternoon in the pantry."

Immediately, I stood up with intention. "Brandon, this is going upstairs to my office."

The big man just rolled his eyes. "God, you're so whipped, it's pathetic."

"Takes one to know one, my friend," I told him. "Now, up we go."

———

FIVE HOURS LATER, Brandon, Nina, Skylar, and I relaxed on the back porch, enjoying a pitcher of ice-cold gin and tonics as a reward for moving in nearly everything in the small moving truck out front. In the yard, Olivia was happily playing with the other kids—Annabelle and Christoph, Skylar's younger siblings, and Jenny and Luis, the Sterlings' children. Every so often, a squeal would erupt from the raucous game of tag under the old willow tree.

"So, what do you think, Zola," Skylar asked. "Are you ready to convert and become a Bostonian?"

I snorted. "Easy there, tiger. We've been here for literally a day."

"I don't think Matthew will ever be able to root for the Red Sox, Brandon," Nina said with a smirk. "He's a Yankees fan, so far as I can tell."

"Well, ask him again after I take him to Fenway next weekend," Brandon replied.

"You can't beat Yankee Stadium," I countered. "I'm sorry, but it's not possible."

The second Sterling had heard I'd lost my job, I'd gotten a call from Skylar insisting I come work for her. It had taken me a few months to come around on the idea (and yes, the promise of a very nice paycheck had helped). But what was I if not a to-the-bone New Yorker? What was my purpose if not to root out the poison in the city of my birth?

But that wasn't an option, at least not for a while. And I knew Nina wanted nothing more than to finish her degree in art history at Wellesley. So, I applied for a reciprocity waiver of the Massachusetts bar, finally allowed, and within a few months, I was officially licensed to practice in two states. I even allowed Nina to pay off the mortgage on the Red Hook house so Sofia and Frankie could have the place to themselves. It was a fresh start for us as a new family, beyond the shadow of the city. And one I had to admit would do us a lot of good.

This mid-sized craftsman that was approximately one quarter the size of her penthouse. Which didn't have a staff quarters or eight bedrooms or seven bathrooms or even a small percentage of the amenities Nina had grown up with.

"It feels like a home," Nina said again when I asked her why she wanted to live there instead of any number of mansions she could have purchased with the sale of the penthouse.

And I, of course, loved her all the more for it.

Before Brandon and I could continue our ongoing argument about which baseball institution was better, the sound of the doorbell filtered through the house.

"I'll get it." I left my drink on the table and jogged back through the house to answer the door.

"Hi!" Jane squealed, and tackled me with a hug as soon as I opened the screen door.

"Hey." I hugged her back, but then set her aside carefully. "Calm down there, sweetheart. You can't shake the bun too much while it's baking, you know?"

About a month ago, Eric and Jane had announced their pregnancy. Now my friend was both expecting *and* about to start her own program at FIT. Eric just continually looked over the damn moon every time he looked at her.

"This is a surprise," I said as I shook his hand.

"I felt bad we couldn't help with the move," he said. "But we brought a pretty good housewarming gift." He gestured to the man in the brown suit. "Where's Nina?"

———

A FEW MINUTES LATER, we were all crowded on the back porch again while Thomas Clark, the estate attorney and executor of Celeste de Vries's estate, introduced himself and proceeded to take out a large document from his briefcase and set it on top of the tablecloth. Jane looked like she wanted to explode from glee. Eric just kept shaking his head like he couldn't believe it.

"She did it to you too," he said. "Just you wait."

"Did what?" Nina asked.

"You'll see, coz. You'll see."

"First," he said, "I have to apologize. This was a very unorthodox way of handling her trust, but Mrs. de Vries was quite insistent when she asked me to draw up her affairs."

Nina frowned. "I don't know what you mean."

"There was another part of the will," Eric supplied, almost as if he couldn't help himself. "You're getting more. So much more than you thought, Nina."

"Wait, what?" Nina stuttered. "I don't understand. Mr. Clark, you told me that if my ex-husband and I split up, I would get nothing. My marriage was very important to my grandmother. She hated scandal of any kind."

"I said that if you *separated* from Mr. Gardner, your inheritance was to be frozen," countered the lawyer. "And that there was nothing about your divorce in the document I gave you. I said nothing about this one, because it was to be kept secret until your divorce was finalized."

He pushed the document in front of us, and we both leaned over to read along as he intoned from a second copy.

In the event that my granddaughter, Nina Gardner nee de Vries, divorces her husband before my original trust is probated, I wish to amend my original bequest to include the following:

To Nina de Vries, my beloved granddaughter: exactly fifty percent of my personal stake in De Vries Shipping Industries, which at the time of this writing accounts for approximately twenty-four point five percent of the controlling shares of De Vries Industries, under the following stipulations:

1. That she remain divorced from Calvin Gardner for the remainder of her life.

2. That she assume an executive position within De Vries
   Industries and a position on the board of directors.
3. That she maintains a permanent residence in New York City.

IF SHE FULFILLS the first obligation but chooses not to work for the
company or live in New York, I instead bequeath ten percent of the
company's shares to do with as she pleases.

BY THE TIME HE FINISHED, tears were streaming down Nina's face, and
she wasn't making a move to stop them. Skylar and Brandon remained
quiet, not completely familiar with all of the complex family dynamics
that would have precipitated such a reaction. But Jane's eyes were
shining too, and Eric watched with satisfaction as his cousin received
her due.

"We wanted to tell you after the divorce," he said. "But Thomas
thought it would be better to add it to the probate proceedings. It was
approved yesterday…so here we are."

Nina seemed to be having a hard time speaking. Or even moving,
for that matter. Eventually, she was able to reach into my lap and took
my hand.

"She loved me," she whispered, so low only I could hear her.
"Matthew, my grandmother. She…"

I squeezed back, then pulled her into my shoulder so I could stroke
her hair. "I know, baby. She did love you. She really did."

"She wanted me to be safe," she said. "She knew something was
wrong with Calvin. So she protected me. She protected my future."

I said nothing, just stroked her hair. This wasn't the first time
Celeste de Vries had gone about protected her family by what struck
me as fairly fucked-up, convoluted means. But I couldn't doubt her
motives. Not now.

Nina sat up, wiping her eyes.

"Mr. Clark," she said. "Is there something I can formally sign
renouncing my claims to the company position?"

"Nina, are you sure?" Eric said. "You guys can stay in New York if you want. Zola could work at the company too. We'll make it a family affair." He reached across the table. "She never meant it to be just me in charge, don't you see that? She wanted you there too."

Nina turned to me. The question in her eyes was clear: Did I want to stay in New York?

Out in the yard, Olivia screamed with joy. Minutely, I shook my head. This was the right place for us, money or not. That hadn't changed, even with the difference of a few billion dollars.

Nina looked back at Eric. "I'm sure. We're doing something important here, Eric. And the company...it was never my passion. Family was, you see. And Matthew and I need some time to build ours."

Mr. Clark pulled out some papers containing what looked like the transfer of ownership of stock into Nina's name, along with another bundle in which she released Eric from any obligation to share company leadership with her. She signed her name with flourish, then accepted the copies of the documents and placed them neatly beside her drink. Outwardly, she looked calm and reserved again, but on top of the documents, her hands were slightly shaking.

"The car will take you back to Logan," Eric told Clark. "The helicopter is there on standby."

With a curt nod, the lawyer stood up. "Thank you, Mr. de Vries. Mrs. de Vries. It's been a pleasure doing business with your family."

———

LATE THAT NIGHT, I awoke to find Nina's side of our makeshift bed—which as of now consisted of only a queen-size mattress on the floor—empty. Down the hall, I could hear a light snore from Olivia's room. But my fiancée was nowhere to be seen.

I got up and followed a distant light shining from downstairs.

Nina stood in the kitchen holding a glass of water, a moonlit goddess in her satin nightdress, blonde hair flowing over her shoulders like water. I watched her for a moment, content just to take in her pure, unadulterated beauty.

Then she turned. And set down her glass, then crossed the kitchen to me with purpose.

Without speaking, she wrapped her arms around my neck and kissed me. Surprised only at first, I was more than happy to reciprocate, slipping my arms around her waist, then lifting her easily onto the counter that seemed to be built at *exactly* the perfect height for this particular activity.

Her long legs wrapped around my waist, drawing me closer as she devoured me whole.

"Matthew," she breathed, like my name was formed by the shape of her mouth.

She grabbed at the chain hanging over my bare chest, capturing the cross and San Gennaro medallion to pull me even closer.

"Nina," I responded as I drew my teeth down her shoulder. There weren't any other words to say. We just needed each other, here in the kitchen. In the middle of this strange, moonlit night.

She groaned as I bent to take one nipple, then the other into my mouth and suckled them straight through the satin. God, she was so lush. So perfect. So mine.

Then her hands slipped down to free me from my boxer briefs, press me between her legs, and then urge me forward so I could slip deep inside her. Right where I belonged.

Her teeth bit hard into my shoulder, and I bit right back into hers. Our bodies ground into one another as I thrust deeper, I didn't have long. She didn't seem to need much more either as I slipped a hand between us and pressed my thumb in concentric circles over her clit.

Her nails clawed my back. I growled at the sudden bite of pain.

"Fuck," I uttered again and again as I pounded into her, demanding that she take every bit of me she could.

But before a wail could escape her like a siren, I covered her mouth with mine, taking her ecstasy with a furious kiss of my own. Tasting her as I came. As we both fell apart together.

I'd give her everything I had. It would never be enough. But I would always keep trying, and I'd be a happier man for it.

———

"So, that was...unexpected," I said a few minutes later as we recovered our breaths, standing side by side against the counters.

Nina smiled through a waterfall of hair before she pushed it out of her face. She wore no makeup in the night, her hair tousled still from the late summer humidity, cheeks flushed from the heat and my attentions.

She had never looked more beautiful.

"I don't know what came over me," she said. "I just saw you...and I needed you."

"Been happening a lot lately, hasn't it?" I asked, picking up her left hand and raising it to my lips. "You haven't been able to keep your hands off me for the last month, doll."

Nina smiled shyly. "I suppose I haven't. Though you haven't been arguing."

"And I never will, baby."

"I was thinking," she murmured as I continued to pepper her hand with kisses, "that we should elope."

I lowered her hand. "Come again?"

"I know we talked about a large church wedding next spring, but I..."

She took both my hands, flatted them palms up, and pressed her hands on top of them, as if measuring the area she could cover with her slender fingers. Then she took my hands, rotated them down, and pressed them into her body. Flat over her belly through the sleek silk fabric.

I looked up. "Wait...are you..."

"You can't be truly *that* surprised. We have used protection sporadically at best the entire time I've known you."

"Well, yeah, but—"

"Matthew," she interrupted. "I'm pregnant. Are you...are you okay with that?"

"Am I okay..." I drifted off, unable to do much more than repeat her words. "Am I okay..." I exhaled, long and low. "Yes, I'm okay. I'm..."

Suddenly, I didn't want any more distance between us than was strictly necessary. I pulled her tight against me, wrapping one hand around her waist, the other around the nape of her neck, to cradle her close.

"I'm so fucking happy I can hardly breathe," I whispered as I rocked her gently back and forth. "And I love you *so* goddamn much."

Nina sighed with clear relief. "Oh, Matthew. I'm so happy too. You have no idea."

Then she pressed her hands on my chest so she could lean back and look at me.

"Please," she said. "I want to start our family whole. We're going to Tuscany next month anyway so Olivia can meet her sisters. Let's do it then. Maybe in that little church in Vernazza. We can take your sisters and your grandmother and invite Eric and Jane. A few friends. Simple. Small. What do you think?"

It wasn't how I originally pictured it. I saw Nina in a big white dress, maybe at Our Redeemer, or if she wanted it, St. Patrick's in midtown. A damn big affair, a way of announcing to the city that seemed to try to thwart us at every move: *this woman is mine.*

But would an affair like that really be for us?

Or would it be for everyone else, just like the way we had lived our lives for the past year and a half?

"All right," I agreed at last. "Let's do it. Let's get married next month in Italy."

Nina smiled, and her face lit up the entire room, brighter than any star in the night sky.

"But you know," I added. "That means I'm going to want to call you Mrs. Zola, doll."

"I don't care what you call me," Nina said as she touched her nose to mine. "As long as we're honest about what we are. And as long as I'm finally yours."

THE END

Want to read about Nina and Matthew's Italian wedding? Check it out in the extended epilogue here: **www. nicolefrenchromance.com/RGExtendedEpilogue**

To receive a first alert email about Frankie and Xavier's story, click here: www.nicolefrenchromance.com/secretbaby

While you wait, explore some of the other characters of the Rose Gold world.

Read Jane and Eric's story here: www.nicolefrenchromance.com/thehatevow
A fast-paced, enemies-to-lovers, marriage-of-convenience romance!

Start Skylar and Brandon's story, FREE here: www.nicolefrenchromance.com/legallyyours
A billionaire-student romance with a twist!

ACKNOWLEDGMENTS

I said the last book in this series was the hardest to write, but I lied. This one was. This one was unbelievably difficult, the cherry on the only book of the series that was completely written during a global pandemic.

No, thank you. Please, not again.

That said, I have to thank some unbelievable people without whom this book would just be sitting half-finished on my computer, never to see the light of day.

To my alpha readers, Danielle and Patricia—thank you for cheering me on and listening to me vent whenever I needed an ear. I could never do any of this without you.

To my beta readers, whose availability is SO appreciated during this trying time. And to my ARC team, whose willingness to read right down to the minute makes all the difference. Thank you SO much.

To my unbelievable editorial and promotional, including my publicist, Dani, marketing director Charlie, editor, Emily Hainsworth, and proofreader, Judy Zweifel, who all rolled with my ever-moving deadlines over the last few months. Your patience and willingness to work fast and efficiently made this book possible in a way nothing else did. You have my everlasting gratitude.

To Jane, Laura, Kim, Crystal, Claudia, and Parker—thank you for being the safe space during this tumultuous year. I legitimately don't know what I would do without your wit and humor.

To my amazing family, including The Dude, who is endlessly supportive, and to my kids, who have this uncanny way of making me a better person. I love you all so much.

And most importantly: to all the readers. Your love of Matthew and Nina's story kept this train chugging on. Thank you for your patience, and thank you for reading. YOU inspire me more than anything else!

Made in the USA
Monee, IL
26 October 2020

46144119R00184